W9-BCR-344

The Bridegroom Wore Plaid

Center Point
Large Print

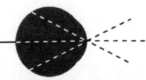

**This Large Print Book carries the
Seal of Approval of N.A.V.H.**

The Bridegroom Wore Plaid

GRACE BURROWES

CENTER POINT LARGE PRINT
THORNDIKE, MAINE

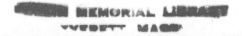

This Center Point Large Print edition
is published in the year 2013 by arrangement with
Sourcebooks, Inc.

The text of this Large Print edition is unabridged.
In other aspects, this book may vary
from the original edition.
Printed in the United States of America
on permanent paper.
Set in 16-point Times New Roman type.

ISBN: 978-1-61173-674-8

Library of Congress Cataloging-in-Publication Data

Burrowes, Grace.
The Bridegroom Wore Plaid / Grace Burrowes. — Center Point Large
Print edition.
pages cm
ISBN 978-1-61173-674-8 (Library Binding : alk. paper)
1. Nobility—Scotland—Fiction. 2. Arranged marriage—Fiction.
3. Dowry—Fiction. 4. Cousins—Fiction. 5. Scotland—Fiction.
6. Large type books. I. Title.
PS3602.U7687B75 2013
813'.6—dc23
                                                          2012046419

This book is dedicated to the families of Scottish emigrants, both those who left home and those left behind. Also, to my great-grandfather, John MacDonald, who left home at age thirteen to make his way in the New World as best he could. The New World—no, the whole world—is richer for Scotland's losses.

One

"IT IS A TRUTH UNIVERSALLY ACKNOWLEDGED that a single, reasonably good-looking earl not in possession of a fortune must be in want of a wealthy wife."

Ian MacGregor repeated Aunt Eulalie's reasoning under his breath. The words had the ring of old-fashioned common sense, and yet they somehow made a mockery of such an earl as well.

Possibly of the wife too. As Ian surveyed the duo of tittering, simpering, blond females debarking from the train on the arm of their scowling escort, he sent up a silent prayer that his countess would be neither reluctant nor managing, but other than that, he could not afford—in the most literal sense—to be particular.

His wife could be homely, or she could be fair. She could be a recent graduate from the schoolroom, or a lady past the first blush of youth. She could be shy or boisterous, gorgeous or plain. It mattered not which, provided she was unequivocally, absolutely, and most assuredly *rich*.

And if Ian MacGregor's bride was to be well and truly rich, she was also going to be—God help him and all those who depended on him—*English*.

For the good of his family, his clan, and the

7

lands they held, he'd consider marrying a well-dowered Englishwoman. If that meant his own preferences in a wife—pragmatism, loyalty, kindness, and a sense of humor—went begging, well, such was the laird's lot.

In the privacy of his personal regrets, Ian admitted a lusty nature in a wife and a fondness for a tall, black-haired, green-eyed Scotsman as a husband wouldn't have gone amiss either. As he waited for his brothers Gilgallon and Connor to maneuver through the throng in the Ballater station yard, Ian tucked that regret away in the vast mental storeroom reserved for such dolorous thoughts.

"I'll take the tall blond," Gil muttered with the air of a man choosing which lame horse to ride into battle.

"I'm for the little blond, then," Connor growled, sounding equally resigned.

Ian understood the strategy. His brothers would offer escort to Miss Eugenia Daniels and her younger sister, Hester Daniels, while Ian was to show himself to be the perfect gentleman. His task thus became to offer his arms to the two chaperones who stood quietly off to the side. One was dressed in subdued if fashionable mauve, the other in wrinkled gray with two shawls, one of beige with a black fringe, the other of gray.

Ian moved away from his brothers, pasting a fatuous smile on his face.

"My lord, my ladies, *fáilte*! Welcome to Aberdeenshire!"

An older man detached himself from the blond females. The fellow sported thick muttonchop whiskers, a prosperous paunch, and the latest fashion in daytime attire. "Willard Daniels, Baron of Altsax and Gribbony."

The baron bowed slightly, acknowledging Ian's superior if somewhat tentative rank.

"Balfour, at your service." Ian shook hands with as much 'hearty bonhomie as he could muster. "Welcome to you and your family, Baron. If you'll introduce me to your womenfolk and your son, I'll make my brothers known to them, and we can be on our way."

The civilities were observed, while Ian tacitly appraised his prospective countess. The taller blond—Eugenia Daniels—was his marital quarry, and she blushed and stammered her greetings with empty-headed good manners. She did not *appear* reluctant, which meant he could well end up married to her, provided he could dredge up sufficient charm to woo her.

And he could. Not ten years after the worst famine known to the British Isles, a strong back and a store of charm were about all that was left to him, so by God, he would use both ruthlessly to his family's advantage.

Connor and Gil comported themselves with similarly counterfeit cheer, though on Con the

9

exercise was not as convincing. Con was happy to go all day without speaking, much less smiling, though Ian knew he, too, understood the desperate nature of their charade.

Daniels made a vague gesture in the direction of the chaperones. "My sister-in-law, Mrs. Julia Redmond. My niece, Augusta Merrick." He turned away as he said the last, his gaze on the men unloading a mountain of trunks from the train.

Thank God Ian had thought to bring the wagon in addition to the coach. The English did set store by their finery. The baron's son, Colonel Matthew Daniels, late of Her Majesty's cavalry, excused himself from the introductions to oversee the transfer of baggage to the wagon.

"Ladies." Ian winged an arm at each of the older women. "I'll have you on your way in no time."

"This is so kind of you," the shorter woman said, taking his arm. Mrs. Redmond was a pretty thing, petite, with perfect skin, big brown eyes, and rich chestnut curls peeking out from under the brim of a lavender silk cottage bonnet. Ian placed her somewhere just a shade south of thirty. A lovely age on a woman. Con would call it a dally-able age.

Only as Ian offered his other arm to the second woman did he realize she was holding a closed hatbox in one hand and a reticule in the other.

Mrs. Redmond held out a gloved hand for the hatbox. "Oh, Gus, do give me Ulysses."

The hatbox emitted a disgruntled yowl.

Ian felt an abrupt yearning for a not-so-wee dram, for now he'd sunk to hosting not just the wealthy English, but their dyspeptic felines as well.

"I will carry my own pet," the taller lady said— Miss Merrick. A man who was a host for hire had to be good with names. She hunched a little more tightly over her hatbox, as if she feared her cat might be torn from her clutches by force.

"Perhaps you'd allow me to carry your bag, so I might escort you to the coach?" Ian cocked his arm at her again, a slight gesture he'd meant to be gracious.

The lady twisted her head on her neck, not straightening entirely, and peered up at him out of a pair of violet-gentian eyes. That color was completely at variance with her bent posture, her pinched mouth, the unrelieved black of her hair, the wilted gray silk of her old-fashioned coal scuttle bonnet, and even with the expression of impatience in the eyes themselves.

The Almighty had tossed even this cranky besom a bone, but these beautiful eyes in the context of this woman were as much burden as benefit. They insulted the rest of her somehow, mocked her and threw her numerous short-comings into higher relief.

11

The two shawls—worn in public, no less—half slipping off her shoulders.

The hem of her gown two inches farther away from the planks of the platform than was fashionable.

The cat yowling its discontent in the hatbox.

The finger poking surreptitiously from the tip of her right glove.

Gazing at those startling eyes, Ian realized that despite her bearing and her attire, Miss Merrick was probably younger than he was, at least chronologically.

"Come, Gussie," Mrs. Redmond said, reaching around Ian for the reticule. "We'll hold up the coach, which will make Willard difficult, and I am most anxious to see Lord Balfour's home."

"And I am anxious to show it off to you." Ian offered an encouraging smile, noting out of the corner of his eye that Gil and Con were bundling their charges into the waiting coach. The sky was full of bright, puffy little clouds scudding against an azure canvas, but this was Scotland in high summer, and the weather was bound to change at any minute out of sheer contrariness.

Miss Merrick put her gloved hand on his sleeve—the glove with the frayed finger—and lifted her chin toward the coach.

A true lady then, one who could issue commands without a word. Ian began the stately progress toward the coach necessitated by the lady's dignified gait, all the while sympathizing with the cat, whose displeasure with his circumstances was made known to the entire surrounds.

Fortunately, Mrs. Redmond was of a sunnier nature.

"It was so good of you to fetch us from the train yourself, my lord," Mrs. Redmond said. "Eulalie told us you offer the best hospitality in the shire."

"Aunt Eulalie can be given to overstatement, but I hope not in this case. You are our guests, and Highland custom would allow us to treat you as nothing less than family."

"Are we in the Highlands?" Miss Merrick asked. "It's quite chilly."

Ian resisted glancing at the hills all around them.

"There is no strict legal boundary defining the Highlands, Miss Merrick. I was born and brought up in the mountains to the west, though, so my manners are those of a Highlander. And by custom, Ballater is indeed considered Highland territory. We can get at least a dusting of snow any month of the year."

Those incongruous, beautiful eyes flicked over him, up, up, and down—to his shoulders, no lower. He tried to label what he saw in her gaze: contempt, possibly, a little curiosity, some veiled boldness.

Shrewdness, he decided with an inward sigh,

though he kept his smile in place. She had the sort of noticing, analyzing shrewdness common to the poor relation managing on family charity—Ian recognized it from long acquaintance.

"How did you come to live in Aberdeenshire?" Mrs. Redmond asked as they approached the coach.

An innocent question bringing to mind images of starvation and despair.

"It's the seat of our earldom. I came of age, and it was time I saw something of the world." *Besides failed potato fields, overgrazed glens, and shabby funerals.* He handed the ladies in, which meant for a moment he held the hatbox. His respect for the cat grew, since from the weight of the hatbox, the beast would barely have room to turn around in its pretty little cage.

Ian knew exactly how that felt.

He handed the cat up to the coachman, closed the coach door, and swung up on Hannibal, because his brothers were already in their respective saddles. Up on the box, Donal waited for the riders to go ahead, lest the mounted contingent have to eat an unnecessary helping of summer dust.

And then they were leaving the crowded surrounds of the Ballater train station, leaving the sound of steam belched from the train, the hubbub of greeting and parting in the station yard, the stomping and tail swishing of coach horses impatient—as Ian was impatient—to be away from the noise.

"What can you tell me?" Ian asked his brothers as they slowed their horses to a walk. The coach had fallen hundreds of yards behind, the aging team needing a modest pace on the many inclines on the road to Balfour House.

"The younger daughter, Hester, is harmless, but not stupid," Connor said. "My guess is she knows she has to wait until the older one is wed before she herself goes on the block. She won't be a problem."

"See that she isn't."

Connor nodded, no doubt resigned to having to dance and flirt—as best he could—with yet another English miss.

"Gil, what about my prospective bride?"

Gil fiddled with his reins, adjusting the balance of curb and snaffle. "Pretty, which should make married life a little easier, at least during daylight hours."

"What does that mean?"

Gil's lips flattened. "She's . . . nervous. Anxious, but many women are not pleased to be making long trips by train. I can't say in five minutes of her company I came to any significant conclusions about Miss Daniels."

Gil had gotten a generous helping of the family charm along with his blond good looks. If there was more intelligence to gain regarding Miss

Daniels, he was the best man to gather it.

Con glowered at nothing in particular. "It was *Mac*Daniels until a few generations ago."

"It's Daniels now," Ian said. "Well, keep your eyes and ears open. The shorter chaperone strikes me as pleasant enough, though those types are easy to underestimate. The taller one is decidedly lacking in cheer."

Con's mouth quirked up. "Serves you right."

"She could be an ally," Ian said. "If she's willing to see her cousin matched to a Scottish earldom, then a fat English dowry is that much closer to our dirty, grasping hands."

Con's smile disappeared as he glared at his horse's mane. "There has to be another way."

"There isn't." Gil's tone was weary. "Thank God that Her Majesty has made all things Scottish fashionable, particularly strutting about the Highlands in summer. The paying guests get us from year to year, from crop to crop, and shearing to shearing. We'd be on the boat to Nova Scotia without them. They will not keep Balfour in any sort of repair, though, and they leave us precious little to send along to the others."

"We're doing all right," Ian said. But just all right. Another blight on the crops, a sickness in the flocks, a new tax from London, and all right would not be good enough. As much coin as they sent to their myriad relations in the New World, there was always a need for more.

"We're waltzing and flirting our lives away," Con said. "It's enough to make that boat to Canada look very, very good."

He'd let his diction lapse: verra, verra guid. As the youngest, Con had come down from the mountains most recently, but it was more than that. This charade took a toll on them all, but on Con worse than Ian or Gil. Con was their horse-master, a man more comfortable out-of-doors among the beasts than swilling tea in his dress kilt.

"Race you!" Gil drove his heels into his horse's sides, shooting out from between his brothers like a blond streak. Con thundered after, while Ian held Hannibal back through a series of impatient crow hops and props.

"Settle, you. A fellow of your dignified years has no business disporting like a cocktail lad of three."

At the sound of Ian's voice, the gelding ceased his antics. They were both getting too old to caper around for the sheer hell of it, but as Ian watched the coach come lumbering up the hill behind him, he wheeled his horse and shot off after his brothers.

"My goodness, the men here are certainly *tall!*" Hester offered this observation to the coach at large.

"And . . . substantial," Julia concurred,

wiggling her eyebrows in an unwidow-like manner. "Verra, verra substantial."

"Naughty, Aunt, mimicking the locals." Eugenia was smiling. Not the bored, arch expression Augusta saw on her so often, but a genuine, affectionate smile.

"Sometimes being a saint grows tiresome," Julia said. "Gus, the Scottish air has put roses in your cheeks. Surely this bodes well for our stay in Aberdeenshire."

"One need not travel this far from the good air of Oxford to acquire roses in one's cheeks," Augusta replied. "I will be surprised if that wretched trip didn't leave the lot of us with permanent aches in unmentionable locations."

This remark occasioned much drollery, which Julia abetted shamelessly while Augusta watched the passing countryside. In its craggy majesty and bleakness—the mountains here sported no trees above a certain altitude—the landscape bore a resemblance to the strapping specimens of Scottish manhood who'd met their train.

This trip had not been Augusta's idea—she'd been dead set against it, in fact—but there was pleasure in spending time with her female cousins. Willard and Matthew, thank the angels, had seen fit to spend this leg of the journey up on the box with the coachman, meaning Augusta could relax just a bit.

Mentally, anyway. The stays biting into her hips

and sides made physical relaxation impossible.

"Pretty country," Genie remarked from her place beside Augusta. "One can see why Her Majesty chose it for her private residence."

Austere, perhaps. Not pretty. "Attractive in its way, but so is Kent."

Something passed through Genie's blue eyes, something that marred the classic English beauty of her features. If Augusta had been forced to name it, she might have called it despair.

And what would such a lovely young lady, the world at her feet after three very successful Seasons, have to despair over?

"You aren't the one being paraded before every title with pockets to let, Cousin." Genie turned her head to look out the other window. "I appreciate that you've abandoned your rose gardens to chaperone Hester and me, but is the duty really so onerous when all you'll be doing is walking in Lord Balfour's woods and dancing with his brothers?"

"Not . . . onerous, though you know I do not dance."

"You did." That from Julia, the traitor. "When you came out you danced quite often, Gussie."

"Nearly a decade ago, when there was no choice but to dance."

A little silence fell, while Augusta felt a despair of her own. This was her lot in life now, to kill confidences from her younger cousins, to leave little clouds of awkwardness and disapproval in her conversational wake. But really, for Julia to bring up Augusta's come-out . . .

"Did you fancy Lord Balfour, Genie?" Hester put the question quietly. Because Augusta was sitting beside Genie, she saw the girl's mouth tighten.

"Cousin Augusta doesn't dance," Genie said. "I do not seek marriage to a stranger sporting a title. I'm sure Lord Balfour is a very amiable gentleman, but I'm not here to become his countess."

Her tone consigned all amiable gentlemen to the jungles of darkest Peru.

"Papa mightn't agree with you." Hester's tone bore no malice. "We're both for titles, Genie. You've heard him lecturing Mama about it incessantly."

"Then you marry the Scottish earl."

Hester, with characteristic good cheer, appeared to consider the notion. "He's handsome, if tall."

"And substantial," Julia added. "Don't forget that. I like his eyes."

"Maybe you should marry him, Aunt," Hester suggested, lips curving. "I hadn't noticed his eyes."

"They're kind," Julia said. "I find that very attractive on a man."

Oh, for pity's sake. The man's eyes were *green*. A startling, emerald green, probably made more striking by his somewhat dark complexion and the thick fringe of dark lashes around them. They were also tired, those eyes. They had a weariness that contrasted subtly with his flashing white teeth, easy grin, and comfortable manners.

"The one with brown hair struck me as serious," Julia said, egging on her charges. "Maybe he'd be a better match for you, Genie. If he's the spare, he'll at least have a courtesy title."

"Connor has the brown hair," Hester supplied. "He has the best nose. Gilgallon looks like he laughs more, and I like his blond hair, but his mouth is stubborn. I'd put my money on him as the spare."

Lord Balfour's mouth wasn't stubborn. Augusta frowned, picturing him grinning as he'd swung up on his horse and patted the beast soundly on the neck. His mouth was wide, the lips a trifle full, and on the left side, he had a dimple that flashed when he smiled. With thick, dark hair ruffled by the breeze, he made an attractive picture.

Julia untied her bonnet and set it in her lap. "What constitutes a good nose, Hester?"

"Proud," Hester said. "Connor has a proud nose, a conqueror's nose. Not a narrow little whining thing like Richard Comstock-Simms has."

"My sister has taken up reading noses," Genie said, her smile back in place now that impending

21

marriage was no longer the subject. "You can make pots of money predicting men's futures by assessing their noses."

"We already have pots of money," Hester retorted. "Which is why Lord Balfour will offer for you. I wouldn't mind having a Scottish brother-in-law, Genie."

"Why not a Scottish husband?" Julia asked, deflecting the temper flaring in Genie's eyes.

"Because Mama will not allow me to marry until Genie is at least engaged. Besides, Genie has had three Seasons, and I've had only one."

Augusta let their combination of banter and bickering wash over her, while she considered Ian MacGregor's nose.

There was nothing subtle about *his* nose. Proud applied, but also, perhaps, aristocratic. His nose occupied the middle of his face as a nose ought, but was a little more grand than the standard nose, having the slightest tendency to hook toward the bottom. She knew this because she'd studied the man in profile when he'd offered his arm the second time.

He'd smiled down at her, offering a polite, even friendly smile to a woman whom he could safely dismiss as a nonentity, which was exactly how Augusta intended he view her. Why his willingness to do so should leave her disgruntled, she did not know, nor was she going to waste time pondering it.

The coach rattled along roads likely improved in honor of Her Majesty's decision to make her private residence at nearby Balmoral. Lord Balfour's proximity to the royal household had figured prominently in the Daniels's campaign to have the girls spend much of their summer here in Aberdeenshire.

As if Queen Victoria would pop out from behind a tree and declare herself thrilled to be making the acquaintance of Hester and Eugenia Daniels.

Julia put her bonnet back on twenty minutes later and tied the ribbons beneath her chin. "At long last, our destination. What a lovely, lovely facade."

Pale gray stone caught bright summer sun, ivy blanketed the northern face, and topiary dragons frolicked along the wings spreading from either side of the main entrance. The house looked comfortable in its setting, secure, affluent, and pretty without being pretentious.

Julia was first to leave the coach, owing to her senior status, but then Augusta motioned for her cousins to leave next. Those oversized, smiling Scotsmen were out there, offering their arms, exuding charm, and generally creating the sort of impression intended to make the ladies forget they were paying a great deal for the privilege of being Lord Balfour's "guests."

"Madam?"

She had expected her uncle or perhaps her cousin Matthew to be the last available escort, but Lord Balfour himself loomed in the coach doorway, his hand extended to offer her assistance.

His bare hand. He'd taken off his riding gloves, allowing Augusta to notice that even the backs of his hands were of a darker complexion than an Englishman would feel comfortable exposing socially.

She placed her gloved fingertips on his palm and suffered him to assist her from the coach. All went well as she stepped down, but as luck would have it, her foot landed on a pebble that rolled beneath her weight as she descended.

Leaving her careening into Lord Balfour.

"Steady there."

She'd pitched ignominiously against his chest, finding him as immovable as a slab of rock.

He smelled better than a rock, though. Leaning against him, Augusta took one half breath to find her balance, enough for her nose to gather the scents of soap, lavender, and something fresh and spicy—heather?—underlain with a hint of horse.

Good smells, clean and bracing. She straightened lest he think her daft. "My thanks, your lordship."

"Surely Balfour will do? It's summertime, and we're far, far from London, Miss Merrick."

She nodded noncommittally. Calling the man

by his title little more than an hour after meeting him was not something Miss Augusta Merrick should be comfortable doing, regardless of the season. She had to like him for offering, though. It suggested some of the warmth in those smiles he tossed around so carelessly might be real.

He put her hand on his arm and patted her knuckles. "I'll have my sister, Mary Frances, show you to your rooms. We keep a country schedule unless our guests request otherwise. It leaves hours of the gloaming to relax and enjoy ourselves."

Gloaming. A soft, northern word. He caressed it a little with the burr in his voice.

"I shall retire early and take a tray in my room," Augusta said. "Train travel does not agree with me." Let his lordship turn that charm on Genie, where all and sundry knew it was intended to focus.

"We'll miss your company at table." He bowed as they gained the front terrace. "And here is Mary Fran, who will be wroth with you if you do not allow her to see to your every comfort."

Mary Fran, more properly Lady Mary Frances—she was an earl's daughter, for pity's sake—was an imposing redhead with the same facile smile as her oldest brother. She collected the ladies with an air of brisk friendliness, and soon had them bustled into their rooms, maids clucking and fussing with an informality that would not have passed muster *at all* back in the South.

Augusta's room was done in the current Highland vogue—curtains, bed hangings, carpet, and even wallpaper sported either a green, black, and white plaid, or echoed the hues of the plaid. As a whole, the room was a little dizzying.

"Is all the staff so . . . familiar?" Augusta asked her maid.

"Familiar, mum?"

"Friendly?"

The girl's freckled face split into a wide grin. "We're to treat you like family, laird's rules. Is there anything else I can do for ye?"

Augusta shook her head and waited while the girl bobbed a curtsy then stopped by the door to check the level of the water in a bouquet of red roses.

And then Augusta was blessedly, finally, at long last, completely *alone*.

Wherever Ian looked for Mary Fran—the kitchen, the formal dining room, the pantries, the larder— the servants reported she'd just gone off to some other location, they knew not exactly where.

And though Ian paid them some of the best wages in the shire, he did not fool himself: if the staff was intent on abetting Mary Fran, then she'd elude capture easily, despite her laird, earl, and brother's pressing need to speak with her.

A flash of red braids and quick, light tread on

the footmen's stairs suggested possible hope. Ian lit up the stairs, two at a time.

"Fiona!" A door banged on the next flight up. "Fiona Ursula MacGregor!"

Silence, meaning the child—who generally knew exactly where her mother had gotten off to—was intent on disregard for authority as well. Ian could expect as much—she was Scottish, a MacGregor, and Mary Fran's own daughter.

He burst through the door on the upper landing, lungs heaving, ready to bellow the rafters down in search of the child, only to stop short.

"Your lordship."

As Ian mentally fumbled about trying to locate the good manners of a charming host, his brain produced the thought: The lady with the anxious, pretty eyes.

"Miss Merrick." Though not the Miss Merrick he'd met at the train station, or even the Miss Merrick he'd escorted from the coach. This Miss Merrick was clothed in a robe the exact shade between red and purple, a regal, substantial hue that flattered her black hair and perfect skin. She looked curiously *luscious,* with her hair piled on her head in a soft topknot, and her spectacles perched on her nose.

"I confess, my lord, to having lost my way." Her smile was more self-conscious than worried. "I was looking for the bathing chamber."

And while another woman might have been

mortified to be caught wandering the hall in a robe, Ian suspected Miss Merrick was more troubled by the loss of her bearings.

He offered her his arm—she was clothed from neck to ankles, for God's sake, and the house was swarming with people. "It's easy to get turned about in this house. When I was a boy visiting my grandfather, I delighted in discovering new rooms and hidden stairways."

And now he was hard put not to resent the entire property.

"Did you also delight in your first experience with train travel? Boys do, I'm told."

Boys were likely a species of noisy, dirty savage to her. "I take it train travel does not appeal to you?"

When he expected her to rap out some sniffy answer, she looked thoughtful. "I enjoy the sense of mobility, of being able to flee my surrounds for a bit of coin. Having come hundreds of miles though, I find I want nothing so much as the solitude, stillness, and fragrance of a hot bath."

Interesting, that she did not profess a desire for her home. "You're in luck then, because we've a monstrous roof cistern, and the old chimneys, stairwells, and priest holes were such that installing some water closets wasn't too much work."

Though it had been expensive. Holy God, had it been expensive. Only Mary Fran's threat to lead a mutiny—from laundry, to kitchens, to gardens—had seen the renovations done.

"Who is this? He looks like a younger version of you."

She'd paused before another extravagance, though this one, Ian was dearly glad for. "That fellow is my older brother, Asher, just before he took ship for Canada."

"A solemn young man, though quite comely."

Solemn? They'd been reeling from the effects of the potato blight, reeling from Mary Fran's scandal with the wretched Captain His Bloody English Lordship Flynn, and reeling from Grandfather's inchoate decline.

"He had much to be solemn about." And the New World had given him only more to be solemn about. "The bathing chamber is this way."

She did not immediately move away from the painting, but stood for another moment, studying a portrait of a young man in Highland attire—not the full regalia; Asher had balked at that notion. Asher had been gaunt, serious to a fault, and proud. Ian hoped the pride at least remained to his brother.

"You have much to be solemn about too," she remarked when she at last deigned to continue their progress.

Ian mustered a smile. "I have much to take pleasure in as well. I've acquired neighbors most fortuitously, we own one of the prettiest patches of ground in God's creation, and my family enjoys good health."

"*You* own it."

Shrewd and noticing—not an endearing combination in a female.

"I am Scottish, Miss Merrick. Everything I do, I do in the name of my family." Even finding lost spinsters and guiding them on their way. "Your bathing chamber."

Ian peeked in and saw that soap, towels, and all the other expensive items Mary Fran claimed were necessary for a lady's bath had been laid out. "Has anyone shown you how to work the taps?"

"No."

And from the look on her face, she would perish of excessive train travel before she'd ask.

"It's not complicated." Ian moved into the marble temple to cleanliness and refined English sensibilities and felt Miss Merrick mincing along behind him. "The one on the right is the cold, the one on the left, hot. You start with cold because the boiler can be cranky, and . . ."

He trailed off, turning both taps only to find someone hadn't opened the upper valves. In the small confines of the water closet, he had to reach over Miss Merrick's head—her hair bore the scent of lemon verbena and coal smoke—to open the feeder taps.

The next few moments happened in a series of impressions.

First came the sensation of the door thwacking into Ian from behind. A stout blow more unexpected than painful, but enough to make him stumble forward.

Then, Fiona's voice, muttering the Gaelic equivalent of "Beg pardon!" followed by a patter of retreating footsteps.

And then, in Ian's male brain, *the woman with the pretty, anxious eyes* became the woman who was soft, lush, and still beneath Ian's much greater weight.

She didn't push him away. She didn't even touch him. The sole indication that his weight was any imposition as he flattened her to the wall, that the impropriety of the moment was any imposition, was her closed eyes.

The final impression threatened to part Ian from his reason: her breasts, heaving against his chest. In preparation for her bath, she'd left off her stays, and the feminine abundance pressed against Ian ambushed his wits.

Shrewd, noticing, and astoundingly well endowed.

When he wanted to press closer, Ian pushed himself away with one hand on the wall and made sure both feeder taps were open. "I do beg your pardon, Miss Merrick."

"A mishap only. I stumbled upon leaving the coach."

She would recall that, while Ian had thought

nothing of it. His damned male parts were thinking at a great rate now, and all because . . .

He wasn't sure why, though lengthy deprivation might have something to do with his reaction—and pretty eyes.

"The valves are open, but mind the hot water."

She nodded, and Ian got the hell out of there before he said something even more stupid.

Two

WILLARD DANIELS WATCHED HIS FIRSTBORN son and heir put an empty glass back on the tray where the decanter—now considerably less full than it had been an hour ago—sat winking in the early evening sunshine.

The boy had graceful hands, which was no compliment. Soldiering was supposed to knock the fancy out of a man, but five years in the light cavalry hadn't quite gotten rid of a certain elegance—fussiness, more like—in the next Baron of Altsax . . . and Gribbony.

Which was why the summer's real objective was something Willard would keep to himself. Matthew had an inconveniently generous dollop of scruples rattling around with all the logic and military strategy in his handsome head. It ruined him, like the red highlights in his blond hair, the slight air of diffidence in his mannerisms, the tendency to silence and distance when a peer of the realm sought and was entitled to hearty assurances from his own son.

Disappointment, Altsax had long ago learned to live with, but failure was out of the question. *Before* Genie or Hester married that buffoon of an earl, before they married anybody, the problem of their aging and awkward cousin was going to be resolved—permanently—lest the Daniels's family finances and social standing continue to be threatened by Augusta Merrick's very existence. She'd turned down the only other possible solution—marriage to Matthew, offered half in jest—though seeing how the pair of them had matured, Altsax had to be grateful. Even his brooding disappointment of a son deserved better than that wretched woman, cousin or not.

Such musings were enough to inspire a man to drain the remaining whisky from the decanter.

To be drunk at dinner would be the height of bad form the first night under the earl's roof, but then, dinner wasn't going to be for at least an hour. Willard reached for the decanter and offered a private though quite sincere toast to the success of his own schemes.

One of the blessings of entertaining wealthy English aristocracy for weeks on end was that Ian could feed his own household well. For a few months of summer and early fall, there were frequent servings of good Aberdeen Angus beef, the occasional lamb, roasted cuts of pork, chicken too young to be anything but tender, and—reason enough to thank God—not a hint of mutton.

Though there had been many times in Ian's life when even a thin mutton stew would have been a fair trade for his soul.

Perhaps it *had* been a fair trade, which was why he was rubbing elbows in evening finery—the kilted version, and bedamned to English fashion—with the half-drunk baron, his tight-lipped son, and his determinedly cheerful womenfolk.

Save the spinster. She at least had the sense to keep to her rooms, where she no doubt was feeding portions of beef to her cat.

The baron rose to his feet a little unsteadily and directed a questioning glance to Ian. "The ladies having departed for their tea and gossip, shall we to the decanter?"

"Of course." But Ian saw Connor eyeing the food uneaten on the Baron's plate. More for the kirk in town, though if they knew it was food served to an Englishman, likely even the wretched poor of Aberdeenshire would turn their noses up at it.

"This is first-rate drink," Matthew Daniels said when all five men were lounging around the library. "Have you ever considered exporting it?"

"Now that's an interesting proposition," Connor replied, sparing Ian the trouble. "There is a market for decent whisky, but there's also a heavy tax imposed, usually at both ends . . ."

Daniels the Younger launched into a surprisingly intelligent debate with Con and Gil about the risks and rewards of exporting whisky, while the Baron—drink in hand—sidled over to where Ian stood by the window.

"That boy." The baron expelled a heavily fumed breath. "Talking trade after dinner with the locals. I wash my hands of him." He turned a long-suffering gaze on his drink, drained the contents, then set the empty glass on the windowsill with a little bang.

"Shall I refresh your drink, Baron?"

"Yes, b'gad. Traveling leaves a man parched, particularly with all them damned, plaguey females. Speaking of which?"

Ian glanced at his guest while he poured a half tumbler of whisky for the baron. He'd chosen the decanter kept farther back along the sideboard, the one reserved for sots who would not be offended by a younger brew. The container itself was fancy and kept just as meticulously dusted as its confreres, but Ian would not have served the contents to Mary Fran's prize sows.

"This is a special batch," Ian said, which was true. "Not for everyday consumption. I'd go slowly."

"Must say"—the baron took a hefty swallow—"for a Scot, you know how to treat your custom."

"My guests," Ian corrected gently.

The baron lifted his glass for another sip then turned to face the window. "As I was saying, about the ladies."

Was business to be broached this soon? A part of Ian was relieved to think the Misses Daniels's father was so determined to see them settled; another part of him was appalled at the man's lack of couth. Not under Ian's roof twelve hours, and already, before it was even apparent Ian would suit his daughter, Altsax was opening negotiations.

"About the ladies?" Ian drawled, joining the baron at the window. Behind them, the younger men had escalated the discussion of whisky exportation into a round of "You damned English/ You bloody Scots," which was great good fun, provided nobody started pounding on anybody indoors.

Mary Fran frowned mightily on broken furniture.

Ian watched as, out on the terrace, Mary Fran started laughing at something Mrs. Redmond had said.

The baron leaned closer, his breath enough to knock a grown man on his arse.

"Just how widowed is your sister, Balfour? She's a toothsome wench, if a man isn't put off by all that red hair. And widows tend to be grateful and enthusiastic, y'know what I mean?"

And by greatest bad luck, the baron had spoken in the overloud confidences of a drunk, his comment falling into one of those peculiar lulls in the other conversation that ensured even the footman at the library door had heard him.

Ian glanced over at his brothers, seeing Con's lips thinning and Gil's hand already on Con's arm.

The insult to Mary Fran had been plain enough that Matthew Daniels's expression had gone from almost genial to the blank, offended mask at which the English excelled, and everybody in the room was looking at Ian.

The baron wiggled his eyebrows and elbowed Ian in the ribs. "Well?"

Morning came blessedly, beautifully early during a Scottish summer, just as sunset came only gradually and late.

This allowed a man playing host to a group of silly English to get in a few hours of meaningful work before appearing in his finery at breakfast. It also allowed him to stay up late tending to correspondence, and to grab what sleep he needed during the brief darkness.

And it permitted him a solitary ride just as the sun was cresting the horizon, a little time to enjoy the natural beauty of dawn in one of the prettiest places on earth, when he'd otherwise brood about the need to ignore slights to his sister from half-inebriated guests.

Ian had scrabbled for some patience and signaled Daniels to get his dear papa up to bed, though the thought of the Baron as a father-in-law was nauseating.

Each year it felt a little more like this was what Ian's life would be: scrabbling for patience, scrabbling to keep up appearances, scrabbling to make ends meet, scrabbling to keep what was left of his branch of the clan together, scrabbling to come up with yet another scheme to wrest coin from some new source for the upkeep of the hall and its inhabitants, scrabbling to hold onto hope that Asher would come home.

He should be introduced as the Earl of Scrabbling.

Soon, in support of these burdens, he'd acquire a countess. Even as the Balfour spare, Ian had accepted he'd eventually marry, and marriage to a practical Scotswoman willing to shoulder some of Ian's burden would have been lovely. Women like Mary Fran understood hard work, sacrifice, and by God, they understood loyalty.

Even that comfort was to be denied him. Eugenia Daniels was pretty enough, but only in a pale, blond, English way. A night in Ian's bed would likely break her in two and leave her crying for her mother—assuming he could muster any enthusiasm for her intimate company.

Ian's morose thoughts were interrupted by a

lone figure emerging from the shadows at the back of the house. A woman . . .

He watched the figure striding confidently along the path into the gardens. She was tall, with a long, glossy black braid hanging down the middle of her back. The end of the plait danced in counterpoint to her walk, swinging up rhythmically with each footfall.

Bloody damn. He recognized the beige shawl with the black fringe and nudged Hannibal into a trot.

"Good morning, Miss Merrick."

She stopped abruptly, her back to him, while Ian dismounted and stuffed his riding gloves into his pockets. He tied up his reins and gave Hannibal a gentle slap on the quarters.

"He won't wander off?" She'd turned, the shawl clutched around her shoulders.

"He's Scottish bred. He'll wander directly to the nearest ration of oats." Ian offered a smile because the lady looked flustered. "Come, Miss Merrick, and we'll walk. The gardens show to advantage in morning light."

Her eyes flicked to the back of the house, and Ian felt a sinking sensation in his chest, which by now he should be adept at ignoring. It was one thing to stumble across him in a back corridor, but she didn't want to be seen walking with him so early in the day, perhaps not at any point in the day.

He took pity on her—she was a lady and not responsible for the prejudices of her sheltered upbringing. "If we take this path to the left, we will not be seen."

Her chin came up, those disconcerting gentian eyes meeting his gaze. "It isn't what you think, my lord."

It never was with proper English ladies.

"What do I think?" He took her hand—devoid of gloves—and placed it on his arm, feeling a spark of—something, something that wasn't entirely gentlemanly—in doing so.

"You think I am reluctant to be seen in company with a single gentleman at an improper hour out-of-doors."

Only the English could make a gorgeous, rural dawn improper. "Early morning is the best part of the day," he said. "It's the only part of the day we haven't already mucked up with our fretting and strutting and carrying on."

"Yes." She stopped and peered up at him, an odd moment. She looked so long and so thoroughly, it took Ian a moment to realize, without her spectacles, she might have difficulty seeing. "That's why I was out, because it's too pretty to stay shut up in that room with Ulysses. But what you think . . ."

It was his turn to peer at her, until manners saved him and he turned her by the arm to begin their walk. He got her behind the tall privet hedge, where they'd have some privacy, and felt her relax marginally beside him.

"I have a certain place in the family," she said, slipping her arm free of his to take a seat on a wooden bench. "Won't you sit for a minute?"

Now that they were private, she wanted to sit with him?

But she clearly did. Her expression was so earnest, her violet eyes solemnly entreating him to spend a little time with her, probably to assuage her lady's conscience.

Ian sat a proper distance away from her, despite the devilish temptation to rattle her by sitting too close.

"Thank you." She let the shawl drape down to her elbows. "I am mindful, Lord Balfour, that you are considering a match with my cousin."

"I am expected to marry," he said carefully, because the mind of woman was a labyrinthine mystery, and this woman could queer his only shot at the Daniels's dowry.

She nodded once. "Of course you must take a wife, but Eugenia is hesitant to marry anybody. She's had three Seasons and any number of offers, but her mama is determined she should have a title."

Ian knew this much, so he kept his silence.

"Genie is young and has odd, modern notions that marriage ought not to serve material purposes. Either that, or her parents' example has disheartened her regard for marriage generally." Miss Merrick's cheeks colored slightly at these admissions.

"May I be blunt?" Because he did not have all morning to exchange civilities with this woman, even if it did appear the Lord had given her a wealth of shining dark hair to go with her pretty, solemn eyes.

"Please. Most people are blunt with me, and I'm not as easy to shock as you might think."

Oh, right. Of course not.

"Is it marriage your cousin objects to, or the intimacies expected of a wife?"

Her eyebrows rose, but only that. Ian waited on her answer, because a marriage in name only would be a relief of a sort—also a bitter curse.

"Now that you raise the possibility," the lady said slowly, "I suspect there is aversion to the . . . intimacies, though both Julia and I have tried to reassure Genie that her fears are groundless."

"I gather, then, that you do not oppose the match?" *And what would a spinster know of those intimacies?*

"I cannot oppose a good match for my cousin. You see, your lordship, I am living the alternative to a congenial marriage. I have given Genie my word I will not maneuver her into a situation where her choices are taken from her, but if you and she were respectfully disposed toward each other, in my heart I would have to

42

support the match. You would be kind to her?"

Kindness? What place had kindness in a discussion of money and security for his family and their kin? But looking into a pair of earnest violet eyes, Ian realized he had something in common with this woman.

She was lonely and alone even among her family. She was *more* alone with family around her, in fact. He reached over and lifted her shawl around her shoulders.

"You'll take cold in the morning damp."

Still, she watched him, waiting on his answer.

"I know little of kindness, Miss Merrick, but I understand honor, and I understand that a smile and an encouraging word can foster good relations when silence and criticism do not. Women are deserving of every consideration. I would show my wife nothing less than perfect courtesy."

She shuddered, likely not at the brisk morning air. "Courtesy can be the unkindest cut, you know. My uncle excels at such courtesy, my aunt as well."

So he had this in common with her too—a distaste for Willard Daniels.

"Marriage would spare you their dubious courtesy, so why aren't you married, then?" Without her hair scraped into a bun or that pinchy expression to her mouth, without her glasses, she wasn't at all bad looking, nor was she as old as Ian had first thought. And those eyes . . .

"I had a Season." She said this the way an old soldier might talk about besting a worthy enemy on a faraway battlefield, her eyes going soft and distant. "I had my come-out, I had a Season like every girl dreams of, but then my parents died, Papa then Mama, and the mourning took two years. By the time I was ready to resume my place in Society, my situation had changed."

He let a silence stretch—not uncomfortable, with her sitting beside him—and moved puzzle pieces around in his mind.

Her situation had changed because when her mourning was over, her cousin Genie had been preparing to emerge from the schoolroom, and it was Genie's papa, not Miss Merrick's grand-father, who would control the purse strings, and both English and Scottish baronial titles.

"Your uncle refused to dower you."

She looked down at her hands where they rested in her lap, her shawl again slipping to her elbows. "Perhaps."

Ian followed the line of her gaze, noting that from beneath the damp hem of her nondescript walking dress, he could see the first two naked toes of her right foot.

A lady of hidden daring, then. He stifled a smile and brought his attention back to the conver-sation. "Miss Merrick. I have a sister, I have a young niece, and more cousins than you can count. I understand that family can be a trial."

She nodded, eyes still downcast. "Uncle explained he would have the support of me for all my years, and then he did the math. Several Seasons plus a dowry would be a much greater burden on the barony than were I to accept the alternative, and he did give me the option of marriage to my cousin Matthew."

Interesting tactic on the baron's part. Ian stored that insight away for further consideration.

"You were not inclined, Miss Merrick? Her Majesty married a cousin, and the union appears to be prospering."

"She married a cousin she'd never met until courting was in the air. Matthew was like a brother to me growing up, and I could not do that to him, not even for the promise of children and the eventual title of baroness. So I am a poor relation, and larking about half clad in the morning dew does not comport with my role."

A minor puzzle formed in Ian's mind: children and a title were probably the greatest inducements that could have been dangled before her, a gently bred English lady—and she'd turned them down.

"I understand costumes and roles." He reached over to pull her shawl up around her shoulders yet again, as she seemed determined to let the thing fall where it may. "I'm disguised as an earl, for example, one who's pleased to open his home to guests each summer when Her Majesty is in residence next door."

It was an admission. Not one he'd planned to make, but her smile told him she was pleased to accept it.

"You should not judge yourself for taking Uncle's coin. He's a trial on a good day, and he'll dine out on his summer with the Queen for years."

"And I'm not really an earl, not yet." He glanced over to make sure she was paying attention, because this truth was one he did not want hidden. "My half brother, Asher, holds the title, but he's been missing for almost seven years. We've started the proceedings for having him declared legally dead, though at the last moment, I expect him to come strolling off a boat, thanking me for my impersonation of him."

"Uncle knows this. He's been spying on you for a bit."

A confidence for a confidence. Miss Merrick rose a notch in Ian's estimation.

"Has he now? I suppose that's to be expected." And Miss Merrick no doubt feared such an uncle would also spy on his niece. "Come with me, and I'll show you where you can pick up a trail in the woods that will allow you all the solitude you want, most of it within shouting distance of the house and stables."

"Another time perhaps." She rose, her expression genuinely rueful. "If I'm seen gadding about with my hair in disarray and my hems getting soaked, there will be questions at breakfast. You won't tattle?"

This was important to her, her eyes suggesting it was tantamount to a matter of safety and peace of mind.

He got to his feet. "A gentleman would never reveal a lady's confidences, Miss Merrick. Never."

She looked relieved, and then indecisive, as if she might say more or take his hand to solemnize the exchange. But she turned, pulled the ugly shawl up, skittered away, then darted back to his side.

Ian had no warning. She rested a hand on his chest then went up on her toes and grazed her lips against his cheek. He got a fleeting impression of warmth and softness and a little whiff of spring flowers before he had the presence of mind to steady her by the elbows. For a procession of instants, she remained next to him, a woman who likely permitted herself no allies and no affection. Ian's hands slid from her elbows to her waist, sharing an embrace that was as comforting as it was unexpected.

She was not prim, fussy, and prejudiced. She was shy, lonely, and uncertain.

Also brave.

It was a sweet moment, and just as Ian might have stepped back and bowed over her hand, she whirled away.

In a flurry of tan shawl and bare feet, she scampered off, reminding Ian of a doe startled at her quiet grazing, then fleeing into the safety of the surrounding shadows.

The Earl of Balfour was a more complicated man than Augusta had wanted to credit. She pondered this realization while she exchanged her old walking dress for a day dress of almost the same sorry vintage.

Her first impression of him was that he had decent manners, a genial disposition, and—like many of his peers—did not suffer from excesses of introspection. And she'd thought him . . . big. Physically big. Tall, broad through the shoulders, solid in the chest, and whether he wore riding attire or the kilts he seemed so fond of, she could see his legs had as much muscle as the rest of him.

Big, *fit,* and handsome in a tall, black-haired, green-eyed Scottish way.

And then he'd caught her in all her ridiculous glory this morning, giving in to the impulse to feel the wet grass on her feet, to sniff a fat, bloodred rose sporting morning dew, to allow the morning sun to kiss her bare cheeks.

Things she could do in exile in Oxfordshire but had missed terribly during these weeks when she'd again been in the company of her family.

The earl hadn't remarked her behavior. He'd

been courteous but honest, gruffly honest. She'd liked the honesty and had tried to convey her approval by returning his candor in full measure. The more serious earl, the man who bluntly broached topics like marriage and Genie's hesitance to become his countess, was a more appealing fellow than the easygoing host.

Too appealing, if her impulsive little buss to his cheek was any indication. What *had* she been thinking, to presume on his person that way? And in what tidy little compartment of proper thought and behavior was she going to stash the memory of their embrace?

He'd been oddly gracious. The first time he'd tucked her shawl up, Augusta hadn't known quite what he was about and had nearly flinched away. The second time, she'd found it . . . intriguing.

Not quite endearing. Endearing was the grave look in his emerald green eyes when he informed her he was not yet officially the earl. Augusta had heard her aunt and uncle discussing this at tiresome length, with Uncle pointing out the man was at the very least an earl's heir, complete with courtesy title, and likely to be the earl in the next year.

So Aunt had pleaded for a yearlong engagement, and Uncle had started ranting.

Augusta gave her hair a repinning after she'd changed into morning attire. She hadn't intended to go to breakfast, but the day had had a promising start. The more she got to know Lord Balfour, the more Augusta was convinced he could make Genie a very decent husband after all.

The man apparently intended to begin his campaign with the morning meal. Augusta watched from her place opposite the laden sideboard as he managed to arrive at the breakfast parlor at the exact same moment as Genie.

"Good morning, Miss Daniels and Miss Hester," he said from the doorway "You both have the radiant appearance of women who've enjoyed a fine night's rest."

"I was asleep before my head hit the pillow," Hester said, sailing into the room. "My goodness, this is *breakfast* in Scotland? I was expecting bannocks with my tea. Genie, do come along lest I eat everything I see."

"Miss Daniels?" The earl waited politely for Genie to pass before him into the room. "May I fix you a plate?"

"Thank you, but I don't typically enjoy much of an appetite first thing in the day." Genie cast Augusta a look probably intended to convey a plea for help—which would not be forthcoming. For the earl to see to a lady guest's plate was perfectly proper and even considerate.

"The scones are very good," he said, quirking an eyebrow. "I'm thinking you'd best have a couple lest Miss Hester remove them as an option."

"Smart man." Hester plucked a pastry from the tray as she cruised along the buffet. "And you'll want to watch the butter, because Augusta slathers it on like she's trying to keep every bossy cow in the shire secure in its employment."

"We have a lot of cows here in Aberdeen. Good morning, Miss Merrick. I hope you slept well?"

And there was not a hint of innuendo, humor, or *anything* in his inflection or his expression. Such an accomplished actor would likely lie convincingly as well, which was a disconcerting realization.

"I did sleep soundly. I kept the terrace door open to humor my cat. I think the fresh air agreed with us both."

"Imagine that—a feline being pleased with something. I don't know as I've seen the like." He turned back to Genie, who was hovering by the array of food. "Some bacon, ma'am? A bit of ham?"

"Just the scone for now, thank you, my lord."

"None of that. You're my guest. Balfour will do, and I shall call you Miss Genie, hmm?" He set her plate on the table and waited to hold her chair, while Genie shot Augusta an even more panicked look.

"Of course you shall call her Miss Genie," Augusta said, reaching for the teapot. "Formalities at breakfast do not aid digestion."

She could not endorse lingering behind a privet

hedge with a handsome earl as an aid to digestion either.

"Hear, hear." Hester waved her fork in a little circle to emphasize her agreement. "I could do with a spot of that tea, Cousin. I've an entire tray of scones to wash down."

"Save some for me," the earl said. "If my brothers descend . . . speak of the devils."

The earl started filling his plate while Connor and Gilgallon came into the breakfast parlor, boots thumping on the polished wood floor.

"Morning, all," Gilgallon said, his blond good looks showing to advantage in riding attire. "Ladies, you each look to be blooming. This tells us Ian hasn't attempted any polite conversation yet."

"Don't let him spoil your appetite," the earl stage-whispered to Genie as he took the place at her elbow. "Scots are nothing if not tenacious, and I'm determined to beat some manners into him."

"I'd help," Connor said, "but I think beating manners into a fellow something of a contradiction. Ian, I am going to tattle to Mary Fran that you've left us only a half-dozen scones, and you, Miss Hester, will be my corroborating witness."

Augusta watched as the earl occasionally dropped his voice to whisper something to Genie, who gradually relaxed under the onslaught of his charm. He topped up her teacup, passed her the cream and sugar, sliced a ripe peach—Her Majesty was said to adore a peach at the conclusion of her evening meal—and put most of it on her plate.

It was breakfast with a side helping of subtle, well-disguised overtures from a man interested in gaining a lady's notice. By the third cup of tea, Genie reached for a bite of peach from the earl's plate then froze with her hand in midair.

"I beg your pardon, my lord." Her hand returned to her lap, while color rose in her cheeks. "I should not presume upon your very breakfast."

Gilgallon reached across the table and plucked the slice of fruit from his brother's plate. "Why not? If you don't, I will, and then there's Con, and Mary Fran, and . . ."

"What about Mary Fran?" The earl's sister posed her question from the door then headed directly for the buffet. "And the truth, Gilgallon Concannon MacGregor, or I'll skelp yer bum but good."

Julia spoke up for the first time. "You'll do what?"

"She'll spank him," Connor supplied, for Gilgallon was munching his peach, or the earl's peach. "Again. Motherhood has made Mary Fran a dab hand with a spanking."

"Quit braggin' on me, ye daft, glaikit mon," Mary Frances said, bringing a full plate to the table.

A few more minutes into the general banter, Augusta noticed the earl leaning over to offer Genie another one of his teasing asides, but Genie kept her gaze on her teacup, apparently wise to the man's tricks. Balfour left off his wooing, for that's what it was, when Matthew joined the assemblage.

Matthew, who might have been Augusta's . . . *husband*.

She regarded her cousin with as much dispassion as she could muster over hot, buttery scones and strong breakfast tea.

He was handsome, tall, lithe, and where she had gotten some ancestor's Celtic black hair, Matthew had been spared such a fate and sported blond hair going reddish at the temples. He'd been spared the peculiar eyes too, his being a perfectly circumspect shade of blue.

She tried to consider him objectively—they were both presently unwed—but the idea of bearing his children left her . . . disturbed. Cousins could marry legally, and royal cousins frequently did.

Matthew had been the one to teach her how to tie her boots, the older boy who'd shown her how to make a fist—thumb *outside*—and instructed her about where exactly a female might knee a bothersome fellow to allow her time to flee to safety. These were not memories conducive to marital inclinations. Not years ago and not now.

And Matthew had grown so serious. The change had started before he'd joined the cavalry, and Augusta regretted it—for his sake and for hers.

"Good morning, Cousin." Matthew took a seat beside her as he spoke. "The teapot, if it wouldn't be too much trouble?"

She obliged, pouring for him in silence. Several seats up the table, Gilgallon was now appropriating his sister's bacon and getting his tanned wrist slapped for it.

"Such violence in an earl's daughter," Connor chided, taking a sip of Gil's tea. "And I've diagnosed Gil's problem. He fails to sweeten his tea, which cannot be good for his disposition."

"My disposition would benefit from a ride directly after breakfast," Gil said, ignoring his brother's larceny. "And I would sweeten my tea, but you lot have plundered the sugar bowl."

"Perhaps the ladies would like to join you on your ride," the earl suggested. He lounged at his end of the table, lord of all he surveyed, a smile lighting his eyes.

How different this breakfast was among Scottish strangers from all the breakfasts Augusta had shared with her relations—and the breakfasts she'd shared with nobody save her cat.

"I would enjoy a tour of the estate," Genie said, pinning a nigh-desperate gaze on Gil. "A tame mount would be best, though."

55

"We'll make it a foursome if the younger Mr. MacGregor will come along," Hester chimed in, smiling at Connor. "Aunt, perhaps you'd like to join us as well?"

Julia appeared to consider this offer as she peered at her tea. "It has been ages since I've ridden. Augusta, will you join us so I won't be the only one left to amble along on an aged pony?"

Augusta was tempted. Oh, how she was tempted. But for her to be riding about with the young ladies when Julia was on hand to do so might be getting above her station.

"I'll leave the girls to your watchful eye," Augusta said. "Perhaps I'll ride some other day."

Three seats up, the Baron folded down his newspaper and frowned at the sugar bowl. "We're to tour the estate? Can't say as I approve of riding after a full meal. You girls mind your aunt, and when you're done, be sure to send along notes to your mama, else she'll be pestering me to death for word of your doings. Pass the teapot, Gussie."

Augusta did as bid. She always did as her uncle bid her, but she also noticed the earl was not making noises to join the riding expedition.

Prudent of him, to only advance his cause so far then leave Genie some time to regain her balance. It wasn't as if his own brothers were going to undermine his prospects with Genie, were they?

Three

IAN COUNTED BREAKFAST A LIMITED SUCCESS, in part because Gil had been canny enough to suggest an outing for the ladies that Ian could easily decline.

Always leave your opponent a graceful out. Grandfather's words echoed in Ian's mind, though Ian wondered how a battle-hardened soldier had applied those words in a life-or-death struggle. They had merit in a wooing, or whatever Ian was engaged in with Miss Daniels.

Miss Genie. Who'd looked only relieved when Miss Merrick had requested Ian's company on a tour of the library.

"Have you many novels in your library?"

Miss Merrick voiced her question tentatively, as if novels were some kind of pornography. Perhaps in her lexicon they were.

"Mary Fran claims we're to stock them for guests. Connor says any Scots household worth its salt has to have a full complement of old Sir Walter. Gil's excuse is that we keep them on hand for Mary Fran, while I admit to reading occasionally purely for recreation."

As she walked beside him along the rows of shelves, her eyes grew wide. "You admit such a thing?"

"There are advantages to being head of the

household." He refrained from giving her a conspiratorial wink lest the poor thing expire from an excess of innuendo, but there was pleasure in showing her what remained of the family library. She ran a single, tentative finger down the spine of each volume he pointed out, her touch slow and reverent, a kind of literary caress.

"Books were my salvation," she said as they paused by the old atlas spread on a gate-legged table. "When Papa died and then Mother died so soon after, I was quite alone. Proper mourning leaves one nothing to do *but* mourn, and I've concluded this isn't a good thing. Grief crowds in closely enough without the rest of life being shoved aside to make way for it. Am I scandalizing you?"

She peeked over at him, and Ian smiled at her. The library door was wide open, a footman posted directly outside. They were discussing novels, or possibly mourning, and she was concerned she might be shocking him.

Ian bent a bit closer and kept his voice down, as if they were exchanging confidences. "I found a great deal more solace in taking care of my father's legacy and brawling with my brothers than I did sitting behind draped windows and reading scripture."

Or getting drunk. He shook off that thought.

"Have you read this one?" He reached over her

shoulder and pulled down a book. "It's credited with sparking the revival of Scottish national pride, indirectly."

"*Waverley?* This is by your Sir Walter."

"It was so popular it gained him a dinner with George IV, and put Sir Walter in the position of managing the King's visit here in '22. I'm told I was brought to Edinburgh as an infant to see George sporting about in royal Stuart finery, but I have no recollection of it."

She frowned at the book in her hand. "George's advisors wanted him away from the Continent at that time, as I recall. He gained a great following here, though, didn't he?"

"Temporarily, at least. In my grandfather's time, we were still forbidden to wear the tartan and play our pipes. That George's visit celebrated the very things long denied us was likely the source of that popularity." But what sort of bluestocking was she, that she'd have a grasp of political history thirty years distant?

He was going to ask her, but she'd opened the book. Her frown became an expression of concentration as she stood right there and began to read. The only sound was the library clock ticking quietly on the wall, and still she remained absorbed in the book.

Ian realized how closely they were standing when he caught a whiff of lilacs from her person, a soft, pleasing scent that went with her retiring demeanor much better than the tart lemon had. She'd caught her hair back in a neat chignon, which left him with a curious desire to see her glossy black braid swinging over her hips again.

Maybe even a desire to have another of those chaste, maidenly little pecks to his cheek?

"I meant to thank you," he said, the words surprising him. *Step back, you idiot.*

She glanced up at him, her expression questioning.

"At breakfast," he clarified. "I presumed to use informal address with your cousin. You aided me in this regard."

She blinked and closed the book with a snap. "I aided the cause of our digestion. I was not raised to stand particularly on ceremony, your lordship. My grandfather was merely a baron, or a . . . what is the Scottish equivalent?"

"A lord of parliament, or lord baron. I hope you enjoy the novel, Miss Merrick."

He turned to go. There was work to be done, and she was regarding him with a peculiar light in her strange eyes.

"My lord?"

He stopped in midstride and turned to face her from a small distance. "Madam?"

From this angle, he could see that a curl had managed to escape from the black netting gathered over her nape. It was provoking, that curl. Lying against her neck, it disturbed the picture of order and calm she presented otherwise.

"I had thought . . ." She dropped her gaze from him to the book in her hands. "I don't mean to presume, but if you were so inclined . . ."

Ian liked women. He enjoyed their company in bed and out, and he treasured the grace and sweetness they added to an otherwise difficult and burdensome existence. Still, something warned him to resist any queer starts on the part of this shy spinster who wandered barefoot in the dew and dispensed kisses at dawn.

He took one step closer. "You are a guest under my roof. You have only to ask, and any aid I can offer, any courtesy, is yours, Miss Merrick." She was also his only ally in his efforts to wed the Daniels' fortune, which fact excused his tarrying with her between the bookshelves.

She mumbled something, so he took one more step closer, and now he could see her cheeks were flaming.

"I beg your pardon, Miss Merrick?"

"Augusta." She raised her gaze to his, her eyes lit with determination. "It might make your informality with Genie less difficult for her if you adopt the same address with Hester and myself. Just don't . . ."

This was costing her, this declaration. For it was a declaration of some sort—maybe of support for his goal, or maybe of something else entirely.

"Just don't?" he prodded. He put his hands behind his back lest he tuck that curl up into its rightful place.

"Don't call me Miss Gussie, or Gus, or Miss Auggie, or—"

She could not have blushed any more brightly red, and abruptly, he did not want to look on her distress. Did not want to cause it.

"I'm Ian." He interrupted her to say this. "I didn't think your cousin would remain at table if I suggested we use first names only, though you may call me Ian if you like, and I shall call you Miss Augusta. My brothers will not refer to me by the title unless they are wroth with me, and it grows . . . awkward, to be Ian to this person, Balfour to that, my lord to the other."

Her blush was fading, though this left a nice color in her usually pale cheeks.

"My grandfather said the same thing, said titles were confusing at best, and a damned lot of nonsense generally." He thought she'd cause herself to blush again, but instead she gave him another of those shy, mischievous smiles. "A lady oughtn't to use such language."

She glanced around, as if someone might censure her for using "such language."

"A guest in my home, particularly in my library, can use any damned language necessary to express herself. I hope you enjoy the book, *Miss Augusta*."

And then he did something impulsive—something a little brave, a little selfish, and more than a little stupid. He gave her a peck on the lips.

A bit more than a peck, really. Enough of a kiss to learn that she had soft, sweet lips and she hadn't been kissed worth a damn in recent memory. Her hand brushed down his chest, a fleeting caress to him, no doubt a simple bid for balance to her.

When he straightened, her hand stayed on the wool of his morning coat for one moment, while both of them stood there, staring at her elegant, bare fingers smoothing down his lapel.

Temptation barreled out of the depths of Ian's male imagination, ambushing common sense with ideas Ian had no business thinking.

He would love to teach her to kiss.

He would love to take down all that black, shining hair and bury his face in it.

He would love to walk barefoot with her in the morning dew and lay her down in the cool summer grass . . .

While the sheer, beaming innocence of her smile said Augusta Merrick had no clue what he was thinking, no clue about any of it.

"I bid you a good morning, Miss Augusta." She looked so pleased at the simple use of her name Ian would have turned from the sight even if there were not hours of work awaiting him elsewhere, and even if he had not flirted with lunacy by kissing her.

Not that anybody would mind if he dallied with her—she was a poor relation, and marriage was a calculating, unromantic business among the titled English . . . and lately the titled Scots, apparently.

He would mind if he dallied with her, and what a damned inconvenience that was.

As he made his way to the stables, Ian acknowledged he and Miss Merrick—Miss Augusta—had something else unexpected in common.

When he and his family had made the decision earlier in the year to file to have Asher declared dead, Mary Fran had insisted it was time for Ian to start using the title. He'd had a courtesy title—Viscount Deesely—but he'd never used it much. With the stroke of a pen on some arcane court pleadings, he'd become not Ian, but—presumptively and presumptuously—my lord, Balfour, Lord Balfour. *The earl,* but for the remaining legalities.

He could go entire weeks without hearing his own name, unless he was in company with his siblings. Inside, inside his very sense of himself, he felt the impending loss of some part of his identity with each use of more formal address. He couldn't reverse this sense of loss; he relied on his family to do it for him by frequent use of his given name.

And now he knew he was not alone in his sense of isolation. Even proper little spinsters from the backwaters of Oxfordshire could suffer the same gnawing fear that if nobody ever called them by name, a part of them would eventually cease to be.

"They ride well for a trio of proper ladies." Gil made the observation grudgingly, because women who rode well were women who'd had the luxury of spare time to learn, indulgent male relations to teach them, and good horses to learn on.

"Mary Fran could have come along if she'd wanted to," Connor replied. "She'd rather terrorize the staff and concoct spells and incantations to shrivel the baron's pizzle."

"Hush, you." Gil nudged his horse forward to keep in step with Connor's younger mount. "Mary Fran hates that sort of talk."

"Then she shouldn't go dancing naked under the Beltane moon, should she?"

Gil did not ask whether Con was speaking figuratively or if he'd really seen their sister comporting herself without clothing by moon-light. God knew, Mary Fran was entitled to a little eccentricity, but Ian would be beside himself if she'd gone that far.

"The widow . . ." Con hesitated, his gaze on Mrs. Redmond, Miss Genie, and Miss Hester riding up ahead. They made a pretty picture even on the less-than-elegant mounts available from the Balfour stables.

"She seems the friendly sort," Gil said, hoping to inspire Con to speak whatever piece he'd intended to speak. Miss Genie was petting her horse, stroking a gloved hand over the mare's crest with a slow, easy rhythm that had the muscles over Gil's shoulder blades relaxing.

"She's the wealthy sort," Con said. "Or was when she married into the Daniels family."

"I've never held wealth against a woman."

Con shook his head, so Gil resigned himself to patience. Con and Mary Fran were close, just as Ian and Asher had been close. Between those pairs of siblings, there had always been unspoken communication, while Gil struggled along parsing meaning as best he could and resorting to blunt inquiry more often than not.

"She said she does not want her niece to be married just for her wealth." Con stretched up in his stirrups then settled back into the saddle. "Said that befell her, and she wouldn't wish it on anybody. I told her I was sorry she'd been treated that way, which is hypocritical when my own brother intends the same thing toward her niece."

Connor would *loathe* feeling hypocritical even more than he loathed running a glorified guest-house for wealthy English pains in the arse. And of course he would apologize for a marriage Julia

Redmond probably hadn't even found truly bothersome.

"She wasn't scolding you, Connor. She was making a chaperone's version of small talk."

Con indulged in one of his infernal silences, which might presage a silent exit, a grunted curse, or a startling profundity.

"She was confiding in me, or something."

Gil knew himself to be handsome, knew Ian was handsomer, and knew Connor was . . . Connor was the braw fellow who ought to be watched and never was. His gruff ways, his indifference to refined dress and manners, and his rare, bold smile earned him all manner of female attention.

But confidences?

Gil ordered himself back to the topic at hand: "Ian isn't an unfeeling brute. He'll make Miss Daniels a passable husband."

But as he spoke, Gil recalled the pathetic relief in Genie Daniels's eyes that morning at breakfast when this outing—*sans* Ian—had been suggested. She'd had the trapped-prey air Gil felt every time he donned evening attire or stood up with a proper young lady at the local assemblies.

A look of such hopelessness, Gil had to wonder at it. "Let's catch up to them." He nudged his mount stoutly with his heels. "You can smooth the pretty widow's feathers, while I flirt with the sisters."

Connor said nothing, urging his horse to a canter and then falling in beside Mrs. Redmond, whose mare was winded enough that walking the rest of the way to the barn would be a kindness to the horse, if not exactly a kindness to her escort.

"Come, ladies, I can show you a path that will let us canter through the woods." Gil offered them the smile useful for getting him his ale before any other patron, but only Hester returned it.

"I'm not in shape for any canters through the woods," she said. "Particularly not after sitting on that train for an eternity. You and Genie go, and I'll keep Aunt company."

"Miss Genie? It cuts through the woods, where Her Majesty sometimes likes to walk and His Highness has been known to ride."

Shameless of him to use such bait, but effective.

"We'll take a groom, of course?" She glanced back at her aunt, whose horse was toddling along beside Con's at the most sedate walk.

"We will," Gil assured her. "Lavelle! You're with us."

The red-haired Lavelle, mounted on a sturdy cob, looked mightily relieved at the prospect of a meander through the woods. He fell in fifty paces back like the good but lazy lad he was. Gil well knew the last man back to the stables had fewer horses to put up.

Genie's mare had to be as fatigued as the other mounts, so Gil kept them to an easy trot until they approached the woods, then slowed to a walk.

He waited for his companion to catch up before speaking. "Our woods abut those of Balmoral, though elsewhere, there are small-holdings between the two properties."

"Have you met Her Majesty?"

"I have." Victoria was downright neighborly at times, for a queen. Just another clucking, fussing, well-to-do mother with a large brood to keep track of and a doting husband at her side. "I've hunted and fished with Albert as well, and met such of the children as are old enough to be out and about."

"The royal couple must be very much in love." Her voice was so wistful, Gil glanced over at her. Her expression matched her melancholy tone, at variance with the sunny, breezy day.

"They're up to at least a half-dozen children, and chronic rumors of more on the way," Gil said. "If they're not in love, they're certainly making the best of their situation." He tried his signature smile on her again, but she just looked . . . sad.

"Do I offend, Miss Daniels?"

She shook her head. "Marriage is such a daunting prospect, and to be married and the monarch . . ."

Marriage was daunting, or marriage to his

brother? Or marriage to any Scottish title? "What about it daunts you?"

She swallowed. "There's no hiding anything in a marriage, not if your husband doesn't want to leave you any privacy. There's no freedom, no hope. You can risk your life giving the man babies, and then he can take them from you and you'll never see them again. You're trapped, a slave with no hope of manumission save his death—or your own."

Gil's brows rose as she spoke. These were desperate words from a woman who'd had her pick of the swains from three London Seasons. "What is your mother doing right this minute, Miss Daniels?"

She turned a puzzled expression on him. "I don't know."

"I'd hazard your father doesn't know, either. For all the weeks he's up here with you, for all the weeks he'll be shooting grouse in Northumbria, your mother will have complete independence from her entire family."

The lady fiddled with the reins. "She will not. Papa has the servants in his pocket, and they'll tattle on her in an instant. He believes a man's home is his castle and his word is law within his own walls."

She turned her face straight up into the sunlight pouring through the pines above them, as if she'd entreat heaven itself for agreement, while Gil struggled for something to say. Things went from bad to worse when she started to cry, which was no damned help at all.

"For God's sake." He caught Lavelle's vacant gaze and nodded in the direction of the stables. The groom obligingly turned back the way they'd come, while Gil reached over and pulled Miss Daniels's horse up. "Madam, this will not do."

He swung off and came around to lift her from the saddle. She was boneless with her upset, sliding down his length like an exhausted child, then leaning on him, weeping softly.

"I can't do this." Her voice was low, miserable, and heartfelt. "I can't impose on your family's hospitality and let my father spend his precious coin when I have no intention of considering your brother's suit. It isn't . . . sporting."

Sporting? What an odd notion in the politics of mutually advantageous matrimony between English and Scot.

"Come sit." He took off his riding gloves and pulled her by the hand to a nicely situated boulder. When she was seated beside him, a shaft of sunlight gilding her hair, he fished out his handkerchief. "What is this really about?"

"I don't know you, Mr. MacGregor, nor would I burden you with confidences even if I did." She took his handkerchief and daintily blotted her eyes. "I apologize for this unseemly display. I simply do not want to marry like this, not your brother, not any titled man my parents might put up to the task."

More tears leaked from the corners of her eyes, and Gil wished he might in that moment follow Asher into the wilds of Canada. "Ian will treat you with utmost civility."

Except when he was swiving the woman witless in service to the damned title. There probably wasn't a civil way to conceive heirs, not for a Scotsman and his wife.

"He will marry me." This last was said so miserably Gil sensed his companion was holding on to her limited store of composure by a slender, taut thread. He settled his hand on her nape, rubbing his thumb gently over the bone that bumped at the top of her spine, much as he might seek to calm a nervous hound by touch.

"You assume because he must marry lucratively Ian will resent his wife or neglect her. This is not so." She remained silent, but he thought some of her anxiety might be easing. "Ian and I have the same mother, as do Con and Mary Fran, but none of us had our mothers for long, or even our grandmothers. We adore mothers, do you hear me? We adore Mary Fran because she's Fiona's mother; we adore wee Fiona because someday she might be a mother too."

Genie opened her eyes and turned her head to peer at him. The sight hit Gil with a visceral punch, sucked the air right out of his lungs. Her lashes were spiky with tears, her blue eyes luminous, and the sadness he saw there . . .

He drew back, lest he comfort her in ways guaranteed to get his face slapped, and then his lights put out by an irate brother with not even a prospective bride to woo.

"You must discuss this with Ian." He patted her hand, resenting her riding gloves because they prevented him from enjoying the feel of her silky skin beneath his fingers.

"I could not."

She swayed toward him and he was not strong enough to stand up, get on his horse, and leave the lady to dry her own tears. He tucked his arm around her waist as her head came to rest on his shoulder.

"Ian is a good man, Miss Daniels. The best. You think the title is what you'll get out of the marriage, but that's not the half of it. He's loyal as hell, hardworking, fair, honest. God knows he's patient and generous with his family . . ." Gil trailed off, because she'd let out a sigh, and the hair on the crown of her head was tickling his cheek, bringing the scent of rose water and warm, clean female to his nose.

"I can't discuss this with him," she said. "I did discuss it with a solicitor, though. Once a woman is married, she is more or less her husband's chattel, even if the contracts try to put limitations on his conduct. And there are far worse cruelties than raising your hand to someone. Trust me, Mr. MacGregor, your brother and I would make each other miserable."

Gil fell silent, willing to steal a few minutes with a pretty woman plastered to him in the privacy of the woods. It should have been toweringly awkward, though she was making no move to leave his side.

"Being the spare can feel a little like being slave," he said after a moment, trailing his hand over her back. "You can't strike out on your own, and you can't quite get out from under the title, though you dare not long for it, either. You sometimes think you'll do anything to see your brothers wed and starting nice big families of healthy boys."

He could not see her mouth, but he could feel her smile.

"I thought Scottish titles could often pass through the female line."

"They can, many of them, and even be held by females. Ours has never been held by a female, though it originated like several dukedoms, when a young married lady caught the eye of Charles II." He kept his arm around her for a few more moments while he wondered at his own motives.

"You are a very good brother," she said at length. She sat up, taking away the warmth of her body along Gil's side. "And I am sorry to be so

74

dramatic. Papa has his heart set on this match, and I . . . I have my reasons, Mr. MacGregor, but I am averse to the kind of marriage my parents have chosen for me."

There was a puzzle here, though Gil thanked God it wasn't his puzzle to unlock. "Are you averse to marrying anybody with a title, or are your reasons specific to Ian?"

"Anybody whom I do not . . . *anybody* seeking to trade a title for my wealth."

She sounded very sure of herself, which left Gil both relieved and oddly disappointed. Though whether he was disappointed for her, for Ian, or—God help him—for himself, he could not have said.

And it hardly mattered, regardless.

"You must explain your situation to Ian," Gil said, rising from their boulder. "He's a canny man, and you wouldn't want for a better friend in a pinch. If anybody can aid you, Miss Daniels, he can."

"He can't help me."

"Not even with a long engagement from which he allows you to cry off and keep much of your settlements?"

She was in the process of shaking out the skirts of her habit as he spoke, but she paused to meet his eyes. "Such arrangements are possible?"

He winged his arm at her, having no idea whatsoever what was possible once lawyers got hold of marriage contracts. His brother, however, he both knew and trusted.

"Ian isn't a good negotiator, he's a *great* negotiator. Our neighbors have been known to solicit Ian's input on sticky foreign policy matters, and in dealing with their various local retainers. He studied law for years, and he can sort out most any situation and draft language to address it."

"Then it's possible? To write a contract such that some of the money will stay with the jilted groom even after a long engagement?"

Why in God's name did she sound so intrigued? Even he knew a woman who jilted her fiancé was effectively ruined. "It may be possible, though Ian has made no secret we need coin sooner rather than later. Still, I suggest you bring up with him whatever is troubling you and solicit his aid. As a gentleman, he's honor bound to help you."

She let Gil assist her into the saddle but said little all the way back to the stables. Gil was going to have to tell Ian something of what had transpired in the woods—that the woman was reluctant, of course. That she'd taken arranged marriage as an institution into dislike for a certainty.

But not that the lady had literally cried on Gil's shoulder. Her dignity alone required he hold that much in confidence.

Four

"GUSSIE, YOU MUST ARISE! CON SAYS WE might spot Her Majesty or His Highness today. After a rainy day, they often take the children for an outing on the walking paths."

Julia's eyes were as animated as any girl's at her first ball, while Augusta stifled the urge to shut the door in the other woman's face. A solitary walk in the woods was apparently not to be had today, though the sun shone brightly enough outside Augusta's bedroom to make the wet grass sparkle invitingly.

"I'll be down to breakfast directly," Augusta said, stepping back from her door. Then a thought struck her. "*Con,* Julia?"

She'd seen the pair of them at dinner, heads together, the quiet Scot occasionally offering Julia a subdued smile that charmed with its very subtlety. It was a just-for-you smile, more personal than the beaming bonhomie of the other MacGregor brothers.

"Connor, then. We agreed it grows awkward to have two Mr. MacGregors at the table, and Con said Gilgallon will become violent if we refer to him as Deesely, which he isn't quite, not really. Or maybe he is."

Augusta watched as Julia moved over to the French doors. For a widow of mature years—

Julia would be thirty on her next birthday—she was positively bouncing along.

"Where is your cat, Gus? I should think he'd be reclining in splendor on that great bed."

"He's likely out sunning himself somewhere. That's why the French doors are left open, so Ulysses may go on his royal progress at his leisure." And so the brisk Highland air could find its way into Augusta's room as she slept.

"He might decide to make his residence here, as Her Majesty has."

Augusta frowned at the French door. Yes, Ulysses might decide he preferred the earl's stables to a glorified farmhouse in Oxfordshire, and if he did, she would miss her cat.

Miss him terribly, which was pathetic.

Julia moved away from the doors. "Let's go down to breakfast, or Con and Gil will have eaten all the scones. I think Hester has quite a crush on Gilgallon."

"Hester has quite a crush on the breakfast offerings."

Augusta found them to her liking as well. The lavish spread of hearty fare was a far cry from the bread, butter, and tea that sustained her at home. Dinners, by contrast, were lighter than their English equivalents, boasting an array of rich, savory sauces and smaller portions.

Somebody had an eye for presentation, Augusta decided as she filled her plate with eggs, ham, and buttered toast. The cuisine was a fine blend of Continental and local, and a decided improvement over even what was served in Aunt and Uncle's house.

For the first time in ages, Augusta's mind wandered into a corner she'd forbidden it to explore out of sheer self-preservation.

If I had my own household, a real household, I'd want the food to be like this. To be hearty and flavorful at the same time. Abundant but not wasteful. Food that was relished down to the last crumb, and lovely in its appearance, scent, and taste. I'd want the food in my kitchens to be prepared with genuine caring for those who consumed it and how it was consumed. I'd take a hand in that myself . . .

She might even set a table like this, with a blue, brown, and white plaid tablecloth as the centerpiece, and everything from the tea service to the serviettes to the curtains coordinated to match.

"Tea, Miss Augusta?"

The earl had appropriated the seat beside her. She'd noticed this about him: he wandered from his expected locations. He'd done it at dinner last night to sit beside Genie for the dessert course, but then he'd engaged her father in discussion, leaving Genie to Gilgallon's silly teasing. The strategy had worked, because when the ladies departed for the drawing room, it was the earl left holding Genie's chair and giving her his arm as escort.

"Tea would be lovely. I was just admiring the skill of your kitchens, my lord."

"That's Ian to you, Miss Augusta." He'd dropped his voice, and when she glanced up at his face, she saw a hint of mischief in his eye. The man had no notion of how to be a proper earl, but then he was a spare, just finding his way with the role.

A spare with a delightful and alarming tendency to reciprocate misplaced kisses.

She took the teapot from where it sat before him and poured for them both. "You are a reluctant earl, aren't you?"

The mischief died abruptly, replaced by an appraising light. "I am not reluctant. I am kicking and screaming, lest you be deceived by appearances to the contrary. I've considered going to Canada to find my older brother, leaving Gil to manage in my stead. He's more ruthless than I am, better suited to the title."

Oh, for pity's sake, he was being *honest*. He stirred his cream into his tea with all the diffidence of a boy waiting for his elders to spring him from the table, and there was a grim set to his mouth that made Augusta wish she'd been less forward.

"I was a reluctant spinster at first." The words were not planned, but they seemed to catch his attention. "I'd stirred some interest during my

Season, and I had always assumed—what girl from a wealthy family doesn't assume?—I'd have a husband, children, a household of my own. I did not adjust easily to my new expectations."

"And none of your adoring swains saw fit to rescue you from those expectations?"

He would ask that. Except his voice hadn't been sardonic or flippant.

"The swains adored my fortune, I'm afraid." And then her stupid mouth would not hush or busy itself slurping at the cooling tea. "Some of them subsequently offered for Genie. I expect they'll make a try for Hester too."

A small silence ensued between them, punctuated by a particularly loud laugh from Julia, who was sitting between the Misters MacGregor down the table.

"I will not offer for Hester should I fail with Genie." His expression was rueful. "I hope."

"Persistence, my lord. You're making progress with Genie, and it's early days yet."

She was so bold as to reach over and pat his arm in company. The idea that this handsome, charming man was admitting of some trepidation was oddly gratifying. Maybe there were worse things than sharing a glorified farmhouse with a cat and an elderly cousin in Oxfordshire.

Miss Augusta—not Gus, Gussie, or Auggie—patted Ian's arm and topped up his tea, little gestures that ought to have irritated him, but they were instead soothing. His siblings had never been the sort to cosset each other, and any tendency they'd had in that direction had fallen away completely when it became obvious Asher wasn't coming back.

"Is it really so bad?" Miss Augusta asked him. She kept her voice down and her expression bland as she reached for her utensils. This was probably a spinster's trick, the ability to lurk beneath notice in her conversations and her mannerisms. Nobody's gaze would pause at the tableau they presented—a host and his guest exchanging civilities over breakfast, nothing more.

"You mean our finances?"

"Your situation." She took a dainty bite of her eggs, casual as you please, while she invited Ian to lay bare his shortcomings as earl.

Or to share his burdens.

He decided her intentions more closely fit the latter.

"It's . . . delicate. Matters are improving, but an estate requires long-term maintenance. We could probably manage well enough over the next few years because my grandfather was a shrewd and practical man, but when the roof needs attention, or if a crop fails again, or Mary Fran or her daughter Fiona require a dowry . . ."

The myriad threatening disasters started to list themselves in Ian's mind: The stables consisted of enormous plough horses, green stock being prepared for sale and near-pensioners, including Ian's own mount. There was no dowry gathering interest for either Fiona or Mary Fran. The roof was going to need attention in the next five years, or after the very next hard winter—and when wasn't a Highland winter hard?

The carpets were all getting worn, and in the family wing there were precious few carpets left. Cook wanted a more modern stove, and the deadfall in the wood was getting thin from providing wood fires for their guests for much of the summer.

Miss Augusta put down her fork, her earnest expression interrupting Ian's mental litany of unmet responsibilities.

"You are a good earl. I recall my own grandfather cautioning my mother to look to the next generation, not the next season. You're a good brother too. Your siblings are lucky to have you."

She didn't pat his arm again, but she might as well have, so nicely did her words settle in Ian's ear. "Despite the pressing burdens, one must soldier on," she said quietly. "Your tea is getting cold, my lord."

Ian. He wanted this quiet mouse with the gentian eyes and innocent kisses to call him Ian. He took a sip of tea rather than admit this to her and did not speculate about what such a wayward impulse might portend.

• • •

The young people were at last away, gamboling like puppies across the park. Watching from his sitting-room balcony, the baron wished them a long and happy ramble. Bleating, laughing sheep, the lot of them. The Scotsmen were big, strapping rams posturing and pawing before the ewes, and the women were brainless twits, just hoping to catch the notice of the fellow of their choice.

But how obliging of them all, to leave him the run of the house so early in his visit. And what great good fortune that Matthew had for once allowed himself a frivolous outing. What was to be done would be done for Matthew, but the man was too stiff-rumped to ever appreciate his father's efforts.

A slow smile spread across the baron's face. The plan was perfect, a work of art. This way, all suspicion would fall on the strutting Scottish earl, making him even more willing to snap up a baron's daughter.

When word of the misfortune befalling one of the earl's guests reached Polite Society, Balfour would never again be able to charge exorbitant sums for simple hospitality.

"Tell me of your home, Miss Genie. How does it compare with Balfour?"

The young lady at Ian's side seemed incapable of uttering a sentence without a considering

84

silence before she opened her mouth. Maybe she was thoughtful by nature, maybe she was intimidated, and maybe this was some hen-witted attempt at coyness falling far short of its mark.

"Which home would that be, my lord? We have the London townhouse, a house in the New Town in Edinburgh, the family seat in Kent, a very nice little set of estates in Oxfordshire, as well as a hunting box in Cumbria, and dower properties for me and Hester in Surrey and Sussex respectively."

Of course they did. "Which is your favorite?"

Another pause, while Ian guided her around a tree root protruding into the path.

"I like them all. The town house is for the Season, so we have great good fun there. My dower property is quite lovely, but I expect you know that."

"I know no such thing, Miss Genie. You could describe it to me."

"I haven't seen it since I was seventeen . . ."

She had the knack of implying questions where they made no sense, like at the end of her last pronouncement. Some query hung in the air:

Shall I describe it to you? Or maybe, *Might we finish conversing now, my lord? Walking and talking at the same time taxes my brain so sorely.*

Except she wasn't stupid. Ian would have bet his best bull doddy the lady wasn't stupid. She

85

was just unforthcoming in his company. At breakfast she'd been laughing and flirting with Gil and Con as shamelessly as her aunt.

"Miss Genie, perhaps there's something you'd like to ask me? My attempts at conversation aren't taking us very far in the direction of getting acquainted."

"Why would you wish to acquaint yourself with me, my lord?"

No hesitation there. "Because you are my guest, because you are a lovely young lady, because my great-aunt suggested we might suit, because we're wandering about here in the woods with no one else to converse with, largely by the design of my enterprising younger siblings."

A slight smile creased her lips. Very slight, but genuine.

She glanced meaningfully over her shoulder at Hester, striding along, opera glasses plastered to her nose supposedly the better to identify Highland birds. "Younger siblings can be the devil, can't they?"

"A mixed blessing, but you and Hester seem close."

This was firmer ground, something they honestly had in common, and Ian mentally kicked himself for not thinking of it sooner. Beside him, he felt the lady relax just a little. Her stride opened up; her grip on his arm became more functional and less decorative.

"Hester is the very best sister, but she is a *little* sister, if you take my meaning. She embarrasses me with her pithy observations—always in company, of course—without even intending to, but she's also my staunchest ally."

"I think your cousin, your brother, and your aunt are all allies too. In his own way, even your papa takes your welfare seriously."

"Oh, he'd better. Mama will sulk for ages if this excursion at Balfour doesn't go well."

The smile was gone, and Ian wondered if Miss Genie recalled with whom she walked. He steered her past another upthrust root.

"What can I do to ensure your visit goes well, Miss Genie? I am your host, after all. Your pleasure is my first concern."

That might have been laying it on a bit thick, but she nibbled her lip and glanced over at him, a considering, somewhat fretful gesture. He waited, hoping they were on the verge of some genuine honesty, a small step in the direction of betrothal, but an important first step.

She dropped her gaze and then stumbled hard, pitching into Ian with an unladylike yelp. He caught her around the middle before she could hit the ground and hauled her up against him.

She stood awkwardly, one foot raised, letting Ian keep her balanced by virtue of leaning into him.

"I am so sorry, my lord. I'm not usually

clumsy. I'm never clumsy, in fact, but I can be preoccupied . . . oh, blast. Excuse my language, but it hurts."

She was going to cry. Ian scooped her up against his chest and carried her to a fallen tree lying sideways along the path. When he had her seated, he fished for his handkerchief, wondering all the while if this was a ploy or a genuine mishap.

"Genie?" Miss Augusta came bustling up, Gil at her side. Ian had never been so glad to see a decent woman in his life. "Dear heart, have you come a cropper?"

"I twisted my ankle, Gussie. I feel so terribly stupid."

"We can heal your ankle," Augusta said, patting her cousin's shoulder. "The stupid part is a chronic facet of the human condition."

Gil whipped out his handkerchief and passed it to the lady, while Ian wondered when his brother had started using monogrammed linen.

"Here, now. Let's have that boot off." Gil knelt on one knee like some damned parfit gentil knight and started on the laces of Genie's walking boot, while Augusta—what was wrong with the woman?—stepped back to allow him.

"Oh, that cannot be comfortable," Augusta murmured, taking the boot from Gil's hand. "You did yourself an injury, my dear."

"I feel so stupid."

Yes, they knew that. Ian was beginning to feel rather stupid himself. He shifted to Augusta's side.

"We can have the grooms bring a pony cart for you," he said. "Or I can simply carry you back to the house."

Genie blushed. Gil's hand on her foot hadn't caused her to color up like that, but Ian's very gallant offer—if he did say so himself—had her cheeks flaming.

"Of course we can't put his lordship to that trouble," Augusta said. "Gilgallon will carry you back to the house, and Lord Balfour and I will locate the others and inform them of your accident."

"You mustn't cut short the outing." Looking fragile and brave, Genie pressed Gil's handkerchief to the corners of her eyes.

"We won't." Hester spoke up from Augusta's other side. "We've a way to go yet before we're along the Balmoral property line. I'll tell Her Majesty you were otherwise detained, shall I?"

"Give her my regrets," Genie said. "His Highness too."

Hester saluted, straightened, and walked off in the direction of the Queen's holding. And just like that, Gil was hefting Genie into his arms, while the lady—Ian's intended—looped her arms around Gil's neck and laid her cheek against his shoulder.

"Only to the edge of the woods, Gil." Ian put some sternness in his voice as Augusta tucked the boot into Genie's lap. "Hail a groundsman to have the pony cart brought along for the sake of the lady's dignity."

"Put ice on that ankle," Augusta added, looping her hand over Ian's arm. "White willow bark tea would be a good idea too." She dropped her voice as Gil moved off with his burden. "Do come away, my lord. Genie is mortified enough."

"What about me?" Ian asked, letting himself be marched on down the path. "What about my mortification? I was the lady's escort, and I was supposed to keep her from harm."

"Genie is not at her best just now, and you did keep her from harm. What if she'd pitched to the earth and struck her head on a rock? No, don't look at them. She would never want you to see your prospective bride so discomposed."

Illumination flared in Ian's brain. Pride he could understand. Genie saw Gil more as a henchman, perhaps, and that was why she'd allowed him to aid her while Ian stood around, surreptitiously stuffing his plain handkerchief back in his pocket.

"I bungled that," he said. "We'd just started a real conversation, and I damned near dropped her on her head. Beg pardon for my language."

He felt a shiver go through Miss Augusta. Perhaps he'd shocked her.

Another shivery little tremble, and then he heard her snort.

"You're laughing at me, Miss Augusta Merrick. A belted earl on his own demesne, and I am an object of ridicule."

"You are *pouting*," she said, letting her mirth become audible. "A great, grand, strapping, handsome man, complete with title, gorgeous green eyes, and loyal minions, and you're pouting because your younger brother stepped into the breach."

"Was her ankle really turned?" He'd been too much a gentleman to inspect it himself. Hadn't even felt an inclination to peek with his gorgeous green eyes, truth be known.

"Oh, yes. There's a lovely bruise rising right below her ankle. She wasn't bamming us, my lord. But if she had been, perhaps it would have been a ploy to find aid and comfort in your arms, had you but offered."

Had he but *offered*? When the lady was cuddled in Gil's embrace as if a dragon were in pursuit of her virtue? "Let's find the others. My sister is loose without supervision in the company of a guest far too much a gentleman for his own good."

Augusta kept up easily with Ian's stride. "Matthew *is* a gentleman, you know. He won't take liberties with your sister unless invited to do so, widow or not, Englishman or not."

"It isn't my sister I'm worried about."

• • •

Augusta closed the door to her bedroom, leaned against it, and smiled broadly.

Wasn't it lovely, to go striding through the woods with a handsome man at her side, one who apparently enjoyed his own property and wasn't bound by the notion that a lady must mince about, clinging helplessly to his arm.

Though she had clung, just a little. How easily Ian had lifted Genie into his arms. How adorable he'd looked, standing by, wanting to help but letting his brother be the one to aid the lady.

Augusta glanced around at the plaid decor surrounding her and decided Scotland was good for her. The MacGregors were good for her, getting her out in company, providing her handsome escorts, putting hearty fare before her at meals . . . Augusta tried to recall why she'd been so reluctant to join this family journey in the first place.

Uncle Willard hadn't urged her to come, but Aunt had—had insisted in fact, and Augusta had sought desperately for some sign from her uncle that he was willing to spend the coin to bring her along. He'd been particularly unforthcoming, his silences considering and unnerving. Julia had asked for her assistance, though, because two girls with one chaperone would always have to be in company, and such an arrangement was not conducive to fostering a betrothal.

Augusta was pleased to see a tea service waiting for her on the escritoire by the windows. The earl's staff was very thoughtful. She must compliment Lady Mary Frances on this, and find a way to do it that wouldn't offend the woman's pride.

Mary Fran was also making an effort to bring Matthew out of the grim mood he'd brought back with him from the Crimea. Uncle had prevailed on Matthew to come home before the official fighting was underway, though everybody spoke of war as if it were inevitable.

Matthew had been smiling at Mary Fran as they'd all wandered back to the house—all save Con and Julia, who'd gotten off to God knew where—and Matthew's smile had been more like the easy, charming smile he'd sported to such advantage as a younger man.

All in all, it had been a wonderful outing. Augusta sat on her big, fluffy bed and bent to unlace her old walking boots. She paused to pet her cat, who was motionless on the floor beside her bed, probably exhausted from chasing every mouse in the Balfour stables.

Ian knew better than to ask a servant where his sister had gotten off to. They were loyal to her, the lot of them—the grinning footmen, the giggling maids, the cheerful tyrant in the kitchens referred to simply as Cook. The stable lads were the worst, mooning after Mary Fran like a pack of schoolboys, when to a man, they were old enough to be her father, some of them old enough to be her grandfather.

But Mary Fran was either in hiding or seeing to the guest chambers, so Ian took himself in that direction only to stop abruptly in the corridor.

Weeping. The sound was quiet but distinct, coming from the other side of . . . Miss Augusta Merrick's door. Ian recalled the location of her room because she'd had that great, fat black cat, and had requested access for him to the outdoors.

He rapped lightly on the door. "Miss Augusta? Shall I send my sister to you?"

He had to strain to hear her words. "Please just go away."

Ian had only the one sister, but she'd trained him properly. That had not been a particularly emphatic command, and in the way of females, it had strongly implied its opposite. Cautiously, he opened the door—the woman hadn't had time to discard her clothing after their walk, or so he hoped.

"Miss Merrick?"

"For pity's sake, close the door." Her breathing hitched. Ian heard it, and he saw it in the twitch of her shoulders where she lay curled on her side on the bed. Her back didn't tell him much, except that she was upset enough to be in tears.

And she was not a crying type of female. "Was it something I said in the woods?"

He hadn't said much really. She was the kind of woman a man didn't feel the need to chatter with. A restful woman, easy to be with.

She pushed up and scooted around, cuddling the furry black beast that had taken such exception to being transported in a hatbox.

"I'm being ridiculous." She pushed her way one-handed to the edge of the bed, and laid the unmoving cat beside her on the quilt. "He was very old, even for a house cat."

"Your cat has gone to his reward?"

She sniffed and nodded as she stroked a hand over the animal's fur. "I'm being maudlin. He was happy to be here, and I don't think he suffered."

And then she curled in on herself, losing her composure again. It broke Ian's heart to see it, to see her struggling against tears when it was just the two of them . . .

In her room, behind a closed door. Good God. The ramifications if somebody came upon them were too awful to contemplate.

His indecision lasted but a moment. If this wasn't a damsel in distress, then such a lady didn't exist. He locked the door behind him and crossed the room.

"You were attached to him," Ian said, wanting to take the mortal remains from the room, but understanding he couldn't yet. He shifted to lean against the bedpost. "When my first pony died, I wouldn't let Grandfather bury him until the parson came from the kirk to bless the ground." He passed her his handkerchief, somewhat the worse for having been balled up and stowed in his pocket earlier.

She took the linen from his hand. "Ulysses was my friend. My only . . ." She fell silent again as weeping overtook her, giving Ian the sense Augusta Merrick would not cry often, but she'd grieve bitterly when tears befell her. She reminded him of Mary Fran in that, so he sat beside her on the bed, the cat between them.

"You'll miss him."

She nodded. "I live in a modest house, not even a real manor, and my third cousin is elderly and rarely leaves her rooms. Ulysses would not let me be alone. He'd come wherever I was when I was home, and when I was not, he'd wait on the porch for me no matter the hour."

"Loyal, then. A good friend."

"He would sleep at my feet on the coldest nights. I'd let him have a little cream when I sat down to tea, like a little girl, having a tea p-party."

She covered her face with her hands while Ian gently shifted the cat. These were confidences wrested from her because she was upset. He had no business hearing them, and she'd be embarrassed to have shared them unless he some-how conveyed that he understood her misery.

He moved closer and put an arm around her waist.

"When I was young, we had a dog. He was *my* dog, given to me because Asher had been given his own horse, and Grandfather said I wasn't yet old enough for that honor. I suspect we simply couldn't afford to feed another mouth in the stable. The dog's name was MacTavish, and he went everywhere with me, though he'd been pronounced too lame to hunt. Asher offered to trade the horse for him, but I wouldn't give up my dog."

"How did you lose him?"

Her head rested on his shoulder while Ian's hand moved slowly over her back. Her bones were more delicate than he'd have thought, and she smelled good, like sweet, new hay and pungent lavender overlaid with lilacs.

"He lived to be thirteen, and though I was a man well grown by Highland standards, when he died, I cried. He was asleep by the hearth, having pride of place as the oldest hound, and then he was gone. It was winter, but Gil and Con had dug some early graves in the fall before the ground froze." He fell silent, recalling the sweep of the wind through the pines on that bitter day; feeling again the painful lump in his throat, the hot tears tracking down his cold cheeks. "Con piped him home."

And for all that Ian had felt as if his very childhood were going into the ground with the old dog, it was a good memory. A memory of how family could comfort and ease heartbreak just by being family.

Though Ian sensed Augusta Merrick's family wouldn't comfort her over the loss of her pet. Matthew might make some quiet gesture; the women would cluck and murmur, but not enough to matter.

"I'll bury him for you. Put him in the ground beside MacTavish and my old pony. I'll have the priest up from town, too, if you like, to bless the plot again."

She was quieter beside him, not giving off so much heat. Ian felt her gathering her dignity and pushed her head to his shoulder lest she move away.

"I would appreciate that, if you'd give him some sort of burial. The priest won't be necessary. Ulysses never did have much patience for my outings to church."

Humor, a small jest, a sign she was recovering her balance. Ian wondered where his own had gone. She sighed, and he resisted the urge to brush his lips against her temple in a gesture of comfort.

Surely, it would only have been a gesture of comfort.

Wouldn't it?

Five

FOREVER AFTER, AUGUSTA KNEW SHE WOULD associate the scent of heather with comfort. Such wonderful, soul-deep comfort, to be held by a man who was easy with the embrace, not stiff and reluctant, not rendered silent and resentful by the prospect of a woman surrendering to her emotions.

Ulysses deserved tears. For years, he'd been her friend, her only link with a happier time, her only tangible proof those times existed outside her imagination.

She blotted her eyes with Lord Balfour's handkerchief, catching another whiff of the clean, outdoor scent of the sachets his sister used to freshen the laundry.

She should move.

His hand gently pushed her head to his shoulder, and Augusta allowed it. She stayed right where she was, sitting beside him, letting his heat and strength seep into her bones.

"I'd forgotten how grief makes the body ache," she said. "It's curious."

"It makes the head ache too, when you try to drink your way through it."

He said nothing more, though his words were enough to acknowledge he'd known loss too. Both parents—like Augusta—grandparents, step-parents, and very likely his older brother.

A trainload of loss. She let out a sigh, feeling the soft wool of his jacket against her cheek. "I will miss him badly."

"You will recall him fondly. Mary Fran will make sure the grave is tended."

"Can you plant heather over it?"

"Of course."

Just like that, not even a manly sigh of exasperation to be heard. Augusta lost a part of her heart to him for his understanding and his patience. She lifted her head and shifted away, using his handkerchief to dab at her eyes.

"May I fix you a cup of tea, Miss Augusta?" He didn't move off, but remained right there on the bed, another sign of the kind of courage that allowed a man to deal with a woman's upset graciously.

Augusta glanced over at the service sitting on her desk.

"No, thank you. It's likely gotten cold by now, and the kitchen sent up only a few drops of cream. I'm a glutton for cream in my tea, but thank you for your thoughtfulness."

She meant to buss his cheek again to emphasize her point, nothing more, but this time, she lingered long enough to notice his skin was a little scratchy with new beard, and cool. The scent of Highland flowers was stronger closer to his person.

And then she didn't move away after her little gesture; she lingered, her mouth near his, offering, despite all sense to the contrary, to allow a moment of consolation to slip toward something most unwise. He rewarded her boldness with a kiss so tender as to be chaste— *almost* chaste—his mouth settling over hers in a soft, unhurried brush of his lips for her comfort. His hand cradled her jaw in the same sort of caress—cherishing and dear without being presumptuous.

He drew back, resting his cheek against her temple. For a moment they remained on the bed while Augusta considered whether she'd just been rejected, consoled, or gallantly spared following a serious lapse in judgment.

"May I take him now, Augusta?"

Oh, how she liked the sound of her name rendered with that masculine burr. Liked it far too well.

Augusta forced her gaze to the cat. Mercifully, the beast's eyes were closed. Had Ian done that for her?

She rose and gathered up the mortal remains of her friend. Ian stood, making no move to relieve her of her burden, his gaze on her. He waited until she passed him the cat, then he held Ulysses with as much gentleness as he'd shown her moments earlier.

"If you'd get the door?" He waited again while

Augusta took a step back, a step admitting that her friend was gone and the practicalities needed to be dealt with. A step that also ignored a growing catalogue of kisses shared with a man who would marry her cousin.

A difficult, painful step.

She went to the door and found it locked, another subtle consideration from a man who owed her less than her family did. She unlocked the door and reached out a hand to smooth it down Ulysses's fur one last time.

"I'll see to him," Ian said. "We'll plant him some heather, and you can visit him before you leave for the South." He leaned around the burden in his arms and kissed her cheek, a different kind of consolation. In his gaze, Augusta saw no censorship, no prurience, no untoward sentiment at all. She saw understanding and regret, an acknowledgement that he too might be capable of poor judgment in a weak moment. And then he was gone, slipping quietly from her chamber, the cat held against his chest.

Augusta crossed the room and stood by the terrace doors, which were still cracked out of consideration for her late cat. She remained there, her palm cradling her cheek, until she saw Ian crossing the back gardens on the way to the stables, the cat in his hands.

What a lovely, lovely man. Kind, patient, considerate, and possessed of a certain knowing quality regarding life and its challenges. Few men had the kind of quiet self-possession Ian MacGregor brought to his earldom. Like Matthew, they could charge off into the heat of battle, guns blazing, sabers at the ready— Augusta had no doubt Ian would acquit himself well in that type of battle too. But how many men could deal with a weeping spinster grieving for her cat, with her clumsy, untoward advances, and neither mock nor take advantage?

Ian MacGregor was going to make Genie a wonderful, *wonderful* husband.

Con paused in his mucking to eye his older brother. "What's that?"

"What does it look like? A dead cat." Ian laid the animal on a bench then hung his jacket on a bridle hook. "Miss Augusta's old beast, by whom she set a great deal of store."

"And the fresh Scottish air did him in?"

"He was old."

Con considered his brother, who'd buried his share of pets and people. They both had. "Shall I get a shovel?"

"Nah . . ." Ian eyed the cat. "Well, yes. It will go more quickly with the two of us planting him, and Augusta asked that we mark the spot with a bit of heather."

"You mean, go pick some heather to lay on the grave?" Their estate boasted showy, expensive gardens full of flowers more impressive than simple, unassuming heather.

"Dig up some heather to plant along with the old bugger." Ian disappeared into the saddle room and emerged carrying two shovels. "Where did you and the pretty widow get off to this morning, little brother? We had some excitement when Miss Genie wrenched her ankle."

Con's brows rose as he realized he'd not gotten his story properly rehearsed in his head before he was supposed to recite his lines. And what popped out of his ignorant gob?

"We got lost."

Ian passed him the pair of shovels, grinning like an older brother ready to have some fun at a younger sibling's expense. "You got *lost*. You, who've rambled and roamed every acre of the shire and every inch of this estate. You got *lost*."

As they ambled down the barn aisle, Con carrying two shovels, Ian carrying the cat, Ian went on. "Did you have to look for the way home under the widow's skirts, Connor?"

"It wasn't like that." Though perhaps it might have been, if Con hadn't gotten so damned angry. Despite her demure and unassuming femininity, Julia Redmond was not a shy woman.

"So she's making you work for it?" Ian cuffed him good-naturedly on the shoulder. "That's only fair. They've been here all of two days, and ladies like determination in their followers."

"Would ye shut up?"

"I'll shut up until we see Gilgallon. He'll be concerned that a fellow who can track deer through a dense Highland fog can't find his way home in his own backyard."

As they crossed to the woods behind the stables, Connor had the sense Ian was just getting started.

"All right," Con said, eyes resolutely on the woods ahead. "We argued."

Ian paused, his expression incredulous. "You don't argue with the guests, me dear. You are Connor MacDean MacGregor, the brooding youngest son. You barely give the ladies the time of day, no matter how fetching they are. Addles them, it does. Your melancholy, hard-to-get posturing drives them to distraction until Gil can step in and apprise them of the alternatives."

"Gil doesn't dally with guests either, though thank God the man's an accomplished flirt."

"What did you argue about?"

"Argue?" Con blinked. "Argue, yes. About."

"Connor MacGregor, have you been over-imbibing?"

"If the whisky's decent, there's no such thing. We argued about money. About how to make money."

And that gave his grinning, teasing older brother pause. "That's probably not gentlemanly, Con, though precious little that's any fun is gentlemanly. This will do."

Ian had led them to the place they'd reserved as boys for the interment of beloved pets. "This is the family plot, Ian, more or less. You sure Miss Merrick's old mouser deserves such an honor?"

Ian laid the cat gently on the earth. "I'm not sure he ever exerted himself to catch a mouse, not when he could swill cream and eat cakes with his lady. He caught her heart, though, so yes, he deserves the honor. Find the old boy a healthy bush of heather, why don't you?"

Connor stalked off, intending to take a good long while to find the perfect bush. Digging a grave for a cat in the high summer was no great exertion, but if Con lingered in Ian's vicinity, he was certain his brother would start in interrogating him again, and eventually, Connor might be tempted to spill the real reason he'd argued with Mrs. Redmond.

Money, indeed.

"I'd say this visit is going fairly well."

Ian accepted a serving of tea from Mary Fran as he offered that observation, then passed the cup and saucer along to Gil—without taking a sip, for once. Gil concluded his older brother was as distracted as his younger brother, as distracted as Mary Fran.

Hell, they were all distracted.

"What makes you say that, Ian?" In the spirit of

the general deception, Gil posed the question as casually as he could.

"I think I made a bit of progress with my intended this morning while we walked in the woods."

To hide his consternation, Gil took a bracing sip of strong, hot tea.

"That was the purpose of the outing," Mary Fran said. She held her teacup before her, then lifted it to her nose. "I do so enjoy it when we don't have to reuse the tea leaves above stairs."

Con declined a serving of tea and turned to scowl at the cold hearth. "There's never enough whisky or wool to sell, never enough weeks of summer to sell, never enough of anything to sell."

"Connor?" Ian regarded Con with an arched brow Gil had long ago learned presaged an interrogation. "I was under the impression we were making slow, steady progress toward better financial health. Is there something you haven't been telling us?"

Con scrubbed a hand over his face then turned and sat on the raised hearth. "No."

Mary Fran set her teacup down. "I saw you, Connor MacGregor."

"Saw me?"

"I thought we didn't dally with the guests." Mary Fran let the fuse on that bomb burn down for a few silent moments, while Gil watched Con and Ian clear their throats and look nowhere in particular.

Gil stepped into the breach, feeling a stab of pity for Con. "She's a widow, Mary Fran."

"So you saw them too?"

"I did not." No, Gil had been too busy fending off an attack from a different and unexpected quarter.

"Connor?" Ian's voice was very soft. "Has the widow put you in difficulties by requesting hospitality you're uncomfortable showing her?"

The relief on Con's face was pathetic, but insight struck Gil at the question. Leave it to Ian to sort through all the innuendo and misapprehension to the truth.

"I'm not in difficulties," Con said. "Not yet. She just . . . She caught me off guard. They aren't like the ladies we've had up here before. At least, Mrs. Redmond isn't."

"You'll tell us if you need reinforcements," Ian said after a considering pause. "We need to stick together if we're to weather this summer successfully, because you're right: This bunch is different. It isn't enough to let them catch a glimpse of Mrs. Peason, so they think they've seen the Queen. They're going to be family, God willing, and they'll solve a lot of problems for a lot of MacGregors. We'd best watch each other's backs."

Gil could not have agreed more.

• • •

Hester slipped her arm through Augusta's as the ladies dispersed after their last cup of tea for the evening. "I need to talk to you, Cousin."

Augusta nodded, for Hester was nothing if not tenacious, and avoiding the girl to go mope over a departed cat—or a few harmless kisses—was hardly doing the job Augusta had been brought along to do.

"Let's fetch shawls and walk in the garden," Augusta suggested. "The evening light lasts forever here, and the flowers are lovely."

"Gil says that's because the days are so long. The flowers explode during the few months of pleasant weather because they have such a long winter to lie dormant."

Dormant. The word landed in Augusta's ear with particular resonance. Tending her garden down in Oxfordshire, she herself had gone dormant in some way she couldn't quite articulate. She puzzled on this until Hester tugged her arm free.

"Aren't we going to get shawls, Cousin?"

"We can manage without. The evening is quite mild." The thought of the dratted tan-and-black shawl was more than Augusta could bear, especially when she beheld the beauty of the gardens in the fading light.

"Genie is going daft." Hester at least waited until they'd cleared the terrace to announce this.

"Genie is in a delicate situation," Augusta replied. "For some reason, she has a horror of marriage, and yet the earl would make a very suitable husband." Wonderfully suitable, and for some reason this rankled. Augusta set this realization aside to consider in private.

"The earl's title would make Genie a countess. That's what's suitable."

As they strolled along, side by side, Augusta detected no rancor in Hester's tone. "Are we out here to discuss your sister, Hester, or something else entirely?"

"Two things. Julia attacked Connor in the woods today."

Augusta managed to keep her expression blank. "Attacked?"

"Pushed him right up against a tree, plastered herself to him from knees to neck—except he's so much taller than she is, so it was more like breasts to belly—and started right in kissing him. They were not chaste kisses." Hester's recitation was remarkably factual, not a hint of glee or consternation about it. "Then she took his hand and . . . well. When he wasn't having any of that, she put *her* hand in a location a lady isn't supposed to even know how to mention, but I've heard the lads call it their—"

Augusta put a hand over Hester's mouth. "Hush, child."

Hester turned her head with Augusta's hand still

over her mouth. When Augusta dropped her hand, Hester's expression remained serious. "My widowed chaperone is wandering in the woods, accosting gentlemen she's known less than a week, and you call me a child?"

"Valid point." Augusta linked their arms and resumed their progress.

"You aren't outraged, Gussie?"

"Are you?"

Hester's expression became perplexed. "I'm surprised, mostly. Aunt is such a nice woman. I never thought . . ."

"You never thought nice women dealt with the need for closeness and affection?"

Well, neither did I. But then a certain kind-hearted Scotsman had found her crying over her cat.

"I don't think Aunt was looking for simple affection."

"Do you judge her, Hester?"

Augusta waited, because Hester was family, and for some reason the girl's assessment of the situation mattered. Augusta thought there'd be no answer when Hester dropped Augusta's arm and strode forward to appropriate a bench near a border of low, pinkish-purple heather.

"I had a Season," Hester said, arranging her skirts.

"And you were a great success." Augusta took the place beside her cousin. "I think your success rattled Genie."

"She's a favorite. I was a deb. She should not

have been rattled." Hester spent another few minutes arranging her skirts just so. "I like kissing."

Ah. Of course. "So do I, with the right gentleman."

Hester's head came up. The surprise in her eyes would have been comical, except it hurt a little to see it.

"So *did* I," Augusta corrected herself. "Stealing a few kisses among the roses and shadows is one of the privileges of being out."

Also one of the privileges of being an invisible chaperone.

Hester's brows knit, and Augusta could see the wheels in her cousin's mind turning.

"You're still pretty, you know, Gussie. You could be wrestling men up against trees if you miss the kissing all that much."

Assuredly *not*. She'd spent much of the day reminding herself that a whiff of that kind of behavior, and Uncle would send her home in disgrace. He'd been very blunt on that point. Very blunt.

Augusta brought her attention back to the matter at hand.

"You're disappointed in your elders, Hester. That's to be expected, but you must forgive us our flaws if you're ever to accept the same peccadilloes in yourself."

"So it's all right to steal a kiss?"

What to say? This was ground Julia ought to be covering, a challenge a widow was far better equipped to handle.

"You don't steal the kisses. They are stolen from you, but you must use great caution."

"I know." Hester hunched forward, elbows on her spread knees in a pose no lady ever assumed in company. "If anybody sees, if the gentleman can't keep his mouth shut, if word should ever get out, I'm ruined."

"The gentlemen generally keep such things to themselves, because the behavior reflects badly upon them, at least in Polite Society. I have my suspicions about what's said among the men when the port is served."

Hester gave a philosophical little shrug. "We gossip over tea; they gossip over port, brandy, or whisky."

"There is danger in kisses, though, Hester."

Hester turned her head to frown at Augusta over her shoulder. "Danger?"

Oh, for pity's sake . . . "Men become impassioned, and their manners desert them."

They took to begging and promising and begging harder, and a lady could lose her virtue in the time it took to brew a pot of tea. A furtive, slightly uncomfortable and very awkward end to years of proper behavior and careful upbringing, and a lady needn't part with a stitch of her clothing to see it done.

But Augusta couldn't put it like that to Hester.

"Maybe Aunt became impassioned." Hester was frowning in thought. "Her manners were certainly nowhere in evidence."

"Nor her dignity, I daresay." But what would it be like, to be so carried away with passion that manners and dignity mattered naught? Connor was a very handsome man, almost as handsome as the earl.

Hester harrumphed out a sigh. "It's silly, to be so hungry for kisses you take to accosting men in the woods."

"Yes. I'm glad you can see that." And what Augusta never wanted her cousin to see was that such behavior was the result of loneliness overcoming good sense, breeding, manners, and even sanity. Loneliness coupled with a sort of desperate courage and irresistible opportunity.

"This brings me to my second concern," Hester said, sitting up.

"Have we resolved Julia's situation to your satisfaction?"

"You'll say something to her? I wouldn't want her to get in trouble."

"I'll say something to her, but my guess is Connor is in the best position to say what needs to be said, and perhaps he already has."

Hester's face creased into a grin. "Suppose you're right, and he's plenty big enough to take care of himself. What I really need to discuss with you is this notion Genie has taken into her head to get herself ruined."

"*Ruined?*" Augusta barely got the word out, so disconcerting was the very idea. "She can't be ruined. Uncle will be wroth with me and Julia both if that should happen."

"I overheard her discussing this with Gilgallon when he came by her sitting room to see about her ankle. She wants him to ruin her so she can't marry respectably. She was begging him, in fact. I don't think he was very taken with the notion."

The baron had spent his morning in the library, some damned book about fowling pieces open before him as he'd waited for a shrieking chambermaid to rouse the alarm.

He'd been certain the English spinster would be found dead in her bedroom, or at the very least, quite, quite ill. Either outcome would do, because it would be little trouble to press a pillow over the face of a badly debilitated woman and finish the job in the dead of night.

The rest of the morning had passed, and no alarm had been raised.

When Augusta had sent word she'd take a tray in her room rather than join the family for luncheon, the baron had been encouraged. She was a damnably stubborn woman; likely even poison would have trouble overcoming such a constitution. The thought of laying flowers at her grave cheered him through the afternoon, flowers to celebrate a family fortune finally made secure.

Then she had appeared at dinner, pale and retiring as usual, her only comment that her cat appeared to have run off to go courting in the stables.

Well. So be it. Calibrating a dose of poison was tricky, a calculated risk. At least she'd be leaving her French doors unlocked as long as she fretted over her cat's whereabouts. A man of parts who could think up one sound plan could easily think up two, or even three.

The baron excused himself from the dinner table and sat smoking cheroots on a bench in the garden. When he spied a certain plump scullery maid scurrying out into the gloaming with the slop pail for the hogs, he rose from his bench, pasted a smile on his face, adjusted himself in his trousers, and set a course to intercept his prey.

Augusta rolled over for the twentieth time in as many minutes and sat up.

She wasn't going to fall asleep, and she wasn't going to bother the kitchen at this hour to make her some warm milk—which, had she requested it, and had the kitchen provided it, she would have been sharing with her cat, had he still lived.

She sighed with the futility of that thought and grabbed her wrapper from the foot of the bed. The moon had risen and was spilling in through her

French doors, which remained open despite the cat's demise.

The air here was so fresh, so bracingly sweet and cool, Augusta let herself keep the doors cracked as a simple indulgence. Acting on impulse, she tossed the afghan—green-and-white plaid, of course—from her fainting couch over her shoulders and made her way to the terrace.

The gardens were beautiful by moonlight, peaceful and silvery like a faery world.

"Good evening, Miss Augusta." The large shadow with the low, pleasant voice detached itself from a bench along the wall.

"My lord."

"Ian," he said, coming closer. "As we are quite alone. I suppose you could not sleep?"

"I could not, which is silly. My usual ability to rest at any opportunity seems to have gone missing." She was also missing her slippers, which was beyond silly. He sauntered up to her, his features arranged into a frown as he studied her by the moonlight.

"You miss your cat. Sit with me and tell me about him." He clasped her wrist in a warm grip and led her back to his bench. This relieved Augusta of the need to demur and fuss and retreat to the solitude of her room, when she really had no interest in such a course.

None at all, and neither did that appall her *at all* when well it should have.

"He was your guardian cat, was he not?" The earl waited until Augusta took a seat, then came down beside her.

"He was a fat, lazy house cat, but he was mine."

"He kept your feet warm."

Augusta's gaze traveled down to her bare toes. She looked over and saw in the earl's expression that he'd also taken in her barefoot state—again. Well, let him be shocked, though he didn't strike her as a man much given to the vapors.

"He kept my heart warm."

She felt the man beside her measuring those words. Were it broad daylight, were it one of their quiet conversations at the breakfast table, she could not have uttered that truth to him. Out here, in the cool and sweet night air, she didn't think to keep it to herself.

"Your aunt is throwing herself at my baby brother."

And he probably would not have said those words to her by day either. "I know. Is this a problem?"

"It means Miss Genie's chaperone is distracted. That could be a problem."

"Or a suitor's opportunity."

"I suppose it might mean that too."

He fell silent while Augusta lectured herself on family duty and tried to forget three—no, four— innocuous kisses.

"I'm concerned that Genie is so disenchanted

with the idea of marriage she's willing to risk her reputation to avoid it." That should be plain enough.

"She's going to drag one of my stable lads off into the trees? They'll go willingly, most of them."

"Not one of your stable lads." She counted on his canny intelligence to provide the details. A flirtation with a stable boy could be hushed up; an affair with the earl's heir could not.

"Bloody damn." He sat forward much as Hester had done earlier, but on him, the posture showed his shoulders to wonderful advantage. He was in shirtsleeves and waistcoat, his cuffs turned back halfway up his forearms. "Please forgive my language. Is your family given to drama generally?"

"No more than yours, probably. I don't find it appealing to observe these goings on, my lord. I love my family, yet I hardly know how to assist them when they're taking such peculiar notions."

She hadn't meant to *my lord* him. He glanced at her in the moonlight, a simmering, considering glance that made Augusta's hand twitch with the desire to smooth her palm over his shoulders. They bore the weight of all the family concerns, those shoulders.

And they bore that weight alone. She shifted a little closer to him under the guise of tucking one foot under her seat. He made no move to scoot away, which meant Augusta could feel the warmth of his body heat.

"Can you speak to your aunt?"

"About?"

Another glance, this one tinged with humor.

"That's the difficult part, isn't it? How do you tell a grown man or a grown woman to mind their duties and stop carrying on like a milkmaid and her shepherd boy?"

"Julia's husband was much older than she, and I gather her marriage was merely cordial. I'm sure she feels . . ." How to describe the feelings that could drive a decent lady to risk her reputation for a little passion with a Scotsman?

"She feels what, Miss Augusta?"

"Like me." Augusta got up, gathering the blanket around her shoulders and taking three steps out into the moonlight. "I sometimes feel like a wild creature with a broken wing, taken captive for the purpose of healing, but now my bones are knitted and the door to my cage is cracked open and I . . ."

He rose. She could feel him standing behind her. "Tell me, Augusta."

"I can't step through," she said. "I forget how to step through into freedom, though I have the certain conviction that I must."

The ideas were forming in her head even as she spoke, and they rang true. They rang so, so true.

"Julia might feel like that. A little desperate and more confused than she can say."

"While I feel as if my freedom is slipping from me, day by day. I don't know how to stop it, but I have the certain conviction that I must."

His hand, big and warm, descended to her shoulder and gave a slow squeeze. He'd spoken quietly. Augusta feared very much he'd spoken from the heart. She covered his hand where it rested on her shoulder, hoping—perhaps as he had—that a simple touch would say what words could not. When he stepped away, she was torn between relief and disappointment.

She turned to face him. "What would you have me do with respect to Julia? Hester noticed her lapse, and that will be a significant reproach in itself."

"I don't ask that you do anything," he said, his lips quirking. "Con and Julia are adults, and provided they use discretion, I expect them to work out their own dealings. What I ask of you is that you keep the requisite close eye on Genie. I would not have my prospective bride err when adequate supervision would spare her the misstep."

"She will not misstep, my lord." And this time, Augusta used the honorific intentionally.

"Then it falls to me to assure her our marriage will be congenial and comfortable for her, which assurances I can honestly give. It's late, my dear. Should we be going in?"

She nodded but made one more push at the door of her cage.

"It should be congenial and comfortable for you too, *Ian*." She wanted him to know this, that she thought him worthy and deserving of happiness.

"I beg your pardon?"

"Your marriage. It should be congenial and comfortable for you as well."

"Intriguing notion." He winged his arm at her, and Augusta realized she was being gently dismissed. "And here I thought the main priority was that my marriage be lucrative for me and socially advantageous for her."

She let him escort her back to her terrace doors, the bleakness in his tone leaving her heart aching for him.

Mostly for him.

On the balcony adjoining his second-story suite, Willard Daniels, Baron of Altsax, blew out a silent puff of smoke from his cheroot.

Women were idiots. That little tableau on the terrace below confirmed this universal truth. Children generally took some direction from a stout caning or a well-delivered slap. Nonetheless, girl children could be relied upon to grow into incorrigible stupidity.

Julia trying to take a reluctant Scotsman for a lover was only to be expected. The better her breeding, the more a decent woman longed for the mud. And an impoverished younger Scottish son definitely qualified as mud, particularly when he sported the hulking dimensions of Connor MacGregor and generally savored of the stables. A peasant in plaid, and she was welcome to him.

Genie and this fool notion of getting herself ruined was a different matter altogether. The girl had her mother's complete lack of sense. If Genie was willing to be ruined to avoid marriage, then her dread of the wedding night couldn't possibly be what put her off the idea of matrimony generally.

She was just being contrary, and a word in certain ears ought to see that contrariness brought to an end.

And then there was dear Augusta, an antidote with a hidden stubborn streak, whose blasted cat had saved her life by sacrificing its own. Guardian cat, indeed.

The baron hadn't been able to see the earl and the antidote as they conversed below him. Moon shadows and the plants intended to make the balcony private had obscured them.

But he'd heard them. Heard Balfour call a dried-up spinster by her given name, heard the quality of the silences between them, heard Augusta's pathetic little confidences and the earl's reciprocal confession.

The earl sported a title and was decent looking in the way a plough horse could be a handsome specimen of brute ability. Such a man was going to dally and flirt and take his pleasures where he found them.

But when the baron's plans for Augusta bore fruit, the earl wouldn't be finding those pleasures with her.

Augusta draped her ugly shawl around her shoulders and tried to convince herself this early morning constitutional had nothing to do with an unbecoming desire to spend time with a certain handsome, charming earl.

An earl whose voice in the darkness promised secrets and pleasures, for all he'd been a perfect if startlingly honest gentleman.

The pleasure of a simple touch, for one.

The pleasure of a confidence shared and a confidence received.

The soul-deep pleasure of, for a few moon-gilded minutes, not feeling so desolately alone in this life.

As she churned along past the gardens, Augusta tried to tell herself to put away these fancies, but the lovely Scottish morning, the scent of the flowers, and quite possibly her own dormant stubborn streak, combined to chase off her better intentions.

He *had* touched her. He *had* spoken with her. He had behaved with complete propriety and still been able to give her a sense of . . . A word bloomed in her awareness. A word spinsters had no occasion to use, a word that warmed her heart and put a wide, purely female smile on her face.

They had shared a sense of *intimacy*. A good intimacy, with elements of trust and consideration about it, not the pawing, undignified liberties Henry Post-Williams had inflicted on her.

She was savoring this insight as she gained the trees, and savoring it yet still as she turned onto the path she'd taken yesterday with Gil.

Intimacy, closeness, warmth—physical warmth, yes, but a warmth of the heart as well. Just describing those few minutes with the earl was buoying her somehow. Opening the door of her cage, the windows of the cell she'd occupied since her parents' deaths.

Augusta raised her gaze to the beauty of the forest around her only to come to an abrupt halt when the elf in the tree started clambering down limb by limb.

Six

"I WON'T TELL ON YE IF YE WON'T TELL ON me."

The burr was so thick Augusta could barely make out the words. "I beg your pardon?"

"We won't tattle, right? Ma would skelp m' bum something fierce."

Augusta caught the sense of that, and realized

the girl—not an elf, despite fat red braids, a smattering of freckles on a perfect complexion, and a pixie grin—was looking for a conspirator.

"If we walk back to the house together, we will neither of us be seen out alone. Perhaps you were concerned I'd get lost in the woods?"

"Ach, you canna get lost in this wee park." The child took Augusta's hand and started back in the direction of the house. "But ye'd best nae be late t' table."

"Your ma will skelp m' bum?"

The child grinned more widely, swinging Augusta's hand as they moved along. "You're a grand lady and a guest of the house. Ma says we must show you courtesy because you're a guest and because your English coin keeps the doddies in their fodder. I love the doddies. I love all the animals."

"Doddy?"

"Fine beef, the Angus. We have red and black both, but mostly black. Sun is kinder to dark coats in winter. Uncle has a fold of the Highland cattle as well." She chattered on, about her favorite calf, and Uncle Con let her pick out a pair of heifers to start her own herd, and cows were better than sheep because the sheep forced the crofters out after the '45. The child wove a tale of agronomy and English aggression that Augusta suspected was mostly true.

"I'm Augusta," she interjected when they

approached the back terrace. "Who are you?"

"I'm Fiona of Clan MacGregor, daughter of the Lady Mary Fran and that good-looking, poaching Sassenach bastard Gordie Flynn, or that's what my uncs call my da. Ma says he wasn't so bad for an Englishman. Everybody poaches, or they used to."

"I am pleased to meet you Fiona of Clan MacGregor. Can we go walking again sometime soon?"

"Really? You want to walk with me?"

"Why wouldn't I? It might seem to you like no one could get lost in those woods, but I'm not from around here, and I need a guide if I'm not to be late to breakfast. Your escort was very helpful."

The child dropped Augusta's hand and pushed a toe through the pebbles on the garden path. "No, it wasn't. I'm a pest. Even Uncle Ian sometimes has to tell me to go visit the ponies. Ma says I'm always underfoot, and Uncle Con says I should have been a boy."

"Who would want to be a boy?" Augusta gave a mock shudder. "They spit and never wash behind their ears and burp and all manner of indelicate things."

Fiona's grin disappeared. "My uncs don't spit."

"They are gentlemen, but we are *ladies*. We know how to make cream cakes and knit lovely blankets and how to give the animals all the best names."

"Yes!" The child spun around with glee, making the gravel crunch beneath her half boot. "Yes! I have to name my cows, and they each had a wee baby, and Uncle Gil never thought up names for *any* of them. Can I show you my cows?"

Canna shew ye m' coos?

Augusta had caught the rhythm of the child's speech and, more significantly, her enthusiasm for the naming task.

"We'll visit them tomorrow, weather permitting. Naming is important, so you must think about it between then and now. We might take the entire week to find names for all the cows in your herd."

"Fiona Ursula MacGregor." The tones were mother-stern, draining the joy from the child's countenance.

"Good morning, Ma."

Lady Mary Fran advanced across the terrace, her expression forbidding. "Into the kitchen. You know you're not to be bothering guests."

"Yes, Ma." The girl's shoulders slumped as she crossed the terrace without another word.

"Please don't blame Fiona," Augusta said when the little figure had disappeared into the house. "She didn't want me to get lost in the woods."

Mary Fran's brows knit. "I almost believe you. She's that tenderhearted, she'd even worry about an Englishwoman."

"We had a wonderful talk about her cows and the sheep and all manner of things having to do with Balfour."

Mary Fran's expression shifted, from guarded to a little bewildered. "I can't keep a close eye on her, not when we're entertaining, and the days are so long, and she's so . . . she's quick, haring all over." She fell silent, her mouth flattening. "You don't have children."

"To my sorrow." Augusta slipped her arm through Mary Fran's and started toward the house. "If I did have a child, I'd want her to be exactly like Fiona. She reminds me of myself."

"You?"

Such incredulity, and not the least ill intended.

"I was raised on a large estate, expecting to inherit that property or at least to manage one like it. My mother did not enjoy good health, so it was probably apparent I was going to be an only child. My father took this in stride—he wasn't burdened by a title—and treated me as his heir, if not his son. I wandered my summers away much as Fiona seems to. I knew all the gardeners and shepherds, the gamekeepers, the woodsmen, the dairymen, the tenants, the beekeeper, the stable boys, groundsmen, the goose girl, and the milkmaids—everybody, and they knew me. Papa took me with him when he rode out, first up before him on his horse, then on a leading line on my own pony. It was a wonderful childhood."

A happy childhood, one Augusta hadn't thought about for years.

Mary Fran walked along with her in silence for a few moments then paused.

"Her uncles spoil her. I worry about that. They can't spoil me, so they spoil her instead."

"And you spoil them."

Mary Fran's smile broke over her face like the sun stealing out from behind a cloud. "Yes. Yes, I do. Every chance I get. And if we don't get into the house soon, we'll miss breakfast."

"You most assuredly will, if you haven't already."

They both looked up at that masculine voice to see the Earl of Balfour lounging in the door to the back hallway of the house, looking splendid in his kilt and morning attire. "And we can't have that." He stepped away to allow the ladies to pass before him inside, then accompanied them into the breakfast parlor.

Augusta chose to sit beside Mary Fran rather than take a place near the earl. He was cordial, of course, holding her chair and offering to fill her plate at the sideboard, but Augusta put him off with a few polite words.

He was going to wed Genie. Once again reminding herself of this truth should have brought Augusta a sense of satisfaction at her cousin's good fortune.

It really should have.

"You need to goddamned woo your infernal bride, Brother." Gil yanked Ian by the arm along the corridor as he spoke.

"I am wooing her." Or Ian would be if she'd venture out of her room for more than the space of a meal. Her turned ankle had been healing for three days, and still she hid.

"You need to woo her trust, Ian." Gil pulled him into the family parlor and closed the door.

"What else does a man woo in a prospective bride?"

"You're not . . ." Gil ran a hand through blond hair already disheveled. In the past few days, Ian's brother—his heir—had been oddly silent, taking the place at meals beside Miss Hester, Mrs. Redmond, or Augusta.

That's Miss *Augusta to you, laddie.*

She'd been acting peculiarly too, taking herself out sketching with another of the ladies or spending an inordinate amount of time with Fiona. Grieving for her cat, perhaps.

Or avoiding her host.

"What's amiss, Gilgallon? The ladies have long since lost the ability to overset you."

"Your intended is dead set against the match, Ian. You need to inspire her confidences."

"Does she love another?"

Gil's expression became stricken. "God, I hope not."

"I'm prepared to observe the same civilities as the next titled gentleman," Ian said, feeling the weight of a long day, a long week, and a long, lonely future press down on him. "When we've a few heirs, she'll be free to share her affections elsewhere."

"With Englishmen, Ian? Have you thought about that? We're brutes in their opinions, and . . ."

Gil fell silent, which allowed Ian to take in the fatigue in his brother's eyes, the blister gracing the inside of his right fourth finger, the relative pallor of his complexion.

Drinking and riding at all hours, then. Gil's recipe for dealing with English under their roof, among other upsets.

"She can dally with Englishmen, Gilgallon, with the stable boys, *with you,* if that's what it takes to secure her fortune. We put on a good show here each summer, and we make some coin. It keeps us going; it keeps us thinking we're making progress. Another blight, a dose of hoof and mouth, a bad market . . ."

"I know. *I know, Ian.*"

"I know too." Ian reached out and squeezed his brother's shoulder. "I'll woo the damned girl until her eyes cross and she lies panting at my booted feet."

He could too. He hadn't been applying himself was all. Giving the girl time, letting her settle in . . . Putting off the inevitable.

"She likes poetry," Gil said dully. "That senti-mental, idle tears, English bastard-fellow. I forget his name."

"Tennyson. I'll read her pretty little ears off until the splendor is damned falling on our castle walls."

"Do that." Gil looked around the parlor like he'd no clue how they'd arrived there. "I'm going for a ride."

Ian headed for the library to pick up a volume of Tennyson, walked resolutely past the ladies' parlor where Augusta—*Miss* Augusta—had been stitching at something in solitude earlier in the day, and prepared to read his intended's ears off.

Though if he recalled his Tennyson aright, the menfolk fought themselves to injury and coma, while the princess remained unmoved up in her tower.

Splendor, indeed.

The library door crashed on its hinges when the Earl of Balfour disturbed Augusta's reading.

"I beg your pardon." He looked disgruntled, like he wasn't in the mood to beg anything of any-body. "I thought you were in the ladies' parlor."

Augusta supposed this was part of a host's function, to keep track of which guest was where. She rose and put aside *Waverley*. "I can remove to the ladies' parlor if you have need of some solitude here."

He'd closed the door behind him too, and removing to the ladies' parlor—to anywhere else—would have been the decision of a prudent chaperone.

"I'll not be but a moment." He scrubbed a hand over his chin and seemed to visually canvass the room. "Fiona isn't lurking under the table, is she? Dragooning you into hide-and-seek or some other nonsense?"

"I think Lady Mary Fran is trying to keep Fiona entertained below stairs for the present. Truly, I can leave if you need the library for business, my lord."

Except she didn't want to leave. It made no sense, but Augusta wanted to linger wherever she could study him, wherever she could observe him. She'd noticed, for example, that in bright sunlight, his dark hair had red highlights, and the lines of fatigue around his mouth and laughter around his eyes were more pronounced.

He blew out a breath, some of the temper leaving his expression to be replaced with humor. "You're my-lording me, Augusta Merrick. I must be exuding about as much charm as my damn— my blasted bull doddy. I'm fetching some poetry to read to Miss Genie."

"Very considerate of you."

He advanced into the room and went to stand by the window. "Come here, if you please."

The command was casual, but a command no

matter how politely stated. Augusta went, rather than dwell any longer on the resentment she felt that Genie was going to be hearing poetry in that lovely, masculine burr, while Augusta had . . . solitude. Tea and solitude, chickens and solitude.

But also a few memories and solitude.

She went to him, stopping a few feet away.

"Here." He waggled his fingers at her but kept his gaze turned toward the window. "I want to show you something."

She came a couple of steps closer. He was being an attentive host, nothing more, pausing in the more important business of wooing Genie to show Augusta some small consideration.

He shifted, putting a hand on each of Augusta's shoulders and guiding her to the sill. "You can see the path behind the stables from here. Just there, where Lavelle is leading that draft team."

Augusta forced herself to stop focusing on the earl's proximity, on the heather and wool scent of him, on the feel his hands, one on each of her shoulders. "Where is he taking those horses?"

"The path winds just inside the tree line for a good way, then jogs over toward Balmoral. There's a lot of construction debris there, some of it worth saving, some of it useful for burning. Her Majesty is generous, and His Highness is practical."

Augusta turned slightly, and still her host did not drop his hands. "What does that mean?"

"We show our appreciation with the occasional gift of whisky. Albert and his wife appreciate decent libation."

She watched his mouth while he spoke, which was hardly polite. Augusta stepped back, out of his grasp. "Thank you for showing me the path. I'm sure Fiona will agree to explore it with me."

"Fiona." His dark brows lowered. "I suppose she will, but you're going on an outing with me tomorrow at first light." He looked surprised by his invitation—if one could call it that—and then resolute.

And yet, an invitation could be declined.

"A walk first thing sounds lovely." She had meant to refuse—to gently, politely, absolutely refuse—though it was impossible to recall why she must when Ian's heathery scent was teasing at her wits. "Where will our outing take us?"

The ambiguity of the question felt vaguely unsuitable, particularly when Ian's handsome features split into a devilish grin.

"I'll show you the path to the high tor. It's an hour's good walking with a fine view of the shire."

Before Augusta could think up a witty rejoinder—his smile was unlike any she'd seen in London ballrooms—the earl strode off toward the door.

"My lord?"

He turned, the smile muted but still in evidence. "Ian, if you please."

"Your book of poetry?"

She heard him curse quite clearly. Only when he had retrieved a slim volume from a middle shelf, departed, and closed the door did Augusta permit herself to smile over it.

Con caught the shadow falling across the stable door out of his peripheral vision and straightened, muck fork in hand.

Julia Redmond stood there in a smart brown riding habit trimmed with green piping. The colors would have looked wonderful on Mary Fran, though Con's sister hadn't had a new habit in years.

The pretty English widow radiated . . . not exactly anger, but tension. "Mr. MacGregor."

"I think you can use my name, seeing as how we're on kissing-and-groping-each-other-in-public terms." He took his time shrugging into his shirt. Petty of him, but no more petty than she'd been.

And then he went back to his mucking.

She clenched her fists and closed her eyes as if praying for fortitude. When she looked at him again her expression was unreadable. "I came here to apologize to you. If you're just going to bait me, I'll leave."

He wanted her to leave. Leave the stables, the estate, Scotland. Hell, she could go pan for gold in California and take her damned insulting English condescension with her.

"Apologize then, but I'm not used to being made a fool of."

She crossed into the barn aisle, walked past him, and stood with her back to him. "I am. I am used to being made to feel like an idiot."

"You expect me to believe a wealthy young English widow can easily be made a fool of?" He set his muck fork aside and went to stand behind her. He smelled of horse and sweat and worse, but still her rose-and-cinnamon scent came to him.

"To you, Connor, I'm wealthy and young. By London standards, I'm old, and compared to the American heiresses, barely solvent. My property is so far north no man in his right mind would spend time there except for grouse season. I'm . . . I have been regarded as foolish in the extreme, more than once."

He could make no sense of her words. "What are you trying to say?"

"I'm turning thirty this fall, Connor, and I have no children."

"Then you're approaching your prime without any bairns clinging to your skirts. Go find some horny Englishman to celebrate with, why don't you?"

She turned, and to his horror there were tears shining in her eyes. "Connor, I didn't know what else to do."

The misery in her voice was genuine, he'd give her that much, but forgiveness was still beyond him. "You didn't know what else to do besides *offer me money for taking you to bed?*"

She bit her lip while one of those tears trickled down her cheek. "I didn't expect you to do something distasteful for free."

"You didn't . . . !" He walked off a few paces then glared at her over his shoulder. "Let me ask you something, Julia Redmond. How would you have felt if I'd offered you money to let me rut on you? Would you have been pleased? Flattered? Would you have entertained my proposition for a moment?"

When she should have been firing off denials and protests, she only peered at him while another tear followed the first. "I feel so . . ."

Ridiculous? Foolish? If she went around making this offer to the gentlemen of London . . .

"Tell me you haven't propositioned anyone else, Julia. Lie to me if you have to, but the idea that you'd hold yourself worse than cheap . . ."

She shook her head. "I tried flirting. I tried innuendo. I tried notes so bold they couldn't be misconstrued. But they always were, or ignored. Ignored is worse."

He let himself return to her side. She was speaking softly for one thing, and she needed his handkerchief for another.

He did not need to catch another whiff of her fragrance. "My estimation of the average Englishman is at risk for a small upward revision if these fellows showed some restraint where your virtue is concerned."

"Little you know." She snatched his handkerchief and tromped over to a trunk along the wall. "It's not restraint if a man finds you too plain to inspire his passion."

Now *this* was utter balderdash. "Lass, the man hasna been born who'd find you too plain for bedsport."

She waved an impatient hand at his words. "Genie is graceful and willowy, Hester is horse mad and great fun, Augusta is well read and poised. I'm none of those things. I'm short, plain, boring, brown-haired, and d-dying of it."

She buried her face in the handkerchief, while Con tried to puzzle out her reasoning. In a convoluted female sort of way, it made sense she'd attribute to herself too little appeal rather than too much. It made female sense, which was likely a contradiction in terms.

He took a seat beside her and patted her knee. "You needn't take on. I've told no one of your folly. They all think you were carried away with your attraction to me."

She looked up, eyes glittering. "I was."

"No, you weren't. Any toothsome fellow would have done, which is why I'm insulted by your offer."

She let her hands fall to her lap and leaned back against the wall. "Not any toothsome fellow, just you. It's all very well and good for men to go around handing out coin to secure a lady's cooperation. I don't see why my offer was such a great insult."

Decent women weren't even to admit they knew of such arrangements, and yet Julia Redmond was decent. Lonely and foolish, but decent.

"I have never paid a woman to tolerate my attentions, and I never will. And the women taking that coin are no longer ladies."

She started folding up his linen in her lap. "Some of them are. They live in their mansions, ordering their servants about, and yet their jewelry boxes are full of tokens of esteem from admirers. It's the same thing."

There was such bewilderment and hurt in her voice, this time he patted her hand. "Do you want to be one of those ladies, Julia? The kind no decent hostess trusts around her husband? The kind mamas never allow their daughters to converse with? Do you want a full jewelry case of tokens?"

She sighed, her head clonking against the wall as she leaned back. "My husband gave me all manner of jewels. He spent my money on me, but he did spend it. And no, Connor, I do not want to be a predatory female. I just want . . ."

He waited while a horse down the aisle groaned sleepily. There were stalls to muck—there were always stalls to muck—but just now, he could spare her a few minutes to hear her . . . apology.

"I want to feel desired, to feel wanted. My husband wasn't young, and passion was beyond him. He consummated the marriage, and then after a few months, it was as if I were his ward or his apprentice. He'd read the financial pages to me until I thought I'd go mad." She stopped and closed her eyes. "Maybe I am going mad."

A suspicion bloomed in Connor's mind. A suspicion of no little wickedness, but one he was going to investigate. "Then he didn't see to your pleasure, this husband?"

"How could reading me the paper be a pleasure? Morning after morning, and then again at night, sometimes the same articles twice in one day."

Ah. Well, then. It put her situation in a different light altogether, but Con wasn't going to make any precipitous moves.

"You need to know two things, Julia Redmond."

She lifted her head from the wall to meet his gaze. "I was an idiot again. I know that. I'm sorry if I offended your honor, but I see things, Connor. Your stable is aging, your domestics are either very young or very old, the windows in the family wing all need a good glazing, your wood is bare of deadfall. There's a need for coin—"

He stopped her with an upraised hand. "That's none of your concern, and yes, you were an idiot, though you're not to be an idiot with any other men. Gil would likely expire from apoplexy if you waylaid him, and Ian is in pursuit of a bride."

"I don't want Ian or—"

He put a finger over her lips. "Two things. First, I accept your apology. We need not speak of this again."

"Thank you. And second?"

He leaned over and kissed her on the mouth, sweetly, gently, not in any hurry but not exactly lingering either. "I would have taken a woman as comely, dear, and determined as you to my bed for free. *Gladly,* for free."

Before she could slap him or kiss him back—he figured the odds of each were about the same—he got up and sauntered away. Had he looked back, he would have seen her sitting all alone on her trunk, two fingers pressed to her mouth and a stunned smile on her face.

But he didn't look back, and he didn't tell her that if ever there was a woman he'd beg for her favors—beg, plead, and all but pay—it would be her.

Ian closed up the little volume of poetry and glanced over at the woman he intended to wed. She was pretty enough, with long, gold-tipped eyelashes, patrician features, and big blue eyes that were at present closed in slumber—blue eyes some would say were unremarkable. She had a decent figure in a long-limbed, English sort of way.

He wished to God he were tempted to steal a kiss. He might have been, had the lady shown the least inclination to steal a kiss from him, but no.

She reclined on her fainting couch, her ankle propped on a pillow. She'd remained unmoving for the past half hour. He'd read her nigh half of Tennyson's damned "Princess," then switched to French poetry recited from memory. She'd closed her eyes by then, and even switching to the Gaelic hadn't gotten her notice.

"Are you enjoying the poetry?"

Her eyes flew open. "The poetry? Oh, a great deal, my lord. You have such a lovely burr."

The *burr* had been beaten out of him in public school, though he could hardly tell her that. "Have you a favorite poem, Miss Genie?"

"I like the simple ones, the ones that make sense."

Her reply had him wondering what Augusta Merrick had been reading in the library, which was absolutely irrelevant to the present situation. "Whom do you like besides Tennyson?"

"I'm not sure I know any other poets." Her fingers twitched at the afghan over her lap, which Ian took for a sign of mendacity. English schoolgirls knew their poetry. "I do appreciate your taking time from your busy day to entertain me, my lord."

144

"My pleasure. Perhaps I should order us some luncheon, it being past noon."

Disgruntlement passed through her eyes, as if having luncheon with him was not in her plans. Good God, how could they fashion any sort of marriage when even an hour in each other's company had them both eyeing the door?

"I'm not hungry, my lord."

"A tea tray, then? I can stop by the kitchen on my way out."

Relief showed on her face. "That would be considerate, my lord. And perhaps you could have the footman scare up my brother and send him to me? Matthew went out riding with Lady Mary Frances, but I'm sure they would have come in by now."

Ian was being dismissed, which was no worse than having been tolerated. A bolt of hopelessness went through him at the prospect of years and years of dismissal and tolerance. How was he to bed her, for God's sake?

"You know, Miss Genie, I would try to be considerate of you under all circumstances."

She glanced over at him uncertainly. "You have been a very amiable host, my lord."

He rose and let himself look out the windows at the summer gardens in all their glory. "Do you want children, Miss Genie? I do. Not just for the title, but for my heart and for my family's heart. I want children to love and guide and leave my legacy to, modest though it will be. Scotland has lost so much, seen so many children leave her shores . . ."

"Every woman of good birth hopes to marry well and have children."

She spoke quietly, miserably.

He turned around and addressed the top of her bent head. "Genie, can't you trust me enough to at least *try?* I'd like to be friends if nothing else, but at the very least I am not your enemy."

She took a breath while Ian waited. If he were any more blunt, she'd hobble out of the room and demand to board her papa's private railcar for the South, but at this rate their marriage was going to be in name only—and Ian wasn't sure he could tolerate that.

"My lord, I am trying. I really am."

She said nothing more. He didn't know what else to do, what else to say, and kissing even her cheek was beyond him. "Then we keep trying. I'll have a tray sent up and find your brother. Is there anything else you need?"

"No, my lord, but thank you."

"For what?"

"I know you're trying too."

Well. She hadn't dissolved in a fit of the vapors, hadn't sent him packing. They'd been under the same roof only a week. Maybe there was hope.

And maybe he was an idiot, blind to all save the need for coin.

Ian asked among the servants, and no one had seen Matthew Daniels or Mary Fran all morning. Two horses were gone from the stables, but only two, which meant Mary Fran had eschewed a groom. Ian spied Con emerging from the dairy in work clothes, his shirt more unbuttoned than buttoned.

"Do you know which way Mary Fran and Daniels went?"

Con stopped and frowned. "I last saw them heading into the woods toward Balmoral. I wouldn't have thought Daniels the kind to gawk at royalty."

"They left after breakfast?"

"They did. I helped saddle their mounts. Why?"

Ian ran a hand through his hair. Connor was not ordinarily prone to missing the obvious. "Because they've been gone for three hours, Connor. They're not gawking at royalty."

Con's brows rose, then he shrugged. "Bully for Mary Fran."

"Yes, bully for Mary Fran, but Fiona's probably loose in those same woods, likely spying in the windows of the gamekeeper's cottage as we speak."

"Hadn't thought of that."

"And neither, apparently, has Mary Fran." Which was intriguing and not in a good way.

"You want me to fetch Mary Fran home?"

"I'll do it. You're hardly dressed for riding, and

I—may God have mercy on my soul—am the head of this family, at least until Asher gets tired of chasing bears in Canada."

"Asher's dead, Ian." Con said it almost cheerfully.

"Asher is not dead, and you smell like a sweaty muck pit. If you see Fee, keep her near the house."

"I'll tie her to the piano; that ought to work."

"Unless you're playing it, in which case she'll chew through her bonds."

The sibling civilities having been observed, Con smiled and sauntered off, his expression in charity with the world.

Ian didn't exactly relish the task of tracking down his sister and her escort, but it was a pretty day, and spending time with his intended made him itchy for a good cross-country gallop. He turned for the stables and paused in midstride.

"Lord Balfour, a moment if you will." Altsax came churning along the crushed gravel walk from the gardens, his complexion florid, sweat beading around his muttonchop sideburns. He swung a riding crop at the occasional gladiolus, leaving a path of decapitated, colorful casualties in his wake.

"Baron, I'm at your disposal."

"Shall we walk, Balfour? The walls have ears, particularly in the stable." He smiled conspiratorially, though there was insult in his observation.

Of course Ian's help would overhear, and of course they'd make it a point to guard the laird's back while they did.

Pushing distaste aside, Ian fell in step with his guest. "Are you enjoying your visit, Baron?"

"Enjoying my visit? Oh, come, Balfour. You needn't play polite host with me. I'm a man of sophistication forced to rusticate in Scotland while my daughter leads you a dance, and for reasons known only to my wife, I am paying handsomely for this privilege."

"Blunt speaking, Altsax." There was nothing wrong with direct speech, but from his future father-in-law Ian had allowed himself to hope for a bit more . . . civility.

"Why dissemble? I tolerate your pursuit of my daughter because you've the highest title of all the hounds slobbering at her heels."

"Lucky me."

"Lucky you, indeed," the baron rejoined, completely missing Ian's irony. "I've a few conditions to the settlements you need to be informed of."

Ian strolled along beside his guest, forcing himself to note the sound of gravel crunching under their feet, the way the breeze fluttered the ivy growing up the north wall of the house, the raven sitting on the weathercock atop the stable. This was a lovely home, a home Ian wanted to pass along to his children. He wanted to provide for his family and provide well. He wanted the next Earl of Balfour to have a good, honorable example to follow.

For these reasons he kept his tone perfectly genial while Altsax huffed and puffed next to him. "I haven't asked for the lady's hand yet, Altsax. Don't you think negotiations at this point are a bit premature?"

"No, I do not. I think you're a complete lackwit for not stealing into her room, anticipating the vows, and having done with this farce. You can dance around the rowan tree with her, or whatever passes for a wedding up here, and I can get back to my own estates and a gentleman's more civilized pursuits in Town. A mistress the caliber of mine isn't going to tolerate indefinite neglect."

"You're encouraging me to take liberties with your daughter?" No wonder Genie was nervous.

"I'm encouraging you to have done with this pretense of a courtship. Marriage is business, man. I know, I've been married for better than thirty years, and I can tell you most honestly marriage is business, and a sorely vexing business at least half the time."

Ian's parents would have argued that conclusion. His grandparents would have laughed at it outright. "What conditions did you want to discuss?"

"Not conditions, Balfour. Demands, and for God's sake find a man some shade."

If a man hadn't left his bedroom trussed up to the nines in the latest fashion in riding attire, he might not be turning red as a beet in the summer sun. "Over there." Ian gestured to a shaded bench but declined to sit beside Altsax. "What are your demands?"

"It's not complicated. You must offer written assurances Genie is marrying a member of the MacGregor family in expectation of a title."

Ian nodded. Of course he could offer those assurances, but he wasn't about to agree to anything with this buffoon so easily. "Go on."

"Genie will be hostess at Balfour House in the summer months. You're not to be hauling her off to the Continent or allowing that sister of yours to run this household when Her Majesty is in residence next door."

Forgive me, Mary Fran, for not planting my fist in this English piece of shit's face. "I'm listening. What else?"

"Genie will attend the London Season with her husband's escort when she so chooses, provided she isn't knocked up."

"I take it your baroness has contributed a mother's perspective on this situation?" Surely that had to be the explanation for such a request.

"God, no. Do you take me for a fool? The whole point of this match is so I might show off my ability to marry my daughter to the title of my choice. She's to come to Town for a few months every year and flaunt her prize, show the world what her papa married her to. Her daughters will hold the title lady, and that's no mean accomplishment for a baron's get."

Show the world *what* her papa married her to. Ian had long considered the London social Season akin to a livestock fair, though he'd never felt the comparison quite as keenly as now, when he'd been demoted from a *who* to a *what*.

"I'll pass these requests on to my solicitors, Altsax. If I accede to them, they will of course affect the settlements."

"Affect the . . . ? You have to be jesting."

"Residing here over the summer means all manner of friends and relations will want to visit us, so they, like you, can claim to have been out walking with Her Majesty. Entertaining costs money, and if Genie is in residence here, that will preclude my family from putting the house to paying purposes. Seasons cost a great deal of money. Traveling hundreds of miles to and from London costs money. Making over this entire house to reflect my wife's preferences rather than my sister's costs money I had not intended to spend."

"Ah, so you weren't going to establish Genie here as your lady?"

"Of course, she would be the lady of whatever house we dwell in, but I have a property of my own, Altsax, among the finest in the shire."

Altsax waved a hand. "Some little farm left to you by your granddame. That will not do, Balfour."

It was thousands of acres of the most arable soil in all of Deeside, with grounds made gorgeous by the mountains rising up just west of the house. It was also profitable as hell. The sparkling jewel in the otherwise tarnished financial crown of the MacGregor family portfolio. It would more than do.

"I'll pass along these requests to the lawyers," Ian said. "You may await our response, assuming I offer for your daughter." He turned in the direction of the stables, needing to get away from Altsax before violent urges overcame his sense of familial duty.

"I don't judge a man for driving a hard bargain," the baron said from where he sat. "After all, you'll have to take on Genie for the rest of your life. Why else would I be paying you a small fortune to get her off my hands?"

He snorted jovially at his own reasoning, while Ian walked off and wondered how in the name of Almighty God he was going to come to terms with such a cretin.

Because he was going to, even if it killed him.

Seven

AUGUSTA WATCHED AS FIONA MADE A CLOVER chain, nimble little fingers fashioning a crown from the lowliest of flowers.

"It's beautiful," Augusta said when Fiona carefully placed it on her guest's head. "I'm queen of the pasture."

Fiona grinned and plopped down on the blanket beside Augusta. "I don't see why you'd want to sketch a silly old pasture. It's just for cows."

"For today, it's for us and our picnic." And it was a gorgeous pasture. Lush and green under a perfect blue sky, the mountains rising around them in summer splendor. "What's the word for cow?"

Fiona had been helping Augusta with some Gaelic. As long as they kept away from the challenge of trying to spell properly, Augusta could build on the conversational skills she'd gleaned in childhood from her mother and grandfather. It wasn't like French or German in sound—it was far more musical—but it did have some commonalities with Latin in structure.

"I can tell you the Scottish words too, if you like," Fiona said. "The uncles say one has to know the Scots to do business with the Lowlanders. They do a lot of business, my uncles."

"Let's stick to Gaelic for now."

Augusta did not examine motives for that decision. It was becoming a habit, this not looking too closely at why she felt and acted as she did. In this manner, she avoided admitting she was attracted to her cousin's intended— *intimately* attracted. She avoided admitting she'd tried to keep herself from the man's company upon this realization, and she avoided admitting such a course was painful.

But not, she hoped, as painful as some other possibilities.

White clover symbolized promises. Augusta promised herself tomorrow's outing with Ian— with his lordship—would be the first and last of its kind. She also promised herself she would enjoy it to the fullest extent possible without asking the earl to compromise his honor.

"I think my ma likes your cousin." Fiona dug about in the wicker hamper they'd lugged to the pasture.

"I hope Lady Mary Frances likes Genie, for they might be sharing a household. Let me peel that orange."

Fiona passed her the orange, her expression solemn. "I didn't mean Miss Genie. I meant Mr. Daniels. He told me about his first pony."

Oh . . . *Oh.*

"He loved his pony very much." Augusta tore into the skin of the orange and cast around for a way to shift the topic.

"If I had a pony, I'd love him very much too. Uncle Gil says I can have Merlin when I'm older and Merlin is older too."

Merlin was a safer topic, thank God. From the corner of Augusta's eye, she detected movement. When she glanced up, her mouth went dry and her heart started up a slow, tense pounding in her chest.

"Fiona? I want you to listen to me, but you must stay perfectly calm."

The child was perceptive. She ceased pawing in the hamper and met Augusta's gaze.

"There's a bull in this pasture," Augusta said, glancing up the hill behind them. "A great, pitch-black fellow with an unhappy expression on his face. I'm thinking he's lonely for his ladies or perhaps resentful we're encroaching on his territory."

"That's Romeo," Fiona said, her voice laden with misgiving. "He's always cranky, but this isn't his pasture. This is the pasture between his proper paddock and the yearling heifers beyond the hill."

Oh, marvelous. They were sitting between a mating bull and his next conquests. The beast swung its great head in their direction and stomped one cloven hoof.

"I want you to start walking for the fence, Fiona. Keep me and this blanket between you and Romeo. Do it now, child, as quietly as you can.

Don't move too quickly. Don't move too slowly, unless he charges. Then, you run like the wind."

God bless the girl, she got up and started walking.

Augusta had known a man in her girlhood who'd lost a leg when he was trampled by a charging bull. For all their size, intact male bovines could be fast and nimble, also very determined.

Well, Augusta was more determined still.

"Hullo, Mr. Romeo." She rose from the blanket, knowing the bull was going to see her movement more clearly than her specific form. She shook her skirt gently. "It's a fine morning for a little stroll, don't you think?" Over her shoulder she saw Fiona was making steady, silent progress toward the gate.

The bull watched as Augusta began to pace back and forth. "We didn't mean to intrude on your solitude, sir, and would account it a great courtesy if you'd allow us to withdraw from your parlor without incident. Keep moving, Fiona."

Another stomp, then a loud, admonitory snort.

"I know. We should have simply left our cards and moved along, not tarried here when you weren't receiving. Fiona, don't you dare stop. When you get to the house, bring one of your uncles back here."

The bull was focused on Augusta, his head raising and lowering, his muscular quarters swinging around as if to launch a charge at her.

"You can have my crown." Augusta pulled the clover chain from her head and swung it in a slow loop from her hand. "I'll sing to you if you like as well. You should have some recompense for our having disturbed your peace." Except her mouth was too dry for her to sing. "Perhaps you'd like my orange?"

She pitched it hard across the bull's line of sight, momentarily distracting him. But only momentarily. As the orange rolled to a stop in the grass, the bull once again turned to regard Augusta. He whisked his short tail against his haunches, and when he stomped this time, he followed it up by pawing a divot of sod from the earth.

I'm going to die. I'm going to die here in a Scottish pasture on a beautiful day with that innocent child looking on.

"Go get help, Fiona. I'll just have a visit with Romeo." Augusta took one step back and knew her life was over. The bull began trotting in her direction, then lowered his head and broke to a faster gait.

Her plan was to dodge him at the last minute, if she could. If she were capable of movement. He came on, making the earth tremble with his charge. Augusta could hear the bellows of his lungs working, see the dampness on his big black snout.

She was going to die . . . She was going to die in Scotland . . .

She was plucked straight up into the air just as the bull swerved off away from the blanket.

"I've got you." The scent of heather enveloped her as she was pulled sideways across a saddle. "It's all right. I've got you."

"Ian." She clutched at him, her heart pounding, her eyes closed tightly as Ian's horse carried them swiftly toward the gate. Fiona swung it open for the horse to pass through then immediately closed it behind them when Ian brought the horse to a halt.

"You're safe," Ian growled. "You're both safe. What in God's name were you thinking, picnicking in a bull's pasture?"

"It's not his pasture." Fiona was frowning up at them, her little face pale. "Romeo has the other side of the hill."

"Then he was napping in the grass off his usual turf," Ian said. "You should have taken a closer look around, Fee." And while he lectured the child, Augusta remained right where she was, bundled into his heat and strength as tightly as she could hold on.

"But Uncle Ian, somebody had to open the gate between Romeo's paddock and this pasture. His gates are always secured with both a rope and a latch because he likes to—"

"I *know* what he likes to do, Fee."

"We're all right," Fiona said, pique and bewilderment in her voice. "Why are you yelling at me? Miss Augusta had a visit with Romeo, and I got out, and then you came along, and it's . . . it's . . . all right. Ma is going to yell, and yell and yell . . ."

She sat down abruptly in the grass, bringing her pinafore up to her face.

"Ian, help her."

He tightened his arms around Augusta momentarily, a little taste of bliss not entirely composed of safety, and then he put the reins in her hand. As he leaned forward to dismount, his chest crowded against Augusta.

He was a big man. A wonderfully, comfortingly, arousingly big man.

"I don't mean to yell, Fee." He hoisted the child to his hip, and she burrowed against him. "You're safe now, and you won't go wandering into a pasture again without keeping an eye out for lonely bulls."

"He wasn't there," she muttered against his neck. "Uncle Ian, I know to keep my eyes sharp, and *he wasn't there* when we chose where to have our picnic this morning. Uncle Gil says Romeo needs the shade on the other side of the hill."

Augusta glanced over at the bull, who was now sporting the ends of a clover chain dangling from his mouth. He was chewing as bovines do, as much side to side as up and down, and looking almost harmless.

She got situated more securely in the saddle, a leg on each side of the horse, her skirts arranged as modestly as possible. Inside her body, where warmth ought to be, she felt cold and shuddery. *What if Ian hadn't come along?*

"Up you go, Fee. You've had a fright, and I'm glad you're safe." He hefted the child to sit before Augusta. "Keep Miss Augusta company, and I'll retrieve your things. Romeo's had his fun for now."

He shrugged out of his coat and handed that to Augusta as well. She bundled it up to hold between her and Fiona, when he snatched it back and shook it out.

"Around your shoulders, madam. You and I will talk later."

He vaulted the fence in one lithe, fit movement then moved toward their blanket in a no-nonsense fashion. "None of your malarkey, laddie. You've had your sport for the morning, chasing heifers that don't belong to you. For shame." Ian continued his scolding while he gathered up their little picnic and tossed their blanket over his shoulder. Whether it was because the animal recognized authority, or didn't feel a mere human male worth his notice, Romeo kept at his grazing without so much as flicking an ear.

When Ian had their effects piled on the safe side of the fence, Augusta resumed breathing.

"You're squashing me, Miss Augusta."

She also loosened her hold on the child. "Apologies. I am discommoded by our adventure. A hot cup of tea is in order, I think. Will you join me?"

Fiona squirmed around to peer at Augusta. "You want me to join you for tea?"

"A private tea, with a whole tray of tea cakes. My favorites have chocolate icing and crème in the center."

"I like the ones that are chocolate everywhere. Inside, outside, and on top. So does Uncle Ian."

Augusta smoothed a hand over the girl's silky crown and looked down to find Ian staring up at them with an odd expression on his face.

"You ladies stay right where you are. We'll send a groom for your things and get you back to the house." He lifted the horse's reins over the beast's neck and led the gelding from the pasture.

"Uncle Ian?"

He didn't even look back. "I'm going to have to tell her, Fee. She's your mama, and I don't lie to my family."

"But then she'll try to *watch* me again, and I hate it when she tries to watch me. I don't want to dust and polish and trot around the house all day. We've company and I'm not supposed to let them see me and it's *boring*."

"Boring?" Augusta knew a reaction in a child when she heard it gathering steam. "How could it be boring to hold court for a little while in your castle after having such a brush with disaster, Fiona? Your uncles Gil and Con will want to hear exactly what happened from you and you alone. They'll wish they'd been the ones to come to the rescue, and they'll try to steal some tea cakes while you tell your tale. You can scold them for their sorry manners. What is the Gaelic word for scold?"

Fiona had a little dialogue on the topic with Ian in their mother tongue while Augusta caught the occasional sentence or phrase. As relief replaced her earlier upset, she let the sound wash over her.

Ian should always speak his first language, she decided. The music of it rumbled from him in a natural flow, more lyrical than the hard edges and clipped intonation of his public-school English, more resonant.

Augusta tugged his jacket closely around her, taking a deep inhale of the scent of Ian and safety: his beautiful voice, his lovely scent, the sight of his muscular shoulders moving under his clothes as he walked the horse along and kept up a conversation to soothe his rattled little niece.

As Augusta had been standing in that pasture, heart pounding, certain her own death was imminent, she'd had the thought she was going to die in Scotland.

And now she'd died and gone to heaven, if only for a few guilty moments.

• • •

Augusta and Fiona would have their little tea party—a great kindness on the part of the adult toward the child who should have been more alert to pastoral dangers—but Ian was going to have a goddamned dram of the good stuff. Several drams.

And not just because the bull had damned near trampled two defenseless females.

Bloody damn . . .

Ian's heart had almost pounded out of his chest when he'd topped the rise and seen Augusta Merrick standing ramrod straight, staring that bull in his bovine face, putting herself squarely in danger for the sake of the child.

And if anything had happened to Fee . . . She was their heart. She was their hope for a happier future, a more secure future where children had enough to eat and felt safe in the love and protection of family.

The third blow to his composure had come when he'd gathered up their hamper, blanket, and sketch pad, and seen what Augusta Merrick had drawn. He'd barely had time to riffle through the pages, but what she'd rendered had trampled him as surely as any bull could have.

She was a talented artist, better even than Con, whose accuracy brought to mind daguerreotypes. She had an ability Con lacked to render emotions incisively, even in inanimate objects.

Balfour House was sketched on its rise, majestic and inviting all at once. A fortress and a refuge, a home of dignity and warmth. She saw it the way Ian *felt* it, not the gutters threatening to sag, the myriad chimneys to keep unclogged, the windows in need of a thorough glazing, but the *home* where his family loved and lived out their lives.

She'd drawn Con and Gil, catching both their humor and a lurking sort of despair, a restlessness overlaid with determination and sheer healthy Scottish male good looks.

Mary Fran was a different sort of study, in humor and in fatigue not just of the body, but also of the . . . heart. And pretty. There was lavish female beauty unstintingly portrayed, enough to make Ian see his own sister in a different and more honest light.

Mary Fran was going to waste, frittering away her best years with a broom in one hand and a tot of whisky in the other.

Augusta Merrick, whose own youth was slipping behind her, saw Mary Fran's life clearly, while Ian—the man responsible for Mary Fran's well-being and happiness—had not.

And then the final page.

Him. Ian, but not any version of Ian MacGregor ever seen in his own mirror. This man was smiling slightly, a warmth in his eyes that belied fatigue and disillusionment, though both were there as well. She'd gotten his nose right too, and yet in her eyes he was a handsome devil, full of mischief and possessed of some wisdom too. He was a leader a family could be proud of, eager for challenges, but patient when needs must, and willing to take on any burden for those he loved.

As he led his horse into the stable yard, Ian realized Miss Augusta Merrick was a romantic. She was a woman who could have argued poetry with him all morning, probably in several languages, and she was a woman selfless enough to protect another's child when children had been denied her.

"Do you have to tell Ma right now?" Fiona sat on the horse, looking perfectly miserable, probably just to twist Ian's heartstrings.

"I'll tell her." Miss Augusta brushed a kiss to the girl's crown that Ian felt in the center of his chest. "I'll tell her after dinner, over tea with the ladies. I'd like it if you could join us, Fiona."

Ian watched as Fiona weighed the options. "I want it over with before bedtime, but if all the ladies are there, Ma won't yell as much."

Ian reached up and lifted the child from the saddle. "Down you go and off to the kitchen. Tell Cook you were out riding with me, and she'll make you a tray." He patted the child's bottom as she scooted off, not exactly gently, which had Fee grinning at him over her shoulder.

"See you at teatime, Miss Augusta!"

"You next." Ian reached up, wondering why—when he'd helped any number of ladies from the saddle—he was tempted to catch this one to him when she put her hands on his shoulders and slid to the ground.

Except he knew why. "Steady?"

She nodded, and he stepped back but let himself take her hand as he led her toward the gardens. When he closed his fingers over hers, he noted two things. First: Her hand was cold in the middle of a bright summer day. Second: She was wiser than he, sensing an attraction Ian hadn't wanted to admit, much less name. Why else had she silently been putting distance between them ever since their chat on the moonlit terrace?

"You don't need to avoid me," he said. He meant the words too. Meant them sincerely.

"Avoid you?" She didn't withdraw her hand, and yet he felt her withdrawing in some intangible way.

"I'm a gentleman, Miss Merrick, and one attempting to court your cousin. I would not trespass . . . I wouldn't presume . . ." He fell silent and led her to a bench they'd occupied before. It sat behind a high privet hedge, shaded and secluded. When she'd gingerly lowered herself to the bench, Ian took the place beside her without asking her permission.

He also took her hand again, lest she stalk off after she'd slapped him.

"I like you, Augusta Merrick. I like you, and I respect you, and what you just did for my niece puts my entire family in debt to you."

It wasn't what he'd meant to say. The two things were separate, the liking her and being in her debt. He'd never been good at delicate innuendo, never would be, but he'd seen those sketches, and they made him a little reckless.

"I like you too, Ian MacGregor." She smiled as she said this, a soft, secret female smile that lit up those violet eyes with some joy known only to her. You'd think she'd never liked a fellow before.

Maybe she hadn't, which was an inordinately cheering thought.

"If you like me, then why haven't you let me show you any more of the woods? Why do you move your place at the table every morning so we no longer converse over breakfast? Why are you from the house for most of every day unless it's pouring? You are my only ally in this endeavor with your cousin. I look to you for guidance, you know."

It was true, in a manner of speaking, but the real truth—the truth a man could tell a friend—popped into his mind as a whole thought: "I've missed you, Augusta Merrick. It has been a very long week, trying to be agreeable to everybody, to fathom the undercurrents in your family and mine, to keep the estate business running smoothly while being the devoted suitor and the charming host."

She was still smiling to herself, her gaze on their joined hands. Her fingers were gradually warming.

"I've . . . not wanted to impose. Not wanted to overstep. You're the earl."

"I'm Ian to you, if you'll recall."

"Ian."

And God bless her, she said it the way Fiona or Mary Fran might. Not E-an, but nearly one syllable and almost rhyming with rain.

"Augusta." It felt good to say her name, but he didn't let himself dwell on that. "You bring your sketchbook when we go on our walk."

"Tomorrow morning?"

"That would suit." That she wasn't going to beg off had his blood bubbling along more happily in his veins. He *had* missed her. It hadn't just been words or a polite sentiment— nor even a purely naughty sentiment either, come to that.

They sat like that, side by side, hands joined, while something shifted in Ian's thinking. She was brave enough to take these small risks to propriety in the name of friendship, brave enough to walk his property with him without benefit of chaperone or family.

A woman who'd face down a courting bull might be willing to chance even greater risks in

the name of something greater—more intimate—
than friendship.

He dropped her hand and rose to his feet, the
direction of his thoughts unworthy of them both.

Also damned hard to ignore.

"You'll be wanting that tea tray, won't you? I
shouldn't keep you out here when you've had
such a fright."

If his abrupt return to sanity disconcerted her,
she hid it well. She rose and linked her arm
through his. "A tea tray and maybe an afternoon
in the library. I'm in the mood to read some
Catullus, I think."

Was she challenging him? "Translations or in
the original?"

"The original. I prefer to puzzle out the translations on my own."

He did not dwell on all the implications of such
a statement, but escorted her up to the house.
Only when she'd disappeared from view did he
realize he'd never caught sight of his errant sister
and her latest Englishman.

Four years ago, when they'd had their first
summer of paying guests, Mary Fran had given
herself permission to like the occasional
Englishman or Englishwoman. Her own English
grandmother had had no patience for prejudice,
saying the rules of Highland hospitality forbade
such pettiness.

"The battlefield is one thing, home and hearth another."

Would that the distinction was as easy for Mary Fran to make. Gordie's perfidy hadn't helped, but it was hard to know if he'd been such a tramp out of maleness, Englishness, or his own simple venery.

Or all three.

"Might I have just a spot more tea, Lady Mary Frances?"

The spinster—Miss Augusta—held up her cup. Mary Fran poured carefully, wondering when the lecture would come. The other ladies had departed for their beds, leaving only Augusta, Mary Fran, and Fiona lingering over the teapot. Fiona had been dogging the woman mercilessly for several days, which was only to be expected.

While Mary Fran held most English in contempt on principle, Fiona was understandably fascinated with her father's people. The child sat in a corner quiet as a mouse for once, a delicate cup and saucer balanced in her lap.

"I wanted to tell you of an adventure I had today while out with Miss Fiona," the spinster said. "You're going to be quite proud of your daughter."

Miss Fiona? Nobody save Vicar called the child that, and never in tones presaging pride.

"I am often proud of our Fee," Mary Fran replied, but she cast the child a sidelong glance.

She *was* proud of her daughter—why didn't she ever tell the girl as much?

"I was determined to sketch the prettiest meadow we could find, and chose my spot without regard for the dangers it might pose." The woman took a sip of her tea, not even realizing that for a mother, that single sentence would create worry.

"Danger, Miss Augusta? Were you on the goat track up to the tor?"

"Nothing so daring as that. We were in a meadow to the east of the house, a lovely place full of clover and sunshine, our picnic not even unpacked when a gentleman came calling."

Gentleman? Who among the local landowners . . . unless it was someone from Balmoral. Please, God, let Fee have remembered her curtsy before the prince or his progeny.

"Another fellow out walking?" Mary Fran took a sip of her tea, only to find her cup empty. She glanced at the dregs, resenting the need to listen patiently to a woman with whom she had nothing in common.

"He was out courting. Fiona tells me he goes by the name of Romeo. Fiona did exactly as I asked her, though, and nobody came to any harm."

"Romeo got loose!?" Mary Fran's cup went clattering to its saucer. "Fiona? You were in a pasture with that bull? What . . ." She realized she was nigh shouting and got to her feet, the need to

172

move undeniable. Fiona was so little, and that damned bull was the biggest, lustiest specimen her brothers had been able to purchase.

Mary Fran sat right back down, comprehending the phrase "weak in the knees" for the first time in her life.

"Lord Balfour says somebody opened his gate," Miss Augusta said. "Romeo's apparently confined with not only stout gates, but gates that are both latched and then tied shut. On the other side of our pasture was a herd of yearling ladies, and they brought out Romeo's protective streak."

"Oh, Fee . . ." Mary Fran gazed at her daughter. Fiona sat looking innocent and tidy in a clean pinny, somebody having redone her braids, her ankles demurely crossed.

She might at that moment have been just as tidily laid out in the parlor. "Fiona Ursula MacGregor, you come here to me." Mary Fran spread her arms, needing to hold her child. Fiona took one hesitant step then swiftly closed the distance.

"Your daughter kept a cool head. She manned the gate for Lord Balfour so Romeo couldn't get up to any more mischief. She didn't panic, she didn't argue, she didn't question. You are raising a very brave and sensible young lady, Lady Mary Frances."

"Fiona MacGregor, what am I to do with you?" Mary Fran hugged her child shamelessly. "That bull could have been the end of you." She lapsed into the Gaelic, though it was rude before a guest. Still, a mother needed to scold in her native tongue, and to be reassured, and to tell her daughter she was loved.

When Fiona had related her great tale with many embellishments and much waving of hands—and even some snorting and pawing—she lapsed into silence, drowsing on her mother's shoulder. Miss Augusta had slipped out somewhere along the second or third telling, leaving Mary Fran to carry the child up to bed and tuck her in.

She didn't always tuck in her own child. One of the maids saw to it if Mary Fran were too busy, just as Miss Augusta had seen to *saving Fiona's life* when Mary Fran had been too busy today.

Feeling guilt about to swamp her composure, Mary Fran grabbed a shawl and took herself to the back terrace. It was nearly dark, and the stars already coming out, meaning Fiona had been up quite late telling her story, working the worry and fear of it out of her system.

And into her mother's.

Augusta had figured out at an early age that she lacked something all the other girls seemed to possess in abundance. Something quintessentially feminine and appealing to the gentlemen searching for brides, something that made a woman truly care which bonnet showed off a new dress to best advantage.

She'd attributed her lack of enthusiasm for shopping or swilling tea by the hour to having spent a great deal of her early years with her father. In the secret depths of her youthful heart, she'd hoped her husband might be the one man who could stir her to passion—about marriage, about bonnets, about wifely duties, about anything the other girls took such delight in.

Mr. Post-Williams had been ardent, he'd been impassioned, he'd been persistent as the devil and also conscientious regarding his tooth powder, so Augusta had capitulated only to be disappointed again.

Disappointed worse than ever.

Lord Balfour was going to disappoint her too—not in the same way of course—but unlike all the men who'd clamored for Augusta's hand, Balfour stirred her passions.

She was out of bed when the birdsong started, eager for their outing. He'd been a gentleman in each of their encounters, whether in private or surrounded by family, but he'd been a *friendly* gentleman. An *affectionate* gentleman, even.

Which was occasioning great, foolish giddiness on Augusta's part.

She wanted him for her own. Wanted him reading her poetry as he'd read to Genie, who'd been oddly subdued by his gallantry and patience.

Augusta wanted his smiles and quiet asides; she wanted his devotion to family and his boundless physical vigor. She wanted his restless, penetrating mind and his humor, and more than anything in her life, she wanted to know him intimately.

This was *very* bad of her, *very* foolish. She desperately hoped she could keep from acting on such mad notions, but the intensity of the feelings consuming her was nigh overwhelming. Fortunately, Balfour showed no signs of reciprocal inclinations, and this was a relief. Augusta had no doubt Uncle would toss her off her property in Oxfordshire if she interfered with Genie's prospects.

She wouldn't interfere, but she would steal a few hours with the earl for herself. She'd have his smiles; she'd have his companionship; she'd even have the occasional opportunity to take his arm or hold his hand.

He was a hand-holder; she'd gathered that much. Lovely quality in a man, but not one she'd ever found in the effete and proper Englishmen who'd kept her company in the past. Balfour was different in so many ways.

Or maybe, *she* was different.

Augusta dressed quickly and considered this possibility. She was older, she'd suffered some bad years, she'd fashioned a meaningful life for herself with very few raw materials. Maybe her hand was more worth holding now, at least to a man who had more on his mind than fabricating tales of having gone walking with the Queen.

She laced up her old half boots—the comfortable ones—pinned up her braid, and slipped out the door to the terrace.

She caught sight of his lordship—Ian—standing in the early morning light at the edge of the terrace. He had a rucksack strapped to his back, but he was bareheaded and bare-handed, his kilt a subdued pattern of gray, red, and black. He smiled as he caught sight of her and held out his hand to her.

This morning, being different was going to be wonderful indeed.

Augusta Merrick was in surprisingly good condition, or she was too sensible to lace her stays to the ridiculous extremes that passed for fashion in the South.

Ian was taking her up the easy way, nonetheless—the long way—the only way that didn't require the nimbleness of a goat, nerves of steel, and some fervent prayers to the gods of weather.

It did, however, require him to hold her hand, to help her over the various rough patches in the goat track, to keep a hand on her waist when the path widened enough to let them walk side by side.

Just for this morning, he'd given up chastising

himself for desiring his intended's cousin. As a married man, he was going to have to discipline himself to look and not touch, perhaps to not touch even his own wife.

The thought coincided with a cloud passing before the sun, turning the summer air chilly in typical Scottish fashion. The Almighty was nothing if not subtle in His humor.

"How much farther to the top?"

She wasn't even out of breath, and they'd been climbing gradually but steadily for nearly an hour. "Not much farther. Let's rest a bit, shall we?"

She looked around and picked out a boulder from among the many possibilities.

"Do you come up here often?" As she spoke, she was unpinning her braid, which had been threatening to lose its moorings. Lifting both arms shifted her breasts gently under her shirt-waist, forcing Ian to focus on the sky.

"Not as often as I did as a boy. The view is magnificent, but the time to make the climb becomes harder and harder to find." The *view* was riveting, in fact.

"You attended university in Edinburgh, didn't you?"

Down came the braid, a thick dark rope long enough to reach her lap.

Bloody damn . . . He pulled his gaze away from the blue hair ribbon twined around the end of her braid, the little bow resting right over her . . .

"I studied law in Aberdeen." He didn't sit right beside her, but took the next boulder over, downwind, so he could catch her lilac scent without being too obvious. "The MacGregors were put to the horn and denied the use of their very name by action of law. The Clearances were conducted by operation of law. The sovereignty of Scotland was obliterated by passage of laws. I thought it behooved a prudent Scotsman to acquaint himself thoroughly with this business of the law."

"England's sovereignty was obliterated too." She held up one of her half boots and upended it with a vigorous shake. Ian wrenched his mind away from the memory of her bare toes. "The Acts of Union were simultaneous and a Scottish monarch put on the throne of the United Kingdom of Great Britain."

She did this. She argued with him, argued history, politics, animal husbandry. They'd argued all the way up the hillside, and he'd never enjoyed a woman's company more—with his clothes on.

"Give me your pins, Augusta."

They'd also dropped any pretense of using titles and polite address with each other. She graced him with an enigmatic smile and passed over a handful of hairpins. He sidled around to stand behind her where she sat.

He gathered up her braid and coiled it neatly at

her nape. "So why don't we call this wonderful island of ours Great Celtland or Great Pictland? Why did we name it after the English heathen of yore?"

"We don't call it great Saxland or Great England."

"Hold still." He forced his fingers to pin up her braid, when what they wanted to do was unravel the thing entirely. Admitting his attraction to her should have made restraint easier—not next to impossible. "You have to concede England certainly has a greater hand in Scottish matters than Scotland does in English matters."

She turned her head to peer at him while Ian was trying to pin up her braid. "One has the impression Scotland would consider taking a hand in English matters boring, a waste of time, and beneath the notice of most Scotsmen."

"Certainly thankless." He finished with her braid and stepped back, adjusting himself in his clothes while her gaze was on the valley spreading out below them.

"You have a very beautiful home, Ian. I can see why you're so protective of it."

"Proud of it. So many of the clans lost everything. Their holdings in the mountains are mostly ruins, their lands overrun by sheep, their people gone across the waters never to return. What the Clearances and the famine didn't take from us, emigration and the Highland regiments have. The MacGregors have been lucky."

She turned to regard him, her violet eyes showing the keen intelligence he'd noted even in his first impression of her. "How were you lucky?"

Eight

THE CLOUD PASSED FROM BEFORE THE SUN. Ian focused on answering Augusta's last question in its least metaphorical sense. How had his branch of the clan been *lucky?*

"The earldom was a stroke of luck, another one of Charles II's generous impulses with a fellow willing to ignore royal interest in his lady. I've often thought most peers never recall another man's given name if he has a title, and thus, we weren't tarred with quite the same brush as the rest of the clan. And our land here is among the best in the shire, mostly because we have an enormous bat cave to the south, which we guard more jealously than a mother wolf guards her cubs."

"A bat cave?"

"The droppings are among the best fertilizer you'll ever find. The local soil is thin at best, but a hundred fifty years of proper management and care, and our land has improved enough to produce a good crop of oats, though wheat still remains a challenge. Others are following suit, but it's a painstaking process."

"You sell this fertilizer?"

"Very dearly, but yes. We also make a present of some to our royal neighbor each year."

"You're paying her back, aren't you? Making reparation to the royal coffers for the earldom bestowed on your family all those years ago."

She would understand that. "It's more a token. If Charles hadn't had such a wandering eye, there would have been no need to bestow placatory titles."

She wrinkled her nose in thought. "Except many a monarch has the wandering eye and doesn't bestow the titles in gratitude, so you feel indebted. Being Scots, and MacGregors, you repay the debt with your most precious coin."

"Perhaps." Being Scots, they also enjoyed the profound irony of gifting the monarch with bat manure. "Are you ready to move on?"

"Another moment. The view is lovely."

She was lovely. Her complexion had bloomed since she'd arrived in Scotland, and her hair shone with glossy highlights. She sat in the morning sunshine, face turned up to the breeze, eyes closed, the picture of a woman awaiting her lover's kiss.

She was clothed in a high-waisted old-fashioned dress that the breeze molded to her figure without interference from hoops or crinolines.

He'd felt that figure against his body, could attest to the generosity of its curves. His intended had been in his arms as well, when she'd turned her ankle, but for some reason, Ian had formed no impression of Genie's feminine attributes.

Bad enough when a man wanted to touch but could only look. Worse yet when he'd touched and not even noticed.

Augusta rose and smiled at him. "Shall we continue?"

"This way." He took her hand in his and led her up the track. The way became narrower and steeper—it was a trail used to herd livestock to higher elevations in summer—but she could have navigated the path without his aid.

"How is it you're accustomed to walking like this, Augusta?"

"I occupy a small manor home in Oxfordshire with an elderly widowed cousin. I'm two miles from town, and unless I'm hauling a load to or from market in my pony cart, I usually walk the distance. Then too, tending to one's animals and one's garden properly requires diligent effort."

He tried to both savor and ignore the feel of her hand in his—which would soon drive him daft. "You have no servants?"

"We have a housekeeper and maid-of-all-work living in, and a day man in most seasons. My cousin has a lady's maid nearly as old as she is. Why?"

"I heard you speaking with Mary Fran the other morning, describing your ramblings as a child."

She glanced over at him and dropped his hand, ostensibly to smooth back an errant strand of hair, though she didn't take his hand again. "I'm not sure which conversation you refer to."

Just like that, she was English to the teeth. Chilly, proper, and punctiliously civil. It made him want to warm her up again, to mess with her hair, to see her bare . . . feet.

Bloody damn, he hadn't been this far gone since adolescence.

"I refer to the conversation where you told Mary Fran you were acquainted with everybody on your father's estate, from the goose girl to the beekeeper."

"And your point?"

"An estate with a goose girl, a beekeeper, and all those other positions is a big place, Augusta. Your parents were wealthy."

"Quite." She smoothed the lock of hair back again, though it hadn't come loose from behind her ear. "Or I assumed they were."

"So why are you living like shabby gentry now? Even if your father suspected you were illegitimate, he would have made provision for you. Your uncle certainly has coin to spare, so much coin he can buy his daughter a relatively well-respected title."

She remained silent while scrambling over a rock-slide blocking the path, then waited for Ian to catch up to her.

"This is not a polite topic of conversation, my lord."

He smiled at her attempt to reestablish the lines. "Augusta, I am *worried* about you. How do you go on? Have you coin of your own? Did you choose this obscurity, or does it chafe? For a single woman to live virtually alone . . ."

She was marching forth again, her back to him because the way was too narrow to walk side by side. She was making an assault on the summit now, no longer out ambling through a Scottish summer morning, and clearly, he had offended her.

"Augusta, forget I asked, please."

She nodded without turning, which suggested Ian hadn't only offended her dignity, he'd also hurt her feelings.

They continued on in silence until near the rocky tor itself, where the way opened up enough that he could take her hand again. She allowed it, which relieved him inordinately.

"Oh . . . *my*." She stopped abruptly right beside him as they gained the base of the tor. At their backs, rocks soared up another thirty feet from the hilltop, and before them lay a vista clear across the shire.

"We haven't views like this in Oxford." She

swung her gaze off to the west, where a rugged line of purple mountains created the horizon. "I have never seen . . . It's beautiful, Ian. Breathtaking. Thank you for showing me this. And you're right, I do want to sketch it. I want to sit here until fall and sketch it as the birches turn golden, and then watch as the snow covers those peaks and the beasts huddle in the hollows. I want to see spring take over the land from up here . . ."

She turned, maybe to make sure he wasn't laughing at her.

"And you want to watch as it blooms into summer," he finished for her. "As a boy, I understood God better once I'd seen the world from up here, and I wondered how so much of my family could leave beauty such as this behind them. The property with all the new construction is Balmoral, and my own home is back that way, to the southwest, near the base of the mountain that looks like a saddle."

"Your home?"

He dropped her hand and shifted behind her, raising his arm over her shoulder. "Just there. On the slope of that mountain. The name of the place translates to something like 'heart's refuge.' The Scots are romantic about the most prosaic things."

And he was inhaling the fragrance of her hair, helpless not to.

"Ian?" She turned her face, exposing her nape. "Before, when you asked about my circumstances? I don't have the answers."

"I ought not to have been prying."

"But you ought to know this." She paced off a few steps, and he should have thanked her for putting space between them. Instead, he resented that space, resented that she hadn't sunk back against him and at least let him hold her as a man holds a woman he desires.

No, it was worse than that: he didn't merely desire her, he *cared* for her.

"What should I know, Augusta?"

She paced off even farther to sit on the rock best suited for viewing the panorama before them. He moved closer but didn't allow himself to sit beside her.

"When I was growing up," she began, "I knew we were wealthy. It was there in obvious ways—you couldn't ride all of our holdings in a day, the house had fifty-some rooms, the stables were gorgeous, and the tenants wanted for nothing. Kent is good land."

"It has that reputation."

"And because I was the only child, I tagged after my papa shamelessly, and he and my mother indulged me. He'd tell me the land would all be mine one day, and I needed to understand how to go on with it. He'd warn me to choose my husband wisely, because any man I married

187

would have to be my partner as well as my spouse. I was a girl. I paid him no mind."

"You're not a girl any longer."

"I grew up quite precipitously when my parents died. One day I was laughing with Mama over which invitation to accept, and the next I was wearing black and dependent on my uncle for my very bread."

"So your father failed to make provision for you?"

"Uncle said Papa's will was invalid, and what little Papa had in coin had gone to pay enormous debts. I never knew if my mother even had a will. I don't understand, because we had money. I saw the account books, saw the strongbox, saw the contents of the safe in my father's study. My involvement in the estate business never struck me as unconventional, though in hindsight, it must have been.

"Then too, Uncle was not related to Papa. I never met my father's family. I think they emigrated like your relations did. I tried writing to the solicitors, but Uncle saw the letter in the mail and asked why I'd do such a thing."

"What did you tell him?"

"The truth: that I did not want to be a burden to him and felt my presence cast a pall over the household."

Despite the lust and mischief coursing through his body, Ian's brain concluded Augusta's story wasn't adding up. The lawyer in him tried to make sense of Augusta's recitation, but no matter how he parsed it, the reality of her childhood didn't mesh with her present circumstances one bit.

"So you withdrew to Oxfordshire voluntarily?"

"They were in *my home,* Ian. Genie chose my bedroom for her own, and I couldn't say anything. She was just a girl. She didn't realize at the time she was dispossessing me, but her parents surely did."

He settled beside her, resisting the urge to take her hand. "It always seemed to me that the worst thing about the Clearances was that they were done with the full backing of the law. They were acts of war, really, to cast people from their homes, to burn their belongings, to force them to flee or starve, but the king's man would read the bills of ejectment time after time, and there was nothing to be done. Your uncle had the law on his side, apparently."

"I cannot fathom how there was any great debt, Ian. Papa was a favorite with the trades because he paid at the time service was rendered. He didn't wait until the end of the year or until he was being dunned. He was a tradesman himself at heart. And he was shrewd and clever and he worked hard . . . where would the debt have come from?"

"Gambling?"

She shook her head. "His mother was a Methodist. We gambled for farthing points over whist, nothing more."

"Women?"

"He was devoted to my mother."

"Taxes?"

"The land wasn't entailed. The taxes had to be paid each year, or the Crown would have intervened. And I saw the books. Papa delighted in explaining them to me and showing me how to keep them. We made money each year—pots of it."

"Books can be manipulated, and it seems whatever the case, when your parents died, your uncle must have somehow inherited through your mother, who would have been his older sister. And he's wealthy now. Quite wealthy."

"It doesn't make sense to me, but I can hardly question my own uncle about his finances now, can I?"

Ian stared out over the dramatic, rolling terrain of his family seat to the mountains to the west. He realized he was in a position to further Augusta's interests, to champion her situation when she couldn't take on the challenge herself.

"You can't nose about in his coffers, Augusta, but I can. I've put off the financial wrangling that goes on before a wedding of significance, but I'll send off a few letters tomorrow and see what I can discover."

"Don't anger him, Ian." She glanced around, as if they might be overheard here on this deserted hilltop. "Uncle has a mean temper, and he's not . . . I don't turn my back on him."

"Neither will I. Tell me something, though. At what point did he offer to wed you to your cousin?"

"At the end of my mourning. I was preparing to move to Oxford, and he mentioned it in passing."

If she regretted passing up that opportunity, her features gave no sign of it. "Had you seen the residence in Oxford before you removed there?"

"No. Aunt made it sound like a cozy manor and assured me I would have adequate staff to see to the place. They were to follow me from Kent with the coach and team I was to have. They never arrived—not the extra staff, not the coach and team. My cousin was in nigh-desperate straits when I arrived. I sold most of my personal jewelry, invested some of the proceeds, and hoarded the rest. We manage."

She managed, Ian realized, because the promised help and support had never been sent, allowing the good baron to all but forget he had a niece. Which raised the question: Why would Genie avoid the opportunity to leave the control of such a father and establish her own household?

There was no solving that conundrum now, and there were better uses of these stolen moments. "Would you like to sketch for a bit?"

"You're changing the topic. Thank you. My finances are not as dire as Uncle might think. I sell everything I don't consume, I teach drawing and piano to the local squires' daughters, I turn all my dresses and sheets, I purchase little in the way of foodstuffs, and I took my trousseau with me when I left Kent. I also watch the funds very closely."

"You cope. It's the Scot in you that can make do with next to nothing and even thrive on it."

He unstrapped his rucksack and withdrew a flask. "There are buttered scones in here along with your sketch pad. That flask holds tea, but I didn't bring any mugs."

He passed her the flask, shamelessly allowing their fingers to brush. She uncapped the lid and tipped her head back to take a sip. "I don't know as I've tasted better, Ian MacGregor. What will you do while I sketch?"

"Nap. The nights are damnably short this time of year, and the days demanding. You're not to tattle on me, either. The laird is expected to be indestructible and have the stamina of a goat."

He pulled a thick, coarse tartan blanket out of the rucksack and laid it on the stubbly grass a short distance from the patch of rocks. When he straightened, she passed him the flask. "Nap then, but do we need to worry about those clouds?"

She pointed east, in the direction of the sea, where—damn the weather all to hell—the clouds were beginning to crowd together into something less than encouraging.

"We don't need to worry about them just yet, but we want to be off this hill before rain arrives. The higher rocky patches have been known to come loose, though it's more a problem in spring after the freezing and thawing."

"May I sketch you, Ian?"

She already had, but now she was asking. He couldn't possibly refuse her.

"Mind you flatter me, lass. Tone the nose down a bit, tidy up my hair. I may soon have English relations to whom that sort of thing will matter."

A dismal prospect, that, especially up here, alone with her.

She opened her sketch pad and rummaged in the rucksack for a pencil. "I'm English, and I like your nose the way God made it." She lowered herself to the blanket. "Here." She patted the place beside her. "Just look out toward your home and tell me about it."

He talked for half an hour, about exporting Aberdeen Angus bulls, about his ambivalence toward the damned sheep, about the darkness of winter in the Highlands and the few relations he had still dwelling farther west. He talked about the famine less than ten years before and the graves that couldn't be dug fast enough. He talked about Fiona and the difficulty he anticipated for her because her parents were only handfasted.

"I've heard of this." Augusta reached out to winnow her fingers through his hair, no doubt rearranging it to suit her composition better. "Explain handfasting to me."

"That's the first time you've touched me, Augusta." He didn't turn his head to point this out.

"We've touched on many occasions. Maybe too many."

She sounded troubled by that observation, so he did look at her. "Or maybe not enough?" Naughty of him, but she should not have left him such an opening.

She shook her head and put the sketch aside. "You must not encourage me, Ian. You've been kind, and I will always treasure the memories you've given me, but you mustn't . . . you must not pity me."

"Why would I pity you?" He pitied himself, truth be known. Now, when he wanted to have her on her back beneath him, and he was supposed to comport himself like some damned choirboy . . .

Some *gentleman*.

She drew her knees up, wrapped her arms around them, and laid her cheek on her knees so she faced him. "You think I'm the typical poor relation, living in very reduced circumstances, having little contact with any larger world, but I like my life, Ian. I'm grateful for it."

He scooted around on the blanket so he faced

her, then leaned back, bracing his weight on his hands. "What do you like about it?"

"It's *mine*. In one sense, I depend on nobody for anything, and to a great extent, nobody has any right to impose on me. I have a sort of freedom few women enjoy. I had my Season. I had offers. I had an understanding with a young gentleman of good breeding and was very prettily courted. I've come to the conclusion that in a few years, if I hadn't been led off to the altar with him, I would likely have withdrawn to Kent, there to end my days arguing with my steward over whether to put the land in pasture or vegetable crops."

She sounded not pleased with her circumstances, but as if she were trying to convince herself to feel pleased. "You deserve more than that, Augusta. You deserve children, a family, the love of those dear to you. You deserve a future beyond that cottage in Oxfordshire."

She was quiet for a long moment, her expression hard to read, while Ian was aware of the storm clouds drawing closer.

"Ian, I am not . . . I am not chaste." She dropped her forehead to her knees.

Of all the things she might have said, he could not have anticipated that, and sorting through his feelings in reaction to her revelation was complicated.

"Was it by your choice, Augusta?"

"More or less." She raised her face to the far

mountains. "The young man and I had an understanding. Our papas were working out the details, and our mamas were planning the ceremony. Mr. Post-Williams was persistent and comely, and on several occasions, we anticipated our vows. He told me it would get better. I did not see much improvement, myself."

He hurt for her. Hurt for the detachment with which she offered this recitation. Mr. Persistent-and-Comely had much to answer for. "But you do not now have the honor of being Mrs. Post-Williams."

"My parents died. When it became apparent I had no dowry, somebody less impecunious had to be recruited for the position of Mrs. Post-Williams. He was very oblique about it, but at least I know."

"What do you know, Augusta?" And where was this Post-Williams now, so Ian might rearrange his comely face?

"I know what happens between men and women, Ian. I'm not going to die a virgin, ignorant of all life beyond my garden and my chicken coop, and yet, my reputation has remained unscathed."

But she didn't *know*. Ian was sure she didn't know half of what *ought* to transpire between lovers. That was glaringly, maddeningly, god-awfully obvious.

Just as obvious as the fact that Ian should not be the one to enlighten her.

"I'm sorry, Augusta. Post-Williams should be horsewhipped, and regardless of your circumstances, the man betrayed your trust."

"I don't dwell on it."

But it ate at her. He could see that. That she'd given herself to someone unworthy and gotten nothing, not children, not pleasure, not a ring, *nothing* in exchange for her trust corroded her soul.

"Augusta . . ." He leaned forward so his face was beside hers, his left cheek to her right. "I wish . . ."

She moved only an inch, to tilt her head closer to his so they touched at the temples. "Hush. There's nothing to say. I wish too."

They remained in that odd, touching non-embrace for a long moment, until thunder rumbled off to the east. Ian raised head and saw the clouds were moving in.

"Time to leave, Augusta. I didn't bring rain gear, and the footing can be treacherous if we get a downpour."

She nodded, got up, and helped him fold the plaid and repack the rucksack. When she started back down the path, Ian didn't even try to take her hand. His misery—for her and for himself— was too great.

A man of parts and sophistication didn't quail when his best-laid plans met with less than complete success. The baron shifted a little in his covert, listening with one ear for the approach of Augusta and her escort from the ramparts. Crouching behind boulders was hardly how the baron wanted to spend his morning, but a man of greatness was capable of sacrifice and dedication when the end was worthy.

The cat drinking the cream had been pure bad luck. Poison was discreet, true, but inaccurate dosing was a hazard, and the necessary stealth meant results couldn't be guaranteed.

And the bull had been a spur-of-the-moment inspiration, more an intent to maim than kill, because an invalid could easily be finished off if injured internally.

But time was wasting. A certain mistress would be getting restless, and so another improvisation was called for. The earl had mentioned—very quietly—to the middle brother to make excuses for him at breakfast because his lordship would be showing Miss Augusta up to the tor, and opportunity had knocked loudly.

This was a certain indication that fate favored the baron's plans.

The earl and the spinster had argued their way up the mountain, from the bits and snatches Altsax had overheard dodging along behind them. The earl was a doting escort, which boded well for Genie's future.

Except very possibly, Genie would end up

marrying the middle brother. Alas, needs must. She seemed attracted to the man, so no loss if the current earl was sacrificed on the altar of the baron's plans as long as Genie bagged her title and the Daniels's family fortune remained safely ensconced in the baron's capable hands.

In any case, one oversized Scotsman with pretensions to decency was no loss at all.

Altsax cocked an ear, hearing the crunch of footsteps on the rock-strewn switchback above him. Augusta had argued the earl to silence, poor man. The death of such a woman ought not even be mourned.

Augusta tried not to think, not to *feel* as she made her way down the hillside. Going down was in some ways trickier than coming up—a metaphor for having said too much and implied even more with the man moving along in front of her.

She could love him. There ought to be some consolation in knowing she was capable of loving a man, any man. She had wondered, after all.

The earl turned to speak over his shoulder. "Watch your step. The footing is loose and tricky here. I've landed on my backside more than once."

Watch your step. Going up, it had been easy to ignore the sheer drop on her left, the way the track was carved out of the hillside so the slope rose on her right almost like a wall. A shower of pebbles rained down from above, causing Ian to stop and turn to her.

"Best we keep moving." He held out a hand, but Augusta hesitated one instant before allowing herself the pleasure and torment of joining her hand to his.

In that instant, several things happened in rapid succession. Another shower of pebbles rained down, this one also containing more sizable rocks. Instinctively, Augusta ducked her head and shrank back against the slope beside her.

Then a peculiar, dull thud from above. Her first thought was thunder, except the sound had a different resonance than thunder, made the earth shake in a different way.

Ian shouting her name.

The impact of his body against hers as he plastered them to the vertical wall of earth and rock.

The feel of him surrounding her, solid rock at her back, solid man everywhere else, as earth, pebbles, and rocks went bouncing down the slope around them.

"Don't move." His voice, a harsh rasp right in her ear.

And the feel of him so close to her they were breathing as one, almost as if they'd just been erotically intimate.

"Are you all right? Augusta, talk to me." Still, he didn't move, and the warmth of him contrasted starkly to the chill and shock moving through Augusta's body.

"I am unharmed." Her voice was calm, detached even. "You?"

"The blanket in the rucksack spared me the worst of it."

She *ought* to be saying prayers of thanksgiving. She *should* be so grateful they hadn't been killed she could think of nothing else. Though what would a life of ought-to-be and should-be get her, but more years, more *decades* tending her chickens in Oxfordshire?

She kissed him. Found his mouth with hers and anchored her hand in his thick, silky hair to keep him from turning his head. A young girl purporting to be a wealthy heiress got kissed from time to time—Augusta wasn't a complete tyro—but kissing Ian *mattered*. This kiss had no pretensions to it about comfort, goodwill, incipient familial affection, or anything else polite and excusable. She was desperate for him to kiss her back.

He growled, and she panicked, twining an arm around his waist to prevent him from leaving her. She drew back only long enough to pant two words.

"Please, Ian . . ."

"Augusta, love, we shouldn't . . ."

And then she was giving thanks after all. His mouth settled on hers gently but firmly. Her desperation became something else entirely, and she realized she was going to be well and thoroughly kissed by a man who knew exactly how to go about it.

His mouth explored hers, moved over her lips slowly, like a weather front passing over the land, then moving on. She felt his nose grazing over her cheeks and forehead, her eyebrows, her jaw. She'd never been nose-kissed before, and it made her insides flutter wonderfully.

Then he was back to business, his mouth on hers, his tongue greeting her lips.

"Open, love."

This was novel and more wonderful still, to taste the tea-sweet essence of him, to feel a part of him making its way delicately into her awareness and into her body.

Between them, she felt a rising ridge of male flesh against her belly, felt it pressing against her in a way that aroused wanting in places female and secret. She moved into him, felt his hand cradling the back of her head, felt sealed to him and still not as close as she wanted to be.

"Kiss me back, Augusta."

His voice, low, harsh, and so very male, sent the wanting out from her depths to her breasts and her mouth and even the palms of her hands. She used her tongue as he had, to trace the contours of his mouth, to learn the taste of him, to join them in a way that felt so right, she wanted to weep with the beauty of it.

And still, it was not enough. Augusta kept one arm lashed around Ian's waist and used her free hand to stroke the wool of his kilt. The fabric was smooth and soft beneath her palm, his hip a lean, elegant curve. He widened his stance, and Augusta realized that a man in a kilt was a man who might be intimately explored. She slid the kilt up along his thigh, bunching the material between their bodies.

His mouth went still on hers while Augusta raised the fabric higher.

The flesh of his erect member was hot. She drew the backs of her fingers up his length, thanking God and Scottish national pride for a fashion that allowed a woman to indulge in such daring.

Her almost-betrothed had not allowed her to touch him. In their furtive joinings, Augusta had been told to hold up her skirts, to be quiet, to be patient for just another minute. The only thing she'd desired was for him to finish before somebody came upon them.

With Ian, her curiosity and desire were going to set the hillside on fire. She wrapped her fingers around his shaft, wanting to tear the kilt off his body.

Only to go still as she felt a breeze on the back of her calf.

Yes. A thousand times, yes.

"So verra soft, ye are," Ian murmured against

her neck. He bunched up her dress another few inches, and more cooling air hit Augusta's legs. She'd worn drawers, of course, but they were thin with age and many washings, little protection against Highland breezes or lapses in sanity.

"Ian, please—"

"Wheesht, love." He drew his hand up the back of her thigh, hiking her leg around his hip. Augusta had never hated fabric more—the thick wool of his kilt, her cotton drawers, her petticoat, her dress—all of it was so much frustration.

And none of it, apparently, enough to daunt Ian.

Augusta felt the brush of his fingers across the slit in her drawers, felt the brush of his nose across her cheek.

"Don't you dare stop, Ian MacGreg—"

His mouth settled over hers, a lazy, knowing mouth full of kisses and mischief. Wonderful, glorious mischief.

"Just this once," he whispered. "Ya ken?"

She nodded, knowing exactly what he was demanding. Through all the fabric bunched between them, she found him with her fingers again. "I understand." He was going to permit them a lapse—one lapse here on the hillside, while the clouds tried to crowd all that bright, brilliant sunshine away.

His arousal was warm, like his fingers as they brushed across Augusta's mons. The blessed, heartbreaking intimacy of that touch left her sagging against him, needing both the man before her and mountain at her back for support. He was touching her, touching her where no other man had touched her and no other ever would.

"Hold on t' me, Augusta."

She heard fabric rip, felt Ian's fingers brush her sex. He was not in a hurry, nor was he the least fussy about acquainting himself with every fold and secret of her intimate flesh.

She wanted him. She wanted him, and she would have him, *just this once*. Augusta hitched closer, hitched her leg higher on Ian's hip, determined to climb him and scale all of his objections too.

His fingers traced her sex again, a touch so intimate, Augusta shuddered with the pleasure of it.

"Shall I pleasure ye, my heart?" He repeated the caress, and while Augusta wasn't sure what he was offering, she divined it was something short of her goal.

"You shall love me." To emphasize her determination, she stroked along his member, going slowly, like he went slowly, then again when she realized her touch had made him go still—or maybe her words.

"Hold tight, Augusta." He shifted them, raising Augusta up a few inches, securing her leg against his hip and anchoring her against the vertical rise of the earth at her back. The ease with which he did this suggested to Augusta he could have held her there all day.

He fused his mouth to hers, sundering her wits with the heat of his kiss. His tongue pushing past her lips held no deliberation or strategy, nothing but lust and a desperation to match Augusta's determination.

"Ian, I can't—"

"Hush." He swept all the offending clothing from between their bodies, jerked his kilt one way, Augusta's dress and petticoats the other. With one strong arm, he settled her more firmly against the hard earth at her back; with his free hand, he traced his fingers around her hip, to the gaping tear in her drawers.

Augusta closed her eyes, the better to savor the scent of good Scottish earth, heather, and Ian. At variance with the harshness of his breathing, she felt Ian's arousal, blunt and warm, probing at her sex.

The sensation of joining with him was a satisfaction of cataclysmic proportions. This was what loving should feel like—an easing together of two bodies for shared pleasure, two bodies ready, willing, and eager to become as intimate as they could be.

While Ian retreated and surged more deeply into Augusta's body, she spared a pang of sorrow for a young woman trying to balance on the edge of a hard desk, her middle cramping with the awkwardness and strain of what should have been beautiful.

"Augusta, are ye crying?"

"Love me, Ian." For she surely loved this, loved the intimacy and power of it, loved that they joined by the broad light of day.

"I am."

She wanted to speak to him of the pleasure he brought her, of the singing, rising, bodily joy that coursed higher moment by moment. She wanted to move with him, to do more than cling to him and revel in an intimacy that felt both inevitable and unprecedented.

All she could manage was a harsh, desperate whisper against his neck. *"Ian—"*

"Let go, my heart." He went on in rough Gaelic, the sound of it joining with the throbbing of Augusta's blood and the rhythm of their joined bodies.

She fought against the pleasure as it coiled more and more tightly, fought against anything resembling a conclusion to this joining, and yet, she was not strong enough to withstand that conclusion for more than a handful of moments.

Dizzying, soaring joy filled her soul while pleasure wracked her body. She clutched at Ian shamelessly, held him hard with everything in her while he buried himself inside her again and again.

And then, silence, except for the pounding of

Augusta's heart. Inside her body, Ian was still; around her, he was a solid, warm presence. Too late, Augusta realized a wide, warm bed, where two people could curl up and catch their breath, had a lot to recommend it.

Her jacket would be filthy, and she did not care.

"Ian?" She brushed her hand over his hair, which still sported a dusting of earth and grit from their near miss.

He let her leg slide down his flank and withdrew from her body. Augusta's skirts drifted down over her legs, propriety trying to fall into place with them, and failing. Ian braced himself with one hand on the earthen wall above Augusta's head.

With the other, he held his arousal, now wet, glistening, and to Augusta's eyes, larger than ever.

She watched while Ian's hand moved on his shaft, an up-and-down stroke that stirred the embers of Augusta's desire.

This was intimate too, particularly when she looked up and saw that Ian watched her mouth as he stroked himself. The look in his eyes was stark with lust and despair, a nigh-animal longing revealed, as well as an even fiercer discipline.

"Kiss me, Augusta. For the love of God, please—"

Rather than stare into those desperate, hopeless green eyes, Augusta kissed him, putting every ounce of passion she had into it, pleading with him to vanquish the despair for at least a moment.

His body shuddered, and Augusta felt the tension go out of him and his hand go still between them. She dropped her head to his shoulder, the heat of him growing more necessary than ever as the sun passed behind the thick gray clouds.

He remained over her for long moments, and then he shifted, though he kept Augusta close in his embrace, his palm angling her head so her face was against his throat. She could feel the pulse there, wanted to touch her tongue to it.

"We canna engage in such folly again, Augusta."

He sounded not angry so much as despairing. Augusta raised her head, wanting him to see in her eyes that she could never regard something so beautiful as pure folly. "You're not engaged to anybody yet, Ian MacGregor."

He huffed out a great, long sigh, one Augusta could feel against her chest. And then he lifted away, far enough that Augusta could feel the chill of the air between their bodies while he stood heaving like a bellows a few inches from her and wiping at himself with a handkerchief.

"I can't be courting your cousin and dallying with you."

Of course he could not, hence the just-this-once aspect of their *folly*. And yet, she had to argue with him, maybe as a way to remain close. "This isn't dallying, Ian."

"Then what would you call it?"

He pushed away, but his feet didn't move. He stood glaring down at her, and even as Augusta understood he had to be angry now, had to find his balance with some emotion saner than desire, she felt the loss of him.

The grief.

"I would call it allowing ourselves a small, temporary taste of happiness, Ian. We deserve that much. Genie doesn't want to marry you. I don't want to spend the rest of my life teaching squires' daughters how to draw bowls of blasted fruit."

"Don't cry." He said something in Gaelic that Augusta would have sworn was an endearment. He hugged her, an embrace very different from the one before it. "I'd end up breaking your heart, Augusta. You're not a lady who can dally and be done with a fellow."

"I told you, this isn't dallying."

"Oh, fine then." He shifted away again, ran a hand through his hair, and aimed a look at her both affectionate and exasperated. "You'd break my heart, all right? That's the God's honest truth, woman. I don't know why it should make you smile. We're in a . . . pickle here. A blasted, damned pickle."

As declarations went, it was only a start, but Augusta took it and held it to her heart.

"I'm not sorry, and neither are you, Ian. That

means it's not an entirely bad pickle." She wanted to smooth his hair back again, to finish dusting away the bits of dirt. As if he knew she was harboring silly notions, Ian caught her fingers and glanced up at the slope.

"It's bad enough. Come along. The rain will start any moment."

He kept his hand in hers while they made a hasty descent. When they reached the trees at the base of the slope, he dropped her hand to escort her very politely back to the house.

By the time they got there, Augusta had stored up an encouragingly fulsome vocabulary of Ian's muttered Gaelic curses. It might take her days to puzzle out translations for them all, and the rest of her life to come to terms with what she and Ian were never going to have a chance to share again.

"I will not ruin ye. We've had this discussion, and ye'll not sway me to yer schemes!"

Gil kept his voice down with effort, but the urge to scream, punch something, break small objects of great value, or run like hell made it difficult.

"And I will not marry your titled brother," Genie hissed. She glanced around, and Gil honestly didn't know if she wanted someone to come upon them in the library or if she had a shred of sense left to dread that possibility.

"I locked the door, Genie. If we're to have a proper argument, we can't be disturbed."

She looked startled, then a calculating gleam came into her eyes.

Gil took a step back while she advanced on him. "You have to talk to Ian, lass. Whatever bee you've got under your bonnet, he's to be your husband, and he's the man to take on your troubles."

"No titled *man* hand-selected by my *father* will take on my *troubles*." She advanced another two steps; he retreated two and a half.

"You say that like men are worse than offal." And yet, Genie Daniels wanted to be intimate with a man, one man in particular—*him,* may God have mercy on his soul. Though maybe she didn't want him in her bed. Maybe she just wanted him to compromise her with some silly kiss, but the girl needed to understand even kisses could be risky.

"Some men are worse than offal," she said, her voice low and taut with anger. "Maybe just a few men. A few is enough." Her expression became determined. "But not you."

"And not Ian!"

She pounced, fusing her mouth to his in an inept mashing of teeth, lips, and will. Gil was too shocked to bodily shove her aside, and then her arms were around him, clinging desperately while she murmured, "Oh, please . . . Please . . ." against his mouth.

"For the love of . . . ." His hand came up to

cradle the back of her head; his fingers plunged into silky blond hair without his willing it. He drew back his head a half inch.

"Not like that, lass. Ye've got it all wrong." Holding her still, he brushed his lips across hers, once, twice. "Ease into it, steal into it. Like moonrise and summer breezes."

He settled his mouth on hers gently, introducing her to the taste of him, the soft, teasing feel of a kiss meant to convey respect and tenderness along with a generous helping of desire. His mouth pled with her to understand, to consider the possibility that kissing could be lovely beyond description.

She held still for him. That alone was enough to tell him she was *considering*. Her lips parted on a sigh, and he offered her his tongue, seaming her lips as further evidence that kissing was the farthest thing from the plundering she'd initiated.

For long, sweet moments he coaxed her into relaxing, into pondering what a kiss could be, and then he touched his tongue to hers. She startled at the contact. She clung to him so tightly he could feel surprise go through her then drain away into a languor that made him want to . . .

Good God.

He was gentleman enough—and aroused enough—not to tear his mouth away and stomp off. Maybe he was besotted enough.

No. Not besotted. This was Ian's intended. An

innocent young lady who knew a great deal less about getting herself ruined than she thought she did. Gil laid his cheek against her temple and let his embrace loosen.

She didn't step back. She merely shifted to rest her forehead against his chest. "Do all Scotsmen kiss that well?"

"Yes." National pride demanded he be honest, but now in addition to wanting to scream and throw things, he didn't know whether to laugh or cry. "Ian's had more practice than any of us, so his kisses will be even better. You need to take your concerns to him, Genie. I won't tell you again."

And still, she made no move to leave his embrace. Maybe she was so innocent—so ignorant—she couldn't feel the nascent erection rising against her belly. Maybe she was as aroused as he—

He stepped back. "You can't go around kissing fellows willy-nilly, lass. You'll get more than you bargain for, and a great deal less."

The look she shot him was brokenhearted, angry, and hopeless. "I know what I'll get, Gilgallon, and I know it would be substantially better than the marital bargain my parents are determined to strike for me."

She thought she knew, anyway. Scottish girls grew up early. Gil wasn't sure spoiled English girls grew up at all, and lingering with this one behind a locked door was the stupidest thing he'd done since . . .

It was the stupidest thing he had done, *ever*.

"Talk to Ian. If you're truly averse to marriage, he won't force it."

"Yes, he will. Papa investigated your finances thoroughly. I'm a fatted calf, and I'm going to be slaughtered on the altar of your brother's ambitions."

He'd never heard such bitterness in a woman's voice, but her myopic view of the situation was the outside of too much.

"Has it ever occurred to you, Eugenia Daniels, that my poor brother is the one being slaughtered on the altar of *your* family's ambitions?"

Her chin jutted. "A man can't be forced to the altar."

"A man who holds himself responsible for the well-being of his clan—what remains of it—can. A man loyal to his family, a man who sees no other options."

"The clan chiefs no longer have any authority."

This was a schoolgirl's recitation of history according to the English, and arguing with her over it would keep Gil from kissing the pout off her pretty face.

"The English are the ones with no authority. Oh, they make laws, they make pronouncements, they send their regiments all over the world to pillage and destroy, but an army is nothing compared to the love and loyalty of a Scotsman for his family. I bid you good day, and I advise you once again to speak honestly with my brother."

She gave him a measuring, purely female look. A look that made Gil think of things far beyond kissing.

"That was not the kiss of a loyal, loving brother, Gilgallon MacGregor."

He cursed long and fluently in Gaelic, then departed, making very sure he did not slam the library door.

Honor was a burdensome thing. It invariably shouted at a man to march off this-a-way when the man's common sense, instincts, and heartfelt preferences were begging him to trot out smartly that-a-way.

Ian struggled with this paradox for the hundredth time as he sat at his desk, knowing he'd been a negligent host for dodging the evening's post-prandial gathering around the decanters.

He did not want to face Daniels the Younger, not when the poor sod was likely reeling from having been caught in Mary Fran's feminine gun sights at close range. Mary Fran was hard on her followers, showed them no mercy in either the pursuit phase or the rejection phase of the goings-on. What came between was something a conscientious and well-intended brother did not dwell on.

Fortunately Daniels was a soldier, a man inured to suffering in silence. By the time he boarded the train for southern climes, he might have regained his dignity if not his masculine self-confidence.

Daniels the Elder was no more attractive company. Ian had a strong suspicion one of the scullery maids was allowing the baron to trifle with her, which created an uneasy ambivalence in Ian's gut. A laird of old would have either given the girl to the baron for his amusement outright or forbidden the girl to share her favors. In either case, the baron as a guest, the girl as a menial in the laird's household, and the entire household as a family and clan would have known where authority and responsibility for the decision lay.

But now . . . Who was Ian to deny a lowly maid the dubious pleasure or paltry coin resulting from the baron's attentions? Yesterday, Ian might have taken the girl to task—Ian would be the one left paying for the resulting child's every need, after all—but after the morning's outing with Augusta, certainty in any moral realm eluded him.

He let his thoughts circle back to her with a sense of inevitability.

He was going to court Augusta's cousin—if the blighted woman ever allowed him a start in that direction—and exhibiting interest in another woman while he did was not . . . honorable—or smart.

It wasn't quite dishonorable, either, though not in these enlightened, bedamned times. Many a man considered the only obligation owed his womenfolk was to keep the decent ones ignorant of and distant from the other variety.

The more interesting variety. The fascinating variety.

The available variety, among whom Augusta Merrick did not and could not number.

Ian stared at the documents before him, so many writs of execution for his remaining chances of happiness. He knew that now in ways he hadn't even twenty-four hours earlier.

And that would have been tolerable, except he was certain marriage to him would make Genie Daniels utterly miserable, and Augusta Merrick . . . Violet-blue eyes soft with sated passion flashed into Ian's mind along with the scents of heather, lilacs, and impending rain.

"Bloody, bleeding damn . . ."

The library door clicked softly shut in exact synchrony with Ian's curse.

"Damn who or what?" Gil stood there, his smile sardonic.

"Life in general. Apologies for leaving you to play host."

Gil sauntered over to the desk and propped a hip on one corner. "How was your outing with Miss Augusta?"

Fraternal concern, this was *not*. Ian pulled his

spectacles off and rubbed the bridge of his nose. "Why do you ask?"

"When you got back to the house, you had dirt in your hair, Ian. I do not profess to be a student of the more arcane erotic arts, but dirt in your hair? One doesn't get good Scottish soil in one's hair striding about the tor and admiring the views."

No, one did not, and damn all little brothers who'd notice such a thing.

"There was a little rockslide, a few boulders bouncing down the hill. We were unharmed, though a few feet in either direction, and the outcome might have been different."

Gil's brows drew down. "A rockslide? This time of year?"

"I haven't gone up there in so long I hardly know how frequent they are. In any event, we did admire the countryside, and we did stride about the tor. The lady has decided opinions." On many topics, and not the opinions Ian might have ascribed to her before he'd taken that hike with her.

"Miss Augusta? The one who lets Fee drag her around by the hand all day?"

"I believe she might be fond of children."

"The maiden ladies often are." Gil's gaze fell on the documents spread around on the desk. "You're burning midnight oil on the settlements?"

"Unless I'm to line the coffers of the blood-sucking toadies in Aberdeen, it falls to me to draft the documents." An exercise that combined penance with futility. "I'd appreciate it if you and Con would have a look as well."

"What's this?" Gil squinted at the page in his hand and moved closer to the branch of candles at Ian's elbow. " 'By signature below, it is warranted that Eugenia Daniels will be marrying a son of the house of MacGregor who is in expectation of a title.' Why not just say she's marrying you, and you're Balfour?"

Ian settled back in his chair, prepared to use Gil for a legal sounding board. Gil wasn't one for documents and heavy tomes, but he was a shrewd tactician able to see a situation from many perspectives at once.

"I have two reasons for the more vague language: First, I am not quite Balfour yet, am I? Asher hasn't been declared legally dead as far as Altsax knows, so the only title I hold beyond dispute is Viscount Deesely."

"Which is a title." Gil set the page down. "The baron didn't specify that you're to be holding *the* title? He'll settle for the courtesy title?"

"I honestly don't think the man smart enough to consider the difference. His darling Genie will be called Lady regardless, and she'll be able to swan around Balfour House when Her Majesty and His Highness are in residence across the glen. Then too, Asher might reappear, and I don't want him obligated to marry the woman."

"Asher's dead, Ian, and even if he weren't, having to wed into the Daniels family would be no less than he deserves for leaving us to wonder all these years."

Gil moved off to stand by the windows, his back to Ian.

"You'd do that to Genie?" Ian asked, rising and going to stand beside his brother. "Bad enough she'll have to marry me, whom she can at least look over and start to fashion into some semblance of a husband she can tolerate. To betroth her to a ghost or a stranger hardly seems like a kindness."

Gil eyed Ian up and down, his expression unreadable. "I've told her you'll be kind to her."

"Of course, I'll be . . . When did you have occasion to tell her this?"

"She's not sanguine at the prospect of wedding you."

Understatement, particularly from Gil, who was blunt even for a Scotsman—also a dodge where an answer to Ian's question ought to have been.

"I understand this, Gilgallon, for she's made no effort to hide her hesitance from me. Nonetheless, she and I have agreed to try, to attempt to become better acquainted, and to establish some mutually agreeable means of going on. If you have a better plan, even if you have a worse plan, I'm happy to hear it."

"I have no plans at all."

He who had little independent wealth, had no plans to wed in the near future. Con was in the same boat, Mary Fran as well. Fiona had their only prayer of amassing some coin, because her entire family would see to it, and they had ten years to work on the problem before Ian would consider allowing the girl to wed.

Ian regarded his younger brother. "Bachelors all over Scotland with no plans are raising up their bairns as we speak, Brother."

"I've no damned bairns, and you know it."

"You're Fee's favorite uncle, Gil. That's a high honor in itself." And Gil unabashedly enjoyed children.

Just as Augusta enjoyed children, for Christ's sake. Ian shoved that thought off a mental cliff, one with a fine view of pleasure, folly, and heartbreak.

Gil's face creased into a reluctant smile at the mention of his ranking among the uncles. "Show me these blighted settlements. I can't promise I'll get them all read tonight, but I'll make a start."

Ian ambled back to the desk and sorted papers. "These are the financial conditions. These are the special terms. I've kept it as simple as I could, but it's binding as hell, and the details can't be ignored."

Gil followed Ian to the desk and picked up the discarded spectacles. "Are you going to require the younger sister to marry you on the same terms if Genie is unwilling or unable to complete the ceremony?"

"Bloody damn . . ." Gil's tone had been casual, but he'd spotted a glaring oversight in Ian's draftsmanship. "This grows worse and worse. Hester's a lovely girl, but she's barely half my age. She's a damned child, Gilgallon. I've no interest in waiting for my bride to grow up before we can get the consummation of the vows over with—and that's assuming I can even manage such a thing."

Gil took Ian's chair and put Ian's glasses on his own nose, giving him an uncharacteristic scholarly air. "You don't have to do this, Ian. We're not starving."

"We're living a precarious farce, Gil. You know it and so do I. The only thing we have to barter for a substantial dose of cash is the title. Even after I'm officially installed as earl, there's no guarantee the solicitors will turn loose of the earldom's trusts, assuming anything remains there in any case."

Gil crossed booted feet on the corner of the desk. "The reports say the trusts are healthy."

"Those reports are written by lawyers. They can say any damned thing they please without actually lying." And Ian was damned if he'd try to wheedle one bloody groat from their aging cousin, the Baron Fenmore, who'd somehow gotten himself appointed overseer of the trusts in Asher's absence.

"Go to bed, Ian. Dawn comes early enough. Don't obligate yourself to marry Hester. Let Altsax be the one to think of that contingency. He wants your title for a trophy so badly he'd probably marry you himself."

"Which would be enough to give a brave man nightmares." *More nightmares.*

Gil pulled the candles closer, and Ian left his brother to the inanities of legal construction. Being able to function as a lawyer didn't mean a man took any joy from the task.

"Excuse me, my lord."

Genie Daniels sat on the top step before the first landing, tucking her dressing gown over her toes. She looked like a schoolgirl caught spying on her elders the night of the ball.

"Genie. You couldn't sleep?"

"I did sleep, but I couldn't remain asleep." Her gaze went everywhere—above Ian's head, to the foot of the stairs, over Ian's shoulder—never to his eyes.

Ian lowered himself beside her, experiencing a reluctant stab of fellow feeling for the other person being dragooned with him to the altar. "A wee dram of the *uisqe beatha* might help with that."

"I couldn't." She was hiding a smile, a small, dim smile.

He felt like he was sixteen and standing up at his first assembly, all awkwardness and uncomfortable silences between frequent trips to the men's punch bowl.

Maybe she felt that way too?

"How's your ankle?"

"Much better, thank you."

"And your head?" Today's ailment had been a megrim.

"Much . . . fine, thank you."

Another silence, laden, struggling. *Hopeless.* Ian blew out a sigh and gave up on polite conversation. "Genie, lass, would you prefer it if I gave you all the flowery words and declarations we both know to be false? I can muster a good show if that will make you less . . . uncomfortable. I was young once. I remember . . ."

He was *still* young, dammit.

"Please, my lord, let's not make this any more false than it already is." Her hands clenched around fistfuls of robe, but she said nothing else.

How could something be made *more* false?

"Will you ride out with me after luncheon tomorrow?" It was all he could think of to offer her. On horseback, she would be assured he'd keep his hands to himself—the idea of taking liberties with her being absurd in any case—and the grooms would stay in close attendance.

"I'll see if my aunt can accompany us." She laid her cheek on her knees in a posture reminiscent of the way Augusta had sat on the blanket that morning, nothing merry about it.

Augusta . . .

Ian got to his feet and extended a hand down to her. "A general outing, then. We'll muster the household and hope the rain moves off. May I escort you up to your room?" Where, if he had any sense, he'd steal a little kiss, presume to touch her hair, or at least take her gently in his arms. At some point they had to become accustomed to touching each other beyond the civilities.

The very idea made him queasy.

"No, thank you, my lord."

She sat right where she was, and Ian was so relieved not to be tried any further, he bid her good night and took himself off to bed. It wasn't until he was tossing himself from one side to the other for the twentieth time that it occurred to him to wonder: For whom did Genie wait on the stairs all alone at midnight?

Nine

JULIA REDMOND WAS A SOUND SLEEPER, SO sound Con had a few extra minutes to doubt his sanity and argue with himself over his presence in her bedroom—fruitless minutes while his cock clamored for him to be about a lusty man's typical business in a willing woman's bed.

Too bad for his cock, that wasn't the plan.

"Connor?" Julia struggled up to prop herself back on her elbows, her braid a thick, coppery rope over one shoulder. "It is you, isn't it?" She blinked in the moonlight streaming through her windows then reached out to where he stood beside her bed to take him by the wrist. "Say something, or I'll think I'm dreaming."

"Maybe you are dreaming." He put one knee on the bed, pausing long enough to pull his shirt out of his breeches and over his head. "Lie back, Julia, and be silent."

There was risk involved. Risk that she'd start shrieking, belatedly recovering her previously misplaced sense of decorum, but Con had seen the loneliness in her eyes, had heard the bewilderment and hurt in her voice when she'd tried to apologize to him in the stable.

"You have one chance to change your mind, Julia Redmond. You shake your head if you don't want me here, or you nod if I'm staying."

He waited as if he had all the time in the world, as if a Chinese rocket weren't trying to launch itself from his breeches into her body. She nodded, slowly, solemnly.

Good. She understood this was no small concession on his part. He pulled the covers aside and settled his body right over hers, caging her with his bigger frame.

"Kiss me, Julia."

He didn't give her time to get all those female gears spinning in her brain; he charged forth, intent on seizing his prize, which was to say, he kissed her. Set his mouth on hers and consigned himself to the sweetest suffering known to man.

She kissed like a young girl, lips sealed, not like a widowed lady who went around propositioning near strangers in the woods. Her reticence pleased him, helped him lecture that trouser rocket into submission and gave him the patience to savor her.

Sweet, was his first impression when he traced her lips with his tongue. Sweet, soft, enticing—like the rest of her. He felt himself getting pulled into the kiss, the exploration and pleasure of it, while he sank a hand into her hair.

"Connor . . ."

"No words, Julia." Except the mention of his name had parted her lips. He didn't invade. He explained and waited for her to catch on, then demonstrated again. On the second try, she got the idea and touched her tongue to his lips, a little lick of warmth that coursed down through his body and made him want to clutch at her.

To shuck his pants and swive her witless.

He let the thought go, thanking the Deity he'd had sense enough to wear trousers rather than a kilt and to keep his trousers on and buttoned. Her tongue grew a tad bolder, venturing to explore the soft flesh inside his lips then retreating uncertainly.

He let out a growl of pleasure at her overture and felt her hips lift against his body.

She wasn't cold. She wasn't the aloof, stand-offish lover he'd worried she might be. She was eager and shy and lovely, which was worse—far worse.

And much, much *better*.

He lifted off her a fraction of an inch, wondering when he'd let himself give her that much of his weight. It was too soon for that—they had a great deal more ground to cover first.

Julia's hand came up, stroked over his hair, then clutched a fistful at his crown, holding him still for her questing lips. She'd apparently found her initiative, forging delicately into his mouth, seeking more of him.

And if he wasn't mistaken, more of herself.

So he let go a little more, put some rhythm into his kiss, put some swagger and dare into it until she was orally consuming him, making little sounds of want and frustration that had Connor wishing his trousers to Halifax.

"Nightgown off, Julia." She lifted her arms in compliance so quickly she almost clipped him on the chin with her elbow. It was a summer night-gown, gone in an instant, tossed who knew where in her willingness to show him her treasures.

And they were treasures. She lay on her back while Con sat on his heels between her legs. He let her suffer a few panting breaths of trepidation while he took lazy, decadent inventory by moonlight: Perfect, full, pale breasts crested with small pinkish nipples puckering invitingly in the night air. Shoulders a touch more broad than he'd anticipated on such a diminutive woman, but tapering to a feminine waist that curved right back out to lovely hips. Not quite an hourglass—she was sturdy and apparently not given to overly tight stays—but so very definitely a woman.

She turned her face aside, which he took for a silent plea for his hands, his mouth. *Him.* She'd be begging before he was through with her, and he'd be cursing.

He shifted forward to hang over her, so they touched only when he gave her his mouth again. *Start slowly,* he admonished himself, teasing his lips over her features. Beneath him, Julia caught the shift, letting him set a more languorous pace. She also took advantage of the distance between their bodies to run her hands over Con's naked ribs.

Her touch shifted gradually from a hesitant request to hungry seeking. She mapped his entire torso with two hands—his ribs, chest, waist, hips. Her fingertips explored his nipples slowly and thoroughly, as if she'd never explored such territory before.

Con had encountered female hands on his person in every imaginable intimate caress, but this . . . *plundering* of him was unraveling his composure. He retaliated by shifting up enough to catch her busy hands in each of his and press them to the mattress on either side of their bodies.

Which left him free to plunder her, to run his nose along the underside of each warm, rosy breast and hear her breath catch in her throat. He did it again, making her squirm delightfully beneath him, and then when he made a third, slower pass, she sighed and went quiet.

Surrender, of a sort.

Only then did he put his mouth to her, by degrees and inches and slow marches, making her wait and whimper while she tried to pull her hands from his. When he finally drew on her nipple, gently of course, she groaned.

"Hush, lass."

She couldn't keep quiet, which pleased him enormously. The sounds coming from her were soft, plaintive, and erotic, escaping in time with the restless shifting of her hips in search of him. He felt the dampness of her curls against his belly and paused, laying his cheek on her abdomen.

The next part was tricky. She was English, after all, but he was betting she'd cast that aggravating detail into the darkness along with her nightgown.

He certainly had.

"Spread your legs for me, Julia."

There was an instant's pause, but only an

instant. He grabbed a pillow for her hips, though he had to show her what he was about.

Some husbands—some *English* husbands—were not worthy of the name.

He sat back to gather his courage in one hand and his self-discipline in the other, then reached out to stroke his fingers over the smooth, soft expanse of her belly. So pale, her skin, and so warm.

She arched her pelvis toward him, her eyes huge in the moonlight.

"Trust me, Julia. For the next few minutes, you trust me."

She did it again, moving under his hand like a cat insisting on its owner's caresses.

He ran his palm up the front of one of her thighs, a nice muscular turn of leg that suggested she enjoyed riding and walking. She was going to enjoy what he had to give her too.

As if he had all the time and fortitude in the world, Con learned the feel of her legs with his hands. His touch wandered over her abdomen, down to her knees, made occasional forays back up to those luscious, succulent breasts. Only when her restless shifting was continuous did he slide both hands up from her knees and brush aside her curls to expose her sex to the moonshine.

He used both hands, focusing his touch on the bud of flesh at the apex of her sex. The shock of it went through her palpably.

"Oh, Connor . . . Connor . . ."

His name, but not just his name. A blessing, a pleading, a promise to him and to the night. She wasn't so English after all.

She held still for an admirably long time while his fingers explored her intimate glory. He could not resist dipping his head to kiss her, though only fleetingly. She was sweet here too, and hot, and ever so ready to be cherished.

Which he did, for long, long moments, until she got a hand fisted around his wrist so tightly Connor noticed it even over the throbbing in his groin. He increased the tempo of his caresses, touching her carefully and then not so carefully at all.

She muttered something that wasn't a prayer, though she called upon the Lord's name in guttural desperation, and then her breath was soughing harshly in her chest as she bucked up hard against his hand.

He rode it out; rode out the thrashing and grinding, the low moans from her, the rising crest of his own arousal. She was fierce and glorious in her pleasure, also greedy and more athletic than a mortal man might withstand.

He withstood it, nonetheless.

When she lay panting and sated, he found he'd hilted two fingers in her heat and pillowed his cheek on her abdomen. While she heaved one mighty breath after another, he felt the small aftershocks spasming through her.

She'd been long overdue. Long, long overdue. More overdue even than he.

"Oh, Connor MacGregor. You . . ." Her hand landed in his hair on a sigh. She caressed his scalp, ran her touch over his ears, and for some godforsaken reason, he didn't want to withdraw his fingers from her. It was a pathetic gesture toward the joining his traitorous body wanted, so he made himself slowly ease away.

"Don't go." She caught his jaw in her palm, pressing his cheek over her womb. He submitted, the ache in his groin shifting to a thick languor throughout his body, almost as if he'd come and come hard.

"I'm heavy." It struck him he was apologizing, but for what he couldn't have said.

"Mmm." She wrapped her legs around him and squeezed in an odd, wordless hug. In her unconventional embrace, he felt a little of his heart—his sanity, his pride, his very reason—slip into her hands.

He nuzzled her belly, stopped trying to puzzle through the politics of it all, and smiled. In moments, she was asleep, which was a fitting reward for her labors.

When he was certain she slept soundly, he peeled himself away and got his shirt back on. A walk in the brisk night air was in order if he were to get any rest before dawn. A long walk, far enough from the house that his common sense and pride could find him and beat him into submission.

It was one thing to strike a blow for the honor of lusty Scotsmen everywhere; it was quite another to be defeated by his own tactics. He padded over to the bedroom door then paused to survey the woman sleeping in the bed.

She was cast away with her pleasure, curled on her side, her breath fluttering the end of her braid where it dangled from her shoulder to the back of her hand. He returned to the bed, shifted her braid, and let himself press one last kiss to her cheek before he repaired to the corridor.

Before he made a complete ass of himself and climbed right back into that bed.

Halfway to the staircase, Con came to an abrupt halt.

"Gilgallon."

"Connor." They both spoke very softly.

"Brother, is that a female you have asleep there in your arms?" Genie Daniels was nothing if not female, and she was curled in Gil's arms like a drunken rag doll.

"She fell asleep in the library." Gil glanced down at the woman he cradled against his chest, and the hopelessness in his eyes was pure torment to see on a proud man's face.

Genie Daniels had done a damned sight more than fall asleep in the library, as had the guilt-stricken, lovelorn Gilgallon.

"The English don't adjust quickly to our short nights." Con put as much understanding as he could into a single sentence. He hadn't seen this coming, and there could be no good end to it. Not for Genie, but more significantly, not for Gilgallon.

"You won't say anything to Ian?" Gil was asking for discretion, for compassion, and it probably killed him to do so.

"What in God's name would I say?"

Gil nodded, relief plain on his features, then his eyes narrowed. "The only bedroom on this corridor besides Genie's belongs to Mrs. Redmond."

"So it does. I guess that makes two of us who won't be troubling Ian with details that can't matter in the least." He gave Gil and his burden a wide berth, left the house, and spent the rest of the night out-of-doors, wrestling with his conscience.

And his heart.

"Meet me in the stables after breakfast." Ian pitched his voice low, so it blended with the general hubbub of breakfast chatter. Augusta, being a quick study, nodded as she accepted an orange from the basket of fruit Ian had proffered.

He replaced the fruit on the sideboard, tried to ignore the scent of lilacs filling his nose, and took his customary position next to Genie.

It was a long fifteen minutes, but at least by now he knew what to expect. If he made conversation with whoever was on his other side—Mrs. Redmond today, and looking particularly fetching—then through occasional asides, polite inquiries, and civilities, he could draw Genie forward into a discussion.

Such a bloody damned lot of work. He would have resented it except for the distinct sense it was work for her too. Down the table, Augusta was excusing herself, murmuring something about drafting a letter to the vicar's wife in Oxfordshire.

Con joined the breakfast party looking a bit peaked, Mrs. Redmond took her leave, and Ian used the opening to excuse himself as well. His intended made not even a token protest at losing his company, which ought to have caused him some despair.

When he got to the stable, Augusta was outside Hannibal's stall, scratching the old blighter's chin. "Apologies if you had to tarry here long. Will you really write a letter to your vicar's wife?"

She left off with the scratching and turned a smile on Ian. "Of course. She's about the only person I have to write to, and the surrounds here are so pretty I feel compelled to convey a description of them to someone."

He'd seen that smile on her face before, a happy

expression at odds with her words. "You will write to Mary Fran when you leave here, Augusta. I'll worry about you otherwise."

The smile dimmed. "If you insist."

"I do." He winged his arm at her. "I'd like to show you the old mouser's grave, if you can spare the time." And he wanted to apologize to her in some way for what had passed between them the previous day—the kissing, the cursing, the cursing about the kissing. *The rest of it.*

He was a sorry case indeed.

"Thank you, Ian. I did not want to impose." She slipped her arm through his, her acquiescence and her proximity settling something inside Ian as they began to move toward the path through the trees. "I'll want to visit him again before we leave for the South."

"Would you ever consider joining Genie's household rather than returning to Oxfordshire?"

Stupid question. He hadn't realized how stupid until he heard the words leaving his mouth.

"I have not. Julia's household is a possibility, but she's so far north for much of the year."

Far north, far away from civilization such as Augusta Merrick had been raised to understand the term, which was probably for the best.

"This way," he said, guiding her along the fork in the path. "The other way will take you eventually to Balmoral."

The longer they walked in the woods, sunlight

slanting through leaves and branches, birds flitting about the canopy, the less restless Ian felt and the more sad. He was attracted to Augusta Merrick in a way he did not entirely understand, but it wasn't just a reaction to the notion of marrying her cousin.

Would to God it were that simple.

"This is lovely," Augusta said, dropping his arm and advancing into a sunny clearing. "Very peaceful and private, for all we're not that far from the house."

Far enough. Ian tossed that thought off into the bushes, where it lay, waiting to pounce the moment his common sense turned its back.

"The cat is over here." He took her hand in his and led her to the far side of the little space. "If you don't know it's a cemetery, it looks like any other sunny patch of undergrowth."

"And you planted him some heather. Will it grow here?" She knelt to brush her fingers over the stiff branches of the shrub, keeping her other hand in Ian's.

"Very likely. It's hardy stuff."

"Thank you, Ian. Thank you more than you know." She rose, using his grip for leverage, and just like that they were standing quite close. Some bird started a cheerful chorus, and amid all the scents of the woods, Ian caught a whiff of lilacs.

"Augusta . . . I hope you know . . . It's not that I don't . . . that is, yesterday . . ." He wanted to drop her hand, and he wanted to lay her down and sink himself into her body until neither of them could recall how to find their way out of the woods. The mingling of desire and regret was new to him and piercingly painful.

"Yesterday," she said very softly, "was lovely."

"Lovely, yes, but it can't . . . Augusta, I want to kiss you again, right here, right now, when what I meant to do was apologize. I sincerely meant to apologize. Please, for the love of God, will you slap me as hard as you can?"

She kissed him, rose up on her toes and gently laid her mouth to his. She brought sweet, soft curves, warmth, and a sense of voracious longing to him, *heartbroken* longing, on a whiff of flowers.

He took her in his arms with a groan and kissed her back, no grace, no finesse, just need and regret expressed by his mouth on hers. He was aware of her hand cradling his jaw, aware of how perfectly her body fit his.

And even more aware of how impossible their situation was.

He broke the kiss just enough to rest his forehead on hers. "Augusta, I am so verra sorry. So sorry. This solves nothing."

She kissed his forehead, which provoked a dizzying confusion of both comfort and torment in Ian's guts. "It doesn't complicate anything either, Ian. I'm sorry too."

She took his hand, and he let her. Let her lead

him back to the path that would take them to the house, and let her drop his hand well before they approached the stables. When they reached the gardens, he let her leave his side, while he remained among the flowers and watched her make her way alone into the house.

Augusta took half the morning to settle her nerves after the outing with Ian, spent two hours trying to compose one prosaic letter, took a luncheon tray in her room and ended up sketching Ian's left hand as best she could recall the look of it wrapped around her right.

He had such lovely hands. She gave up on the letter and kept the sketch, but called a halt to her hours of self-indulgence and went in search of Mary Fran.

Whenever Augusta thought she'd found a minute alone with Mary Fran, it turned out Matthew was lurking in the vicinity, or the baron, or the baron and Matthew both. Uncle finally declared the library too stuffy for reading the newspaper, and Augusta seized her moment.

"Matthew, may I have a word with you?" She aimed a smile at the cousin who might have been her spouse and subtly twisted the tail of his conscience.

"Of course. Lady Mary Frances was good enough to show me the portrait gallery yesterday. Shall we walk there?"

He escorted her up through the house, considerate and careful with her, though she'd seen the brooding frown he'd aimed at Mary Fran before departing the library.

"Were you always such a gentleman?"

His eyebrows rose as he strolled along beside her. "I hope I was. I gather from your question there is some doubt."

"Not doubt, just a failure of accurate recollection. Are you enjoying your stay here?"

She intended it as a polite, passing question, but Matthew's lips quirked, and his gaze lit with humor as they perambulated past some dark paintings in heavy, gilded frames. "I'm enjoying it immeasurably. Far more than I'd intended."

"You came on a holiday not intending to enjoy yourself?"

"I came to make sure Altsax didn't force Genie into marriage with some old curmudgeon who thinks bathing unhealthful and a wife's purpose to ensure the succession when she isn't peeling potatoes in his root cellar."

Interesting. She'd sold him short by not attributing such fraternal concern to him. "And you are satisfied on this point?"

"Balfour is not a curmudgeon." It was half an answer. An intriguing half. "But what of you, Gus? Did you come on this outing expecting to enjoy yourself?"

Matthew had never been stupid. Augusta

wondered what conclusions he'd drawn about her dealings with Ian, what he'd overheard, what he'd seen.

"I came expecting to provide some reinforcement to Julia as she tried to chaperone two girls in a strange household. I was not opposed to the idea of enjoying myself."

He shook his head, pausing before a smaller work depicting three children playing with a brown-and-white spaniel. "When Altsax told me you'd decided to retire to the country rather than resume the social whirl, I was concerned for you. I didn't think your parents would want you to make a shrine to their memories. I should have insisted you make at least one more try at finding your own spouse."

"One more try?" *What on earth had Uncle told him?*

"After Post-Williams went to Altsax and said he'd accept a quiet wedding out of respect for your loss, the baron explained to him you weren't willing to be rushed. And thus the man left the field, concluding you were trying to tell him you didn't suit. It fell to me to listen to Henry's drunken ramblings on the matter. He truly was fond of you, but I didn't see as he had much choice. I gather you regard the matter differently?"

Somehow, she manufactured a reply. "I don't hold it against him." *But what on earth was Matthew saying?*

"He read me a letter he intended to send you. Pathetic, the things a man will say when he fancies his heart's broken and there's decent libation on hand. So why did you drag me up here?"

She could barely comprehend Matthew's question, so thoroughly had his recitation disconcerted her. She cast back over her last discussion with Henry Post-Williams . . . He'd muttered things about having to speak with Uncle, their situation being very different from what he'd anticipated, and then he'd been gone, leaving it to Uncle and Aunt to explain his continued absence.

"Gus? Woolgathering?" Matthew was looking down at her, concern in his blue eyes.

"Your version of my distant past does not comport *at all* with my own recollections."

"It wasn't that long ago." His frown deepened, which meant he was applying his mind to the situation. Matthew had a formidable mind, so Augusta seized on a formidable distraction.

"Why are you hovering around Mary Fran?"

His eyebrows rose then crashed down. "I am not hovering around her so much as hovering in the vicinity of my father."

"Uncle?"

"He made an inappropriate advance toward her earlier in our stay. She did not inform her brothers, or Genie's chances at the earl would have been thoroughly queered by now."

"And Uncle quite possibly called to task for his misstep."

Just then, Augusta would not have minded seeing her uncle brought up short. What could he possibly have been about, to chase Henry off under false pretenses when the love and consideration of a devoted husband would have been such a comfort to her? She'd written Henry no letters—a proper young lady would not have corresponded with a young man not of her family. So what if they'd had to live humbly? She was living humbly and virtually *alone* in Oxford— alone with a pesky lot of chickens.

"Insulting your hostess, and an earl's daughter at that is not a misstep, Gus. It comes closer to being a fatal error."

"Nobody duels anymore. Her Majesty frowns on it."

"This is Scotland, not the civilized confines of Kent. Nobody thinks it's his right to prey on any female he sees, and yet Altsax easily could."

There was a curious bitterness beneath Matthew's observation.

"Why not let your father deal with the consequences of his actions and be on your merry way? You've seen that Balfour will not force Genie to the altar."

Balfour would force *himself* to the altar though, and he'd woo Genie's consent once he realized

Genie's life would be hell if she failed to marry the earl.

Matthew sighed and walked off a few paces to study a portrait of some fellow in bright blue-and-red tartan regalia. The figure in the portrait looked a little like Ian, but this older Scot's fierceness was almost decorative compared to Ian's. Ian's ferociousness was kept leashed, kept buried only to surface in his devotion to his family—and in his kisses.

"I do not want any titles, Gus. I never have. The title was the stated reason I was jerked away from my regiment at a time when intelligent leadership would have made a difference in the fighting. The needless, *lunatic* bloodshed—"

He stopped and closed his eyes, then joined his hands behind his back and clasped them tightly.

"Matthew?"

"I digress." He let out a pent-up breath and turned to face her. "I do not care for any titles, Gus. The Lords is mostly a waste of time. The common man is running this country more each day, the monarchy is becoming an anachronism, and the peerage with it."

She stared at him, wondering at the man he'd become. "Why, Matthew. I do believe you are a radical. This is so . . . unexpected. And so heartening."

"Heartening? I'm afraid Altsax wouldn't agree

with you. He scoffs at my interest in trade and considers agricultural science a contradiction in terms."

"Uncle is old school. But, Matthew?"

"Cousin?"

"Why did you never come visit me in Oxford?"

Before this surprising exchange with him, she hadn't realized it mattered, though it did. It mattered, and it *hurt* that her remaining family had shunned her, hurt in the way of a familiar ache for which no treatment had been availing.

He cocked his head in puzzlement. "You wanted your privacy. Mama and Altsax insisted I respect that. You never answered my letters or Genie's. After a couple of years, we just gave up."

She'd never received any letters, except a few from Hester, who would have been off at school. "I gave up too."

Unease coiled low in her belly. It was one thing to conclude she'd had no understanding of her parents' complicated financial estates, but Matthew's words suggested her correspondence and her marital prospects had been tampered with as well.

And her uncle—Matthew's own father—would have been in a position to do that tampering, but why would he have done such a thing?

Matthew considered her from closer range. "There's more you're not telling me. With Genie and Hester, I can winkle their confessions out of them, though Hester's getting more stubborn. With you, I could never tell what you were thinking."

"Sometimes, I hardly know what to think."

"Are you trying to find a way to warn me off Lady Mary Fran? I won't be offended if you are, but I'll be disappointed."

"Warn you off?" For pity's sake, she'd been so absorbed in her own situation she'd hardly considered . . . "She's a wonderful woman, Matthew. Don't let anybody or anything warn you off, least of all Uncle's fuming and carrying on."

"We are agreed on that."

The relief in his eyes was touching. Such a soldier he'd become, but he remained her cousin too. Still, it was with Ian she wanted to discuss these revelations, not with her own family.

Matthew went back to studying the Highlander. "I haven't said anything to anybody yet about my interest in Mary Fran. I don't intend to either, not until the lady gives me some encouragement."

Ah. A proud soldier, the best and most determined kind. "Perhaps, Cousin, I can aid your cause."

He shot a look over his shoulder that would have been hopeful had it not been so hesitant. "I am not in the habit of refusing aid, not in something that counts for so very much."

"Then leave me the occasional moment alone with Mary Fran. She and I have things to discuss."

And he was a prudent soldier too. He escorted Augusta back to the library and retreated without asking even one more question.

"No. Try again." Mary Fran sat across Ian's desk from Augusta, speaking very slowly and clearly in Gaelic. "Beloved of my heart."

Augusta mimicked her, and Mary Fran grinned. "You're getting there. It isn't a prissy language, it's a passionate language. You can't be standing guard over every vowel and consonant. You must go by ear and by feeling. What's next?"

For a spinster, Miss Augusta's choice of vocabulary was odd: Please. Thank you. Thank you most graciously. I love you. All very prosaic, but then: I *desire* you. I need you. Love me—in the second person singular emphatic command form.

Shocking, really, but the woman had saved Fee's life, and when asked for a few lessons in Gaelic, Mary Fran had hardly been in a position to refuse.

"You have to do me a small kindness," Mary Fran said when Augusta had mastered her phrases for the day.

"Of course. Name it." Augusta smiled as she spoke, making it hard to recall the woman was

English. She didn't look English, not with that lustrous black hair and those odd violet eyes. She didn't smile English either.

"I like to make sure my guests are accommodated in all ways possible." Mary Fran tidied up Ian's stack of correspondence to give her hands something to do. "I was curious about some of Mr. Daniels's preferences."

Mary Fran felt her face heating while Augusta's smile became a grin.

"I've known Matthew all my life. Ask away."

"What is his favorite dessert?"

Miss Augusta was so generous with her replies, so detailed and thorough, that an hour later, Mary Fran was still taking notes.

After a morning of struggling for conversation with his intended, Ian was hardly inclined to humor her glowering older brother. What Ian wanted—what his soul shrieked at him to do— was to find Augusta and kiss the daylights out of her. And if he couldn't do that, then he wanted simply to behold her. To feast his eyes on her female shape, to catch a hint of the lilac-and-meadow scent of her to hoard up in his memory against all the years they'd be apart.

He did *not* want to exchange pleasantries with Young Daniels or hear a lecture from the man about an earl's responsibility to curb his widowed sister's rapacious tendencies with the fellows.

"A word with you, my lord?"

"This way." Ian gestured toward the gardens and purposely did not turn behind the privet hedge. "I trust you're enjoying your stay?"

Best give the man a broad opening and get it over with.

"Immensely. Your hospitality is superb and your family a delight."

Ian glanced over sharply. Englishmen stole and cheated as if the world was owed to them in its entirety. They could lie too, but they didn't lie well. They'd never had to learn the knack, when they could just pillage and plunder under legal decrees instead. Young Daniels was smiling a soft, genuine, introspective smile. He wasn't even trying to lie.

Mary Fran hadn't run him through yet, poor bastard.

"I'm pleased to hear you're having a fine time. So how may I be of service to you?" Please God, don't let the damned man be asking to court Mary Fran. Daniels was English, and she'd show him not one shred of mercy.

"As a man considering offering for my sister, you are in a position to make certain inquiries."

"I am." After tossing and turning half the night, Ian had gotten up at dawn and started drafting those inquiries. He wasn't *nearly* finished.

"I trust you will find all in order with respect to the barony's finances, my lord, but I have occasion to feel some concern regarding my cousin's situation."

"Your . . . cousin?" Ian's irritation vanished, replaced with a taut focus. "Miss Augusta?"

Daniels nodded, his expression hard to read. "Shall we sit?"

Damned English and their infernal good manners. "Of course."

Ian's guest sauntered over to the nearest bench, which was at least in shade and not visible from the house. He flipped out his tails, shot his cuffs, and generally tormented Ian with his fussing.

"What I'm going to relate to you is a family matter, one that has troubled me for some time. You're courting my sister, or working up to it. Years ago there was another man, Henry Post-Williams, in a similar posture regarding my cousin. I think you'd be well within your rights to make some inquiries, because the situation was all but solemnized, and he withdrew his suit. My hands are tied, you understand."

Ian nodded once to show he did understand. Altsax would not countenance his heir asking difficult questions. Young Daniels frowned as if gathering his thoughts for a moment then went on.

"Post-Williams was a decent fellow of modest means, but he was smitten, and I thought Gus was too . . . Truly smitten."

Ian listened. He didn't listen like a suitor intent

on finding leverage before undertaking settlement negotiations—though he could smell leverage playing right into his hands. He listened like a lawyer, sifting facts and details, putting things in sequence and measuring cause and effect. He asked a few questions and listened some more.

When Daniels had thoroughly unburdened himself, Ian had to concede the Englishmen had been right to be troubled.

Bloody damned troubled.

And to hell with polite epistles to various solicitors and connections of his aunt's in the South. Ian dashed those off—going into battle against an unscrupulous enemy a man needed every weapon he could find—but when the letters were posted, Ian also sent off a note to his neighbors.

"This is preposterous! *Pre*-posterous!" The baron slammed his glass down on the sideboard for emphasis. "The negotiations have opened, Balfour. You can't tell me now you need time for further inquiries."

"I only just met the young lady, Baron." Balfour might be a barbarian in kilted evening attire, but he could affect a convincing lordly drawl. "Of course I have additional inquiries. Then too, I've only just met you."

Damn the man! He put a world of innuendo into

his tone and took a leisurely sip of his drink. The baron made a show of pacing to the window, where the interminable Scottish evening was coming to a close, the fading light showing the grounds to spectacular advantage.

Altsax had chosen so carefully. Chosen a man whose holdings were distant from Kent and London, a man who spent very little time anywhere but on his own property. He'd chosen from the Scottish peerage—a minor aristocracy if ever there was one—but grabbed for the highest title he could find. And the whole point of that careful sifting and sorting had been to ensure there would be *no* questions.

Balfour was supposed to be pathetically grateful for his good fortune, *ask no questions,* and cheerfully bestow his damned title on an obedient and unprotesting new wife.

The baron turned back to his host. *They'd see who could condescend to whom.* "You're looking for a way to cry off. Not well done of you, Balfour."

"I can hardly cry off when there's no betrothal yet, can I? More brandy?" Balfour lifted an elaborately cut crystal decanter in one hand, the one he'd referred to as distinctive.

"Just a bit."

Altsax let a silence stretch while he watched Balfour pour the amber liquid into his glass. Rather than bring him his drink, though, Balfour put the stopper in the decanter and left the baron's serving sitting on the sideboard.

"I've directed my solicitors into the usual areas of interest," Balfour said. "Finances, social standing, voting record in Parliament."

"Voting record? A man votes his conscience and his duty, Balfour. My voting record can be of no interest to you." Not that the baron troubled himself to vote unless the issue affected his own pocketbook.

"One wouldn't want to publicly oppose one's father-in-law on the important issues, would one?" Balfour frowned at his drink. "That's assuming I ever join the Scottish delegation to the Lords and find the strength to tear myself away from my doting wife, hmm?"

Instincts served a man of sophistication and parts as well as education and shrewd observation, and the baron's instincts were telling him something in the wind had shifted. Genie was spending most of her Scottish holiday in her damned room, not in flirtation with Balfour.

And earlier this week, Balfour had taken most of a morning to march around the hills with an opinionated spinster of limited means—and even more limited life expectancy.

Starting a rockslide that might have ended the earl's life along with Augusta's hadn't been the most prudent course. Altsax could admit that in hindsight, but this dithering and questioning . . .

An idea bloomed in the baron's awareness, a connection between seemingly unrelated events. If Augusta were to die in the near future, Genie would be cast into mourning. The wedding would have to be immediate and very quiet—very inexpensive—or the earl would have to wait at least a year for his money.

One didn't generally mourn a cousin for a year, but one could. If one were very devoted to that cousin, one certainly could.

Altsax crossed the room to pick up his drink and salute Balfour graciously. "Make your inquiries, Balfour. Take all the time you need. When we're enjoying your hospitality so thoroughly, what's the rush?"

Though Genie was going to have done with cowering in her room. Rebellious females weren't attractive to anybody.

Ian had thought meals were the worst. The long, leisurely suppers where the best of the estate's produce was put before strangers to be consumed without thought on their part, and a parody of gracious company was manufactured for hours on end.

Augusta shot him curious looks, not hurt, not angry, but . . . considering. He tried not to look at her at all, but failed miserably. His body seemed to know where she was even when his gaze was resolutely turned elsewhere.

His hands ached for the feel of her, and his heart . . .

God damn his bloody, stupid heart.

The meals weren't the worst, and the nights weren't the worst. At night he at least had the privacy of his thoughts and the pleasure of his dreams, dreams in which familial duty didn't force him to make choices his heart knew were a recipe for misery.

The worst part of his day was the hour after dinner, when he was required by manners to retire with his brothers, the baron, and the baron's son to the parlor designated for exclusively male congregation. Altsax smoked and hadn't the courtesy to take his filthy habit onto the terrace.

Daniels—he was really no younger than Gilgallon—brooded and read correspondence in the corner, while Con, Gil, and Ian tried to make conversation that included guests but didn't wander onto familial topics. In previous years, the exercise hadn't seemed anywhere near as nerve-wracking.

"I'm for bed." The baron weaved a little as he got to his feet. "The thin air here has me fatigued, Balfour. Meaning no insult." The idiot smiled and took an uncertain step toward the door.

"I'll light you up," Gil said, getting to his feet. He rolled his eyes at Ian, out of Altsax's line of sight, and plucked a single candle from the mantel.

Daniels rose and folded his letters and reports into a leather satchel. "I'll join you. Balfour, good night, and thank you again for a pleasant day. Another pleasant day."

When Ian was left alone with Con, he realized his brother had the look of a man with something to say.

"Spit it out, Connor. I'm about dead on my feet from the effort of being charming the livelong damned day."

Con cocked his head and regarded Ian with the aggravating acumen of a younger sibling. "It never seemed to wear on you before."

"I was never stalking a bride before." Ian considered another drink and decided against it. "Let's go out on the terrace. Altsax has left this place reeking."

Con nodded but said nothing further until they'd gained the fresh night air.

"Are you stalking your bride, Ian?"

"Fair question." *Awkward,* fair question. "She rode between me and Gil yesterday, she walked in the garden with me today after lunch, she sat next to me this morning at breakfast, and yet all the while, I have the sense she's not really *here.*"

"Like I have the sense you're not really here?"

Ian blew out a breath and scrubbed a hand over his face. "What are you trying to tell me, Connor?"

Con ambled off a few steps and kept his back

to Ian. There was light coming from a few of the windows, which meant had he been facing his brother, Ian might have had a chance to read his brother's expression. He read his posture instead— tense, burdened, tired.

"Connor, we've always been honest with each other. I'm too exhausted to settle anything with fists tonight."

"And Gil's not on hand to referee. Do you want to marry this woman, Ian?"

"I want to provide for my family. I want to *have* a family. It's one of the many burdens attendant to bearing a title. Fee needs cousins."

"Yes, and we all want Asher to come home, but that's not going to happen. If you don't marry Genie . . ."

"I'm going to marry Genie if it kills me."

"I've been a wee bit naughty." Con didn't sound even a wee bit contrite—he sounded bemused. Ian walked around his brother so they were facing each other.

"At least somebody's having some fun. Am I to be an uncle again, Con?"

"Not on my account, but Gil saw me leaving Mrs. Redmond's bedroom of a night."

Ian chose his words carefully and spoke with studied neutrality. "You would not force yourself on an unwilling woman, and Mrs. Redmond is a widow." Widows were fair game; *spinsters were not.* Not even the ones who'd been misguided into surrendering their virginity long, lonely years ago, much less the ones who'd indulged in a single, understandable, *unforgettable* lapse thereafter.

"So you wouldn't banish me to the west for trifling with a guest?" Con made the question an even greater study in neutrality.

"Who'd keep the stable lads in line if you took to the mountains?" Con's shoulders relaxed a trifle at Ian's rejoinder. "So have you trifled with her?"

"I have not." *Yet.* Ian understood his brother clearly. Connor enjoyed the ladies, and the ladies enjoyed Con. The lucky little widow's fate was sealed. "Or, I haven't trifled with her any more than she's trifled with me."

"One likes a sense of fairness in one's recreation."

"So if Gil tattles, you'll be surprised? He hates keeping confidences."

"If Gil tattles, I shall reel with indignation that you were so clumsy as to be caught by your brother somewhere that might reflect poorly on a lady's reputation. Now get to bed. I have to practice my reeling in private."

Con grinned, nodded, and sauntered back toward the house, punching Ian on the arm as he passed him.

At least somebody was enjoying himself this summer. Ian eyed the house behind him and concluded more fresh air was in order. He had just decided which shadowed bench would best serve for a bout of sighing and brooding when a voice came out of the darkness.

"For a man intent on marriage to my cousin, you've done precious little proposing to her."

Ten

MATTHEW AND HIS PRETENTIOUS LITTLE schoolboy sack of letters turned right at the bottom of the stairs. The baron watched his son disappear down a gloomy corridor, wondering why such a devoted papa as himself was abruptly being cursed with multiple displays of rebellion among his progeny.

When the baron and the Balfour spare got to the first landing, the baron headed left. "I'd like to bid my daughter good night, if you don't mind."

MacGregor extended the candle toward him, but even an audience of one would be useful for what the baron had in mind. "This will take only a moment, Mr. MacGregor."

The stupid Scot had no choice but to follow, though when they reached Genie's door, MacGregor set his candle on a low table and waited, arms crossed, lounging against the far wall.

Gilgallon MacGregor wasn't very sociable. No matter, his presence alone was sufficient for what would transpire.

"Eugenia?" Altsax rapped lightly on his daughter's door. There was no need for his nosey sister-in-law to add her presence to what was about to happen—assuming the little slut was even in her room. "Eugenia, come to the door."

She did, clad in nightgown and wrapper, a thick blond braid over one shoulder. She was a perfectly lovely female confection suitable for any impoverished Scottish earl's countess.

"Hello, Papa." Her puzzled glance took in MacGregor, silent in the shadows a few feet away.

"Daughter, are you enjoying your holiday so far?"

"Yes, Papa."

"Well, I am not."

"I'm sorry, Papa." She cast another nervous glance across the hall. Genie was a little brighter than her mother in a simple, animal sense. Thirty-plus years of marriage gave an astute man an instinct for how to correct the women burdening his household. With Genie, threatening to forbid her the company of her vapid, silly friends had usually been adequate to ensure her obedience.

"You *should* be sorry, my girl, for you are the cause of my discontent. You are here to woo your earl, not to tat lace in your sitting room. Do I make myself clear?"

She nodded, her gaze on him now. "Yes, Papa. Very clear."

He saw wary relief in her eyes that this little lecture was over.

Not quite, silly girl. He struck without warning, a solid forehand slap to her pale cheek. Forehand was the way to go with women. Backhand ran the risk that rings would cut open flesh and knuckles would leave bruises. By contrast, the flat of a man's palm delivered sufficient punishment and made a nice, satisfyingly loud—

MacGregor moved so quickly Altsax had no chance to muster a defense. In the blink of an eye, the baron found himself face-first against the wall, an arm hiked painfully behind his back.

"Strike her again, Altsax, and you will not live to regret it long. Eugenia is a guest in this house and due the protection of my family. *We do not strike our women.*"

"Let him go, please." Genie's voice was soft, with a hint of tears behind her words. "Gil—Mr. MacGregor, you will please let my father go. This is a family matter."

The weight threatening to dislocate the baron's arm eased away. He turned and twitched his smoking jacket into place.

"Your brother will hear about this, MacGregor. All of Polite Society might be hearing about it." Altsax treated the brute to a fulminating glance then glared at his daughter for good measure. He noted with some satisfaction her cheek was already red, even in the shadowed corridor.

"Daughter, I bid you good night and caution you to assiduously heed my guidance. You won't always have barbarians such as that"—he jerked his chin at MacGregor—"to interfere with your father's authority."

He strode off, leaving his chastened daughter to deal with her champion. The earl had to tolerate his brother as a spare, but once Genie had said her vows and dropped a few bull calves in the Balfour pastures, there would be no more need for Gilgallon MacGregor.

None at all. What a cheering thought for a man to take with him to his slumbers.

Ian loomed out of the darkness before Augusta, a big, unhappy shadow in the gloom of the terrace. "Eavesdropping, Miss Merrick?"

Miss Merrick, not Augusta. The rebuke hurt, as did the formality with which it was delivered. "You assumed you had privacy out here, your lordship."

He muttered something that started with "Bloody . . ." and fell away on sigh.

"Canna sit with you?" He did, taking the place right beside her. "I'm out of sorts and distracted, but I wasn't ignoring you. You're not a woman scorned, Augusta, believe me." He took her hand, wrapping it in both of his. The gesture seemed to comfort him as much as it did her.

"I'm a woman invisible," she said. "I expect

you to eventually marry my cousin, Ian. I'm not trying to interfere with what you and she see as your duty, but it could take months for you to get engaged. Aunt will want to make a fuss, to have the wedding in London, and that takes time."

"You aren't invisible. Not to me."

That was good to hear. She ought to feel pathetic—except she didn't. She felt . . . determined, which was gratifyingly far from pathetic.

"How are you?" She hadn't thought to ask, but he seemed weary and somehow without his usual defenses.

The look he gave her was both sad and humorous. "I'm well, thank you, and you, my dear?"

"You're stubborn, Ian MacGregor. But I'm stubborn too when it comes to what I truly care about."

His arm came around her shoulders. "Lass, I have noticed this." He sounded like he was admiring more than he was complaining.

They sat like that, while Augusta slowly teased from him the concerns of his day. Con was flirting with Julia, the kittens in the stables were beginning to stir around and get underfoot, Mary Fran was leading Matthew a dance, and Fee had run across one of the neighbor's daughters and taught her how to make mud pies and dirtballs.

Prosaic, mundane things, such as a husband

might share with his wife, except the feel of him beside her, the feel of his body heat warming her, was anything but prosaic. Her hands ached to learn the contours of him, to map his muscles and tendons, his joints and features. She wanted to know the tastes and sounds and textures of him until she knew them as well as she knew her own body.

She wanted the feel of his arousal, warm and hard against her belly one more time.

When Augusta realized neither of them had spoken for several moments, she wondered if he were imagining the same lovely, intimate things she was. She lifted her head. "You need your rest, sir."

He smoothed her hair back over her ear. "Let's not be discussing what I need. You should go in without me."

He leaned over, and Augusta was certain he was going to kiss her forehead. She'd take even that, so hungry was she for any affection from him. Shameless, really, but what had years of protecting her dignity gotten her except happy chickens and a tidy garden hundreds of miles to the south?

He brushed his mouth against hers. "Forgive me, Augusta . . ."

She would *not* forgive him. She would kiss him within an inch of her sanity, rejoicing in each moment their mouths fused. His hand, big and warm, slid down her arm and brushed over her fingers.

He was so careful with her, Augusta almost didn't comprehend it when that same hand closed gently over her breast. Through her nightgown and wrapper she could feel the heat of him. His touch was intimate and cherishing, and ignited a hot, needy wanting for more of his touches, more of him.

She arched into that heat, wrapping her hand over his to bring him closer. Longing rose up with a sharp, piercing ache. She wanted his hand on her skin, she wanted—

Augusta ceased listing her frustrations, rose up and straddled him where he sat on the bench. His arms came around her with gratifying swiftness, and the kiss resumed with reckless heat. Night-clothes were marvelous attire for plundering kisses from a Highland earl—no stays, no pantalettes, no layers and layers of fashion to thwart a woman's passionate impulses.

Augusta rose higher on her knees, feeling the secure support of Ian's arm low on her back. She sank both hands into his hair, intent on kissing him within an inch of his—

The pleasure of plunging her tongue into his welcoming heat distracted her at first, but as Ian gentled the kiss, Augusta became aware of a whisper of night air on her left knee.

Then on her thigh.

Ian's hand was warm, caressing her leg, shifting her nightclothes then stealing *under* her night-clothes. Augusta went still, hanging over him, waiting and focusing every scintilla of her awareness on his callused palm caressing her thigh.

Mr. Post-Williams hadn't touched Augusta intimately with his hands. He'd taken himself in his own hand and pushed at her with his erection—his member to her most intimate flesh. That he'd touch himself but not her had struck Augusta as vaguely shaming, as if her most intimate parts were dirty and not to be acknowl-edged, even as he'd taken his pleasure of her.

Ian had no such reservations. Augusta might have begged, had she the ability to speak, but she didn't need words. His fingers teased through her curls, a soft, skilled caress that made her breasts feel heavy and her insides weightless.

"Ian—"

"Wheesht, hinney." His kiss was sweet, his touch sweeter still. With one blunt finger, he traced the creases and folds of Augusta's sex, until she was damp, panting, and ready to shed every stitch of her clothing.

She was about to tell him as much when his touch shifted, so he cupped her mons. The feel of his hand there, where Augusta rarely touched herself except to wash, was both arousing and comforting. She waited, poised on the precipice of things forbidden, wonderful, and necessary for her soul.

Ian kissed her again, an achingly tender kiss that did nothing to assuage her disappointment at the feel of his hand sliding down her leg then tugging her nightclothes down to cover her knee.

"Into the house with you, Augusta. I'll not be taking you on a hard bench in the garden."

In the limited light, she saw when his own words registered with him. He shook his head and scrubbed a hand over his face—the same hand that had just touched her so carefully and intimately. "I'll not be taking you anywhere at all."

Ever again. He left those words mercifully unsaid.

She'd pushed him as far as he could go, and he was right: This time, they were not far, far from the house, out in the hills with nobody but the birds of the air to see them. Anybody could come along for a bit of fresh night air. There were balconies on this side of the house.

Then too, as a younger woman, Augusta had been coerced into sharing her intimate favors. She had no intention of coercing Ian, ever.

She kissed his cheek and rose, conceding nothing. She was in her room, pondering her latest encounter with the man who was never very far from her thoughts, when another idea intruded:

Augusta had overheard Connor's confession to Ian, the one about visiting Julia in her bedroom. Connor had started his recitation with the fact that Gil had seen him coming out of Julia's room. The only other occupied room on that floor belonged to Genie. What had Gilgallon MacGregor been *doing* outside Genie's room so late the previous night?

What was he *doing,* letting his hands wander over Augusta Merrick's person in unseemly and intimate paths? She'd been so eager for his kisses, so yielding and feminine and warm . . .

Twelve hours later, and Ian was still reliving the most fleeting caress of a breast he'd executed since he'd been a hesitant boy of fourteen. The most fleeting and the most memorable.

Augusta Merrick was willing to risk her very livelihood just for a chance to share the same intimacies with Ian that Genie Daniels would go a lifetime disdaining. This paradox made Ian's insides churn and his hand fist around his pen where he sat at his desk. Right and wrong were supposed to be clearly distinguishable, like up and down, Scottish and English, and yet . . .

He was not engaged to anybody, and at this rate, he wasn't likely to be soon.

Augusta was not an innocent; she knew what she risked.

And Ian was sure in his bones she hadn't

270

offered herself to any other man since her feckless beau had deserted her upon learning of her poverty. Ian stared at the letter he'd written to the feckless beau—a man Matthew had sworn was honorable—and signed the damned thing. Before Ian could change his mind, he sanded the signature.

"I beg your pardon."

The object of Ian's frustration—and his pre-occupation and his delight—stopped just inside the library door, limned in the soft light of early afternoon. "My lord, I wasn't aware you were still working in here. Shall I leave?"

Yes.

"Come in. I've just finished my correspondence for the day." He rose and came around the desk, lest she see the piles of paper putting the lie to his words. "Can I help you find a book?"

So polite they were, but she seemed amused by it. "Or answer a question."

He did not allow himself to speculate what manner of question she might ask him. "There's a tea tray on the sideboard. Mary Fran sends them in when I forget to appear for luncheon. I'd be obliged if you'd share it with me lest my sister get to fretting."

"If you like." She took a seat on the sofa while Ian brought the tray over. If he were smart, he'd toss a cushion on the raised hearth and keep the table between them.

If he were smart, he'd be howling with the Canadian wolves alongside Asher.

He ensconced himself directly beside Augusta on the sofa.

"We're an imposition, aren't we?" Augusta asked. She poured for them both, the epitome of the graceful lady. "Guests show up at a time when you need to be tending to the crops and the weeding, not wasting entire mornings wandering up into the hills."

He took a teacup from her, letting their fingers brush because he was an idiot. "Are you fishing for reassurances, Augusta?"

"No." She smiled at her teacup as if she'd just found a pot of gold. "I think you dispensed those rather convincingly last night."

Was that what he'd been doing? "What was it you wanted to ask me?"

She passed him a sandwich. White bread piled with thin slices of roasted beef, a thick slab of local cheddar, a dollop of tangy mustard, and a generous helping of butter. He set the plate aside untouched, though it bore a feast by the standards of years past.

"I'm enjoying your sister's company tremendously," Augusta said. "I've wanted to ask her about handfasting, but didn't want to give offense. What is it, exactly?"

Ah, a legal question. He seized on it.

"It's not what most people think it is. Old Sir

Walter put it about we handfast by marrying for a year and a day, and then merrily discard our partners for another temporary union if the first doesn't suit. That might have been the custom long ago, and perhaps it still is in some places, but the legal concept is different."

"Tell me about it."

It was an excuse to look competent and knowledgeable in her eyes, an excuse to share a meal with her.

"A handfasting is a legal marriage, recognized by both church and civil authorities. It consists of an exchange of future vows to wed, followed by either a formal wedding ceremony or consummation of the engagement. It is held in contempt by the same authorities who recognize its validity."

"Why?"

She would ask that, even as she placidly sipped her tea.

"It's said to promote licentious behavior."

Her brows drew down in puzzlement. "It starts with an engagement, the same as most other unions require. How can that promote licentious behavior?"

"Because, lass, it provides a frisky couple the option of claiming—when they're caught in flagrante delicto—that they'd previously exchanged those vows to wed. Upon being discovered at their mischief, they become wed by act of law. It gives them a way to save face they would not have otherwise had."

"I . . . see."

"Why do you ask?"

"Mary Fran has made occasional reference to her late spouse as being a sly, handfasting, er, rascal. I did not understand . . ."

"You still don't." He rose and crossed to the window, his gaze on the back gardens that kept so many of his cousins and relations employed—for a few months each year, but only a few months. And they were grateful for what little he paid them.

"Ian?" She'd followed him, had crept right up beside him without making a sound. "I don't mean to pry."

"It's a predictable tale." He could not put an arm around her waist—they were standing by a window, for God's sake—so he clasped his hands behind his back. "Mary Fran chafed badly under Grandfather's idea of how a proper earl's granddaughter ought to conduct herself. The more stern his discipline, the wilder she became. The business with Gordie . . . It was supposed to be a minor rebellion, wild oats, a statement of her independence—she was all of eighteen, quite grown-up in her own eyes—and at the regimental ball, her little scheme misfired."

"Misfired?"

"As soon as Mary Fran realized Grandfather

274

wasn't going to have an apoplexy over her peccadilloes with Gordie, it became apparent Fiona was on the way, and that was that. A handfast marriage was produced from thin air, complete with legal documents and sworn witness testimony, despite the fact that Mary Fran's taste for English mischief had since abated. Fee is legitimate, but barely."

"And Gordie?"

"He was off to Canada with his regiment before Fee was born and did not survive his first winter. I send his family regular reports about Fee's progress, which are works of creative fiction. They've never mentioned sending coin to assist with her upbringing, which is all to the good. If they had, I'd have cause to be nervous."

"Why should it make you nervous?"

"Englishmen bearing gifts make most of the world, civilized and otherwise, nervous. They come either to collect specimens for their infernal museums or to make peace in the name of my lovely, conquering royal neighbor."

Augusta turned to regard him then crossed the room to retrieve his sandwich plate. "You should eat."

"So should you." He held out the sandwich to her, and damned if the woman didn't bite off a piece. She watched him as she did then chewed slowly.

"It's good, Ian. You finish it."

He was *doomed*. He stuffed a bite of sandwich in his mouth and returned to the sofa. In a bit of divine mercy, she took the hearth opposite, resting her chin on her updrawn knees.

"What's the hardest thing, Ian?"

She *would* use his name. "About?"

"About being you? About all this?" She waved a hand around the library and sat back. "I've been thinking about that lately: What's the hardest thing about my life in Oxfordshire? It's a peaceful little life, I want for nothing material, and my neighbors are good, kind people."

"But?" He gestured with the second half of the sandwich, and she shook her head.

"But it's hard too." She gave him a sunny smile, one that belied the truth of her words. He got an abrupt image of her moving briskly around her little holding, the hems of her nondescript dresses muddy in the chicken yard, her ugly shawls growing more deplorable by the year . . .

If I could afford a mistress, even . . . But he could not.

"It's not so difficult, being the laird." He tried on the falsehood he told himself several times daily. Spoken aloud, it sounded hollow. "Or it wouldn't be, if I'd been raised to it. Missing my brother, not knowing what happened to him, that's hard."

She looked at him steadily, and his mouth kept forming words. "It's hard being the one to keep hope alive for the others. Hope that those who've emigrated are faring well in foreign lands, hope that this year's crop will be better than last, this year's prices at the yearling sale, this year's receipts. We live very much in the future, and yet we dwell in the past too. That's difficult as hell when you've a past like ours."

She wasn't even touching him, but he could feel her as a soothing presence in his mind.

"I hate it, the hoping." He scrubbed a hand over his face. "When things go well, I hate it even more, because it's all going to come crashing down around us—it always does. We were just getting on our feet when the damned potato blight came through. Potatoes have never been our crop of choice, but they kept the least among us with the poorest soil and the fewest hands fed and able to procure a few necessities. We're getting on our feet again, barely, and I dread finding out what hardship the Almighty has in store for us next."

"Because it's increasingly difficult to rise to the challenge." She finished the thought for him, her tone neither judgmental nor bleak, merely stating a fact.

He patted the place beside him, wishing he could take this whining, useless little digression back and stuff it in that place in his mind where the worst of the despair dwelled. "I will make you melancholy with this lament."

She shifted so she sat beside him. "More tea?"

It was an English response to just about every dislocation in life, because the English could afford to use a fresh helping of stout black tea for every pot. He did not want to be any more rude and presuming than he already had been, so he nodded.

Sitting right there beside him, she prepared them each a second cup. She passed him his, took a sip of her own, then set it aside.

While Ian stared at his tea and wondered why in God's name he had waxed so philosophical with her in the middle of the day—so petulant and needy—she shifted just a little, so her head rested on his shoulder.

A big sigh went out of him. This was what he wanted. This was what would make all the hoping easier to bear—some honest companionship, some comfort, somebody at his side when the hoping got too hard.

He tilted his head a shade too, so his jaw rested along her crown. They could have this much, for a few minutes anyway. Her breathing soon became regular, and still Ian didn't move. She was a warm, sleepy weight against his side when it occurred to him he hadn't asked her: What was hardest about her solitary, bucolic existence in Oxfordshire?

"Answer a question for me, Connor MacGregor, and no lies, please."

Julia had caught him in the billiards room, which doubled as the armory for the house, with everything from claymores to ceremonial dirks displayed on the walls, and large gun cabinets standing in two corners.

"Mrs. Redmond, a pleasure." Con focused on the fowling piece he'd broken down for cleaning, but his heart picked up a few beats as she advanced into the room. They hadn't spoken more than civilities since he'd let himself into her room the previous week, and he'd been unable to decipher her odd glances and considering looks.

"Are we married, Mr. MacGregor?"

"What! Sweet suffering Jesus in a kilt . . ." He set the gun barrel aside and crossed the room to close the door. "*That's* your question?"

She nodded, perfectly, ominously serious.

"Mrs. Redmond, you are English. I am Scottish. *Scot-tish*. Why would we marry except under duress?"

Duress. An odd feeling came over him—part despair, part protectiveness—toward her. He came to stand beside her, close enough to see the flecks of gold in her brown eyes. "Julia, are you carrying some other fellow's bairn? Is that what drives you? A need to look out for your child?"

"Am I carrying . . . ? You think I'd lie about *that?* For God's sake, Connor, I know how to deal with a child."

Which wasn't a no.

"How would you deal with a child?" He'd tried to keep his tone neutral, but the emphasis on the words *deal with* had been marked by disdain. A growing fashion in the South encouraged women to deal with a lapse of virtue by jumping into the Thames as the tide went out.

"If the herbalist can't help, then a lady goes for an extended trip to the Continent, or even the Americas. She can have the child adopted in a foreign land—the Papists are very good about such things—or she can claim it's her cousin's child and so forth."

"And you'd do that to your own child?" God help the woman if Mary Fran heard such a recitation.

"No, I would not. Not ever, though I don't expect you to believe me. I'm English. *En-glish.* In your eyes, incapable of a selfless, moral deed even toward my own child—which I am not carrying."

He looked her up and down, saw the hurt in her eyes—hurt he'd put there. "You're capable of being very generous and trusting," he said carefully, because he'd no wish to insult her. He turned from her when she didn't react to his words. "What was your question?"

"Are we married?"

He ambled over to the table where the gun lay in parts and shot her a sardonic smile over his shoulder. "If we were married, Julia, I'd sure as hell not be wasting a pretty day by me lonesome, cleaning me weapons, now would I?"

"Might you please be serious?" Her hands were fisted and her teeth were clenched as she stalked around the table. "Mary Fran was talking about handfasting with Matthew, and she kept lapsing into Gaelic terms and law Norman, and I don't know what all. Something to do with promises and intimacies, and I propositioned you, and then we were intimate. *Are we married?*"

"Would you mind so very much if we were?" The question slipped out not as a taunt, but as a genuine expression of curiosity. It stopped her midpace. She drew back, two fingers going to her lips.

He watched a progression of emotions chase across her face: surprise, intrigue, bewilderment, and something else, something . . . more innocent than calculation. Wistfulness, maybe? Something that came under the surprising heading of: *If Only . . .*

"Would it be so bad, being married to me, Julia?" He prowled up to her and set his hands on her hips, not examining his own motives too closely. Step by step, he backed her up to the billiards table. "Did you mind my attention very much the other night? You've never told me if you liked it." He didn't let her answer. He kissed her instead, kissed her the way he'd been dreaming about kissing her for the past week.

She did not even try to prevaricate. There was no stiff English upper lip, no protest for form's sake. Just his name, "Connor . . ." on a soft sigh as her arms went around his neck. He hiked her up onto the table without breaking the kiss and made a place for himself between her legs.

From somewhere in the back of his mind, his conscience was starting up an unholy din of recriminations and warnings. Oh, he'd stop before the consequences were unbearable, he was *almost* sure of it.

But he'd wondered: Had she been repulsed by his attentions? Satisfied beyond the physical, left wondering—as he'd been—if there could *be* something besides the physical? Had she been haunted by the sweetness of what they'd done until it hung in her mind, beclouding all the moments since with a haze of longing and wonder?

Her hands were tugging his shirt free of his waistband, then coursing over the bare skin of his back and chest as if she were parched for the sensation of his flesh under her palms. "Missed you, Scot."

He ran his finger over the swell of her breasts above her stays, hating the fabric that kept him from her skin. "Missed you too, English."

He started frothing up her skirts around her waist, hoping, hoping, and when his hands found her bare legs, he wanted to dance the fling.

"God bless a woman who forgets her drawers."
She covered his mouth with her own. "The Scottish air makes me frisky—or perhaps the Scottish company. Make me forget my own name."

Conscience and common sense gave up on a whimper. Before Con and Julia were done, both were incapable of speech, much less of recalling something as trivial as a name or a nationality, though Con was careful—when he'd restored her clothing and his, and had assured himself she wasn't going to dissolve into the vapors and neither was he—to reassure her they still weren't married.

"We have to talk." Gil appeared before Ian's desk, looking like a specter in the candlelight.

"So talk." Ian switched to Gaelic, the language of their childhood, the language of their family. A much better language for confession and strategy than English.

Gil glanced at the door, which he'd closed behind him. "You'll want to hit me, and maybe you'd better."

Ian tossed his pen on the desk and tried to keep himself from smiling. Gil liked nothing better than a good brawl, a short, emphatic physical expression of emotion that saved thousands of words and a great deal of awkwardness. It also restored fine fellow feeling over the shared medicinal dram that usually followed, and the shared scolding from Mary Fran following after that.

"You're the one who forgot to latch Romeo's gate?" Ian watched Gil's features and saw he'd guessed wrong. "What is it, then?"

"I assaulted a guest."

Ian came around to the front of his desk, unwilling to sit like some headmaster grilling an unruly first former. "Did Matthew make the mistake of engaging you on the matter of the Clearances?"

Gil shook his head.

"Famine aid?" Of which there had been precious next-to-none for Scotland.

"No . . . it's . . ." He threw himself onto the sofa. "I pitched Altsax against the wall and threatened to do worse."

Gil was quick with his fists—and very good with his fists—but he'd long since outgrown a young man's rages. Ian leaned back against his desk and crossed his arms.

"What did he do, Gilgallon? I'll not believe you just took a casual notion to end our trade, destroy our reputation, and lay yourself open to charges."

Gil winced, and by the light of the nearby hearth his features were looking too sharp.

"He slapped Genie." Gil sat forward, running both hands through his hair and then bracing his elbows on his thighs. "He called her into the corridor under the pretense of bidding her good night, made sure I was paying attention, then belted the hell out of her for not being more diligent in her pursuit of you. Very pleasant about the whole thing too. Very calculating."

"He *struck* her?"

Gil's head came up. "I am not a liar, Ian MacGregor. I'm a fool and a barbarian and a Highlander strutting around in a gentleman's clothes, but I do not dissemble with me own laird."

Ian lowered himself beside his brother, trying to make sense of information that appalled even as it roused his curiosity.

"I believe you. What did you do?"

"Fetched him up against the wall and threatened his miserable titled ass if he ever raises a hand to another female under our roof again."

"You didn't strike him?"

"Genie intervened. Said it was a family matter."

"We can have you halfway to France by morning if you think the baron will press charges."

Gil shook his head. "No more deserting. When Asher stopped writing, it about killed you."

Three letters they'd had from Asher over the course of several years—only two Ian could tell his family about—then nothing. He pushed that thought away, as the brother beside him was the one he could assist.

"When was this?"

"Two nights ago. I've been waiting for the Queen's man to fetch me to the gaol."

"You can cease your waiting." Ian considered the line of his brother's shoulders, shoulders that had been bearing a significant weight in silence, when it was the laird's responsibility to keep his family members safe.

"What? Of all Scotsmen, I'm suddenly granted the right to assault titled Englishmen with impunity?"

"You were set up, laddie. He wanted you there for an audience, to shame his daughter, to make sure I knew, firstly, that he was willing to go to significant lengths to ensure the match, and secondly, that I am not his daughter's choice. As a negotiating tactic, it's brilliant."

Gil shot to his feet. "Bugger negotiating tactics, Ian. He enjoyed hurting her, enjoyed even more humiliating her, and enjoyed most of all that I was powerless to intervene on her behalf."

"What did you do when you'd sent him packing?"

Gil glared at the hearth, where peat had been added to the fire now that guests were abed. They might smell the peat smoke in the morning, though the maids would be by early to air out the room.

"I did nothing. I fetched Mrs. Redmond, went to the icehouse—Genie didn't want the servants alerted—and I spent the rest of the night riding so I wouldn't drink myself into a temper."

"Good thinking. You acquired a witness to testify that Genie's face was sporting a welt, that she was upset, and that she'd just bid her father good night. Moreover, Mrs. Redmond could testify that Genie was not in fear of you, so even if Genie refused to implicate her father, the constables won't be visiting us any time soon."

"This is not a matter of criminal defense, Ian. This is not even a matter of a lady's honor. For all legal intents, her father can strike her at will."

"I know, lad. It's a matter of her safety. I'll deal with it."

Gil shifted so he was leaning one arm along the mantel, which allowed Ian to see his brother's face again. Of the three of them, Gil was quickest to laugh, the quickest to anger. He was beyond anger now, having literally galloped past that familiar territory into something that looked to Ian like bewilderment. Or despair.

"I don't like it, Ian. I don't like that we're marrying into a family that thinks treating women in such a fashion is allowable, not for any purpose."

"We're not marrying the baron, Gil." For that matter, *we* weren't marrying anybody.

"If you proposed, he'd have to leave her alone."

"And that is just what he wants. I told him I was doing more digging into his finances, and this is his response. A harrying tactic and a shrewd one, but it won't be effective at achieving his goals."

"Why not?"

"The baron has no allies in this house. Not even his own son—whom I will tell of this encounter—would countenance this behavior. Then too, the women are on our side as well."

"The women? What can they do?"

"They've been dealing with stupid, violent men for generations. Genie and Julia might not enlist the aid of the others, but I will."

Gil looked doubtful but placated. "You'll tell Mary Fran? She's diabolical when it comes to giving a man regrets."

"Mary Fran, Hester, Augusta. They'll look after Genie when we can't, and the negotiations are going to become even more plodding."

"Keep her safe, Ian. It did pass through my mind to whisk your fiancée off to France."

"What stopped you?"

"I don't know."

Interesting answer, but Ian didn't ponder it. In the five minutes following Gil's departure, Ian instead tried to dissuade himself from his next maneuver. When that mental exercise proved fruitless, he blew out the library candles and headed for the door on the terrace leading to Augusta's bedroom.

Eleven

AUGUSTA FOUND, IN JUST A FEW WEEKS IN Scotland, she'd lost the knack of sleeping well. At home, she'd crammed as much productivity into her day as possible and fallen into bed exhausted, only to repeat the pattern day after day, week after week.

But in Scotland she had leisure time, time to read and time to relearn Gaelic, time to wander, and time to desire a man she was increasingly convinced needed rescuing from his own tenaciously held misconceptions about honor and family duty.

Not that Augusta would be marrying him. He was still an earl, and she was a poor relation well past her come-out. He needed coin, and she had none. But he also needed love and companionship, things Genie couldn't give him, though some other wealthy young lady might.

A shadow glided past Augusta's French doors. A big, man-shaped patch of darkness that started Augusta's heart thudding in her chest. "Who's there?"

"Come out to the terrace, Augusta."

Ian spoke just above a whisper from right inside her doors, his shape barely discernible in the moon shadows.

"Not the terrace," she said, hiking up on her

elbows and keeping her voice down. "I've a suspicion Altsax sits out on his balcony, smoking cheroots. Come away from the door."

And by all that was holy, she wanted Ian MacGregor in her bedroom. Wanted him in her *bed,* wanted his hands and his mouth and his very breath on her body.

He didn't move, so she tossed her covers back, locked the door to the corridor, and drew Ian by the wrist away from her French doors. When he stood frowning down at her in a shaft of moonlight, she closed the doors behind him and went up on her toes to kiss him.

Not his cheek. She'd kissed his cheek before. Cheek-kissing was for spinsters content to feed their chickens and weed their beans. Cheek-kissing would not create the type of memory to warm her heart for years to come—much less warm his. She pressed her body to his, sealed her mouth to his.

"You've gotten so bold, Augusta Merrick."

"You come climbing in my bedroom windows, and you call me bold?"

She saw his teeth gleam in the darkness. "You hauled me through your door."

She shifted a few feet to sit on the bed, lest she become bolder still and inspire him to flee from the room. "What brings you here, Ian? You've been avoiding me generally, which is silly when Genie's equally bent on avoiding you."

"She is." He glanced around the shadowed room then took a seat on the bed beside Augusta. "Have you any idea why?"

"Julia and I have discussed this. Genie has observed her father's example as a husband for years. That is argument enough against matrimony on general principles."

"Aye, 'tis." He took her hand in his, his tone distracted, though how he expected her to think clearly when he rubbed his thumb over her palm like that was a mystery. "And yet, her papa is dead set on getting us wed."

"Why do you say that? You are by no means the only title in want of coin, Ian."

"He's considering others?" He shifted his grip to brush his thumb back and forth across Augusta's knuckles, a small caress that made talk of plans to marry him to poor Genie feel blasphemous.

"My aunt has a whole list, but I don't know about my uncle."

"Your uncle is a sly bastard, Augusta Merrick. He struck Genie while my brother Gil was helpless to aid her, and I'm sure this was calculated to hasten the nuptials."

"Because even Uncle would not attempt such behavior if Genie were your fiancée." She shook her hand loose from his, rose, and got settled leaning back against her headboard, the covers over her legs. "So why are you here, Ian?"

The topic was enough to give even Augusta's burgeoning desire pause. Of course he'd protect a young lady as defenseless as Genie. It was a part of Ian Augusta found irresistibly attractive. And of course nothing less than such a mission would bring him to Augusta's bedroom in the dark of night.

"I'm here because I need your help."

He did not sound pleased to be admitting this. Augusta drew her knees up under the blanket and linked her arms around them as she sat back against her pillows. He was powerless to refuse Genie help; Augusta was powerless to refuse him anything he asked.

"How can I help you, Ian?"

"You, Julia, Hester, and Mary Fran, even Fee, you can keep Genie safe. You don't let her be alone, you don't let there be a moment when Altsax can pull the same maneuver again. Keep the footmen near at hand as much as you can. I'll cozy up to the girl, but I can't be alone with her for more than a moment here and there. You explain to her these stratagems are my doing and not an attempt to coerce her into marriage."

"But she *is* being coerced."

"Augusta, I know that, and because she's being coerced, I'm more certain than ever Altsax is hiding something. If anything, I'm more inclined to caution over the engagement than I was before I met the baron."

Augusta nodded, trying to keep the relief from her eyes. When she looked up, Ian had shifted closer, so he was sitting at her hip.

"I have no right to ask this of you," he said, reaching out a hand to tug her braid over her shoulder. "And I had no intention of getting into any mischief when I came skulking in your door tonight, Augusta, but the thought of being wed for years without even affection . . ."

He fell silent, his hand still on her braid. He used it to gently tug her forward into what Augusta hoped and prayed and wished was kissing range.

"I won't put demands on you, Ian. I won't develop expectations, I won't ever . . ." He silenced her descent into pleading and begging by settling his mouth over hers.

He touched his mouth to hers glancingly at first, as if a little taste might do, but then on a groan, he was back, his mouth on hers.

"I wasn't going to . . ." He spoke against her teeth. "God . . . Bloody . . . let me *in,* Augusta."

She smiled, and he was there, tasting her, smiling in return, and looming up closer until without breaking the kiss, Augusta was on her back amid the pillows, Ian's chest and his kiss pinning her to the mattress.

"Overdressed," she muttered, pulling at his shirt.

"Aye." He levered up to untie the bows of her

293

nightgown, and it was as if a referee had rung the bell at the end of a bare-knuckle round. They separated enough to make eye contact, both breathing deeply, hands tangled in the other's clothing.

The smile died from Ian's eyes, but not the heat. "Augusta, if we do this . . ."

"If we . . ." was such a long, wonderful way from "we can't . . ." but Augusta kept her expression solemn.

"If we do this," she took up the thought, "it can't mean anything but some comfort stolen against the circumstances. It can't lead to anything. It can't mean anything, whether you marry Genie or some other woman."

His hand settled against her cheek. "It will mean worlds, Augusta. Between us it will mean worlds, but it cannot go any further, and I'm still not convinced—"

"Shirt off, Ian. Everything off, in fact. If we're only to allow ourselves one lapse with a bed, pillows, and privacy, then let it be a glorious one."

Except in the back of her mind, where she had to be honest with herself even when it hurt, she admitted she was thinking one lapse might lead to a few more. She was committing that folly no sane woman of limited means and accumulating years allows herself: she was *hoping*.

"Don't look at me like that, Augusta." He stood

to pull his shirt over his head. "I don't deserve it. No mortal man could deserve such an expression."

His hands went to the waistband of his trousers, and Augusta watched, even as his fingers stilled. "Shall you do this, lass?" One corner of his mouth kicked up wickedly. "I feel like a present wrapped up and waiting for my lady's gleeful reception of what lies beneath all the decoration."

"My hands would shake, Ian. You do it."

"The things you say . . ." He sat to yank off his boots and socks, then stood again right beside the bed. He turned his body so he was facing Augusta and waited. She pushed the covers aside, divining his purpose, and swung her legs over the side of the bed. While she sat before him, Ian undid the bows down the front of her nightgown. An eddy of night air cooled the heated skin of her breastbone, then lower, until her clothing was parted from throat to hem, the material pooling in her lap.

And yet, he didn't push it aside, didn't draw it off her shoulders.

She met his gaze in the moonlight, knowing even in the shadows, her blush must be evident. He held the back of one hand against her cheek as if to confirm it.

"Please, Ian."

His hand dropped. At a casual pace, he unfastened his trousers, pausing occasionally to glance at her.

As if she could have looked away.

"Unwrap your unlikely treasure, Augusta. I certainly intend to do the same with mine."

He wanted her naked too. Ah, bless him, bless him. Augusta slipped her hand into the fabric of his loosened clothes, finding her way down the plane of his lower abdomen, over flesh taut with muscle and warm with life. Her knuckles encountered hair—soft, springy, then . . .

She worked his clothing down another couple of inches and went exploring again. She found the thick column of his erect flesh, rising from a nest of down. Carefully, she extracted him from the clothing, until his penis was angling up along his belly—thick, hard, and oddly beautiful in its unabashed arousal.

"I'd light candles for you if I dared," he said. "Indulge your curiosity, Augusta. I want you to learn this of me."

"To learn this part of you?" She drew a finger up the length of him, watched as the muscles of his belly rippled in response.

"That too, but I want you to learn it *with* me. Touch me again."

"Get on the bed."

He stepped out of his clothes, becoming a piece of animated sculpture rendered alive by moonlight. There was not a spare ounce on him; he was all muscle and bone, efficient movement and conserved strength.

And he was climbing into *her* bed. "On your back."

His was so big, he made the entire bed shift and jostle as he moved. The mattress bounced as he flopped onto his back and crossed his arms behind his head. "Do we need terms, Augusta?"

"Terms?" She was becoming drunk on the bounty before her. He ranged the length of her bed, making a large piece of furniture abruptly much cozier. He'd stayed above the covers, so she saw everything from the soft hair of his underarms to the geometry of his chest and ribs, to that lovely, lovely man-part of him, on down to legs thick with muscle and feet larger than any Augusta had studied before.

She leaned in to sniff at his chest.

"Terms, my lady, like nothing said or done, no act or omission between us in this bed tonight will be cause for regret or recrimination. This is a gift we give each other."

"I get a much larger present than you," she said, surveying him.

"Give me your hand, Augusta."

Curious, she did. He took her hand, and without letting her pause or draw back, wrapped it around his erection. "Stroke me, and I'll tell you how it feels."

"Stroke?"

He showed her, showed her how tightly to hold him, showed her the parts that were particularly sensitive, the same parts he liked to have touched and cupped and fondled. He showed her how God put together the male organs involved in procreation and explained their functions and habits to her.

It was an initiation of sorts, and she treasured him for making the time for it. She was going to leave her bed in the morning a far wiser and more confident woman—also much sadder, but she pushed that realization firmly to the side.

"I like this," she said, stroking a finger over the hair at his armpit. "It's very soft and very dark." Incongruously soft. "Particularly compared to your chin." She ran the pad of one thumb over his shadowed jaw. "You are hard in so many places, Ian."

"While you are soft." He held her gaze as she traced her hands for the dozenth time down the stair-step muscles along the outsides of his ribs. Lean, powerful, and utterly open to her for these few hours. She'd gathered her courage long enough.

"You want to see me, don't you?"

"Of course I *want* to." He smiled but didn't shift his position. "If you're feeling too modest, I'll content myself with learning the feel and taste and touch of you. A canny Scot learns to improvise."

The *taste* of her?

"Don't worry, Augusta." He drew his finger

down the crease in her brow then down her nose. "I want only to pleasure you. Keep your night-gown on if you like, or dive under the covers before you take it off. It matters naught to me."

"You think I'll want it off soon enough." And she would. In the next instant, she wanted it off.

"You want it off now, lass. You're wondering why I didn't peel you to your skin when I had the chance."

"Why didn't you?" She resisted the urge to gather her disheveled clothing around her just to thwart him.

"For two reasons. First, to assist me with my self-discipline, so I might have as much patience as you need tonight."

"That was flattery. What's the real reason?"

"Because you deserve to learn some pleasure, Augusta, some little touches of decadent wicked-ness. I'm guessing you permit yourself on the occasional hot night to leave off the nightgown. Ah, I'm right. But you think it a pragmatic concession, nothing more."

"I like it, a little, to be honest." She did gather the folds of her dressing gown over her middle. "But I also feel foolish. For whom am I being wicked?"

"For your own pleasure, my lady. Just as being half undressed is a pleasure of a different order."

His hand, big, warm, and a little rough, eased along her waist, until he was a sweet, stealthy intruder under her nightgown. "Breathe, Augusta."

She let out the breath she'd been holding then went still, the better to focus on his fingertips sliding up her ribs.

"Ian . . ." She closed her eyes as his movements edged her nightgown away from her body, dragging the soft fabric along her breast.

"Hush and let me look," he said, his burr thickening. "You're beautiful, Augusta. Never doubt it."

While she waited in silence behind closed eyes, he slowly parted her clothing, peeling back layers of propriety, loneliness, and uncertainty as he did. "Beautiful," he said again. Then he went still, his hands framing her on either side of her ribs. She opened her eyes and met his gaze.

"There you are." He sounded so pleased with her for simply opening her eyes. So proud. He moved his hands up to cover her breasts, his touch easy and reverent at the same time.

"You make me want to be naked all over, Ian MacGregor."

"Soon." A single word, enough to inflame and soothe, both. His gaze dropped to her breasts, and she had the courage not simply to allow it but to enjoy him feasting on the sight of her. His hands moved gently, a rasp of his palms over her ruched nipples, a single finger caressing the undercurve of each breast, and then—glory of glories—a slight, glancing pressure to each nipple.

"Ian . . ."

"I know, love. You can have more of anything you please, but let me learn you now."

He arranged her on her back as he had been, but made no move to push her nightgown from her shoulders. As fascinated as she was with the intimacies they were sharing, Augusta still kept a drape of cotton over her sex.

"I'll see all of you when you're ready to show me."

He lay full length beside her, wonderfully unselfconscious of his own nudity. When Augusta had thought of being intimate with Ian, she'd had a vague notion of kissing and holding and moving under the covers in a silent, darkened room.

How ignorant she'd been, how unimaginative! This nakedness was a wonderful expression of closeness beyond her experience, a closeness she'd longed for without being able to describe.

"Let's have some kisses, shall we?" Ian leaned over, and Augusta braced herself for the pleasure of his mouth on hers. She closed her eyes the better to savor what he offered, only to feel his breath on her nipple one instant before his mouth landed there.

The pleasure was . . . shocking, intimate, so intense she whimpered with it.

"Augusta?" He raised his head to peer at her. "You don't like it?"

She took his head in her hands, arched her back,

and begged with her body for more of those kisses. Any words were beyond her, so dumb-struck was she by what was passing between them.

She gave herself up to him, to his ability to sense when she was becoming overwhelmed, when he needed to veer off to a different touch in a different territory.

"You're not the chatty kind in bed," he concluded long moments later, almost as if speaking to himself. "But your body speaks volumes, my love. You like this . . ." He arched over her and kissed her deeply while he plied her nipple with his fingers. "Though you're not so sure about this . . ."

He shifted, letting his hand trail down her midline and dally a little at her navel.

"Augusta?" He addressed himself to the lower curve of her nearest breast, speaking right against her skin. "What does my body tell you?"

His hand didn't stop moving; it kept on trailing south, to tease the curls shielding her sex. He'd flirted with that before, stroking and patting and even massaging the flesh over her pubic bone. The variety of his caresses inebriated her, the skill with which he plied them . . .

He'd asked her a question. "What?"

"What does my body tell you?" He'd gone a little Scottish on her, "ma bodie."

She opened her eyes. "Your body tells me you

know far more about this business than I dreamed there was to know." A whole sentence, clearly spoken while he tugged a little here and there.

"What else?" He didn't bother to hide the smug humor in his voice.

"That you're patient and naughty, also inventive."

He smiled, teeth gleaming in the darkness. "Such flattery." He took her hand and guided it to his erect penis.

"You're aroused. Still."

"Seems I am." His finger dipped lower—when had she parted her legs? "Seems you are as well."

She was . . . damp. Augusta frowned, some of the erotic haze lifting from her brain. With . . . Oh, she forgot his name—the anemic blond fellow with the clammy hands—she'd thought something must have been wrong, because it had felt like he'd been pushing sandpaper into her body.

"Is it bad that I'm aroused?" She could ask Ian that, now.

"For God's sake, woman. Do you think I'm turning m' balls blue . . ." He stopped and smiled crookedly.

"Do they really turn . . . ?" She could not imagine such a thing, but there had been *so much* she hadn't imagined.

"No, hinny, it's a phrase to describe when a fellow's asked too much of his patience. When do you bleed, Augusta?"

She didn't even blush at his inquiry. The question was intended to protect her from dire consequences—her life among the yeomanry had provided at least that much insight.

"Soon. I expect I won't be joining the shoot."

"You are a woman of providential good timing, my heart. There's more I'd share with you, but it grows late."

Was he *leaving?* She bundled into his long body, hiking a leg over his hips in a display of need that would have been unthinkable an hour earlier. "I don't want you to go. Not yet."

"I'm not leaving this bed until I've attended to your pleasure, Augusta Merrick, and my own as well. But I'm debating . . ."

She loved hearing his words rumble in his chest while he held her. Loved the scent of heather clinging to his skin, loved the solid warmth of him. But this debating . . .

"What are you debating about, Ian?"

"When you were with your beau, how was it?"

She drew slightly away. "Surely this is not a fit topic . . . ?"

"Love, we're abed after midnight with my clothes in a heap on the floor. There are no unfit topics except for how quickly a Scottish summer night passes. Did he cover you, put you on your knees before him, sit you in his lap, have you ride him—?"

She put her hand over his mouth while her mind's eye tried to picture the wild things his words suggested. "I sat on the edge of a desk, and he stood between my legs. I got a cramp in my leg all three times, and my stomach hurt because I had to hold my skirts away and there was nothing to balance on." And the desk had been hard, and the entire business furtive, hurried, and worst of all—disappointing.

"A cramp . . . Damned English. It's a wonder there are any wee English babies about. I suppose we'll go with tradition then, unless you decide you want something else."

"Tradition?"

He shifted, looming over her on all fours. "All you have to do is spread your legs a bit and hold onto me. You tell me if I'm getting it wrong. Pull my hair, swat my backside, bite my ear."

"Skelp your bum?"

"Aye."

"Ian?" He went still while the covers settled around them.

"Love?"

"This isn't what I expected."

He shifted back, frowning. "I'm not a formal man, Augusta. The earl isn't who I am, it's a responsibility . . ."

"Hush." She had to brace herself up on one elbow to lay two fingers over his mouth. "This is so much more than I'd envisioned . . . What was I thinking? To imagine I had anything to give you under circumstances like this?"

"Ah, but you do. You give me so much, Augusta." He caged her body with his, and now, now when he'd set about kissing her, his mouth on hers, his body blanketing hers, she wanted to tell him things, to make sure he understood that this was the greatest gift . . . trust, tenderness, and pleasure. These few hours would illuminate decades of a solitary life in the prosaic shires to the south, give the years meaning, give Augusta herself meaning.

For these few hours, she loved and she was cared for by a good, worthy man.

She wrapped her arms around him, fiercely glad to feel the warm, blunt head of his erection graze the skin low down on her belly. She wanted this, wanted him, craved him. Craved to be as close to him as she could be.

"That's it . . ." He probed lower, an easy nudge and retreat a little off target. "Hold me, Augusta. We're in no hurry."

Oh, yes they were. "I want . . ."

"There." He found his mark but barely seemed to notice. "That's what you want, aye?"

"How can you . . . ?" She fell silent as he did it again, a friendly little greeting between bodies, almost something more, but not . . . "Ian . . . *please.*"

"Hmm?" He dipped his head to kiss her, giving her his tongue to draw into her mouth. She put her demands to him orally, undulating her hips in counterpoint to his movements.

"Greedy," he growled. "Lovely quality in a naked lady."

"Ian MacGregor." She tried to lunge at him when next he came nudging and whistling around the neighborhood.

"Bossy is a verra dear quality too."

She ran her hand down his arm, found his hand, and brought it to her breast. Bossy, *indeed*.

"A woman of discernment."

With her fingers over his, she closed his grip on her nipple, and abruptly, all the teasing went out of him. She'd beat him at his own game, if a game it had been, and then the only sounds in the room were the rustle of the sheets and the sounds of their breathing.

He crossed the line from teasing to penetration. Crossed it by small, slow increments, while Augusta made demands on his tongue and kept his fingers closed on her breast. A tantrum was welling up inside her, a hot ball of undifferentiated wanting for him, for his body, for closeness so consuming . . .

She went up in flames, the conflagration sparked by the indescribable pleasure of his body joining with hers. When she started a low keening against his neck, he added power and depth to his thrusts, until Augusta felt as if each push and retreat ricocheted not just through her body, but through her soul as well. The pleasure built until she didn't know if she was straining toward it or away from it, until she became the pleasure itself—incandescent, consumed, and consuming.

When she was limp and panting beneath him, Ian kissed her cheek. "My dearest, impatient love, did you think I was trying to be aggravatingly deliberate for the hell of it?"

Without warning, Augusta found herself weeping. Blast him to perdition—for the tears were Ian MacGregor's fault. She wept for all she hadn't known, wept for years as no one's dearest anything, wept for reasons that had no words. He was too generous with her, too patient, too caring, and this joining was much, much more than anything that had passed between them before, more intimate, more precious.

"Augusta Merrick, what am I to do with ye?" He angled an arm under her shoulders and enfolded her in his embrace. "You must stop putting it about that you're English. Such tender sentiments belie the Scot in you."

He pattered on, about she knew not what, and all the while, the heat of him throbbed inside her, and his callused fingers brushed away her tears. He moved lazily from time to time, sending spikes of renewed wanting through her.

"Ian?"

"Love?"

"I'm all right."

"Tears aren't unheard of in bed," he said, bending his head again to brush his mouth over her forehead. "When it's a good, honest loving, there can be tears."

He was trying to explain something to her, but she couldn't hold it in her mind. The din was growing in her body again, the need and joy and courage were cresting higher and higher, and now she knew the destination could be shared, knew the intensity of the pleasure he offered her.

They developed an entire bodily language of intimate caresses and sighs, smiles and teases. Worlds and worlds opened up for Augusta, until a snake slithered into her garden with the first gray glimmerings of approaching dawn.

"You should be going," she said. It was easier to admit this because Ian was spooned around her, his chest to her back, while she faced the French doors with their relentlessly lightening shadows.

His lips brushed her nape. "I don't want to leave you, Augusta."

She'd told him she wouldn't cling and cry, so she reached deep into the wells of self-respect and determination Ian had replenished so generously for her. "I'll help you dress."

He went still behind her, then she felt the covers

lift and forced herself out of the bed. In the gloom, she passed Ian his boots and socks while he tugged on his breeches. He let his hands fall to his sides while she buttoned a few of his shirt buttons, and then, with no further ado, their time was over.

Still he didn't go. He sat on the bed and caught her by one wrist. Her braid had long ago fallen victim to his clever fingers, so when he pulled her down onto one hard male thigh, her hair spilled over her shoulder between them. He swept it back.

"I have something to say to you, Augusta. You'll not want to hear it."

"Then say it quickly. If you're found in here, there will be no dealing with the consequences."

He nodded and pushed her head to his shoulder. "We agreed this time together can't change anything, can't make a difference, but, my lady"—he brushed his lips over her temple—"do you recall your description of the times you were with that sorry Englishman?"

"I do."

"Augusta, I very much fear that if I'm forced into that sort of proximity with any other woman but you, I'll be the one with a cramp in my heart and nowhere to balance."

She smiled despite the lump in her throat. He was lying. He'd make it as beautiful for Genie— or whatever woman he married—as he had for her, damn him, damn Genie, damn, damn, and damn.

"I'm not coming down to breakfast," she said, rising from his lap.

"Sleep in, then, and may your dreams be sweet." His tone was so sad, so tender, Augusta didn't trust herself to answer him. She walked with him to the French doors, where he paused and gathered her to him. "Augusta . . ."

He said something else, in Gaelic. She understood him, and she understood as well he would think the sentiment indecipherable to her.

"No more words, Ian, except thank you, and I will cherish this memory more than you'll ever know."

He nodded, kissed her lingeringly on the mouth, and then she was alone.

"You will always be my dearest love."

In solitude, she said again aloud the words he'd given her. They lit a determination in Augusta she hadn't known she was capable of. She could not be his wife, but she'd be . . . *bloody damned* if she'd allow him to consign himself to a life of heart-cramps and self-denial. Let him find another wealthy bride, a woman willing to love and laugh along with him, to be his friend and his countess both.

Rather than Genie, who—a fool a thousand times over—loathed the very thought of marriage to Ian.

. . .

Ian considered going to his room for an attempted nap, but when a man's world had been stood on end by a violet-eyed lady who sought nothing from him but memories and discretion, a nap would not serve.

He saddled Hannibal and lit out of the stable yard like the demons of hell were after him.

Which they were. Marriage to Genie Daniels had been a difficult but necessary duty before; it loomed like torture now. *Impossible,* unthinkable torture. Coupling with Augusta just now had crossed a line. They weren't reeling from a brush with death; they weren't deceiving themselves or each other about the probable outcome of their situation.

If nothing else became clear during Ian's ride, he headed home knowing what his options were, *and what they were not.*

Connor leaned on his muck fork and frowned as Ian swung down. "Have you taken to abusing your only decent mount?"

"We walked the last mile."

"And galloped five before that."

Ian looped the reins over Hannibal's head, and Con fell in step beside them as they walked into the barn. "I can put him up for you."

"I'll tend to my own mount, Brother. You're up early."

Con's lips thinned. "The upcoming shoot means

312

the chores will back up for a couple of days."

The shoot and the dress ball they held the night before. The local gentry came by for the free food and the dancing. The English in the area showed up in hopes the royal neighbors might put in an appearance, which they had at least once a year.

"The deer herd can use thinning," Ian said, unbuckling the gelding's girth. "And the meat never goes to waste." Nor the hide, nor the bones, nor the antlers, even.

"We're going to waste." Con muttered that sentiment, prompting Ian to peer at his brother over the horse's back.

"Care to explain yourself, baby brother?"

"This engagement, Ian. I'm having second thoughts."

Ian hefted the saddle off Hannibal's back and took it to the saddle room lest he shout his agreement. "You're not the one who'll be marching up the aisle in full dress regalia, but say on. If you've some other way to fatten our coffers, I'm all ears."

"We don't need to fatten them this way," Con said, scowling at the barn floor. "We're managing, Ian, and have you thought about what this is like for Genie?"

Ian's older-brother instincts twitched to life. Con had an agenda here, but Ian was going to be all damned day figuring out what it was. "If I have to, I will make Genie Daniels as congenial and considerate a husband as anybody could, Connor MacGregor."

If he had to, which he would *not*. Somehow, he would not.

"But you don't love her. You're not choosing her, you're choosing her money."

Ian snatched a brush down from a peg. "And she would be choosing my title, as if I were some damned breeding bull guaranteed to throw broad quarters on all the heifers my own has been paid for me to service. Find me a hoof pick."

Con pulled one from his pocket and bent to lift one of Hannibal's sturdy forelegs.

"I don't have a good feeling about this, Ian. Have you considered Genie might love another?"

"Yes, Connor. Yes, I have, and I have considered that I might love another given the damned chance, none of which will feed the doddies next winter or put a decent portion in Fee's pretty little hands."

Connor set the first hoof down and straightened to glare at Ian over the horse's neck. "The haying this year is the best we've seen since the famine, and that whisky you found in the back cellars is worth its weight in gold. If we encounter a hardship, we've only to apply to the earldom's trustees and—"

"Fenmore will expire of glee should we be

reduced to begging for our own money, most of which I'm told is perpetually tied up in 'long term investments.' Give me that hoof pick."

Connor passed it over, trading Ian for the brush. "Gil said you want us both to read the settlements."

"I do. They're sitting in plain view on my desk. I expect Daniels will be having a look at them before we're done." Ian answered easily but suspected Connor was simply angling around the topic to strike again from a different vantage. The urge to burden his brother with confidences and confessions was tearing at Ian's soul, so he turned the conversation to a different topic. "I smell a rat in the baron's financial situation, one he's desperate for me not to find."

"Which means you're determined to find it. Pity the poor rat."

Ian put down the last of Hannibal's muddy hooves, dipped the bit in a bucket of water, and started wiping down his bridle while Con finished brushing the horse.

"I am determined to find the rat, Con, but not just because only a fool trusts an Englishmen bearing gifts. Daniels told me Miss Augusta was engaged to a decent prospect after her come-out, but her not-very-devoted swain was waved off under peculiar circumstances, just as marriage would have solved a great deal of difficulty for the woman."

"Waved off by whom? Women get odd notions, particularly when they're grieving."

"What do you know of grieving women?"

Con paused while brushing the horse's muscular neck. "Julia—Mrs. Redmond—is grieving."

"Still?" And how would Connor know such a thing? "She must have loved her late husband."

"Not him." Con started back to the brushing with inordinate focus. "She grieves her youth, her innocence, the choices she was never allowed to make for herself, the years wasted . . . She grieves a great deal, and I'm not even sure she comprehends this."

"Oh, that's subtle, Con. Just as Genie will grieve endlessly married to me?"

Con glanced up, one corner of his mouth quirking. "If the shoe fits, Ian."

"Right now, Connor, not one damned thing in my life feels like it truly fits."

Nor did it feel like it ever would. And yet, last night, with Augusta's naked body snug and warm around him, nothing had ever fit better.

Twelve

AUGUSTA VENTURED INTO THE LIBRARY ONLY after she'd taken trays for both breakfast and luncheon. She hadn't hidden. She'd spent the morning wandering the woods with Fiona, searching out fairy rings and finding a small dance of stones Fiona promised her was full of good magic.

Maybe it was. Soaking in the beauty of Balfour, spending time with the child, Augusta gradually found some sort of balance. Enough to risk running into Ian in the library, enough to be relieved when he wasn't there.

"Will I disturb you if I read here for a bit, Mr. MacGregor?"

Gilgallon rose from the desk, a blond, tired, sleeker version of his older brother. "I'll be glad for the company, Miss Augusta. What are you reading?"

"It's a grammar for the Gaelic, though Mary Fran says this is for the Irish version."

"Irish and Scottish aren't that different. Even an English grammar would be better than trying to plow through these marriage settlements. Ian doesn't believe in leaving details to sort themselves out."

"Marriage is a complicated undertaking," Augusta said, eyeing the thick sheaf of documents in Gil's hand. She wanted to burn them, as if without executed documents, there could be no wedding.

Which, come to think of it, there wouldn't be.

"It shouldn't be this complicated." Gil set the papers down on the desk and paced to the window. "It feels like this is just one more way the English are conquering us."

He spoke with his back half to her, his tone bleak.

"I'm very sure Genie is the one feeling seized and carried off, Mr. MacGregor." Augusta winced a little at her word choice: To "seize and carry off" was the genteel translation for the Latin verb *rapio*.

"I'm not trying to be rude." He smiled over his shoulder, though his eyes remained bleak. "It just seems to me that when much has been taken from a man—most of his family, the best of his lands, two hundred years of being a clan, his older brother—that choosing a mate ought to remain to him for his own pleasure. It shouldn't be a matter of marrying for coin."

Disjointed images—of Gil watching Genie, Gil carrying Genie from the woods, Gil faithfully taking the place beside Genie each morning at breakfast—coalesced in Augusta's mind.

"You're in love with my cousin, aren't you, Gilgallon?"

He said nothing for a long moment, while Augusta reeled with the irony of it. Was *this* why Genie was so reluctant to marry Ian?

Gil's smile was a sad echo of his brother's. "I care for them both, Miss Augusta, or I hope I do. I hope I'm honorable enough to wish this marriage didn't have to be, for both of their sakes rather than for mine."

Augusta studied the lean planes of his face

while wheels turned in her mind. "If there were a way to spare them, a way that protected Genie from her father and left your family without financial obligations to hers, would you take it?"

"There isn't a way, and even if there were, Ian is convinced his title is all we have left to sell for a cushion between us and the next disaster."

"He doesn't even have the title yet himself."

"Yes, he does." Gil glanced over at her, clearly measuring how much to tell an outsider. "Asher has been declared dead. We got that word yesterday, which means Ian is Balfour in truth, though the formalities yet remain. We agreed to keep that much from the baron. If he thinks we're waiting for word on Asher's death, then we have another reason to stall negotiations."

"I think Ian will have done dragging his feet now, Gilgallon."

He studied her with an intensity that put Augusta in mind of his older brother. "You call him Ian now?"

She nodded, finding it necessary to stare out the window across the beauty of the gardens stretching out behind the house.

"We're a pair, aren't we?" His green eyes were full of understanding and commiseration. "At least you can scurry back south and never set eyes on them again. Until they have some sons, I'm doomed to stay close at hand, being the spare and Ian's henchman. I'm not sure there's enough

319

whisky left in Scotland to make that prospect bearable."

Scurrying. She loathed the notion, but comparing miseries with Gilgallon would get them nowhere. "You've read the settlements in their entirety?"

"I'm on my second trip through. Ian is a careful draftsman. It's heavy going."

Augusta marched to the desk, found a pair of reading spectacles there, and hooked them around her ears. "My father used to make a game out of explaining contract clauses to me and quizzing me on the legal language. My impression is that lawyers delight in creating heavy going. Sooner begun is sooner done."

His smile was slow to bloom, starting in his eyes then drifting down over his face like summer sun filling a valley from up over a high, cold tor. That smile lightened his countenance, taking away years and worries and woes as it cascaded down his features.

"Genie said you were formidable."

"She did?" Augusta picked up the sheaf of papers and passed half to Gilgallon. "One wonders how she came to such an odd conclusion."

"I am concerned for you."

Augusta looked up to find Matthew peering down at her where she sat at the big estate desk in Ian's library.

"Why would you be concerned for me, Matthew?" She tucked the settlement documents under a pile of letters and blinked up at him in what she hoped was convincing innocence.

"Gilgallon told me you'd been in here all afternoon, noodling away at some dusty old grammar. I find you with ink stains on both hands, circles under your eyes, and your usually tidy coiffure attempting disarray before sunset."

"Sunset is quite late in these surrounds." Still, Matthew had a point. She'd been in here for hours, absorbed in the minutiae of legalities that should not concern her in the least.

"We have an hour before we must dress for dinner, cousin. I was hoping for a game of chess on the terrace."

Confidences, then. He wanted to pry them from her, or alert her to some situation that might devolve to her discredit—such as Genie falling in love with the wrong brother.

"A change of scene appeals," Augusta said, getting to her feet. Matthew led her directly to the terrace from the library, pausing only to get a chess set down from the shelves. They'd no sooner started setting up pieces than a footman appeared with a tea service.

"Mary Fran has spies everywhere," Matthew said, and this put a rare smile on his face. "No guest will go hungry or thirsty on her watch."

"You're enjoying your stay here, then?"

Matthew paused with the black queen in his hand. The set was old, ivory and onyx, gorgeous little carvings so detailed the pieces had ferocious, bellicose expressions on their faces—all save the queens. The one in Matthew's hand was smiling.

"I did not expect to make a friend of an earl's widowed daughter," he said, putting the queen on the board. "Mary Fran got me talking about . . . the past."

Augusta abruptly understood the sadness in Matthew's smile. He'd finally chosen somebody to confide in about his wife, who had not survived the posting to the Crimea, while Matthew had. Mary Fran, being widowed herself, would be a sympathetic ear. "I'm guessing Mary Fran makes as impressive a friend as she would an enemy," she said carefully.

Matthew looked up, the smile reaching his eyes. "Exactly so, as do I. I need to know, should I have to depart temporarily to deal with the press of business, that you will be all right here."

Depart temporarily . . . ? "Matthew, if you've finally found a lady with whom you are congenial, then now is not the time to depart, temporarily or otherwise."

"I'm investigating options, Gus, not blowing full retreat, and yet I don't like the idea of leaving you here without anybody to keep an eye on Altsax."

"I can handle Uncle." Brave words, brave, untrue words.

"If this business with Genie and the earl doesn't come off according to the baron's plans, he's going to blame you, Gus, at least in part." Matthew spoke very quietly as he started lining up his pawns.

"I know this. He'll blame me, Julia, Genie, Balfour—everybody but himself. Julia has the resources to deal with him, and there's a limit to what he'll do to his own daughter if he wants her to remain marriageable in the eyes of Polite Society."

The pieces were set up, but Matthew was studying Augusta, not the board. "When did you learn to give nothing away, Gus? I used to be able to tell what sort of game we'd have by the way you set up your men. I can't tell if you're in the mood to trounce me or if you're just humoring my request for a game."

"I'm considering options too, Matthew." She opened with the white queen's knight, which had her cousin frowning in consternation.

"I have money, Gus. Altsax scoffs and mutters about my dabbling in trade, but I'm good at it. You're not to consider yourself on his charity any longer."

She lifted her gaze from the board to regard a cousin she'd stopped seeing years ago. "Could you invest a sum for me?"

"If that's all you'll let me do, then yes. I should not have let him remove you to Oxford without making sure myself you were content to be removed. Allow me to make amends. I own properties as well, Gus. You need not rusticate in Oxford, not when I have handsome farms to let in Surrey and Hampshire."

Augusta sat back, utterly flummoxed by the conversation. "I may have need of one of those farms, Matthew, at least for a time."

He pursed his lips and studied the board for a long moment. "You'll be careful, Gus. I don't trust Altsax farther than I could throw him." He put his hand on a pawn, withdrew it, then made the move.

"Neither do I, Matthew. Not any longer."

She didn't trounce him, but she did win. And all through the game, Augusta's mind was in motion. The years in Oxford had not been wasted—she'd been wrong about that. In those years, she'd been learning to think for herself, to fend for herself, to manage life with the few tools available to a single woman of very limited means.

She'd been gathering strength so slowly, she hadn't even noticed it herself. And now, she was willing to risk all she'd gained to make sure Ian had a chance at happiness.

She loved him. That was how strong she'd become.

"Were you spying on me?" Augusta stood in the doorway that led from the library to the terrace, the chess set in her hands, her expression disconcerted.

"I was enjoying the sight of you. You were very absorbed in the game, and I had the distinct impression you relished your victory." They were alone. Ian didn't castigate himself for the honesty when all too soon, there might be no further occasion for it. He took the chess set from her and set it up on its customary shelf. "Will you share a drink with me, Augusta?"

"Yes."

Bless the woman, she hadn't even glanced at the clock, and the first bell would soon sound for dinner.

"I'm warning you, what you're about to taste is considered very fine potation."

He went to the sideboard and she joined him. "Everything I've had here, food and drink, has tasted good to me, better than anything I've had in the South."

Well.

"It's the Highland air. Puts the appetite on a person." He poured her a finger of the best they had to offer, then did the same for himself.

What would it be like to share a wee dram with her every night, to watch her mind working out

325

the path to victory over a chessboard on a long winter evening?

"Shall we make a toast?" she asked, bringing the glass under her nose. "My goodness, that is strong."

Strong, complex, and satisfying—like her. "To your happiness, Augusta Merrick." He spoke softly, as sincere a toast as he'd ever offered. The coming days would likely bring a great deal of upheaval for them both, and inevitably, Augusta would return south, but this moment Ian took for himself.

"To yours." She lowered her lashes and took a sip. "My, my . . ."

"Do you like it?"

He liked watching the emotions play across her features. Liked it too well.

"I do. I'm sure I do, but it's complicated." She assayed another taste. "It's fruity, smoky, sweet . . . I could probably drain that whole bottle and not describe the contents to my satisfaction."

"If you drained the whole bottle, you'd likely be unable to speak." And the idea of Augusta Merrick tipsy was intoxicating in itself.

"You must not look at me like that, Ian."

"How am I looking at you?" He tipped his glass to his lips but didn't take his gaze from hers.

"With tender eyes. Your gorgeous green eyes are soft . . ." She glanced around, color staining her cheeks. "I suppose that's the drink talking."

"The drink doesn't work quite that quickly, Augusta, not even on nice English ladies. Would you like more?"

She shook her head, but her words lingered in Ian's mind: tender eyes. He knew what she meant. He hadn't regarded anybody or anything with tender eyes for so long . . .

"Will I see you at dinner, Augusta?"

"You will." She looked like she might say something more, like she might go up on her toes and grace him with one of those sweet, chaste kisses of hers, but she just put her empty glass on the sideboard and left Ian alone with his drink.

He finished his whisky in a single swallow and set the glass down solidly beside Augusta's. They'd get through dinner, they'd get through whatever lay ahead, but Ian was more convinced than ever that his future would not include marriage to Augusta Merrick's cousin.

Nor to any woman upon whom he did not gaze with tender eyes.

Waiting would make a lesser man unsure of himself, but as the week progressed, the baron became more confident of his plans. Friday was to be the grand ball—as grand as these rustic surrounds could produce—and an organized hunt was planned for Saturday.

The shoot was just too perfect an opportunity to

pass up, and then, with Augusta laid out in the parlor, it would be simple to explain to the earl that time had just become of the essence. If he wanted to get his Scottish paws on good English coin in the foreseeable future, he'd quit his fool posturing and snooping, and get Genie wedded and bedded in short order.

And as for Genie . . . The hens were keeping her in a protective circle, clucking and fussing and being sure to order tea when the baron came around. No matter. In a few days, the Daniels family would be mourning, the MacGregors would be trying to explain how a guest had been killed by accident in their woods, the earl would take off running for a special license, and Altsax would rejoice.

"We need to talk." Ian drew Genie's arm through his and kept his expression friendly. When she would have pulled away, he smiled down at her as convincingly as he could, when he wanted to shake her until her teeth rattled. "Show a little faith, woman. I'm not your enemy."

Her features smoothed out into that bland nonexpression at which English ladies forced to accept dubious company excelled, and she fell in step beside him. "I understand from Gilgallon there's a litter of kittens in the stables. Perhaps you might show them to me, my lord?"

"Their eyes have been open for a few weeks,"

Ian said, willing to work with any gambit. "They're leaving the nest more and more, and if we're patient, we'll likely catch them playing."

She made an effort thereafter at the small talk: Fiona was such a delightful child. Did he enjoy haggis?—haggis, for God's sake—Did he have a favorite among all the flowers in his lovely gardens?

And all the while he was wending his way at a crawl toward the stables and filling the air with inanities, Ian couldn't help but compare this lady with another.

Augusta would have marched along right beside him, arguing with him or grilling him on the follies of Scottish church politics. She would have spoken her piece; she would have delighted in his touch; she would have borne the faint scent of lilacs when he bent near . . .

"What do we need to discuss, my lord?" Genie's blue eyes were full of trepidation by the time they reached the stables.

"You're not sleeping much, are you?" He dropped her arm and wasn't surprised when she moved off a good six feet down the barn aisle.

"I am not. The surroundings are unfamiliar, and the sun comes up quite early. I'm sure I'll accustom myself to Balfour over time."

Could she sound any more dismal? "Genie, do you want to marry me?"

She turned her back, and to Ian's eye it looked

as if she'd hunched in on herself. "I do not want to marry you, but I shall marry you."

"For God's sake, why?"

She faced him, the expression in her eyes appallingly bitter. "You're the best of a bad lot, Ian MacGregor. I have to marry someone, I know this. Papa regards it as my purpose on earth to drag some impoverished title into the family, as if I were bringing down game with his rifle and shot. I haven't any more Seasons. He's made that plain. Hester is more than of age, and I must be safely wed before she can be paraded up to the altar. You are not only my best chance, I very much fear you're my last chance."

He advanced on her; she held her ground until they were just a foot apart then stepped back. "I was not asking why you'd condescend to accept my suit, madam. I was asking *why* you do not want to marry me. I know your position—the entire household knows your position—I do not know the reasons for it."

She shook her head. "It's not personal to you. I don't care to marry any title my parents choose for me. The precedents don't bode well for our union, and some genuine affection—not the manufactured kind—is not too much to ask of a man for whom I will give up every freedom."

Her expression was not so much angry as it was . . . resolved. Determined.

"What precedents would those be? I personally

know the man who married the highest title in the land, and the union prospers more shamelessly each year."

Her chin came up. "I am not a queen, and I do not appreciate your making a jest out of what will likely turn into a petty tragedy."

Oh, bloody damn. Her big blue eyes were aglitter with inchoate tears. Ian reached out a hand, intending to make some conciliatory contact with her shoulder or her arm, but she flinched away, her gaze wary.

Ian took a step back and considered the woman whom common sense said he was supposed to marry. "The precedent you refer to, Genie, would that be your parents?"

She gave a jerky nod, which caused tears to spill down her cheeks. After another considering silence, Ian held out his handkerchief, dangling it from his fingers like a white flag.

"Thank you." She snatched it from him and blotted it against her face with both hands, reminding Ian of Fee weeping into the apron of her pinafore.

"Your parents' union was arranged, then?"

Another nod, but she lifted her face from the white square of linen and aimed a look both accusatory and condemned at Ian. "Mama's family was thrilled that she had landed a man in expectation of a title. They provided her an obscene dowry, and everybody thought it amusing when she would not come down to breakfast after her wedding night."

The unease Ian lived with daily, the unease that had been gathering since this entire scheme with Altsax's daughter had been hatched, congealed into dread. "She *could* not come down, is that it?"

Genie put more distance between them, walking off a few paces to stand outside Merlin's stall. "I attend my mother at her bath, my lord, because she is too ashamed to let the maids see what my father does to her, what he has been doing to her for years. The bruises—"

Her voice broke, and her reserve, her damnably English, cool, impersonal reserve made him want to howl. "I'll not raise my hand to you, Genie. I promise you that, but if we go through with this, our marriage could be very, very personal."

She shuddered, making it plain she took his meaning. "I know you need heirs. *If* marriage becomes unavoidable, I'll tolerate my duty if you insist." She'd spoken so quietly she'd nearly whispered.

I'll tolerate my duty if you insist. Genie's grudging capitulation to duty blew through Ian's thoughts like a gust of frigid Highland air. She would lie unmoving, tolerating his rutting when she must, the candles snuffed along with any hope either of them had for happiness.

As if Ian could bring himself to join with any woman under circumstances such as those.

He was not going to marry her. He'd been working up to this realization even before joining Augusta in bed, but he knew it now with the same certainty he knew the sounds of his siblings' voices and scent of the heather on the Balfour hillsides. For the sake of his children, his honor, his sanity, and even his obligation as a gentleman to the woman before him and to her cousin, he would not marry Genie Daniels.

Ian sorted courses of action in his mind while he regarded Genie standing just a few feet away. The best plan he'd been able to devise was desperate and fraught with risk, and while it might leave Ian free of Altsax's marital schemes, it would also leave him with nothing to offer any other woman, much less a woman he loved.

He lopped off that thought for consideration another day. While *he* knew he could not marry Genie Daniels, Genie herself required convincing.

"Let's try something." Ian kept his voice down, glancing around to make sure they were still alone. "A little experiment." *Before he lost his nerve.*

"What sort of experiment?"

He gave up on the words that were getting them nowhere and moved close enough to kiss her, steadying her with his hands on her shoulders. She stiffened at the first touch of his lips on her cheek, stiffened more when he didn't immediately remove himself, and then started trembling when he smoothed a hand over her back.

"I'm sorry." She jerked back long before Ian could steel himself to join their mouths. "I am so sorry, but just as you have promised not to raise your hand to me, I have promised myself I would marry only for love." She turned away, though Ian kept one hand on her arm.

"Genie, lass, I'm sorry too, but surely you see now we're going to have to come up with something if we're not to be a great deal sorrier here directly."

She nodded, her gaze on the dirt floor. "Papa wants to make an announcement at the ball this weekend."

This was news—bad news. "I haven't signed the documents."

"He'll make the announcement anyway to force your hand."

"And if I gainsay him?"

Her hand went to her cheek—probably the very cheek her father had struck while Gil looked on helplessly—and she shook her head. "You think I'm the one Papa can coerce, my lord, but if you back out now, he'll have it all over Town the hospitality at Balfour was abysmal, the sheets damp, the food poor, and the company mere peasantry. He can ruin you with a word. He's done the same to many and enjoyed doing it."

Insight struck with a strange sense of liberation:

if Ian coerced Genie to the altar, he'd be no better than Altsax.

"I can't marry a woman who's being forced to say her vows, much less a woman who detests my touch, Genie. I won't do it to you, or to myself."

Her expression became impatient. "Yes, you can and you will. The alternative is to jeopardize your family's standing and security—which you might be willing to do—but you won't leave me to my father's machinations. He might not have chosen you for your honor, but it's the reason he'll get you to say vows you abhor."

She wasn't stupid. Too late, Ian realized his intended was a very perceptive woman. Also very frightened, and the prospect of spending years married to her . . .

He asked a question he hoped was theoretical. "Did you want a white marriage, then?" Images of Augusta popped into his mind, her hair cascading around her naked breasts, her smile wicked in the moonlight . . .

Bloody damn.

"I do not seek a white marriage," Genie said. "One hears talk such unions can be annulled, and your brothers aren't married. If you are to have heirs, they need to be of my body."

The idea made her as sick as it did him. He could see that by the careful lack of expression on her face. "Genie Daniels, I cannot—I *will not*—marry, much less consummate a marriage with a

335

woman who's being forced. We're at an impasse, and until we resolve it, I'll not sign anything, regardless of what your papa announces."

A calico kitten came stotting out of the saddle room, followed by a second, a marmalade tabby. "Lass, I am so sorry."

She kept her gaze toward the kittens rolling and playing on the ground, each arching its back and hissing and spitting before leaping merrily on the other. "I'm sorry too," she said, turning and leaving. Ian swore viciously for long minutes then grabbed a muck fork and started stabbing at the horseshit that seemed to be accumulating all around him.

Con had taken to watching for Julia without even realizing it himself, and it wasn't hard to find her, because she was almost always in Genie's vicinity. He wasn't surprised then, to find the lady who had most recently graced his dreams sitting on a bench outside the foals' paddock, a book of poetry facedown in her lap.

"Mrs. Redmond, good day."

She smiled up at him. "Connor. Good day to you too."

His chest expanded to behold that smile. She'd fallen asleep on his shoulder in the billiards room, then awoken blushing and stammering. As soon as he'd set her hair to rights, she'd scampered off, and he'd been left wondering ever since.

Wondering and aching.

"I don't find you in solitude very often," he said, taking the place beside her.

"I have been remiss in my duties as chaperone." She set the book aside. "Genie is visiting the horses on her intended's arm, though, so I have a few minutes to spend with Mr. Burns."

"I'll read to you if you like." Because he was that far gone, he'd read her smarmy old Robbie Burns. To have her drowsing in his arms again, he'd read her *English* poetry naked on the front drive. "Genie has already gone up to the house."

"I hardly see how your brother is going to bring the girl around if they don't spend more than five minutes together at a time." She started to rise, but Con caught her by the wrist.

"We need to talk about that."

She sank slowly to the bench and made no move to retrieve her hand, so Con linked their fingers where their hands rested between them. "We need to have a private discussion, in fact. Are you all right, Julia?"

She closed her eyes and let out a sigh. "When you pitch your voice like that, Connor, so low and intimately, I am not all right in the least. My innards get to fluttering and my brain stalls and all I can think about . . ."

He rubbed his thumb over the soft skin of her wrist. "All you can think about . . . ?"

"All I can think about is having a billiards room built into all my residences."

"Interesting idea. Have you missed me then, Julia?"

She didn't hesitate. She nodded, cheeks flaming. "You destroy a lady's sense of decorum, Connor MacGregor. I see you in my dreams. All the hours I spend trailing Genie around the gardens, sipping tea with her, and reading novels to her in the library, I am watching for you."

Con kept his eyes on the stables, lest he allow her to see what this confession was doing to his . . . composure. "We have a problem, my dear."

She glanced over at him, her scrutiny guarded. "I'm not expecting, if that's what you're hinting at."

"Would you like to be carrying my bairn, Julia?"

He'd put the question to her to knock her off her pins, to get the dreamy look out of her pretty brown eyes, but the smile curving her mouth— full, soft, sweet, and sincere—had him feeling poleaxed where he sat.

"Don't answer that question if you value my dignity, Julia Redmond. We truly do have a problem. I happened to be up in the hayloft, catching forty winks, when Ian and Genie came strolling by to visit the horses. Were you aware your niece has a specific aversion to an arranged match with a title?"

Julia's head slewed around, and the dreamy expression was nowhere to be found. "A specific aversion?"

"Said the precedents didn't bode well, and she's promised herself to marry only for love. Ian kissed her cheek—mostly to make a point, I'm guessing—and it was painful to watch. Seems the baron's brand of domestic discipline has put the fear of arranged marriages in his daughter."

"You saw . . . ?" Julia fell silent, worrying her bottom lip. "Augusta and I have suspected Altsax's example has put Genie off an arranged match, but Genie wouldn't divulge any particulars."

"It gets worse." Con leaned across her to retrieve the book, also to feel her breast pressing against his arm. "Genie has decided to put her trust in a man, but not her intended."

"Gilgallon." Julia loaded a wealth of despair into the name. "I saw them after Altsax walloped Genie, and I'd say they're equally smitten."

"So what are we to do? Ian will end up marrying the girl just to keep her safe from her own father."

"I don't know what to do." Julia looked around them and gave his hand a surreptitious squeeze. "Maybe we could discuss it further over a game of billiards?"

"It's stinking worse the more I stir it." Ian tossed the latest missive down on his desk and accepted the drink Mary Fran passed him. "I can find out all I want about a wee piece of Kent that serves as the Altsax seat, but the Gribbony barony and its Scottish holdings are a confounded mystery."

"What does Daniels have to say about it?" Con posed the question quite, quite casually, but Ian saw Mary Fran brace herself.

"Young Daniels has departed for the South. He said he'd be back by week's end. He took a proper leave of me as his host, so I can't think it was anything more than business, just as the man said."

Mary Fran looked grateful for Ian's observation. Gil looked thoughtful. "Genie says her brother has been kept out of the business of the barony, says Altsax won't allow his son the least involvement with the estates, or with Trevisham, either."

"Trevisham?" The name was familiar.

"The place Altsax acquired from the Merrick family," Gil clarified. "Until Genie's come-out, it was where they lived part of the year. She says it's a lovely estate, and the baron has boasted that it's quite profitable."

"I'm looking into that."

Mary Fran regarded him from where she stood by the hearth. "You don't sound very pleased with matters, Ian."

"I am not pleased at all. Genie has made it clear she's marrying under duress, the baron will take

340

it out on our social standing if the wedding doesn't take place, and every instinct I have says there's something underhand in Altsax's finances."

"I am against this wedding." Connor spoke quietly then glanced around at his siblings. "Ian is being put in the position of having to force a woman to the altar. It isn't honorable. We don't need the coin, we just want it. Compromising honor for discretionary coin makes us whores."

Ian wanted to lift a toast in agreement with Con's summary of the situation, wanted to take his siblings into his confidence. And yet, if Ian's plan, shaky as it was, didn't come to fruition, then his confidences would have been for naught.

Gil pushed away from the windowsill where he'd been lounging. "If Ian *doesn't* marry the woman, can you imagine her fate at Altsax's hands?"

"That is her brother's concern," Mary Fran said. "I'm confident Matthew can keep his sister safe if the situation is explained to him clearly enough."

"Matthew," Gil spat, "who isn't here."

"This gets us nowhere," Ian said. "I haven't signed anything, nor will I until I understand Altsax's source of wealth. I'll speak to Daniels when he returns, and we will comport ourselves graciously to our guests until he does. Mary Fran, are we in readiness for the weekend's festivities?"

Ian saw his siblings exchange fulminating glances. Yes, he'd just pulled rank, and yes, Connor's position was the one supported by honor and integrity. Yes, Matthew Daniels's disappearance was very untimely—as far as Ian's siblings knew—and yes again, the Baron Altsax was a viper under their roof.

And notwithstanding any of that, notwithstanding all plans and wishes to the contrary, come Friday night, Ian might very possibly have to permit the baron to make Genie's betrothal announcement before every titled guest in the shire.

Thirteen

"EXPLAIN SOMETHING TO ME." IAN'S WEIGHT dipped the mattress as he sat on Augusta's bed. "How is it your uncle claimed Trevisham was deep in debt eight years ago, but Genie says it's the most profitable of his holdings now?"

"Ian?"

"Don't shoo me away, Augusta Merrick. You avoided me for most of the day. I have questions for you."

Augusta struggled to a sitting position, only to see Ian shucking his clothing where he stood beside the bed. "Is it necessary that you be naked to interview me, Ian?"

"No." His hands stilled at his waistband, his

expression shuttered. "But I would dearly like to be."

"This is not wise." It was the best she could do, a little remonstrance. A sop to common sense at complete variance with what her body—and her heart—desperately wanted.

"I do not see a wise course before me, Augusta. Not in the direction of your cousin, not in the direction of your bed, not in the direction of the docks where I am very tempted to take ship as my older brother and so many of my clan have before me."

"Then why are you here?"

Because I cannot remain away from your side.

Augusta was slow to translate his Gaelic. Slow and unsure.

"I'm here because something greater than wisdom compels me to be here, Augusta. I'll leave if you like, and I won't come back, but as early as this weekend Altsax might attempt to announce a betrothal and then . . ."

"Then, no more heeding things greater than wisdom."

"I fear not." He rolled his head on his neck. "I *vow* not. You have my word on that. Regardless of the outcome of Altsax's schemes, I will do nothing to jeopardize your standing in the eyes of your family."

So their time was running out, as they'd both known it would. "Come to bed." She patted the place beside her. "What do you want to know about Trevisham?"

He did indeed interview her, though Augusta almost didn't realize what he was about. He started by asking her to recount her memories of the place, to describe its metes and bounds, the size of its herds and the reckonings of its various harvests. She was surprised at how much detail she recalled.

"And what of Altsax?"

"It's a pretty little place in a pretty corner of Kent," Augusta said, drawing a pattern on Ian's chest as she spoke. "Very little of the land around it was entailed with the manor, though, so it was sold off in lean times until it became not much more than a home farm and some tenancies. Mama said her younger brothers were welcome to squabble over it."

"And Gribbony?"

"I never saw it. Papa said we needed to make the trip some year, as it was part of my birthright, but then it became time for my come-out, and life unraveled shortly after that."

"Unraveled. That's a good word." He sucked in a sharp breath as Augusta's hand drifted lower. "A very good word."

"Ian?"

"Beloved?"

How she loved it when he spoke in his native language. "Last night, you mentioned something about a woman being on her knees before the man. How would that work?"

As a young fellow at university, Ian had quickly realized he needed to exercise judgment in his amatory affairs. Reasonably good looks, some charm, and a title dangling a few branches over on the family tree meant women took an interest in him often before he took more than a passing interest in them.

It became second nature to keep a running mental catalogue.

That one, for all her flirtation, would want him to read to her in bed rather than romp.

This one would be great fun, until it was time to part, in which case she'd turn into an emotional barnacle.

The other wasn't so very pretty, but she had a great sense of humor and wouldn't cling.

Augusta's hand drifted down his abdomen, nigh stealing his wits.

"Last night, you mentioned something about a woman being on her knees before the man. How would that work?"

He trapped her hand before it could wander any lower. "That's a dangerous question, Augusta." Dangerous to *him,* because Augusta wasn't fitting into any of his catalogue compartments. She wasn't a romp; she wasn't a fling; she wasn't anything casual at all.

She was a woman with whom he could *build* something, build a life. A woman with whom he could be not just a casual partner or a cordial spouse, but a lover. A woman with whom he could share such trust; anything would be possible between them.

And while he was fending off a great load of regret—he could offer her nothing but poverty and long winters, assuming he could disentangle himself from Genie—Augusta wrapped his cock in a firm, warm grip. "This part of you fascinates me."

She was asking him for permission. He was helpless to deny her when their time was so limited. "Do what you will with me, Augusta, but turnabout is fair play." Assuming there was an occasion for it.

He suffered her exploration all over again, more intimately than he'd done the previous night, because her touch revealed more confidence—confidence in her welcome and in herself as a woman. She ran her fingers over his length, exploring the soft skin of the crown, then along his shaft to sift through the down at the base.

"These are the oddest bits."

His balls, of course. "They're a man's most delicate bits too. That feels good."

She cupped him. "Will you show me that business about being on my knees before you?"

"Of course." And lest she start making him a

list, he shifted her so she was straddling him. "Kiss me, Augusta. I'll show you the world if you'll kiss me."

Her expression was a combination of confusion and curiosity. Ian flexed his hips, and the confusion faded.

"We can join like this, can't we?" She seemed delighted at the idea.

"Kiss me, *beloved of my heart*." She leaned down, braced herself on her hands, and brushed her mouth over his. She was smiling, the baggage. Ian flexed his hips again, teasing her sex while she teased his mouth.

"Ian MacGregor . . ."

Whatever else she might have said was lost in her sigh as Ian used one hand to gently knead her breast and the other to guide himself to her. This wasn't the most prudent position if a man wanted to protect his lady from conceiving. It was difficult to withdraw, difficult to *want* to withdraw.

Impossible to want to withdraw.

With Augusta, what *was* possible was to put her pleasure ahead of his own. While she hung over him, her kisses temporarily suspended, he set up a languid rhythm. By half inches, he penetrated her body then retreated, all the while using his hands to caress her breasts, to anchor her to him, to stroke his fingers over the planes and angles of her face.

"Ian, this is . . ." Her voice was a whisper in the darkness.

"Tell me."

"I want to move." She shifted closer to him, onto her forearms. "I *must* move."

"Move then." Though he didn't stop his own flexing and withdrawing. The pleasure of it was wondrous, such a combination of satisfying and arousing, he could maintain such a pace all night.

She hitched closer still and moved right into his rhythm, deepening the penetration and obliterating any fool notion that he could last all night.

"I like this, Ian."

She got her teeth on his earlobe; he closed his thumb and forefinger around one rosy nipple in self-defense. "I like it too. I like it so much I want it to last, Augusta."

He wanted it to last for the rest of his life.

Except Augusta, clever lady, chose that moment to discover she had muscles in places designed to drive a man beyond any restraint. She let go of his ear and fused her mouth to his just as she used her body to glove his cock with a momentary tightness.

"Augusta, you must not . . ."

She did it again, and again, and *Ian* came unraveled. He lashed his arm low across her back and drove into her, hard, and then, when she started keening against his throat, harder still. Pleasure engulfed him, then drowned him when he felt her body fisting around him in tight, wringing convulsions.

His awareness of everything save the woman to whom he was joined dissolved, leaving only pleasure, wonder, and oneness for a few shining moments until Augusta collapsed onto his chest in a boneless, panting heap.

It helped to feel the warm, comforting weight of her on his body. Helped Ian recover from the unprecedented intensity of his orgasm, helped him fix his attention on something real and precious.

"Tell me I didn't hurt you, *my heart*." He stroked his hands over the length of her back, traced her spine with his fingers, and buried his lips in her hair. "Augusta?"

She snuggled closer and nuzzled his neck, which was answer enough. They remained entwined for a long time, while Ian tried not to regret what had just passed between them.

It was one thing to long for what was forbidden. It was another thing entirely to taste the forbidden fruit and learn just how luscious it was.

"Ian?" She kept his earlobe between her teeth as she spoke.

"My heart?"

"Now will you show me the part about being on my knees before you?"

• • •

He showed her how it worked when she was on her knees, clinging to the headboard of the bed and trying not to scream, and how it worked when he let her drowse on her side as he loved her gently from behind. By the time dawn came stealing along, Augusta felt as if she'd changed yet another increment from the timid mouse tending chickens in Oxford.

Changed for the better.

"I want you to know something, Ian MacGregor." She sat beside him on the edge of the bed while he shrugged into his shirt.

"This sounds serious."

"It is. I'm going to try to stop you from marrying Genie."

He was silent for a moment. She could feel him weighing his words before he spoke. "Augusta, I believe we agreed . . ."

She put her fingers over his lovely, lovely mouth. "Hear me out. I know you must marry for money, but I also know you deserve to marry a woman who understands it's a privilege to be your countess."

"It's no bloody damned privilege to pay coin for a man's title, lass. I deserve the women who deserve me."

"Stubborn, MacGregor, but what about Genie? Doesn't she deserve some chance at happiness? She'll be miserable married to you."

He scrubbed a hand over his face, looking haunted in the bedroom's shadows. "I know this. I've tried to reason with her, but I get the sense she wants to marry me to protect me from Altsax's vituperation, and I'm to marry her to protect her from his violence."

"Matthew can take measures to protect his sister."

"You're the second person to make this pronouncement, but I've yet to hear it from Daniels himself. Daniels, who had damned well better get back from his infernal business before Mary Fran's heart breaks, or I'll hunt the man down myself."

"He'll come back." Augusta stroked her hand over Ian's disheveled hair. "He promised Fee he'd be back."

"That's something. We none of us would disappoint Fee apurpose, but about this other, Augusta, you must desist. The baron is not to be trusted. Genie says he'll announce a betrothal at the ball just to force my hand, and I have to agree with her."

"Announcements do not vows make. If I have this week, then give me this week to see what might be done."

He peered at her for a long moment, looking as if some further admonishment hovered on the tip of his tongue, and then his lips quirked up. "I can't stop you, can I?"

She smiled at him, a radiant, joyous benediction because he understood he *could* not stop her, and because he would not try. "Of course, you can't stop me."

"Then promise me you'll be careful, my heart. I do not trust Altsax one bit. Do not trust that even the most clever scheme will be enough to see that man put in his place. Promise me you'll take *no* risks while you're seeing what might be done, and be damned careful."

The Scottish peerage could put on all the airs and graces it pleased, but from what Altsax had seen in the Balfour household, there was little of true aristocracy about it. The servants, for example, were friendly and eager to please.

In the Altsax household, they knew better than to be eager, for God's sake.

The child—Fiona, little more than a bastard—was indulged by the household at large, supervised by the household at large, and had the run of the household at large. Altsax almost pitied Balfour, having to find a spouse for such a hoyden. She already had her mother's wicked red hair, as if that weren't burden enough.

And the younger sons . . . They trailed after the earl like loyal hounds, guarding his flank, taking his orders. In a proper household, one would be consigned to the church and the other would be off in the hinterlands serving Queen and Country.

They'd each make an effort to produce a few sons as duty required, but here among the Scots? Not a legitimate male child among them.

They simply had *no* idea how to go on.

Which was part of their backward, titled charm.

A footman knocked on the library door, paused inside the room to bow to the baron, then deposited a salver of mail on the estate desk dominating one end of the room. The baron kept his eyes trained on the book in his lap until the man took a silent leave.

The amount of mail Balfour had to read each day was appalling, and most of it appeared to be personal correspondence. Smudged, faded, and travel worn, a prodigious number of missives bore the simple return address: MacGregor, Boston. Or more common yet, MacGregor, N.S. Canada.

They apparently propagated like fleas when there wasn't a title involved. Altsax shuffled through the stack of letters, seeing two from his own solicitors, which was all well and good.

They would pass along to Balfour exactly what Altsax wanted them to and nothing more. He sorted through more mail until he came to a cream envelope bearing . . .

The Seal of the House of Gotha and Saxe-Coburg?

From His Highness, Albert . . .

Altsax had to sit, never before having had the

privilege of seeing, much less holding, a piece of truly royal correspondence. Royal mail to a bumpkin of an earl. It symbolized every injustice ever done a lowly baron.

He set the missive down. It was likely a regret for the weekend's ball. Royalty could hardly be bothered to watch the locals every time one of them took a notion to sport about in his plaid—though it would be the occasion of Genie's engagement.

Altsax picked up the envelope then set it down again.

This ball would see all his plans and hard work brought to fruition, while Balfour stood helpless to do anything but smile and accept congratulations.

Altsax stole a glance at the door then rummaged in the desk for a penknife. Sealing wax was sealing wax, and Altsax had been slitting seals and reclosing them since he'd been a boy. How else would he have learned the terms of Merrick's will and where it had been stored for safe-keeping?

He scanned the contents of the Prince Consort's epistle, then got up to pace. It wasn't simply a rejection of the weekend's invitation. It was a regret for the ball but an acceptance for the next day's hunt—along with a tidily noted addendum to the body of the letter. Those few words contained information that could bring everything the baron held dear—his wealth, his rank, his influence, his *title*—crashing down around him in disgrace if he were not exceedingly careful.

He pocketed the letter and headed for his room.

Mary Fran's full lips were compressed, and her expression suggested to Augusta that she hated the summer ball. Not the planning and organizing of it, not seeing her brothers in all their Highland finery, not seeing how excited Fee got as the day drew closer.

She hated the ball itself.

"You are glowering, my lady. Have I done something to offend?" Augusta posed the question gently, lest Mary Fran direct that glower at her.

"All this nonsense offends," Mary Fran said, glancing around the ballroom. "There won't be a flower left in the garden, and the ice alone will beggar us."

"He'll come back, Mary Fran." Augusta couldn't keep the words behind her teeth, given the memories Mary Fran had of balls and swains and the consequences those associations had to bear for her. "Matthew is honorable. If he told you and Fee he'd be back, he will be."

"I'm that obvious?"

"You're that in love."

Rather than meet Mary Fran's gaze, Augusta busied herself arranging flowers for a small centerpiece. To her pleasure and surprise, Mary Fran had been willing to follow Augusta's suggestion to keep the centerpieces low and therefore simple, and to use mostly heather to keep the air fresh and the tenor of the gathering Scottish.

"You wouldn't begrudge me your cousin's affections?" Mary Fran put her question quite casually and nudged at the flowers on the next table over.

"Let's take a break," Augusta said. "And no, we will not ring for tea."

She linked her arm through Mary Fran's and led the way out to the terraces, where footmen were setting up torches and tables, and maids scurried in all directions. Mary Fran drew out her pocket flask when she and Augusta got to the first bench behind the privet hedge.

"A medicinal nip is in order." Mary Fran passed over the little leather-covered flask, and Augusta opened the thing without even glancing around to see which of the maids and footmen were remarking this departure from strict decorum.

"Powerful medicine." And there was a kind of nourishment in its heat that had nothing to do with keeping the belly quiet.

"Each time we put on one of these fancy-dress affairs, I hate it a little more." Mary Fran had never sounded so weary of spirit, so dis-enchanted.

After a few more desultory exchanges, Mary Fran closed her eyes and tipped her head back to rest it against the sturdy gray stones of Balfour House.

"Matthew will lead you out, and then you won't hate it so much ever again," Augusta said.

Mary Fran was quiet for a moment before replying. "What gave us away?"

The whisky was making them brave, or foolish. In either case, Augusta wasn't going to dissemble. "You look at Matthew the way I look at Ian."

"You don't wait up for me." Ian's first boot hit the floor with a thump. "Is that because you know I'll spend every minute I can with you—despite all sense and intentions to the contrary—or because you believe each visit is the last?"

His second boot came off, and then he was removing his clothing in an order Augusta had come to know as his routine: waistcoat, shirt, stockings, breeches. He was completely at home in his skin, which only made what she had to tell him all the more difficult.

"You might have reason not to stay with me tonight."

He looked up from where he was using the wash water across the room, his expression wary. "And why is that?"

She searched for words while he frowned at her. "I am indisposed."

"Indis—oh." His expression shifted from guarded to sympathetic in a blink. "I can fetch you a wee dram. Mary Fran swears by it when she's crampy."

"No, thank you. I'm not uncomfortable, just untidy."

"Augusta Merrick, if you think I'm going to let that stop me from joining you in that bed . . . The ball is in a few days, the shoot the following morning. Our time is running out."

"I read over the contracts again today." Twice, and she couldn't escape the nagging feeling there were loopholes in them somewhere. Loopholes large enough that she could sight some happiness through them—for Ian, for Genie, and maybe even a little bit for herself.

"You should have the documents damned well memorized by now. Scoot over." He took over the bed like an incoming tide. She could scoot or not; it made no difference, because he'd put her exactly where he wanted her. With equal parts strength and care, he'd shift her around on the bed, move pillows, and rearrange covers until things were to his liking.

"What do you know of the Gribbony barony, my heart?" He enveloped her from behind, his arm coming around her waist.

"You've asked me that before. I'm not even

sure where it is—not far from the border, I think."

"North or south of the border?" Through her nightgown she could feel his hand move lower, over her womb.

"North. It's an old Scottish title. That's all I know of it. My grandfather was quite proud of it, and Papa referred to it as part of my birthright."

"You're sure it's Scottish?"

"A Lord of Parliament, which I think can only be Scottish."

"Aye, our version of a barony. You'd tell me if you hurt, wouldn't you, Augusta?"

She sighed as his hand began to gently knead her belly. "I'd tell you that feels lovely."

He was silent for a long moment, his hand working wonders, his very presence a comfort beyond words. "I never meant to hurt you, Augusta. I'm more sorry for that than I can say."

She rolled over to peer at him in the moon shadows. "It isn't like that, Ian. To think of you having to marry another . . . that is painful, but I want you to be happy. To think of never having shared this bed with you, to think of never having known you intimately . . . that would be *unbearable*." She meant every word, despite the lump in her throat, despite the tears pricking the backs of her eyes.

This was what it meant to love a man, to be in love with him, but those words would only hurt him.

"I do not deserve these sentiments, lass."

"You do not deserve to be forced into marriage with a woman who cannot appreciate you."

He again looked like he'd say something, then sighed and nuzzled her neck instead—an admission that they were once more at *point non plus*. She arranged him in her arms, his cheek pillowed on her shoulder, and held him until sleep claimed them both.

Ian sifted and sorted through his mail one more time, but the contents remained the same.

"What are you looking for?" Gil closed the door as he entered the library.

"I don't know. A sign from God, a letter from the damned solicitors, something from that Post-Williams fellow . . ."

Gil sidled over and propped a hip on the desk. "Post-who fellow?"

"He jilted Augusta, though he thinks she did the jilting."

"That doesn't make sense. Who jilted whom is hard to mistake, but what relevance is it to you?"

"Augusta Merrick's situation troubles me."

Gil crossed his arms, pursed his lips and quirked one eyebrow. Ian shoved out of his chair and crossed to the sideboard.

"She's the poor relation, Gil, but she had marital prospects that mysteriously disappeared exactly when she needed them most. I'm in a position to investigate this mystery, and I owe the woman."

"What do you owe her?"

"Excuse me?" Hester Daniels stood in the door, looking young, pretty, and uncertain. How much had she overheard?

"Miss Hester, you're looking quite fetching today." Ian smiled at the girl, glad to have somebody derail Gil's interrogation.

"Miss Hester." Gil's signature smile would have blinded entire convents of nuns. "What have you there?"

"It's a letter addressed to his lordship." She advanced into the room, pulling the door closed behind her. "I'm not sure how it came to be with my own correspondence, but I thought you should have it." She passed Ian a plain missive with a return address in Kent.

"My thanks, Miss Hester. Will you be joining the ladies on the lawn when we shoot this weekend?"

She grimaced. "The sight of dead animals . . ."

"We'll spare you that," Gil assured her. "We field dress the game in the woods, and it goes straight to the venison locker or the kitchens. Have you ever fired a gun, Miss Hester?"

"Papa is a crack shot, but no, I've never felt the inclination."

"Perhaps you'll let me show you how it's done?" Gil somehow put humility into his

361

flirtation. The man was truly amazing. "When we're finished in the woods, I'll find you."

"I'll be guarding the desserts." She dipped a little curtsy and left them alone, taking Gil's smiles with her.

"What was that about?" Ian asked. He frowned at the envelope she'd passed him. Whom did he know in Kent?

"Hester goes with Annie down to the village to get the mail each morning," Gil said. "If something showed up in her correspondence, it's because she put it there."

"What are you saying, Gilgallon? I do not attribute nefarious motives to that girl, though her father is another matter."

Gil's frown became thoughtful. "Maybe it's her father's tampering she's trying to protect us from."

"What do you mean?" But as he asked the question, Ian had a mental vision of the baron sitting by the windows reading, every morning after breakfast. Reading while the post would have been brought in . . .

"The baron tampered with Augusta's mail," Ian said slowly. "She's almost sure of it. The only letters to get through to her were from Hester, who was off in boarding school. Her cousins never got her letters to them, either."

Gil grimaced. "One or two letters going astray is not unusual . . . Whom is this one from?"

Ian opened the letter, a single page in a tidy, legible handwriting.

"Henry Post-Williams, Augusta's jilt. I honestly didn't expect to hear back from him."

"What does he have to say?"

Ian started reading, and when he was through, he began cursing in four different languages.

"I took the liberty of having Genie execute the contracts." The baron smiled at his host as he fired off that cannon, but Balfour did an admirable job of showing no reaction.

"Is that prudent, Baron? I might make changes to the documents after she's put her hand to them."

"And then she'd have to initial each change, or I'd have grounds for accusing you of bad faith."

Balfour appeared to consider the baron's friendly reminder, passing over a tumbler of whisky as he did. "Did you have her signature witnessed?"

"Of course, Balfour. She's of age, so I had my valet and footman serve as witnesses. Excellent drink, as always."

"To your health." Balfour saluted with his drink, the man's hands remarkably steady for an earl who'd just lost his every freedom. He'd marry Genie; he'd vote the way Altsax told him to; he'd be seen where and when Altsax directed.

All in all, the earl was about to become a neutered Scottish hound on a very short, tight English leash.

The pleasure of that image was almost . . . sexual.

"You will understand if I am not quite ready to sign the documents myself?" Balfour sauntered over to the window. "I have yet to hear from any reliable source regarding the income from the Gribbony barony."

Nor would he. Altsax pasted a comparably bland expression on his face and joined his host at the window. "The Gribbony barony is more ceremonial than anything else, not even a true barony, really, but one of those old Scottish squiredoms. The income is negligible. I can give you my word on that."

Balfour studied his drink. "That leaves me with a mystery, then, Altsax, because the income reflected from the Altsax properties is also negligible—your solicitors were forthcoming in that regard—and I'm unaware of investments that would account for the rest of what you claim is the family's income."

"What exactly are you implying?" Altsax injected as much frost as possible into his tone. "You bruit it about that my finances are anything but spotlessly in order, Balfour, and I will shut down this little hostel you're running in the Queen's backyard, ruin your brothers' prospects in trade, and see what remains of your sister's reputation dragged through the sewers."

Balfour smiled slightly and took a measured sip of his drink. "Bad form, Baron, threatening the prospective groom before the documents are signed. I want the funds Genie will bring to the marriage—on that let there be no mistake—but I'm beginning to see those funds might come at too high a price."

So the gloves were to come off? Altsax smiled and touched the back of his host's hand with one finger, as if they were conspiring together over some shared secret. "Rattle those old claymores all you like, Balfour. I understand tattered Scottish pride and the need to posture, but balk at this engagement now, and I will bring you and what remains of your family to your bony Scottish knees."

He clinked their glasses, tossed back his whisky, and left the room with the satisfaction of having the last—and only important—words.

Balfour would come to heel, the engagement would be announced at the ball, and the very next day, amid the confusion and camaraderie of an organized hunt, dear Augusta would find her eternal reward.

What a fitting end to a very tedious excuse for a holiday.

Fourteen

"YOU NEED TO KNOW WHAT'S AFOOT." IAN snagged Con by the arm as they ambled down the aisle of the horse barn.

"From your expression, nothing good."

"I cannot marry Genie Daniels, and there will be damages."

Con stopped midstride, treating Ian to a close perusal. "What brought on this insight?"

Ian dropped his brother's arm and paced off a few steps. "Several things. I have to marry for money, but you're right—marrying Genie Daniels isn't the answer. I gave Altsax a perfect opening to explain to me that his primary source of income is Trevisham, a property he inherited—or claims he inherited—from his older sister, Augusta Merrick's mother. He not only failed to mention the property, he also intimated the Scottish barony he holds is of no consequence either."

"You suspect something underhand?"

"I don't need to suspect it. Henry Post-Williams had an understanding with Augusta at the time her parents died. Their fathers were at the point of drawing up the agreements, and Mr. Merrick made very clear to Post-Williams that Augusta was an heiress of significant wealth. He was explicit that the entire estate of Trevisham would be hers, consistent with her mother's wishes and his own. He also suggested Augusta was due other income, but we'll probably never get to the bottom of that mare's nest."

"So the baron got away with stealing from his niece?"

"It would appear so, as the deed has long since been a fait accompli. To his credit, Post-Williams confronted the baron after Augusta had removed to Oxfordshire. He asked Altsax why a wealthy young woman was living in obscurity in the shires, but Altsax assured him it was consistent with Augusta's dearest wishes."

Ian watched while Con's features reflected consternation, then intense concentration.

"A liar and a cheat, then, but how does this get you off the marital hook?" Con stretched out a hand to old Hannibal, who came over to investigate his callers.

"It doesn't, exactly, but it might give me a great deal of leverage."

"And leave Genie where? Gil's about to elope with the girl, will she, nil she."

"No, he's not. Not yet." Ian hoped and prayed he was speaking the truth.

Con scratched the horse under the chin, which had the beast half closing its eyes in bliss. "There's a shoot coming up, Brother."

"I am aware of this."

"You aren't planning anything foolish are you?" Con's tone was particularly casual.

"If I were?"

"I'd have to ask you to refrain from foolishness. If you get yourself convicted of a felony—say manslaughter, for example—then we very likely lose the title and the lands."

"Not necessarily. I'd be tried in the Lords, and they seldom convict their own. And if I met with an untimely accident, then Gil would inherit the title and the bride who goes with it."

Con's hand on the horse's neck stilled. "He would inherit so much guilt he'd choke on it before the first child was conceived."

"Don't bet on it."

"He's not here." Mary Fran muttered the words to her oldest brother, the one she could trust not to lose his temper under any circumstances, particularly not in the entrance hall when guests were expected momentarily.

"Daniels will be here shortly, Mary Frances. Trust me." Ian's expression was genial, but there was a glint in his green eyes Mary Fran knew not to ignore.

"What do you know that you're not saying, Ian? The guests will be arriving soon, and I haven't time for intrigues and nonsense. Altsax is preening and smirking like he knows something we don't."

"He probably knows many things we don't. Are the musicians here?"

"A twelve-piece orchestra, for the love of God. A simple quartet wouldn't do?"

She was arranging the folds of his small kilt, repinning the clan brooch, fussing with the Scotch pine in his bonnet until Ian closed his fingers around her hand. "Settle, woman. A twelve-piece orchestra of our cousins is twelve more stout fellows to keep the peace if matters grow unruly. All will be well, despite how bleak things might seem now."

"You should be marrying Augusta." She'd surprised him, that was some satisfaction, though his expression quickly shuttered.

"You'd best be keeping such sentiments to yourself, Mary Frances MacGregor."

"Flynn." She spoke softly. "I married a Flynn. My daughter is a Flynn."

"And as far as I know, I'm not marrying anybody, not in the immediate future. It might cost us greatly, but there's no amount of coin that would justify taking our chances with Altsax on his terms."

He meant it, which was a wonderful relief. "Do Con and Gil know?"

"They applaud my decision, though I'm not sure they'll sing the same tune when Altsax starts in with his ranting and lawyering."

"You're not going to publicly humiliate the man, are you? He's worse than the average Englishman, Ian. Matthew doesn't trust him in the least."

Ian flashed a smile at her, a false, friendly smile that alerted her to the front doors opening.

Not Matthew, but rather, the first of their guests. Mary Fran took her place beside her brother and tried not to let her anxiety show.

The ball gown was borrowed, but nonetheless magnificent.

"You must wear it." Hester stroked a hand over the midnight-blue velvet. The trim was a bright red-and-blue four-square tartan plaid, crossed at the bodice and flowing up over the shoulders of a gracefully scooped neckline. The same plaid detail plunged in a dramatic inverted vee to the hem, accentuating the hourglass turn of a lady's figure.

"I haven't anything of my own grand enough for a ball," Augusta said. "And I haven't danced for years." And she should not let herself be tempted by Mary Fran's generosity.

"You'll offend our hostess if you don't wear it," Hester said. "I think the trim is one of the MacGregor tartans, maybe the one for dancing."

"Not the dancing plaid—that's green and white. This is the one for the local branch of the family." Augusta's fingers trailed along the hem. "I suppose I could watch from the minstrel's gallery."

"Nonsense. You will sit with me as a chaperone would. Julia has eyes only for Connor of late, and

I'm sure she'll be dancing with him every chance she gets."

"She might save him one waltz, Hester. She's not going to flaunt propriety while Altsax is at hand."

"There's something I've been meaning to tell you." Hester stepped away from where the dress hung on the wardrobe door and sat herself on Augusta's bed. "I miss your cat."

"I miss him too, but that wasn't what you intended to say."

"Do you recall getting letters from me when you moved to Oxford?"

"Yes, I do. They were a particular comfort, as I received almost no other mail."

Augusta crossed the room to sit next to her cousin. Somewhere along the way, Hester had grown into a young lady of both sense and beauty. If Hester had something to say, Augusta intended to listen.

"Well, you got letters from Mr. Post-Williams, after you went up to Oxford."

"I did?"

Hester nodded, her gaze on the pretty ball gown hanging a few feet away. "Papa is not a gentleman."

"You needn't point out the obvious, Hester, though if I were any kind of influence on you, I'd tell you not to disrespect your elders."

"He reads other people's mail. The letters from

Post-Williams? I saw three when I wasn't off at school, and I don't think any of them were forwarded to you. When we'd visit at Trevisham when I was a little girl, I'd catch Papa going through the mail before Uncle came down to breakfast. I think he's still doing it."

"Going through the mail?"

Hester nodded, her expression disgruntled. "I saw another letter from Post-Williams, this one addressed to his lordship. I kept it back then passed it along to Lord Balfour. I hope that was the right thing to do."

"If you saw it into Ian's hands, then that wasn't wrong." But what could the letter have said, and what had the three letters Altsax had pilfered said?

"He's a widower, you know."

Augusta peered over at her cousin. "Who is?"

"Mr. Post-Williams. He's widowed. He was making the rounds earlier this year, supposedly looking for a mother to his children. I think he's lonely."

"He's . . . widowed?" Augusta waited for this information to register, waited for some elemental shift in her heart, to know the man who'd offered for her, the man to whom she'd given her virginity, was again available and seeking a wife.

But she felt . . . nothing, except a vague wish he'd find eventual happiness, or at least a decent mother for his children.

"Augusta, Mr. Post-Williams doesn't need to marry for money this time. He's quite well set up now. Genie's friends were very explicit in that regard."

"Then I wish Genie's friends the joy of him. When it came down to it, he was set to spend his life with me one day and willing to accept his congé from Uncle and Aunt the next."

Hester's gaze was troubled. "Is that how it was?"

"More or less." But what had his letters said? And had the baron forged replies supposedly from Augusta in response?

"You should renew your acquaintance with him, Gus. He might be a prospect, and you can't tell me you'd rather raise chickens in the shires than be a mother to a decent man's children."

Augusta opened her mouth to reply then shut it as a truth settled around her heart.

"Yes, Hester, I can so tell you that very thing. Being a glorified governess to another woman's children is not preferable to raising my chickens, not when I'm expected to be grateful for the attentions of a man who deserted me years ago."

And this insight was squarely, purely, and utterly Ian MacGregor's fault. Augusta smiled at the realization.

There was no longer any need to defend her bucolic little life from criticisms and pity. It was a life that had allowed her to love and love fiercely when she'd been given the chance, to experience the soul-nourishing joy of mutual desire and respect, however briefly.

Augusta rose from the bed and took the ball gown down from its hanger. "You'll help me figure out what to do with my hair?"

Hester hopped off the bed and made straight for Augusta's vanity. "Of course, I'll help—and you won't be hiding in the minstrel's gallery."

"I won't."

But Augusta would steal another half hour for herself in the library, where she would read those benighted damned contracts just one more time.

The reception line had disbanded, the guests were swilling spirits at a great rate, and the musicians were tuning up. The ballroom was a lovely sight, decorated with both the finest flowers from Ian's gardens, and the finest flowers of the local gentry as well as the English community that formed each summer around the sovereign's retreat to Balmoral.

Altsax appeared at Ian's elbow, looking choleric in his evening attire. "I think an announcement just before the supper waltz makes the most sense."

The man had an eye for the dramatic, since Ian stood at the top of the grand staircase, every eye upon him. He'd open the dancing, of course, usually by dancing with the highest-ranking lady in the assemblage—which was sometimes his own sister and once had been the Queen herself.

"It's risky to count your chickens before they hatch, Baron. If we should for some reason be unable to come to terms, there are plenty of representatives of London society here who will recall your announcement, and it will not devolve to your daughter's credit."

"We've come to the only terms I'm willing to offer, Balfour. Genie has signed the documents, and it would be a nice touch if you'd do likewise this very evening."

A nice touch, and the death of Ian's hopes, dreams, and honor. "Except you've shown the next thing to bad faith, Baron, by withholding financial information critical to my decision."

Altsax visibly expanded, like a cat puffing out its fur to appear larger and more menacing. "You dare to accuse me of bad faith? You, who charge your in-laws for the very bread you put before them?"

He was keeping his voice down, as Ian had known he would. The baron was acutely aware of appearances, one of few advantages Ian could count on.

"I have no in-laws as we speak, Baron, though I think Connor's getting ideas about Mrs. Redmond."

That stopped whatever tirade the baron had

been winding up to. "Julia is going to stoop to taking that . . . that kilted brute to the altar?"

"That brute is my baby brother, Baron. Smile. This is a social occasion, and these people are my friends and neighbors."

The baron didn't smile, but he wiped the incredulity from his face. "I'll take matters into my own hands, Balfour. Make the announcement myself."

"And won't that look odd, with nary a single Scottish groom to be seen when you do?"

Ian walked off, letting the baron sputter himself to silence. From the corner of Ian's eye, he saw Mary Fran standing by the door, her expression perfectly serene except for the anxiety pinching the corners of her smile. Daniels the Younger had better be showing up soon, or Ian would be the one sputtering.

He conferred with the concertmaster—his third cousin, Doungal MacGregor—and made sure the drink was flowing freely. Ian was running out of ways to stall when he spotted his quarry.

In a gown that appeared to have been sewn onto her, Augusta looked magnificent. She'd piled some of her hair softly upon her head but left long, fat curls draping down over her pale shoulders. Ian took the space of two breaths just to drink in the sight of her.

Magnificent, lovely, beautiful . . . neither English nor Gaelic had vocabulary sufficient to do justice to the lady, or to the feelings the sight of her engendered in Ian's heart.

Doungal caught Ian's nod and signaled to the orchestra to put down their drinks and take their places. While the entire room looked on, Ian crossed the empty dance floor to Augusta's side.

"My lady, you are a vision."

She dipped a graceful curtsy. "My lord, I am indebted to your sister for my borrowed finery."

He leaned nearer but spoke loudly enough to be overheard by the crowd. "Perhaps your finery is borrowed, but as for what's in it, we can give fervent thanks only to the Almighty. May I have this dance, Miss Merrick?"

A little color came into her cheeks, though she remained composed. Her smile was sweet and genuine, not a ballroom showpiece intended to condescend. "I would be honored."

He led her out to the center of the room, her gloved hand resting on his knuckles. He'd quite honestly expected a little more of a fight from her, but he wanted the baron—and the baron's society—to understand that Augusta Merrick had allies. Admirers, even, because Con and Gil were going to see to it the woman danced every dance.

"I need to speak to you." Augusta's voice was calm, but as he took her in his arms, Ian felt the tension in her body.

"Can't we just enjoy a dance, Augusta? The damned baron is yapping at my heels, Genie's looking tragic, Gil is muttering about hanging felonies, Mary Fran can't take her eyes off the door, and Con has gone calf-eyed over the widow."

The orchestra started the introduction. Augusta curtsied, Ian bowed, and the waltz began.

She was like holding music in his arms. Sweet, lyrical, warm, and feminine, but substantial too. Ian thought back to his first glimpse of her— gangly, awkward, graceless, and plain but for her startling eyes. How wrong he'd been, except he had the sense she hadn't even seen herself accurately that day at the train station.

"You're fretting," he said as Con and Julia joined them on the floor, followed by Gil and Genie.

"I've done something, Ian." Like Mary Fran, Augusta's anxiety was well hidden unless a man knew where to look. "Something you will not like, but I assure you, I had the consent of all parties. All the relevant parties."

She spoke so earnestly while she floated in his arms.

"Well, we're even then, because I'm going to do things tonight I can't expect anybody to approve of."

"Ian?"

"I'm the head of this family, Augusta. I have to do what I think is right for the whole family."

"What does that mean?"

He pulled her a little closer on a sweeping turn, wishing he could just waltz her out to the gardens and explain himself to her—though he couldn't. Not until Matthew Daniels was again in their midst.

"It means whatever you hear the baron saying, whatever announcements he might trump up, you must not lose faith in me. I cannot marry Genie."

She searched his face, seeming to come to some conclusion. "No, you cannot." She smiled a little—wistfully, it seemed to him—and came more fully into his arms. It wasn't so much a matter of their bodies being closer as it was of her allowing him more responsibility for her balance.

And for the rest of the dance, he was torn between the pleasure of holding the woman he loved in his arms—for he did love her—and the need to keep a sharp eye on the baron.

And on Mary Fran.

And Con.

And Gil.

And even on Fiona, who was spying on them from the minstrel's gallery, her face pressed between the balusters.

"Ian?"

"Beloved?" He kept his voice down, because many in the room would understand the Gaelic.

"Whatever transpires later tonight, please know that"—Augusta met his gaze only fleetingly—"I will never care for another as I do for you."

He should have grabbed those words to his heart and hoarded them up for his own pleasure. Instead, he frowned down at her.

"You're scaring me, Augusta Merrick. What have you done?" If she'd taken on the old bastard Altsax by herself, he was going to shake her, assembled nobility be damned.

Before she could answer, the music drew to a close, and yet, Ian did not let her go. "Augusta, tell me."

She reached up to run her fingers down the soft wool of his plaid waistcoat. "I did what I had to do, Ian. Don't be angry."

And then she was gone, leaving Ian to realize the baron was scowling mightily and angling to intercept her. Smart lady, she shifted course for the punch bowl, which was thronged with neighbors all too willing to get to know the woman whom Ian had broken protocol to dance with.

"He's still not here." Mary Fran spoke through clenched teeth as Ian gained the edge of the ballroom.

"He sent a telegram, Mary Fran. He'll be here." Ian gave her shoulder a squeeze. "Stay close to Augusta. She's done something to incur Altsax's wrath, and I can't be by her side every minute."

Mary Fran looked intrigued, then nodded and moved off toward Augusta.

One disaster averted. Gil was escorting Genie

off the dance floor, trading partners with Con as if by arrangement. Genie was still looking haunted, probably dreading the dance Ian himself would share with her.

His moment came before supper, when he'd danced and flirted and charmed and smiled until his teeth ached—all the while intercepting desperate looks from Mary Fran and trying to keep watch over Augusta. The neighbors—mindful of whose plaid Augusta wore—were keeping Altsax from Augusta's side, and Ian's opportunities to speak with his former intended were dwindling.

"May I have this dance?" He recited his part of the litany, but Genie just stared at him, so he moved a little closer. "For God's sake, smile, or your papa will be here to know the reason why."

Her lips curved woodenly.

It was a landler, an old-fashioned partner dance enjoying a revival on the Continent, a dance that would allow Ian some chance to warn the lady of the brewing storm.

"Pay attention, Genie." He smiled and nodded, then turned away in the prescribed steps of the dance. "When you see your brother in the ballroom, get you to Gilgallon's side. Tear a hem, develop a megrim, do what you need to do to get to Gil."

She nodded, holding his gaze, but Ian honestly couldn't say if she comprehended his words.

"I'm not going to marry you, Genie Daniels."

"What will you do?"

Ah, so there was intelligent life behind those frightened blue eyes.

"You'll be safe," he said. "Gil will make sure of that."

"You should marry Augusta."

He nearly stumbled, so great was his surprise. "Miss Augusta can look forward to being courted by a Mr. Henry Post-Williams, a wealthy man much respected in English social circles."

Impatience flashed across Genie's features. "Don't be an ass, Ian MacGregor. She belongs with you, and you belong with her. I saw you coming across the park when you came back from that hike, and she'd nearly been hurt by the landslide. You didn't want to let her out of your sight."

He lost his rhythm for a moment then recovered. "I need to marry money, and Augusta deserves to resume her place in proper society. You'll keep an eye on Gil?"

"I always do."

Her smile was sad but genuine, and Ian realized whatever her hesitations and fears regarding marriage to the titled stranger chosen by her parents, they surely did not apply where Gil was concerned.

Which was a fine thing, considering she was going to end up wedded to the man.

• • •

"You're up to something." The baron's breath would have knocked a Highland regiment flat, but Augusta stood her ground among the potted ferns at the edge of the ballroom.

"I'm enjoying my first ball in years, Uncle. I think Hester and Genie are having a fine time as well."

His fingers closed painfully around her arm just above the elbow, where her evening gloves would hide any bruises. "Let them dance. This time tomorrow, Genie will be all but leg-shackled to Balfour, and I can depart for more civilized surrounds shortly thereafter."

Augusta turned so she broke his hold. "Genie has already signed the contracts."

"Of course she has, and I had her signature witnessed. Her tears of happiness were very affecting." He made another grab for her arm, one Augusta thought might have been rendered a tad clumsy with drink. She lifted her wrist corsage to her nose, blocking his maneuver easily.

"The groom has signed the documents as well, Uncle. His own brother witnessed his signature. You need not fret any further over Genie's future."

"The groom . . . ?" Altsax's expression turned crafty. "I knew he'd see reason. Has a certain animal cunning, Balfour does. And the settlements are really most favorable to him monetarily."

"I've wondered about that." Augusta took a step back and shook out her skirts. "Where does the money come from, Uncle? Your baronies are not that lucrative, and you claim Trevisham was riddled with debt. How can you afford to buy Genie this title and still plan on doing the same for Hester?"

His expression became, if anything, uglier. "You're as bad as Balfour, insinuating and implying about you know not what. The contracts are signed, and I don't owe you any explanations, my girl. You've been luckier than you know to rusticate away these years. Luckier than you deserve."

He spun on his heel, listed a little into a man standing to his left, righted himself, and stalked off, leaving Augusta to eye the door and wonder how much longer she could bear to watch Ian dancing and smiling as if he hadn't a care in the world.

Ian had spent supper at a table reserved for him, his siblings, his intended bride, her father, sister, and aunt. Augusta was noticeably absent from the family group, but Mary Fran was at his elbow, her every other glance going toward the door. Con and Gil were looking no more settled than their sister, while Julia and Hester's attempts to carry the small talk were flagging.

The baron raised his wine glass and aimed a tobacco-stained grin at Ian. "Balfour, I commend you on a delightful evening, but it's time to accept your fate. People are drifting off to the gardens, and the dancing will soon resume. Let's have an announcement, shall we?"

Where the hell was Augusta?

"Matthew!" Mary Fran's whisper carried directly to Ian's heart, the relief in her gaze suggesting she'd known exactly what Ian had charged the man with before his departure.

"Fine, Baron." Ian took a sip of good whisky. "An announcement you shall have." He dithered, straightening his sporran and fussing with the tucks of his kilt until Daniels had made his way across the dining room.

"Balfour, apologies for my tardiness. Baron, sisters, Aunt, Lady Mary Fran, I bid you a very good evening." Daniels's grave tone was at variance with his convivial words. Contrary to the rest of the gathering, he was in riding attire, his hair windblown, his clothes still reeking of dust and horse.

"Daniels, I trust your sortie was successful?" Ian put the question quietly as he got to his feet.

"Entirely successful, my lord."

Ian passed him his unfinished whisky, catching a surreptitious wink from Daniels as he accepted the glass.

The man did have Scots blood in him, a cheering thought given the occasion.

"My lords, my ladies, friends, and neighbors." Ian's voice carried across the room, creating a hush worthy of a royal proclamation. "It is always a fine occasion when we gather with our dear ones to celebrate the joys of summer, and this year my family is particularly blessed. It is my privilege and my pleasure as head of the MacGregor family to announce that Miss Eugenia Daniels, daughter of Willard Daniels, Baron of Altsax and Gribbony, and our guest for these past few weeks, will be joining the MacGregor family. Her brother, Matthew, has been good enough to procure a special license for the occasion, and I'm sure you'll join with me in congratulating *my brother Gilgallon Concannon MacGregor* on his great good fortune."

Ian started the applause, grateful he'd thought to position his brothers between Genie and her father. Daniels was standing by the baron's chair, a restraining hand on his father's shoulder.

When the clapping and cheering—and ribald good wishes—died down, Ian spoke again.

"You will excuse us as a family if we repair to the library for a wee dram. Doungal has his musicians at the ready, and the footmen have been told nary a guest may go thirsty. Enjoy!"

More applause, which provided a perfect backdrop for Con and Daniels to hustle the splenetic baron from the room. Gil had his arm around Genie, and Hester and Mary Fran took over the task of accepting congratulations as the other family members processed from the room.

All in all, it had gone better than Ian could have hoped, *but where in the hell was Augusta?*

The library door was closed and latched, Con and Daniels positioned on either side of the door when the baron started in ranting.

"You cannot get away with this, Balfour! I'll sue you for breach of promise. I'll drag your family's wretched Scottish name through so much offal you'll be happy to raise pigs in Nova Scotia. You'll be the laughingstock of the realm before I'm through with you, and you"—he turned a vicious glare on Genie—"you'll be lucky if I can sell you to a poxy old squire for breeding purposes after this night's work."

"Enough." Ian advanced on the baron, whose nose was positively glowing with ire and strong drink. "Your daughter's happiness should mean more to you than any damned title. I've not signed the contracts. You have no grounds for breach. Genie cannot testify against Gil once they're wed, so you have no case."

"Have no case!" The baron positively shrieked. "I'll try this in the courts! I'll try this in the court of public opinion! I'll—"

Gil moved so quickly Ian couldn't stop him. In the blink of an eye, Altsax was crammed against the paneling, eyes bulging, his breath wheezing from his lungs.

"You will shut up, old man. I've *signed those contracts myself,* before a sober, adult witness, and they are legal and binding."

"But you're not Balfour!" the baron hissed.

Gil eased his elbow from the baron's throat, and a moment of odd silence descended.

Augusta had done this. Ian's brain reeled to think she'd seen Gil's hand set to the very contracts, something Ian hadn't thought to do. Ian's mind started parsing the legalities, the details, the language he himself had written even as Gil spoke quietly to his future father-in-law.

"This is a fait accompli, Baron. Your best course is to put a good face on it and wish your daughter well."

"I will never capitulate to this farce. Those contracts were unassailably clear. I read them myself."

But so, apparently, had somebody a hell of a lot smarter than the baron.

Fifteen

"ALTSAX"—IAN KEPT HIS TONE CONCILIATORY as the library went silent with tension—"you specified that the groom had to be in expectation of a title. Gilgallon here is Viscount Deesely and my heir. That's more than expectation, Baron.

You specified that Genie had to be hostess at Balfour during Her Majesty's residence at Balmoral. I have every confidence Mary Fran will be handing over those reins at the first opportunity. You further specified that Genie had to be free to attend the social Season in the South, and I can assure you—should she desire to exert herself so—Gilgallon will happily escort her to every single function."

Gil stepped back and went to Genie's side, leaving the baron looking rumpled and mortally disgruntled.

"We've brought the parson along with the licenses," Ian went on. "You can look a fool, Baron, or appear to be a doting papa. It's your choice, and regardless of your choice, Gil and Genie will be marrying and living happily ever after."

"As will Julia and I." Con stepped forward and put an arm around the widow. "Assuming she'll have me."

The baron's face was a study in shades of ire. While Ian watched, murderous rage faded into consternation, then disgust, then—after a short battle with renewed anger—contempt.

"Have your farce, then, the lot of you. Your double farce. Litter the shire with your mongrel get. Dance about in your heathen skirts while you swill your vile concoctions and amuse Her Majesty with your barbarian regalia. Hester and I will be departing immediately following the nuptials, which I assume will be tomorrow."

"After the shoot," Ian said. "And don't trouble yourself with an announcement in the *Times*, Baron. I will see to that detail."

The baron sniffed, straightened his cuffs, and left the room at an angry stalk.

"Drinks." Mary Fran made directly for the sideboard, going for the family decanter. "I was hoping the man would have an apoplexy, but he's too cussed to be so accommodating." She glanced over at Matthew. "My pardon for insulting your father."

"I've had my doubts about that," Daniels said quietly, "but a drink would be appreciated."

Con sidled up to his brother while Julia passed out the drinks Mary Fran poured. "You knew I asked Daniels to procure a license for Julia and me?"

"I suspected." Ian smiled at his brother, realizing belatedly that Con was asking for not just his brother's approval, but his laird's blessing. "You've chosen well, baby brother."

"She's English." Con seemed perplexed by this.

"In the dark, we're not English or Scottish, Con. We're just men and women, and we have the same needs and the same hearts. How are you going to deal with having a rich wife?"

Con's eyebrows rose, and his lips tilted up. "We'll manage. Julia is full of ideas about what to do with her money, but she says if the Queen can turn over all her correspondence to the Prince Consort, then surely a lowly wife can seek her husband's guidance on important matters."

"She's getting around you already, Connor."

"And it's the damnedest thing, Ian. I don't mind in the least, and my game of billiards has improved tremendously."

Whatever that meant.

Con took to studying his drink. "About that wealth, Ian?"

"Julia's wealth."

"Not under the law, it won't be. She'll control it, but it will be mine in name. She's very clear that we're available to see Balfour over any rough spots in the coming years. I don't trust the baron to pay up on Genie's settlement."

Ian wanted to wince and to laugh. He should be insulted. He should be ashamed. He was head of the family, not some charity case for his brother's wife to take under her wing. But the pride—the arrogance—simply couldn't be mustered. He was too happy for Con. "Please tell Julia her generosity is much appreciated. Let's hope I've no need of it."

Con looked relieved. "I thought you'd belt me, but Julia insisted."

"I am blessed in my family," Ian said, his gaze traveling to where Gil and Genie were standing as close as propriety and physics allowed.

"Congratulations, Gilgallon. Genie, welcome to the family."

They approached, still tightly seamed to each other.

"Gil explained to me you had Matthew procure the license for us," Genie said. "Please don't be offended if I say I'm looking much more forward to having you as a brother-in-law than as a husband."

"A gentleman would know how to reply to that," Ian said as Con drifted back to his lady's side. "I'll content myself with kissing the bride when the nuptials have been attended to."

"On the cheek," Gil muttered. The way he glared at Ian was heartwarming. If Ian had had the smallest doubt about the rightness of his plans, they evaporated at the sight of Gil's protectiveness.

"When did Augusta have you sign the contracts?" Ian put the question casually, but the answer mattered.

"Just after the receiving line disbanded. She came flying out of the library and dragged me back in. We rounded Con up to witness my signature. It was a nice touch. My compliments on your brilliant draftsmanship."

"It had nothing to do with my draftsmanship, Gil. Augusta saw the possibilities without realizing I'd arranged for your special license."

Genie blanched. "You were willing to risk a lawsuit with my papa over this?"

"I expected a lawsuit," Ian said. "But I am trained in the law, so it loomed as just another nuisance, and being laird means dealing with a great number of those. I was not prepared for Augusta to insert herself into the equation and incur the baron's wrath as she did."

Genie's eyes clouded with concern. "You must have that settlement, Ian. You'll need it to defend against Papa's mischief."

"Absent a true disaster, I'll not be taking my brother's coin," Ian said. "Though the offer is appreciated."

"This isn't good, Ian." Gil's brows drew down. "You'll take at least some of that settlement for all the trouble you've been put to this summer, even if Altsax has sense enough to accept defeat gracefully. I thought Augusta was acting on your behalf when she had me sign those contracts."

"She wasn't, and you are to cease talk of splitting settlements. If the baron grows unruly, I'll deal with it," Ian said, but the need to find Augusta and make sure she was safe was becoming a compulsion. He turned to Daniels, who was conferring with Mary Fran by the sideboard.

"Daniels, my thanks for procuring the documents."

Daniels, Ian noted, had linked hands with Mary Fran. "My apologies for the close timing. If you'll excuse Lady Mary Frances and me, we'll go see that order is maintained in the ballroom in your absence."

Mary Fran was watching Daniels, a wistful smile playing around her mouth. "The MacDeans cannot hold their whisky," she said, "and Old Farquar gets to flirting where his missus can see. Somebody had best be keeping an eye on things."

Something had shifted between Ian's sister and Daniels, something sweet and lovely, which Mary Fran would apprise her brothers of in her own good time.

Ian kissed his sister's cheek. "To the ballroom with you, then. My thanks to you both."

"Ian?" Mary Fran caught his eye. "Thank you. For everything. If I never said it before, thank you from the bottom of my heart."

"Here, here." Con raised his glass, and Gil did likewise, the solemnity of their joy hitting Ian physically. They were his family, he'd seen to their happiness, and nothing else in his life should matter in comparison. The moment was bright with love and the satisfaction of plans for once turning out well, but beneath the pleasure and relief, Ian was still anxious.

He acknowledged their salute with a nod. "If you'll excuse me, I'm off to find a certain meddling chaperone so I might thank her as well."

And then shake some damned sense into her.

• • •

"I had to run the whole way from the minstrel's gallery to the reading balcony, and I almost didn't beat them to the library." Fiona held up Augusta's dancing slippers. "I'm going to have plaid slippers too, when I learn to dance the waltz. I'm already working on the clan dances."

"Clan dances?" Augusta asked from where she sat at her vanity.

"Flings and reels and sword dances and such." Fiona bounced off the bed and raised one hand over her head, put the other on her hip, and executed a few graceful steps. "I want to wear the dancing tartan because it goes with my eyes."

"I'm sure you'll look lovely."

Augusta took down the last pinned curl, glad for the child's company, but anxious too. "So the baron didn't threaten anybody, Fiona?"

"He turned red," Fiona said, skipping to the wardrobe. "He used a very ugly tone of voice, but the uncles talked him 'round. Then there was a lot of smiling and kissing and toasting after the baron left. Uncle Ian said Gil and Genie will live happily ever after, and Con and Matthew said they will too—not with each other, with Mrs. Redmond and Mama. Will Mrs. Redmond become a MacGregor?"

"She will." *Lucky, lucky Julia.*

"Will I become a Daniels?"

"I don't know." Augusta started brushing out

her hair, though her arm felt heavy, and a nameless sense of unease crept through her mind. Would Ian be angry with her? He'd had the situation in hand if the special licenses were any indication, and Augusta had gone charging off alone without even consulting him.

"If Matthew adopts you, Fee, then you might well be a Daniels. We'd be cousins then, though at some remove."

"I've lots of removed cousins. They go to America mostly, and Ireland, though some go from Ireland to America and Canada since the 'taties all rotted. Matthew said I'm not to worry about that, because he has pots of money, and that means I'll have pots of money too."

"You're lucky then, but Fiona? There are far more important things than having pots of money."

"Yes, like having pots of cream." Fiona grinned and twirled across the room. "Or a pony."

"Fiona." Ian stood at the door to the terrace, still attired in his Highland finery minus the bonnet. As much as it was a relief to see him, his sudden appearance—looking so stern and regal in his formal attire—was disquieting too. "You should be in bed, child, but you'll want to wish your mother good night."

"She won't yell at me for staying up so late?"

"She might, but only a little. Tonight is for celebrating, not scolding."

396

Augusta was relieved to hear that, because Ian's expression was oddly solemn for a man who had much to celebrate.

"Good night, Miss Augusta." Fee hugged Augusta briefly, treated her uncle to the same affection, and skipped out the door.

"She's happy," Ian said, crossing the room to lock the door. "But what about you, Augusta Merrick?"

"All it takes to make Fiona happy is the hope of a pony some day." Augusta resisted the urge to get to her feet as Ian stalked back across the room. "My needs are a little more complicated. I take it Gil and Genie are betrothed?"

"You know they are." He glowered down at her, plucked the hairbrush from her hand, and moved to stand behind her. "I'm grateful to you, Augusta, for taking an interest in my family's welfare, but the baron will get wind of your hand in things."

"I told him the contracts had been signed. I'm sure he's figured out I saw it done."

Ian's arms folded around her shoulders. "You took a very great risk."

He sounded . . . worried, exasperated. He did not sound pleased, and yet the scent of him as he curled against her neck was making it difficult for Augusta to think.

"I could not see any legal risk, Ian. The contracts were written so Gil could sign them."

"So you divined, but I wrote them, and I did not realize they could be interpreted that way. When Matthew told me he was haring south to procure a special license for Con and Julia, I charged him with getting one for Gil and Genie as well. You trumped my simple schemes beautifully, Augusta."

"Are you angry with me?"

He straightened, looking very tall in Augusta's vanity mirror. "I am *worried* for you, Augusta. The baron will take out his ire on somebody. I'm thinking Hester had best bide with her brother at some length—Altsax could use his youngest in some scheme to torment Genie and Gil." He started brushing her hair, making long, slow strokes from her crown to her hips. "I enjoyed dancing with you tonight, Augusta Merrick."

"You made a spectacle of me, opening the dancing that way." She closed her eyes against a growing lassitude.

"You were cheated out of years of dances, and the MacGregor plaid has never been worn to such graceful advantage."

She opened her eyes to see he was at least half smiling at her in the mirror. "Flummery, MacGregor. Arrant flummery."

"Promise me something, Augusta." He set the brush aside and crouched beside her chair so their eyes met. "Promise me when you go south, you'll take utmost care. Stay with Gil and Genie in the

London townhouse, bide with Con and Julia at her residence in Northumbria. Matthew assures me he has any number of places for you to stay where Altsax won't be able to find you. Your safety matters to me, my heart."

Augusta leaned forward to bury her face against his neck. The look in his eye could not have been more concerned. His voice was low, urgent, and sincere, but what he *wasn't* saying . . .

He expected her to go south, to put this summer idyll behind them, and really, why should he expect otherwise? He still needed to marry money, and she was still a poor relation. She'd wanted him free of Altsax's schemes, and her wish had been granted in that regard. Spectacularly, wonderfully.

Though abruptly, it felt like the wrong wish.

"I'll be careful, Ian. Matthew has assured me I need not go back to Oxfordshire."

"That's . . . good." His arms came around her. "I'll rest easier knowing you're safe."

He was silent a long moment, while Augusta was at a loss to know what he waited for.

"I'll just be going then." He said the words, but still he did not rise, and Augusta tightened her arms around his shoulders. She shook her head, words clogging in her throat.

"What, my heart? I canna divine your thoughts."

"Don't . . ." She drew in a ragged breath. "Don't go, Ian."

"All right then." His voice was a little unsteady as he stroked his hand over her hair. "I'll not leave you just yet, and you'll not leave me."

What did a man say who had nothing to offer the woman who'd risked everything she had to see him and his family happy? What did he say to the woman he loved?

There were no words worthy of the moment, so Ian let his hands speak for him.

"Let me finish with your hair, my heart. You should always wear it down, like the pagan queens of old." He resumed brushing her hair, though it seemed to him her arms slid from his neck reluctantly.

He made love to her hair, one slow, sweet stroke at a time, until it gleamed in a midnight cascade from her crown to her waist. When she'd said nothing for a long moment, he started braiding it, slowly, carefully. Not too snug, not too loose. If ever there was a perfect braid, Ian created it for Augusta.

"You're for bed then?" He planted a kiss on that shining crown as he spoke.

"I don't want you to go."

The first words she'd spoken in perhaps twenty minutes, and they comforted.

"You want me to stay with you tonight, Augusta? You need your sleep after such a day."

She rose and faced him, her eyes impossible to read. "I am still indisposed, but yes, I want you to stay with me."

He searched her face for clues. No woman but Augusta had ever sought his company through the night without a thought for her own pleasure. "I'll stay."

Of course he'd stay. If it broke his heart, if it tore his soul to shreds, if it drove him mad, he'd stay with her as long as he could.

She helped him undress, asking him about each piece of his formal Highland attire, examining it closely before hanging it in the wardrobe. The sight of her hands stroking over the wool did things to Ian's insides. Not even purely erotic things, but tender, personal things.

He washed off by the hearth, while she sat at her escritoire in her night rail and wrapper and watched him. Candlelight made her hair shine with fiery red– and-gold highlights; the shadows and hollows on her features made him think of wanton angels.

When his person was clean—he'd been slow and thorough for her sake—she came to him and put her arms around his waist. "Come to bed, Ian."

Wifely words, considering they were not to make love. He put that thought aside and let her lead him by the hand to the bed. When they lay down side by side, Ian wondered if that's all it was to be—a shared bed—when Augusta shifted to lay along his side.

"Hold me."

"If I could, I'd hold you forever." Gaelic, to preserve just a little of his dignity, for there was no longer any hope to preserve. The worst of his financial worries were gone, thanks to Julia's and Genie's proffered generosity, but Augusta's cousins would see to her welfare now, and her former suitor would make good on the offer the baron had snatched away. The man's letter had been a pathetic monument to regret.

And a woman never got over her first lover.

"Ian?"

"Here, love."

"I wasn't trying to interfere when I had Gil sign those contracts. I shouldn't have doubted you, but I couldn't just . . . I couldn't passively accept what fate handed out, not again."

"You saw the better solution," Ian said, stroking his hand over her bare arm. "I'm not angry, Augusta. I am in awe." He kissed her to stop himself from saying anything more, and she kissed him back. They composed a symphony of kisses—warm, tender, intimate, and even playful, but for Ian, every single kiss also bore the taste of good-bye.

Augusta awoke alone, which she tried to tell herself was not entirely a bad thing. She assayed

402

her emotions and found her heart was at once too empty and too full for tears. She had preserved Ian from having to marry Genie, and that had been her goal.

Except he hadn't needed her help or her interference, though he didn't seem perturbed with her over it. He'd even been willing to indulge her sentimental request to spend another night with him—a night of kisses, touches, sighs, and warmth, a night of the kindest farewell she would ever know.

Outside her window, in the golden glow of the summer dawn, a rifle shot exploded. A gun large enough to take down a deer.

Somebody was likely sighting in his weapon, using a target to ensure the aim was accurate. Augusta's father had been an avid hunter, and once told her half the pleasure of sighting in a new weapon lay simply in all the racket it created.

"You're awake!" Fiona slipped in the door, grinning hugely. "The shoot will start soon, and that means we set up the picnic next. Have you ever eaten dessert in a tree?"

Augusta mustered a smile for the child. "I have not. You will remedy this oversight with me, won't you?"

"I will, but you have to wear clothes that won't catch Mama's eye. The men are in their hunting plaids. I chose a brown smock and a green pinny."

403

"Let's see what I can find for camouflage."

Fiona chattered on, about the ball, about her cousin Doungal letting her conduct the orchestra someday if she practiced her piano, about her mama not yelling at her because Matthew—"He's going to be my papa!"—kept kissing Mama's cheek.

Augusta paused with her hair half-pinned up. "Fiona, may I tell you something?"

"Of course. We're friends, aren't we?"

"We are, and all I wanted to say is that I'm very, very glad you're my friend. I hadn't made any new friends for quite some time before I came on this holiday. It's wonderful to have you for a friend."

This smile was bashful, hinting at a mature beauty that would emerge in just a few years.

"I like having a new friend too. That brown dress will do for today. It won't show the dirt if you sit in the grass for your picnic."

"Or in a tree," Augusta replied. She made short work of getting dressed, because Fiona was ricocheting around the room more energetically with each gunshot, darting from the bed to the window and popping in and out of the wardrobe.

"They must be hunting already," Augusta said.

"Uncle Ian doesn't use beaters," Fiona replied from the depths of the wardrobe. "Says the bunnies and such need a sporting chance. Your clothes all smell good, like flowers."

"Your mama uses flowers to keep your whole house smelling fresh." Augusta glanced around the room. She'd soon be packing up, should probably start on it immediately so there would be less to do after the wedding.

Weddings.

The thought brought her mind to a stillness, while the recognition of all Augusta would not have—with Ian, at Balfour, in Scotland, with the MacGregor clan sprinkled all over the shire—washed over her, and her door clicked open again.

"You're awake."

The last person—the very last person Augusta ever wanted or expected to see in her bedroom was Willard Daniels. He stood just inside her door in tidy hunting attire, but his eyes were bloodshot, his complexion splotchy, and his mouth curved in a cruel smile.

And in his hand was a large, lethal-looking pistol.

"Uncle. I believe the hunt has started. What brings you here?"

And please, Almighty God, she prayed, give Fiona the sense to remain hidden in the wardrobe, because the baron's purpose had to be evil.

"The hunting is just under way, and you and I have a little excursion to make. You will accompany me right out that door to the terrace, Augusta. So accommodating of you to insist on a bedroom on the ground floor. It has made all manner of schemes possible."

"I'm going," Augusta said. "Let me at least fetch a hat to keep the sun off my face."

"Oh, by all means." He waved his gun, the peculiar light in his eyes as he continued to smile proof positive the man wasn't sane. Augusta crossed to the wardrobe and made a show of rummaging among her effects.

"Don't follow. Stay safe." She whispered the words to Fiona who was crouched, wide-eyed among Augusta's boots and shoes. "He has a gun."

Fiona nodded and shrank into a smaller ball.

Augusta grabbed a bright white, wide-brimmed straw hat, which she hoped would make her conspicuous. She closed the door to the wardrobe except for a small crack and put the hat on her head, jamming a hat pin through the crown.

"I assume we're taking a walk, Uncle?"

"You do a great deal of assuming, Augusta Merrick, but in this instance you're correct. We're taking a little walk in the woods, and you're finally having the damned accident you were supposed to have much earlier in our visit to this benighted province. I swear you have more lives than that damned cat of yours—though he at least knew enough to succumb to poison. Now march, my girl, and keep your mouth shut."

He waved the gun again, and even as she

vowed to avenge her murdered cat, Augusta noted Altsax had his finger on the trigger. She snatched her ugly old tan shawl from the foot of the bed and slipped out the terrace door, one step ahead of her uncle. As soon as they were outside the house, he manacled one hand on her arm, the loose folds of his shooting jacket hiding the gun.

He steered her toward the path Ian had shown her through the woods soon after her arrival. It started off close to the house, meaning there was little likelihood anybody would see Augusta with her demented escort.

Please God, keep Fiona safe.

The baron hustled Augusta along in silence for some yards, his grip on her arm destroying her balance to the point that she stumbled. From the corner of her eye, she saw Fiona streaking around the corner of the stables, making straight for a woods crammed with hunters who were armed to the teeth and likely shooting at anything that moved.

"Your Highness." Ian bowed to his neighbor. "This is an unexpected pleasure." A gun went off about fifty yards to their right, while the Prince Consort acknowledged the bow.

"Do you know, Balfour, how the number of children in a household can make the summer months seem particularly riotous? My wife has remarked on this phenomenon herself, but she seems to think it a wonderful thing."

Albert was tall, good-looking, with a fashionable set of side-whiskers and a kind of bluff, German common sense to him. He was also possessed of sufficient strength of character to husband the lady reigning over the most far-flung empire known to humankind. Ian had liked the man on sight.

The Prince Consort was known to appreciate decent libation too, as well as deer stalking, fishing, and grouse hunting.

"My thanks for that brew you sent over," Albert continued. "Are we trying to murder every creature in the woods?"

"We're celebrating," Ian said. "There were betrothals announced at last night's ball. Missed you, of course, and your lovely wife."

Albert frowned as another gun went off at a greater distance. "I sent you regrets, at least for the ball, and a note accepting your invitation today. It was with all that prosing on from the College of Arms."

Ian passed his companion a flask and settled on a boulder. The hunt would sweep past them, pushing the game toward the edges of the wood. "I didn't get it."

"You didn't get a royal epistle? Time to fire your domestics, Balfour, except I forget: up here, you hire your distant family members so you at least get some work out of all those you support."

"We hire them," Ian said quietly, "so they don't follow all our cousins and leave the realm entirely."

Albert had the grace to grimace, then took a sip from the flask. "You need to scare up that letter, Balfour. You're harboring a baroness without portfolio. Her uncle is larking around under some false colors, and my wife is inclined to frown on such behavior among the peerage. Excellent stuff."

"Keep it." Highland hospitality—and political common sense—required such generosity. "What baroness am I harboring?"

Albert grinned and pocketed the flask. "Augusta Merrick, of course. Victoria got your epistle a week or more ago, the telegrams and pigeons were sent off, and I sent you the answers. The Gribbony barony is Scottish, while the Altsax title is English. Doesn't happen very often, unless the titles are quite old."

"I knew the Gribbony title was Scottish," Ian said slowly, "but what does that have to do with Augusta?"

A racket started up in the undergrowth to their right, and Albert immediately had an ornately decorated rifle against his shoulder.

"Uncle Ian! Uncle Ian!" Fiona gasped as she emerged at a dead run from the bushes. "Don't shoot me. He has Augusta, and he has a gun!"

Albert lowered his rifle and shot Ian a quizzical look. "You've got trouble, Balfour."

Fiona pelted into her uncle, tears streaking her face, her breathing harsh. "The baron's going to kill her, and you have to save her!"

"Fiona, calm down." Ian propped his rifle against the boulder and scooped his niece up. "Take a breath and let it out slowly. There's my girl. Again."

"He's going to *kill* her. He came to her room and made her leave with him."

"Balfour, what's the signal?" Albert was pointing his gun at the sky as he spoke.

"Three shots," Ian said. "As close together as you can." Ian walked off a few paces with Fiona, while the prince gave the signal ending the hunt.

"Which way did he take her, Fee?"

"Up the path behind the stables. He has a big gun, and Augusta is going to *die*."

"No, she's not." Ian kissed the child's forehead. "She is bloody damned not going to die while I have breath in my body."

Albert, a man exceedingly familiar with small children, reached for Fiona. "Give her to me. I'll gather a party at the stables."

"We haven't time for that," Ian said, passing Fiona over. "Keep the women safe, explain to my brothers what's afoot, but don't alarm the neighbors."

"Mama will yell at me," Fee said, curling into

410

His Highness's neck. "I was really bad, going into the woods when you were hunting."

"She won't yell at you," Albert said. "My word as a papa. Have a care, Balfour. Decent neighbors are hard to find."

Ian smiled at that and melted into the woods.

Sixteen

"YOU TURNED THAT BULL LOOSE ON US, didn't you?" Augusta gathered her shawl more closely around her, but nothing was going to penetrate the chill in her bones. *I'm going to die in Scotland after all.*

"Of course I turned the bull loose on you," Altsax said. "I also literally tried to move mountains to put period to your miserable existence, but Scotland has ever been unwilling to accommodate the plans of her betters."

"Because she has none," Augusta said. "Must you drag me at such an unseemly pace through this bracken?" She raised her voice as much as she dared, hoping the noise might alert someone from the hunting party.

"She has none? When all her best and brightest have long since deserted this heathen realm? The only Scots left behind are those too poor or stubborn to abandon the place. May disease and poverty soon finish them off. Come along."

He jerked her elbow hard enough to send

Augusta to her knees, where she briefly considered wrestling him for the gun.

"Get up, you stupid bitch. This hunt won't last all morning, and your tragic demise can't happen just anywhere. You have to be found in an area the hunt has passed through."

Thank God for that.

"If you don't let me catch my breath, I'm going to expire right here." Augusta sat back, chest heaving with a drama that was only slightly feigned. Let him think her stays were too tight, though thank God she'd never held with the extremes fashion demanded of young women.

"If you don't get moving," Altsax said, shifting to stand right over her, "I'm going to sacrifice finesse for effectiveness." He cocked the gun.

That little click, a small, common sound, settled something in Augusta's mind. She was going to die. Very well. Everything born to earth died sooner or later, but she was going to die fighting.

She hadn't fought. Hadn't fought when she was shuffled off to Oxford, hadn't fought when her fiancé deserted her, hadn't fought when her uncle claimed all manner of impossible things about Trevisham, hadn't fought when she thought her cousins had turned their backs on her.

Hadn't fought to keep the man she loved when she'd had the chance, but rather, had meekly concluded he'd be better off sorting through the heiresses and debutantes, when what the man needed was somebody to love him, not to be a banker in the marriage bed.

"Uncle." Augusta got to one knee. "You may go to hell."

She surged upward, pitching her hat at his face at the same time she jammed the hat pin straight into his gut. For an instant, she saw victory, while the baron cried out in indignation and pain. Augusta moved off, thinking to put as many trees as she could between her and the baron's bullets.

Only to fall flat on her face three feet away.

"Oh, well done, Augusta." The baron's voice was smug with delight. "A brave show, at long last, but brought low by a damned tree root. My condolences on your failure and on your impending death."

"Not so fast, Baron." Ian loomed right up out of the undergrowth not two feet from where Augusta had fallen. "You have two shots, but you'll need both of them to bring me down. I'm that big, that mean, and that determined you will not escape justice." He moved a step closer. "Augusta, get up and run. I'll stand between you and this idiot's gun, and then I will kill him for you."

She somehow got her legs under her, though relief was making her knees unreliable, and fear was making her heart pound in her chest. "Don't let him kill you, Ian."

"Not a chance."

"For God's sake." Altsax tried for a lofty tone,

but Augusta heard the quaver of fear in his voice as she got to her feet. She picked up the old shawl and balled it up in her arms. "You don't know what she is, Balfour. You don't know what she could do to me. You're supposed to be a member of the peerage. Have you no respect for a fellow peer?"

"To the extent you refer to yourself," Ian said, shifting so he stood between Augusta and the baron, "none whatsoever. Give me the gun, and I might let you live."

"Don't trust him, Ian."

"Scat, Augusta. I'd spare you the sight of his blood and sound of his begging."

"I might like to hear that."

"You're both mad," the baron said, raising his gun. "I'll shoot you through the heart, Balfour. Married to your heir, my Genie will be the countess then, and nobody will listen to some bitter old spinster's version of the tale. I'll have Augusta committed . . . and she *will* meet with an accident in very short order."

Augusta gave Ian little warning taps—one, two, three—between his shoulder blades, then pitched her wadded-up shawl into the air straight over Ian's shoulder. Ian took advantage of the distraction to tackle the baron where he stood. The gun went off, and Augusta's heart lodged in her throat.

"Ian!" He lay over the baron, who was blinking

rapidly up at the canopy above him. "Ian, for God's sake, say something. For God's sake . . . please."

Ian groaned and shifted back onto all fours. "Bastard actually fired."

"You're hit! Oh, God, you're hit." Augusta tried to get him to his feet, which was futile, since he outweighed her by nigh six stone.

"Augusta, my heart, I am not hit." Ian wove to his feet. "Altsax, before more witnesses gather, I suggest you make your peace with the woman you've wronged."

"Never," the baron gasped where he lay. "She was going to ruin everything. Everything . . ." His breath came in a desperate rasp while blood welled from a wound high up on his left shoulder.

Ian's hands landed on Augusta's hips and turned her into his body. "Don't weep for him. The bastard's too tough to oblige us by dying."

"I'm not weeping for him." She smacked Ian hard on the shoulder. "I'm weeping for you! He was trying to kill you!" She fetched up against Ian's chest, and his arms closed around her.

"He's been trying to kill you, you mean, and I suspect this is not his first attempt."

Augusta nodded and clutched Ian more desperately. "He said he tried to move mountains to kill me. He p-poisoned Ulysses. He hates me."

And this—which should have been obvious—

had her sobbing uncontrollably against Ian's chest.

She heard him crooning to her in Gaelic, felt him lift her and move with her away from where the baron lay. When Ian settled with her on a boulder, Augusta lashed her arms around his neck and still could not stop crying.

"*Hush, beloved. You're safe.* You're safe, and he'll never hurt you again. I vow this, I swear it."

Ian's voice, not his words but the sound of his voice, the soft, Gaelic music of it, the care and concern in his tone, gradually calmed her. When Augusta looked up, a half circle of men stood a few yards off, their expressions grave.

Gil, Con, Matthew, and another kilted gentleman who looked familiar, all wearing expressions of solemn concern, and each sporting a weapon in his hand.

"There's been an accident," Ian said, his gaze going to the fourth gentleman.

"Of course. There has been an accident," the gentleman said, irony wreathing his slight German accent. "Most unfortunate, but these things occur to those who are careless. We will provide all possible aid to the injured. You'll see to the lady, Balfour?"

Ian nodded and rose with Augusta in his arms.

"I can walk," Augusta said, her voice a mere croak.

"You can walk," Ian retorted, making no move

416

to put her down. "You can cheat death, you can outwit a man bent on your destruction, you can subsist on hope and tough chicken for years, you can see my brothers happily married despite all odds to the contrary, and you can bloody damned well let me carry you."

"Yes, Ian." She tucked her face against his neck, more than willing to let him do just that.

The three weddings held in the days following were very quiet: Matthew married Mary Fran in the family parlor; Con and Julia married on the terrace; Gil and Genie were married at the foot of the garden.

And Augusta tried to get used to people addressing her as "my lady."

"You're the Baroness Gribbony, a peeress in your own right," Ian had told her the morning of the shoot. "Your mother either didn't know or didn't care that the Scottish title went to the eldest and could be matrilineal, but as she was eldest and you are her only child, the title comes to you."

"I don't want it."

Ian's smile was sad. "That's the hell of it. With titles you have them, and then they have you, and there's not a damned thing you can do about it."

He hadn't come to her room since the evening following the hunt almost a week past. That night, he'd come to her in silence, held her close all through the darkness, and departed before the sun had risen. She'd waited for him to come again then realized he wasn't going to.

He'd said all the good-byes he was going to say to her.

So she made arrangements to go south with Con and Julia—not as far south as London, but to Julia's holding in Northumbria. Chaperoning a honeymoon wasn't the way Augusta wanted to spend her autumn, but the idea of her little property in Oxford, without even a cat for company . . .

And then were was Trevisham. She wasn't ready to go back there either, though Matthew had explained to her privately that it would one day soon be hers again.

While Altsax recovered under strict guard, the safes in Kent had been opened, revealing the original copy of the very valid will left by Augusta's parents. The baron had secreted the will, lied to her and the courts, created a guardianship of her property, and then set about reaping the rewards of his perfidy—making damned sure Augusta wasn't viewed as a marriage prospect by any who might get to questioning her finances.

And in a subtle bit of cleverness, Altsax had started alluding to his possession of the Gribbony barony only years after Augusta's parents had died, and then only on a few discreet occasions. Sooner or later his ruse would likely have been revealed, at which point he could pronounce himself repentant over having misinterpreted the vagaries of an old patent.

Ian and Matthew had conferred privately regarding a proper fate for the baron, but Augusta could not muster enough sentiment to care what befell her uncle, as long as his path never again crossed her own.

"Augusta?" Ian stood at the edge of the terrace, looking weary and dear in waistcoat, shirt, and plain work kilt. "Have you a minute, my lady?"

"I hate it when you call me that."

One corner of his mouth quirked up a very little. "Shall I call you Baroness?"

"I like it better when you called me 'my heart' and 'my love.'" She ducked her face, staring at her hands where they rested in her lap. Fatigue— or perhaps desperation—was taking a toll on her manners.

Ian came down beside her on the bench and let out a sigh. "I should not have presumed. I ask you to forgive me for it."

She glanced over at him, feeling tears threaten. They were close at hand these days, as was a grinding, dragging fatigue.

"I will forgive you for that remark, Ian MacGregor. Honest sentiment should never be a cause for apology between a man and a woman who've been as intimate as we have."

He was quiet a long while, the fresh scent of

him coming to her on a breeze that bore a hint of autumn. Autumn, when everything died away and Augusta would be far from Ian and all she held dear.

"There's something I want you to know, but I haven't known quite how to put it," he said.

Augusta's gaze shifted to Ian's hands—strong, callused, and yet elegant, and beautiful to her. *For God's sake, take my hand.* Augusta smoothed out her skirts lest she grab for his hand instead.

"In the woods," Ian said, "when the baron and I struggled, I think he was trying to turn the gun on himself."

"To attempt suicide?"

"He isn't sane, Augusta. I have been forbidden by no less than the Prince Consort to blame myself for not seeing Altsax for the menace he presented. I'm finding it difficult to respect the prince's guidance on this issue."

"Albert is your friend."

"If such a man can have friends, I would be honored to think I'm among them."

"He's English."

"By act of Parliament."

They fell silent, while Augusta felt her heart breaking in her chest. They discussed suicide and princes, but not what mattered.

"You've a letter, Augusta. I think you'll want to read it in private." He withdrew an epistle from his pocket. "Before you read it, though . . ."

"What, Ian?"

He peered over at her, his expression impossible to read, and then his arms seized her, and his mouth was crashing down on hers. Hot, demanding, and so, so welcome. Augusta wrapped her arms around him and put everything she was, every scrap of love and determination she felt toward him, into her answering kiss.

And then he drew back and stood. "Read your letter."

She glanced at the letter—Henry Post-Williams was bestirring himself to write to her *while Ian was walking away*.

"Hang the damned letter, Ian MacGregor. You don't kiss me like that after days of leaving me to toss on my own all night and then just walk away."

Ian stopped in midstride, his back still to her. He turned slowly, his expression fierce. "The letter is from a prosperous English gentleman seeking to offer you his addresses, *Baroness*. I suggest you read it."

She marched up to him, held the letter up before his gorgeous Scottish nose, and tore the paper right down the middle. "Hester says his hairline is receding." She tore it again. "He's looking for a free governess." She tore it yet again. "And he can't *kiss* worth a farthing." She flung the pieces over her shoulder. "I shudder to think of the poor woman who has to content herself with Henry Post-Williams's company for the rest of her life. She'd be better off raising chickens in the shires."

She put her hands on her hips. *"I love you, Ian MacGregor."* She spoke the Gaelic carefully. *"I will always love you. You are the beloved of my heart."* It was the limit of what she could manage in his native tongue. "I will leave tomorrow if you ask it of me, but I will spend my life regretting that I allowed you to send me away."

She went up on her toes and kissed him softly but soundly on the mouth. "You will regret it too."

And she was not going to leave the field, but if she didn't sit down, the knocking of her knees was going to see her laid out flat at his feet—a metaphor she'd rather avoid. She marched back to the bench and sat, glaring at him where he stared at her.

He took one step toward her then halted. "I have nothing to offer you, Augusta. I'm poor."

"You're wealthy in your family, Ian. You are surrounded by people who love you and are loyal to you."

He took one more step toward her. "I know nothing but hard work, and hard work is all I foresee. Until the last member of my family is well fed, safe, and secure, it's all I can allow myself."

"You think subsisting in a farmhouse for years

is easy? Weeding my own gardens, milking my own cow, slopping my own hogs? I could manage in a croft, Ian, and consider it a wonderful life if I could share it with the man I love."

He shook his head, his hands fisting at his sides. "Augusta, I'd keep you pregnant until we had so many mouths to feed . . ."

"I've wasted years feeding *chickens*. Give me all the children the Lord sends to us, Ian. Green-eyed boys and girls with humor and pride and stubborn streaks as wide as their papa's."

He took the last step and sank to his knees before her. "I said . . ." He stopped, his voice hoarse. "I said an earl not in possession of a fortune must be in want of a wealthy wife. I was not . . . I was not wrong." He paused again, swallowed, and slid his arms around her waist. "I was right, my heart. I need a wife with a wealth of courage and honor, a wife with abundant loyalty. I need a wife so canny and resourceful that even when her title and her wealth are stolen from her, she has the courage and wits to fight for me and mine . . . to love . . . to love me. Ah, God, Augusta . . ."

He gathered her to him, his embrace fierce. "I can offer you nothing," he said. "Nothing except my love and my pledge to bend my entire being to your safekeeping and happiness, but for the love of God, will you marry me? You don't need my title—you have one of your own—you don't need the shelter of my house—you've one of those too. You don't need . . ."

She kissed him into silence. "I need, Ian. I *need* from the bottom of my soul. I need your love. I need your arms around me. I need you beside me in this life. I need to bear your children. I will be your wife, gladly, joyfully. It will be my privilege and my honor to be your wife."

A great sigh went out of him, a sigh of such surrender Augusta felt tears drifting down her cheeks. She burrowed closer, craving the scent of him, the heat of him, the touch and sound and essence of him drawn so deeply into her awareness it could become a part of her.

He rose with her cradled against his chest and carried her, not to the bedroom where she'd been a guest and become his lover, but to the estate chambers where the earl and his countess would dwell for their remaining days at Balfour.

They passed Gil and Genie on the stair, both of whom beamed at them like idiots. Outside the billiards room, they encountered Con and Julia, who whooped with unladylike glee and managed to land a glancing swat on Ian's backside. In the family wing, they met up with Matthew, Mary Fran, and Fiona, all dressed for riding. Matthew grinned, Mary Fran got teary, and Fiona dragged her parents off toward the stables, muttering something in Gaelic about new friends and lovesick uncles.

When Ian laid Augusta down on his enormous bed, they made love—there was no other description for the tenderness and joy with which they coupled. They made love endlessly as the afternoon shadows stretched across the room and the quiet of the house settled around them, and then they made love some more.

"Ian?" Augusta drew her hand over his chest hours later. A marvelous thing, that chest, so strong and yet susceptible of being tickled.

"My heart?"

"We won't be poor."

He smoothed his hands over her hair—it had come tumbling down long ago—and cuddled her a little closer. "It won't be so bad, if we're careful and lucky. By Scottish standards, we'll be comfortable."

"No." She levered up to peer at him, realizing only then that Ian had no idea she'd inherited not only Trevisham but the substantial income from the Gribbony barony as well. "We'll be fine."

"Scots live on love and stubbornness." He kissed her cheek. "We've plenty of both."

She subsided against him. "We can live on love and stubbornness, or we can live on love, stubbornness, and all the income from my properties. I've more than one, you know."

His hand went still in her hair. "I know you've the Gribbony estate, but it's a Lowland holding, probably nothing much left of it but some farms and a few bleating sheep."

"It's four thousand acres plus a dozen tenancies, Ian." She walked her fingers up his sternum. "A wool mill, a flour mill, and a distillery."

He trapped her hand in his. "A distillery? You wouldna tease about such a thing?"

"I thought you knew."

"I knew about the title, but this . . ."

She peered up at him. "Is it all right? I think you had your heart set on being poor and working your fingers to the bone and riding Hannibal until his muzzle was completely gray."

"Had my heart set on . . ." He growled and rolled so she was under him. "Here's your first lesson in being a Scottish countess: I will take such good care of your properties, Augusta MacGregor, that you will see how wonderfully well the Scots can adapt to wealth. I will dazzle you with my ability in this regard, as will my family."

"Augusta MacGregor?" Oh, she liked the sound of that, loved it, particularly when Ian said her name in that soft, deep burr.

"We pledged to marry then consummated the pledge. By Scottish law, we're married, woman. I am your husband from this moment forward, and all your troubles belong exclusively to me."

He sounded fiercely pleased to be telling her this. Augusta was pleased to hear it too. "Then you won't mind that I'll be asking you to look in on Trevisham, will you? Matthew says it's thriving, and . . ."

He kissed her, and then—and for decades to come—he dazzled her with his abilities in regards that had not one damned thing to do with monetary wealth and everything to do with what really mattered to them both.

Author's Note

Readers will pardon me for taking a small liberty with the facts by laying railroad tracks as far west as Ballater in the 1850s. In truth, the line didn't get to Ballater until the next decade, and in the present day, Royal Deeside is served by buses rather than trains. If you go to Ballater, you'll see the train station has been converted in part to a museum dedicated to preservation of the area's Victorian history. One of Her Majesty's train cars is on display, and visitors can even take a peek at the royal parlor and the royal potty, a beautiful creation of mahogany, marble, and stained glass.

The present rendition of Balmoral Castle was undergoing construction as Ian and Augusta's story unfolds. The centuries-old hunting box originally gracing the property would be demolished upon completion of the present structure, which Albert had designed for his wife and their growing family. In part because of Victoria's affection for Balmoral and all things Highland, Victorian society became enthralled with tartan decor and "walking" in the Highlands.

And in a second small deviation from fact, I've moved the royal visit to Balmoral up by a few weeks. Victoria and Albert typically did not repair to Balmoral until midsummer or even early autumn, though early in her long widowhood, Victoria spent so much time at Balmoral as to cause her ministers and officials concern.

I am confident, as much in love as they were, neither Her Majesty nor His Highness would be offended at these small deviations, made—as they were—in the interests of telling a love story that ends with a resounding happily ever after.

Grace Burrowes

Acknowledgments

An author doesn't try her wings in a new direction without a lot of trepidation, and after working on a long Regency series, even early Victorian Scotland was new ground for me. I am indebted to my editor, Deb Werksman, for her support in this venture, and of course to all my book people, who've once again turned a rough manuscript into a beautiful romance novel. Skye, Susie, Cat, Danielle, Madam Copy Editor, many, many thanks. Dominique, you are among my blessings. Steve, thanks for the guidance and support that has seen this book to its happily ever after.

I am also indebted to a taxi driver in Aberdeen by the name of Abbey. He drove me up to Balmoral and back to Aberdeen, with a running narrative of each little hamlet and landmark along the way. I could have listened to him all day for his accent alone, and that was before he lapsed into the Doric.

I'd also like to thank the staff on grounds at Balmoral Castle. Never was a tired, disheveled, none-too-travel-savvy author made to feel more welcome, or given more congenial surrounds in which to write. I left with many happy memories and a burning passion for more trips to Scotland.

Center Point Large Print
600 Brooks Road / PO Box 1
Thorndike ME 04986-0001 USA

(207) 568-3717

US & Canada:
1 800 929-9108
www.centerpointlargeprint.com